The Dirge of Defeat

All day the stream of tattered, weary men in grey had poured by the great plantation house of Fairview. The spring sunshine burned down pitilessly on what once had been a proud, supremely self-confident army.

A young Confederate officer, hardly more than a boy, but with his face prematurely etched with the lines of tragedy, stopped for a sip of water.

Jane Meade's mother watched him eagerly drinking from the glass she handed him and said, "My son was a lieutenant, too, a little younger than you, I reckon. He was killed in Petersburg in January."

A strange look came over the young man's face. "Don't weep for him, ma'am," he said. "Tears are for the living. . . ."

For Jane's mother, the struggle was almost over. But for Jane Meade, it had only just begun. . . .

TEARS ARE FOR
THE LIVING

TEARS ARE FOR THE LIVING

MARGARET BANISTER

POPULAR LIBRARY • NEW YORK

POPULAR LIBRARY EDITION
December, 1976

Copyright © 1963 by Margaret S. Banister

Library of Congress Catalog Card Number: 63-14183

Published by arrangement with Houghton Mifflin Company

ISBN: 0-445-08536-3

Prologue

On her hundredth birthday Miss Janie sat in her wheelchair by the window of the front parlor, dressed in her best gray silk. She sat quietly, though the house was filled with activity, with the sound of the telephone and the constantly ringing doorbell, the arrival of gifts and flowers and telegrams. She was surprised at the to-do being made over her hundredth birthday, surprised too at her pleasure in it. Out of the lonely years it was pleasant to emerge into this flurry of attention and expressed affection. Pleasant but wearying.

She had put on the gray silk dress that morning to honor the day. When she looked into her jewel box she had chosen the moonstone brooch edged with diamond chips which had been Avery's present to her when Elizabeth was born, the first and indeed the only piece of jewelry he had ever given her.

What obscure impulse had prompted the choice she could not say. It was from no upsurge of reminiscent emotion about Avery, who had retreated so far into the shadowy stretches of the past that he was merely a fact to her, not a person. He was part of the record. He had come into her life and he had gone out of it. For a time he had been life itself to her, the unfolding miracle, the embodied dream. He had become the beginning of disillusionment and the grand climactic tragedy. These things were part of the record too. They could not touch her now, and yet she had chosen the moonstone brooch to wear on her hundredth birthday. It glimmered cloudily in the lace at her throat.

The October sun flooded through the east windows and cut diagonally into the south window at which she sat. The day was fresh with the crispness of autumn, but warm enough for the window to be open so that an aimless little breeze could reach Miss Janie. Outside the yellowing leaves fell lazily from the tulip poplar trees and the old copper beech was burnished in the sunshine. The street noises, the sounds of people, cars and lumbering buses, were muted by the stretch of lawn in front of the old house.

Miss Janie sat relaxed in the morning sun, not moving, hardly thinking, letting little wisps of thought drift through her mind. The fragrance of the flowers in the room was almost overpowering, but she loved it. To her it seemed to gather together all the fragrances of all the flowers she had known. Lilacs and syringa in the spring, Ascension lilies and roses when Grandpa was laid out in this room, the white roses and bridal wreath of her wedding bouquet, Mama's potpouri of dried rose leaves, her lavender and lemon verbena for the linen, the trailing arbutus on the slope of the hill beside the stream. The violets that Jane loved and Tommy Tyler always sent her, the spice of pinks in the garden, the delicate fragrance of box bushes warmed by the sun. Lovely scents, lovely flowers, lovely memories. Lovely and sad they had been, now she no longer felt the sadness. Peace filled her. The old house was speaking to her:

"Well, damn it—I beg your pardon, Lizzie—but what do you expect me to wear, a frock coat in June?"

"Mama, there are a lot of men coming down the road." This was herself speaking.

"If you go, you can never come back."

"They say they are going to shoot you, and damn if I don't believe they will."

"Certainly not too soon, Mr. Calhoun. I am glad to see you."

"Old stick-in-the-mud," Henry had said. "Little old stick-in-the-mud. Don't let's change anything, that's what you say."

"Mama, I have something to tell you. I am going to be married." This was Elizabeth speaking to her. Young Avery had said: "Mama, I am going into the church, into the ministry. I am going to be a minister." It was little Jane who said: "Oh, Mama, Mama, I love him so and I can't marry him. I can't. He'll never be any different."

6

"Sir, there is death in this house." Mama speaking to the Yankee officer.

How many times had there been death in this house, how many times new life? Six generations had called it home. All the living and dying that had gone on here, the loving and borning, the laughing and dancing, the crying and laying out of the dead; all the washing and scrubbing and dusting, the polishing and partying, the cooking and eating, the coming and going. All the full currents of life narrowed now to one thin thread soon to be broken, her own life. When she went Fairview would go, as Meriden and Ashby Hall and so many other places had gone. Well, let them go, their substance had long since gone. "We've got to learn what we can keep and what we must give up," Henry had said long ago. Henry was always wise.

There seemed to be a lot of activity going on at the back of the house, doors opening and closing, china rattling, subdued voices. Miss Janie paid little attention to them. The voices of the past were louder in her ears.

Part I

1

It was hot for April. Janie's mother had let her take off her winter underwear that day, and now she was sitting on the steps of the front porch with her pantaletted legs stretched out, feeling light and airy with the weight of flannel gone. She had finished her practicing and she was trying to decide what to do with the rest of the afternoon.

It was too late to walk up in the woods where the trailing arbutus grew, and she had just about decided to call Baizy's Lucy and some of the other children to play a game of hopscotch when she heard the sound of a horse coming down the road. She waited to see if it was going to turn into the driveway, and sure enough it did. Janie was delighted; somebody was coming to see them. She jumped up to run in the house and tell Mama, but then she saw that it was her father who was coming and that scared her a little. Papa never came home this early. Sometimes he didn't even come for supper, because he liked to stay at the office in town until the paper was all set for printing. Something must have happened. Dear Lord, don't let anybody else be killed, she prayed.

Janie sat still and watched her father ride up the driveway. He came up to the steps and got off and went into the house. He didn't hitch Black Prince or call Zeb to take him or anything. He just got off and passed Janie as if he did not see her, and went through the open door into the shadowy front hall.

"Elizabeth," he called.

Janie followed her into the house. Emily leaned over the railing upstairs and when she saw Papa she ran down.

"Elizabeth," he called again. Papa was the only person in the world who called Mama Elizabeth.

She came through the door from the back hall and hurried toward him. "Mr. Meade," she said, "what has happened?"

"General Lee has surrendered," Papa said. "Yesterday, at Appomattox."

Slowly Mama's hands went up to her face. She pressed them against her mouth and stood looking at Papa.

"It is the end," he said. Then he went upstairs, climbing the steps slowly, as if it were hard work.

Mama sat down on the hall sofa. Nobody said anything; there didn't seem to be anything to say. After a while Emily spoke.

"Well, at least, Mama, it means the end of this awful fighting."

"It means the end of everything," Mrs. Meade said. She put her arms on the arm of the sofa and her head on them, and began to cry. Janie had never seen her cry like that. Even on the terrible afternoon when word came that Jon had been killed at Petersburg she had not cried like that, with great racking sobs that shook her whole body and jarred the sofa. It frightened Janie. Mama had always tried to be brave. That is what she always said when anything happened: "We must be brave." "Remember, Janie," she would say, "no matter what happens, we must face the world with courage." She was not trying to be brave now. Janie felt that she was letting all the tears come that she had been holding back for years.

After a while Emily went over and patted her shoulder. The touch of Emily's hand seemed to pull Mama up out of her deep well of misery. She sat up straight, fumbled in her dress for a handkerchief and wiped her eyes.

"I am sorry, children," she said. "This is no time to give way like this." She stood up, smoothed her hair and straightened her dress. "I don't know what we will do, but we must go on the best we can."

Mrs. Meade went out through the door to the back hall and closed it behind her. Emily went into the back parlor. Janie was left alone in the wide front hall. Sunlight slanted in from the west through the open door of the library, and

11

gleamed on the polished oak floor. The only sounds were small outdoor noises, the twittering of birds in the poplar trees, Frisk barking somewhere off in the distance. The sunny afternoon lay quietly over the land.

General Lee had surrendered. Yesterday Papa had been sure that would not happen. Richmond and Petersburg were lost, but the General was making his way west, Papa said, supplies were coming to meet him, there was still plenty of fight left in the Army. Now it was over. "It is the end," Papa had said. The quiet was the quiet of emptiness.

Janie followed Emily into the parlor. Her sister was standing in front of the fireplace, looking at herself in the gilt-framed mirror over the mantelpiece. As Janie entered she faced Emily's reflection, and to her astonishment saw that she was smiling gaily at her own mirrored face.

Janie stared. "You're laughing," she said wonderingly.

Emily whirled around and with a little rush caught Janie in her arms and squeezed her. "Oh, Janie, Janie," she said. "I don't care, I know it's awful, but I am *glad* this war is over. I'm so tired of people being killed and houses being burned and everybody starving to death. I am tired of being sad, I want to be happy again."

"But how can you help being sad now?" Janie asked. "With our loved ones gone and the war lost and General Lee surrendered. It's a sad time."

Emily held her off to look at her. "Mercy me! Listen to the child. Not ten years old, and hear her talk!" Then she hugged her again. "You poor little thing. You were only six years old when the war began, weren't you. I don't suppose you remember what it was like to be happy. But I do."

Emily released Janie and started to do a little dance step, pirouetting across the room, her full skirt billowing around her. "I remember when the world was a lovely place and I was gay and happy. Happy, happy. I want to be that way again and I am going to be."

She stopped dancing and ran out of the room and up the stairs. Janie thought she was behaving very strangely, but then Emily had been acting strangely a lot recently. Mama said she had not been like herself since she went up to Winchester in the winter of '64 to visit Aunt Em and Uncle Murrell.

"It's that man," Janie heard Mama say to Papa, who nodded with a sort of grim expression on his face. When Janie asked what man, however, Mama said: "Never mind. Don't ask so many questions, Janie." She thought that was very unfair, because she had not asked many questions.

Emily was the oldest one. She was grown up. Jon was eighteen months younger than Emily, and he was nineteen when he was killed. Peyton would have been fifteen if he had lived. She was the baby. She would be ten years old next October, and she did remember what it was like to be happy. She had always been happy until this last terrible year; even now she knew how to be happy for a little while at a time. You had to be careful, though, not to think, at least not to think about real things that were happening around you. You had to pull your thoughts up and away and let them float around like little white clouds in a clear sky, not doing anything or going anywhere, but just floating. She decided that was what she would do now.

Janie went out of the front door and circled around the house, under the poplar trees and past the old copper beech, to the back yard. There she found Baizy's Lucy sitting under the oak tree near the well house. The sun was sinking now and it was getting cool. She selected a spot of sunlight and lay down in it. Lucy started to speak, but Janie stopped her. "You mustn't talk. I want to—to meditate."

She closed her eyes. That was what you had to do first, if you wanted to forget about things and be happy. You shut your eyes and lay still and stopped thinking about anything. It was hard to do. Little wisps of thoughts kept drifting around in your mind, but she had found that if you lay perfectly still and kept brushing them away, after a while they stopped coming and your mind would be bare and empty and quiet, like the dim emptiness of the old icehouse when all the ice was gone. Then you opened your eyes and looked up at the sky. On a clear day all you could do was look up. Up and up and up. Janie always felt that if you looked long enough and hard enough you could see farther and farther into the blue, and some day you might see what was on the other side. If there were clouds in the sky it was fun to go along with the clouds and wonder how it felt to be floating up there high above the earth and what it looked like from up there.

Today the sky was blue and cloudless. Janie looked as hard

13

as she could into the blue distance, but thoughts kept coming into her mind, not drifting thoughts that you could push away but heavy, determined thoughts that settled down in front of you. She kept remembering how Papa had looked when he came home, and how Mama had cried. She kept wondering what would become of them now that the Yankees were right down the road at Appomattox, and there was no Confederate Army to protect them.

Presently she sat up. "It's no use," she said. "I can't meditate today." Janie was fond of that word, she had heard the minister use it. "I keep thinking."

Baizy's Lucy didn't say anything. "The war is over," Janie told her. "General Lee has surrendered."

Lucy nodded. "Maw done tol' me," she said. "What gwine happen now, you reckon?"

"I don't know."

"You reckon 'em Yankees is comin' back agin?"

Janie knew she had been trying not to ask herself that question, but now that Lucy had asked it there was no use pretending any longer. That was the thought she was finding it hardest to keep out of her mind. The two little girls looked at each other in horror. The worst thing that had ever happened to them was the time the Yankees came last summer. Last June it was.

2

A man had ridden out from town that morning with a message for Grandpa. General Meade, who had been a general of the Virginia militia, was too old to fight in the Army, but he, together with the other old men of the town, belonged to the Home Defense. All that morning the Court House bell had been tolling to summon all the men left in town, but Fairview was too far away for the bell to be heard, so they sent a messenger for Grandpa. Hunter's Yankees were coming. General Breckenridge had arrived to defend the town, and his men were throwing up breastworks to the west, but he had only a small command to face Hunter's thousands. General Early was coming down from Charlottesville, but until he could get here they must hold the town. Every man who could carry a gun was needed. Would General Meade please come.

Grandpa listened to the message in silence, nodded to the messenger, and went out to the closet in the back hall to get his musket. When he returned to the front hall he picked up his straw hat from the hall table and stood looking at Mama and Janie.

All her life her grandfather had been to Janie a being set apart. He was the Voice of Authority, beyond which no authority went, except that of God. He was tall and straight with white hair and a white mustache and very blue eyes that seemed to see inside you when he looked at you. When Grandpa came into a room you felt as if something important

15

had happened. Nobody questioned what he said and nobody argued with him. He was always kind. He would smile at Janie and pat her head and sometimes tweak her ear. He gave her splendid presents; it was he who had given her the pony, Trotter, that she loved more than anything she owned. He was kind from somewhere far off, however, on some higher level of being. Janie always felt shy with him. Watching him now going off to fight the Yankees, she had nothing to say. Mama said nothing either. Her face was pale, and she just stood looking at Grandpa.

"If anything should happen to me, Lizzie," he said, "you know that Snead and Purcell have my will. Richard Snead knows all about our affairs, he will help you until Jonathan comes home. And Tom Scott, you could call on Tom for anything."

Mama put her hand on his arm. "General," she said, speaking for the first time, "you can't go like that, in those clothes."

Grandpa looked down at himself. He had on a white linen suit. He always wore white linen in the summer, black broadcloth in the winter.

"Well, damn it—I beg your pardon, Lizzie—but what do you expect me to wear, a frock coat in June?" When he got excited Grandpa could not help saying damn, but he never got so excited that he forgot to apologize to Mama. "I haven't worn my uniform for years, I don't know where it is and I have no time to look for it. It isn't necessary to get myself dressed up like a tin soldier." He bent down and kissed Mama, patted Janie's head, and started toward the door. When he got almost there he turned, with a smile on his face. "Besides, it's blue," he said.

The next time they saw Grandpa he was lying, still and straight, on a stretcher; his blue eyes were closed, his face looked like carved marble, and there was blood all over his white coat. Two men they had never seen brought him home in a wagon, with his horse tethered to the back of it. The men were pretty old, and they looked and talked like countrymen.

"Mighty sorry, ma'am," one of them said. "Mighty sorry. We ain't had much fightin' yit, but them Yankees didn't have no trouble pickin' off the tall old gentleman in the white suit."

"They're liable to be here tomorrow," the other said. "Ain't aimin' to scare you, ma'am, but we cain't hardly hold 'em back, less General Early gits here in time."

The Yankees did come the next day. They never got into the town, because General Early got there first, but they came to Fairview and went a mile or two beyond, to the very outskirts of the town. Mama and Emily and the house servants worked nearly all night getting ready for the Yankees. Her mother made Janie go to bed, but she couldn't sleep, and she got up two or three times to see what was going on. Before daybreak Jackson and Arthur took all the flat silver, wrapped in flannel and the silver service in flannel bags, and buried them under the grape arbor on the other side of the cutting garden. The epergne and candelabra and vases were too big to bury. They hid the best china and the crested Peyton compotes in the basement, in a dark place behind the woodbin. The rugs had already been taken up and the summer matting put down on the floors, and the blue velvet over-draperies in the parlors and the French brocade hangings in the dining room had been taken down for the summer, so they were safe.

"Unless they burn the house," Mama said. That was what frightened her most, that the Yankees would burn down the house. General Hunter burned houses right and left, she said.

She sent Zeb into town with word of Grandpa's death and Tom Scott, who managed the newspaper while Papa was fighting with the Army, came out with the undertaker, bringing messages from the aunts. He would not let any of them come with him on account of the Yankees, and Mama said he was quite right.

They laid Grandpa out in the front parlor, with the branched silver candelabra at his head and his feet, and filled the silver vases and alabaster bowls with flowers and put them around the room. By breakfast time everything that could be done had been.

They ate breakfast off of the second-best china with knives, forks and spoons from the kitchen. After they finished Mama insisted on Tom Scott's going back to town. He wanted to stay with them.

"No, Tom," Mama said. "You are needed in town, and there is nothing more you can do for us right now. They won't hurt us personally, and whatever harm they may do to

17

the place they would do whether you are here or not. I shouldn't think that even Hunter's men would have the heart to burn down a house where an old gentleman lies in his coffin, would you, Tom?"

"No, ma'am, I don't think they goin' to burn you down, but I don't like the idea of you bein' out here by yourself with all them Yankees runnin' round loose."

"I am not by myself, Tom. I have Emily and Janie, and Jackson and Arthur and all the other servants will be with me. If you don't go before they come I don't know how long it will be before you can get there, and what will become of the paper? You must go quickly, and get in touch with Mr. Harrison, will you, Tom. Ask him to come as soon as he can. Even if the Yankees take the town I'm sure they would let a minister come to perform a funeral service."

After Tom Scott rode away there was nothing to do but wait. Janie stayed out in the kitchen with Baizy and Dolly Ann and Baizy's Lucy. Mama was too occupied to be much comfort to her, and Emily was no comfort at all because she kept saying that this was ridiculous, the Yankees would not harm anything. She had stayed in the house with some of them for weeks last winter when she visited Aunt Em in Winchester, and they had been very gentlemanly. Nobody paid any attention to her when she said that, and presently she got mad and went up to her own room.

Baizy's Lucy was even more frightened than Janie was. Every now and then during the morning they heard scattered gunfire and each time the sound came Lucy would put her hands over her ears and look scared to death. Nobody had much to say. Baizy went on cooking dinner, and the rest of them just sat around. Sometimes Jackson and Zeb came in and sat with them.

Mrs. Meade had stationed some of the little colored boys down the road to watch out for the Yankees and let her know if they saw them coming. Along about noontime they came running back to the house. They had not seen any Yankees, but they had seen a big cloud of dust coming up over the hill where the road turned on the other side of West Field. Their warning was not necessary, however, because by that time they had all seen the smoke billowing up against the sky to the west, where Greenway stood. That was where Sara Anne Williams, Janie's best friend, lived, two miles away. Janie saw

18

the smoke from the back porch and knew that the Yankees must have set fire to the Williams house. She ran to tell Mama. When Mrs. Meade looked out of the window and saw the smoke Janie thought she was going to cry. Instead, she went into the front parlor and stood looking down at Grandpa.

"General," she said, just as if he could hear her, "I pray God they will leave you in peace until we can put you in your resting place."

A little table had been placed at one side of Grandpa's casket with the big family Bible on it, opened at the eleventh chapter of John, where Jesus said: "I am the resurrection and the life: he that believeth in me, though he were dead, yet shall he live." Mrs. Meade went to the table and knelt and prayed for a while. When she stood up she sent Janie to call the servants, and she began giving them directions.

"Zeb," she said, "you and Jake go out to the stable and the barn. Don't do or say anything but be there, and if they start to set fire to any of the buildings, get the animals out. Arthur, sound the farm bell and tell all the Negroes to go to their own cabins and shut their doors and stay there quietly. Then you come back here. Jackson, you stay with me, and Baizy, you and Dolly Ann and Susie go on back to the kitchen."

"Miss Lizzie, ma'am," Baizy said, "we'd ruther stay nearby you."

That is the way they were when the Yankees came. Mrs. Meade, with Emily on one side and Janie on the other, stood squarely in the center of the hall, with Jackson and Arthur, very stiff and straight, standing a few feet behind them, and the women standing in the dining room doorway. Baizy's Lucy was behind her mother and peeped around her to see what was happening whenever her curiosity overcame her fright.

They could hear the men coming up the driveway. The front door was closed and black crape streamers were tied to the knocker. The soldiers paid no attention to that. They opened the door and came surging into the hall, laughing and talking. When the first ones saw the members of the household standing in front of them they paused, and then, when they looked into the parlor and saw the casket and the lighted candles, and the Ascension lilies and syringa around the room, the laughter left their faces. The men behind them, who could not see what was holding them, began calling and pressing forward. A young officer pushed through the men and came into the hall. There was a smile on his face and he made them an ironic little bow.

"Good day, ladies," he said. "A reception committee, I see."

"Sir," said Mama, "there is death in this house. I trust you will follow the dictates of ordinary human decency and leave us with our sorrow, undisturbed."

The officer stopped smiling. After a moment he went into the parlor and stood looking down at the white face of the old General. When he came back to the hall he bowed again, without the smile.

"All right, men," he said, "leave the house alone."

The soldiers in the hall turned and began to push their way. They looked as if they were glad to go. There was muttering among those behind, who had not been in the house. The officer waited until the last of the soldiers had gone, then he went out and closed the door behind him.

"Didn't I tell you so, Mama?" said Emily triumphantly.

Her mother did not answer her. She went into the parlor again and stood by the General's coffin, looking at him.

"Strong in death," she said, "as in life."

Zeb came running in from the back hall. "Miss Lizzie, 'em Yankees is takin' ev'ything, horses, mules, wagons, ev'ything to eat. They jes' goin' right straight through barn and stable and storehouse. Pigs and chickens, ev'ything."

Mrs. Meade closed her eyes for a moment. Then she opened them and said: "All right, Zeb. There is nothing we can do. Absolutely nothing. Just be grateful if they don't burn down the buildings."

A terrible thought came to Janie. "Zeb, they haven't taken my pony, have they? Oh, Zeb, have they taken Trotter?"

"I'se mighty feared they has, Lil' Miss. They's takin' ev'ything they kin git their hands on."

Janie gave a cry and started to run.

"Janie," her mother called, "come back here. Don't go out there."

Janie almost always did what her mother told her to do, but now she hardly heard her. She kept on running.

"Go after her, Zeb," Mrs. Meade said. "Bring her back to the house."

Janie lifted up her full skirts, showing a length of white cotton pantalettes almost to her knees, and ran as fast as she could across the back yard and out to the stable yard. Blue-coated soldiers were everywhere. Loaded wagons were creaking down the farm road; the storehouse door was open and men passed her with sacks of flour and sugar and cornmeal on their shoulders. Soldiers were in the chicken yard and the henhouses, and the air was filled with the squawks of chickens and the squealing of pigs. Janie paid no attention to any of it. She dashed into the stable and there stopped short. Silence and desolation met her. The big, dim stretches of the stable, usually so full of the rustling and stamping and breathing of animals, were quiet and empty. The carriage horses, Grandpa's riding horse, the little mare that had been Peyton's, the workhorses, were all gone, and Trotter's stall was empty. The silence came down on Janie like a weight; it settled around her and pressed in upon her. She could not stand it.

Turning, she ran out into the stable yard and bumped into a Yankee who was pulling a mule along. She struck out at him blindly, yelling: "Where is my pony? Don't you dare take my pony."

The man pushed her aside roughly, and went on pulling the mule. Another soldier standing near spoke to her kindly.

"You better git away from here, little gal," he said. "This ain't any place for a little gal. You better go on back to your maw."

Zeb caught up with her and took her hand. "Come on, Lil' Miss. Come on, les us go back to Miss Lizzie. We can't do nothin' heah, we can't do nothin' atall."

Janie let herself be led back to the house. When she reached the back porch she sat down on the steps and began to cry. Zeb stood looking at her helplessly. Baizy came out of the kitchen, sat down on the steps by her side and put her arm around her.

"Ne'mind, honey," she said. "Ne'mind, lil' gal. Yo' papa will git you another pony."

"Oh, Baizy, who'll take care of Trotter? Who will feed him his oats and rub him down and give him sugar?"

"They'll tek keer o' him, honey. Don't you worry 'bout that. Some other lil' gal up in 'e Nawth'll git him, and she'll tek keer o' him."

The thought of some other girl having her pony seemed so terrible to Janie that she cried harder than ever. Her mother heard her and came out on the porch and took her in her arms.

"You must not cry like this, precious," she said. "I am so sorry, so sorry about the pony. But, darling, there are so many things to cry about. Suppose we all just sat down and cried, what would become of us? And that is what we would do if we let ourselves go."

So Janie sat up and stopped crying, but even now, nearly a year later, she still missed the pony.

The next day the Reverend Mr. Henry Harrison came out from town, through the Yankee lines, and Grandpa was buried in the family burying ground. That day also the Williams family came over from Greenway to stay with them for a while, because Hunter's men had burned down the house and all the buildings at Greenway. Later they went in town to live with Mrs. Williams' father and mother, old Mr. and Mrs. Lewis, on Sycamore Street. Janie missed Sara Anne terribly. Nothing had ever been the same since that time. Now the two little girls sitting out in the back yard in the April twilight were remembering these things.

Janie tried to be consoling. "I don't reckon they will come back here again, Lucy," she said. "There ain't much left here now for them to take."

All the same, she was frightened. The Yankees were at Appomattox, and Appomattox was only twenty miles down the road to the east.

3

Baizy was bustling around the kitchen, trying to pretend that she was busy. Miss Lizzie was in the storeroom, just off the kitchen, measuring out supplies for the day for the family and house servants, and Baizy did not want to talk to Miss Lizzie. I ain't sayin' nothin', she thought. I knows what I know, but I ain't sayin' nothin' to nobody. Not a word, I ain't. No, ma'am.

Miss Lizzie knowed she wan't busy. How she gwine be busy when there wan't nothin' to cook? No good meals to fix, no hot bread to set a-risin', no company comin' and goin', no hongry boys yellin' at her for sump'n t'eat. There wan't nothin' to eat. Ain't been a thing wu'th eatin' in this house sence the Yankees was there last summer. Lawd, Lawd, what she wouldn't give for a taste of hog-meat. Bacon fryin' on the stove, smellin' so good it make your mouf water, good fresh snaps cooked in fat meat, grits runnin' in butter. "Shet yo' mouf, Baizy," she told herself. "Don't do no good thinkin' 'bout things like 'at. Don't do no good thinkin' 'bout anything, and 'at's a fact."

She put the dried beans in a bowl to soak for dinner. Marse Jon'than done gone down the hill to the cabins, she see him go past the kitchen window a few minutes ago. Lawd, Lawd, what gwine happen now? He looked mighty worrit and tuckered out, and it was Gawd's truf he'd had enough to worrit him. Comin' home from the fightin' last fall with his

23

arm all broke to pieces, tied up in a splint, to find ev'y kind of bad thing happen, Ol' Marse kilt and lil' Mist' Peyton daid and sto'house and barn and stable empty, not so much as a shoulder of bacon on the place, not so much as a cow or a hog or a chicken, or a mule to work the fields. And young Marse Jon gettin' killed last winter, and now the Army done surrendered and the Yankees was a-settin' just a lil' piece down the road. Marse Jon'than done tuk losin' the war mighty hard. Mighty hard. Come home from town that afternoon, two-three days ago, and go up and laid hisself face down on the big four-post' bed and stayed thar all night and all the next day. Wouldn't come out, wouldn't speak to nobody, wouldn't eat nothin'. Mighty hard. Gawd A'mighty, you wouldn't 'spect so many bad things to happen to this fambly, use to be so happy.

Lil' Miss was a-settin' on the stool over by the window, lookin' like a lil' lost soul, po' lil' lonely gal.

"If we had some flour and sugar and eggs and milk we could make a cake," she said.

Baizy laughed. "You means ef we had some flour and sugar and eggs and milk I could make a cake. You cain't make no cake."

"I can make a cake, but not a very good one."

"You cain't make no cake, you cain't make no biscuits. I don't know what you kin make."

Baizy was teasing her, trying to make her set up and look lively, a little, but Janie agreed.

"I know. I'm not very good at cooking."

"Ne'mind, ne'mind, lil' gal, you'll learn," Baizy said, with quick sympathy. She was scrubbing the wood of the trestle table with lye. "Whyn't you and Lucy go out and play in 'e back yard?"

"What will we play?" Janie asked.

"Well, fo' Gawd's sake, cain't two lil' gals think of sump'n to play?"

"I don't feel much like playing."

Baizy nodded. "You right. This ain't no playin' time, for nobody."

No playin' time, not even for lil' gals. Bad times, these was, mighty bad, and the Lawd knows what we gwine do. All the people leavin' this heah plantation, sneakin' off in the dark, goin' into town. What they gwine do in town? Talkin' 'bout

24

bein' free. Free! Who free? What free? Free from what, free *for* what? Who gwine free her? How that tall, skinny gent'-mun a-settin' up in Wash'n'ton gwine free Baizy from the things the Lawd done put on her? How he gwine free her from that good-for-nothin' black man she been lovin' so long? Gwine right on lovin', cain't stop. Big Jim, the biggest, drum-beatin'est, dancin'est, laughin'est man she ever laid her eyes on. Lawdy, Lawdy, what he could do with that lil' ole drum of his'n. Ra-ta-ta-ra-ta-ta-ra-ta-ta-*ta* with the fingers, bum—bum with the palm of his hand. Rhythm like you ain't never hyeard before, dancin' like you ain't never seed before. Drumbeat in the dark, callin' in the blood, mock orange sweet in the air, banjo music in the distance! Oh! they was good times, they was, when Baizy and Jim was a-lovin' each other. Young and happy and a-lovin'.

No worritin' then, no pain or sorrow, no heavy hand of the Lawd laid on them. And when that lil' gal, her Lucy, was a-comin' Miss Lizzie say they gotta git married. That suit Baizy fine, and Jim, he laugh and slap his laig and say: "Cert'ny, ma'am, cert'ny, we git married." So Miss Lizzie brung the preacher from the Baptist meetin'house at the crossroads to Fairview, and he say the words over them and they was married. Miss Lizzie brung them up the hill and give 'em one of the house servants cabins, and put Baizy in the kitchen to help Aunt Cynthy, who was gittin' old, and put Jim to work in the stable, and that was bad, because later on when that yalla gal come along Jim didn't have no trouble git-tin' a horse to sneak off and ride over to Greenway to see her in the night.

There had been other gals before her. Baizy knowed that, right from the first. Jim didn't fool her none. It made her kinda mad, and kinda mis'able, but it didn't make no real sho'nuff diff-unce because Jim was still her man. He was just foolin' around with them other gals, but it was diff'unt when that yalla gal at Greenway come along, walkin' like she was steppin' on aigshells, swinging her hips and lookin' slantwise out of her smoky eyes. That was diff'unt. That was when things got bad, and kept on gittin' worse right up to that night, like a lotta other nights it begun, when Jim came home from the stable and washed hisself and eat the good supper she fix for him. He set around for a while and then he stood up and reached for his drum and began to beat it, ra-ta-ta, bum—bum, and did a slow kinda shufflin' dance. Drumbeat and dance got faster and faster, tell Jim was cavortin' round that room like nothin' you ever see, most shakin' the roof down. When he stopped he put back his haid and laugh long and loud, and slap hisself on the laig and go out in the dark and rid to Greenway to see that gal, and never come back. Never come back, because he found another man with that gal, and he kilt that man, one of Mist' Williams' field hands, just reached out and choked the life right outa him with his big hands. Then he rid back to Fairview and put Old Marse's horse in the stable, but didn't come to the cabin where Baizy was a-settin' up waitin' for him. He lit out for to run away. She never did know whar he was goin' or what happen to him because in the mornin' when they found that daid man at Greenway and ev'ybody set out to look for Jim they found him a-floatin' in the river, daid. For all he was so big and strong Jim never did know how to swim, he was always scairt of the water, and how he got in the river she didn't know, but there he was, drowned in the water, in the dark.

"It's the hand of the Lawd, Sister Baizy," said the preacher; "the hand of the Lawd. Brother Jim was a sinner, and that's a fact. He took a life, sister, he took a life, and the Lawd done struck him down. You got no call to grieve because he was drownded. It was better for him to go that way. If the Lawd hadn't acted the white folks woulda."

That didn't do her no good, though, because she knowed how Jim felt about the water, and knowing, she thought that what the white folks woulda done to him for killin' a man wouldn'ta been no worse than what the hand of the Lawd done.

Miss Lizzie was mighty good to her during that time, mighty good. She come out to the cabin where Baizy was a-hollerin' and a-cryin' and brung her hot soup and said how sorry she was, and told her not to bother about the kitchen or about anything tell she felt like it; Aunt Cynthy could tek keer of Lucy and they'd send her food out to her and she could just rest quiet in the cabin tell she felt like comin' out.

"Ain't no use my tellin' you he wan't wu'th your grief, Baizy," Miss Lizzie say, "'cause I knows that when a woman love a man she grieve for him whether he wu'th it or not."

That's what Miss Lizzie say, and it was Gawd's truf.

Baizy knowed he wan't wu'th it, but she went right on grievin' just the same, and right on lovin'. That been seven-eight years ago and she ain't been free of that man a minute sence then, that Jim, that big black man with the white teeth and the laughin' eyes and the long, strong hands, the drum-beatin' hands, the love-makin' hands, the killin' hands.

So now they was all talkin' about bein' free and done snuk off and gone into town, and Marse Jon'than must know it by this time because it was a right smart while ago he went by the kitchen window. What they gwine do in town? Ef she went in town what happen to her and Lucy? Who gwine feed 'em, who she gwine wuk for? Ambrose he say the new Guv'-mint gwine tek keer of the colored people, gwine tek the land away from the white folks and give it to the colored folks. Forty acres and a mule for ev'ybody. What she gwine do with forty acres and a mule? She didn't want no forty acres and a mule. She wanted the cabin where she live with Jim, and her own vegetable patch when they git some vegetables, and this big kitchen, warm in winter and cool in summer.

All the same, ev'y now and then she kinda unnerstood how them people felt, gittin' up and goin' into town. Ev'y now and then she kinda wondered how 'bout she might go. But ef she go into town, who gwine tek keer of the fambly? Who gwine cook for 'em, even ef they ain't got anything to eat but dried beans? How Marse Jon'than gwine git along anyhow, how he gwine run this big place 'thout no help? How Miss Lizzie gwine git along?

There was a noise outside and Baizy looked through the window. Marse Jon'than was coming across the back yard. He was carrying a little black baby in his arms. The baby was yellin' and he was stompin' along, mad as a wet hen. You could tell how mad he was from the way he walked. Gawd A'mighty, what we gwine do? she thought. Lawd, Lawd, what gwine happen now?

4

Elizabeth Meade stood in the cool, dim storeroom and measured out a supply of cornmeal for the day. She was carrying on a silent conversation, partly with herself and partly with God. Cornmeal! Cornmeal and dried beans. Dried apples one day and dried peaches the next, and always cornbread and dried beans. Not batterbread, just plain old corn pones. Thou who knowest all hearts, oh Lord, know that I try not to complain, but dear Lord, if we have to eat corn pones much longer I think I'll scream. It was bad enough during the fall and winter, but then Mr. Meade could occasionally get something in town, a chicken or a piece of meat or some root vegetables. Recently there hasn't been anything to get in town, what little was there had to go to the wounded soldiers in the hospitals. How long, oh Lord, how long has it been since we have had a chicken or a piece of meat? Not even a piece of salt pork. And there isn't going to be enough cornmeal to last us all until the new crop comes in, not nearly enough. Mr. Meade says he is going to have to tell most of the field hands and their families that they will have to go, and I reckon that's the only thing to do. Poor things, what will become of them? Mr. Meade says the Freedmen's Bureau will take care of them. He says they are better off than we are, nobody is helping us, and that's a fact, oh Lord, that's a fact. Nobody but Thee, Father in heaven, our trust is in Thee.

Elizabeth became conscious of the sound of a child's

crying. It came nearer; she heard the kitchen door open and Mr. Meade's angry voice demanding: "Whose child is this?"

She went to the storeroom door. "For heaven's sake," she said. A little colored girl was sitting on the kitchen table, screaming. "Who is that?"

"That is what I am trying to find out," Mr. Meade said.

"Look lak 'at good-for-nothin' Lindy Lee's baby," Baizy told them.

"Well, she has been abandoned," Major Meade said angrily. "I found her in a cabin all by herself, yelling bloody murder. Her mother has gone off and left her."

"Her papa, too," said Baizy.

He looked at her sharply. "You knew?"

Baizy nodded. "I knowed they was all a-gwine."

Major Meade turned to his wife. "I needn't have worried about having to tell some of the field hands to leave. They have all gone."

"All gone?" Elizabeth asked incredulously.

"Every last one of them, except old Aunt Mary and Uncle Willie. They're too old to go anywhere. And Zeb's boy Amos, of course, and this child."

"You mean they left without saying a word?"

"Not a word. Not a word."

"Even Arthur?"

"Even Arthur," the Major said grimly. That hurt. Arthur was his foreman, his right-hand man.

They stood in heavy silence. The baby was still crying. "Can't you stop that howling?" the Major said irritably.

"She hongry," Baizy said. She went over to a crock and took out a piece of cold cornbread. When she gave it to the baby the little thing stopped crying and began to suck the bread.

Elizabeth looked at the child in perplexity. "Do you suppose we could find her mother?" she asked.

"Wouldn't do no good," Baizy said. "That chile's mama nor her paper never gwine tek keer o' her. Never has. Somebody else all-time had to feed and fix her."

"What are we going to do with her?"

"Give her to the Freedmen's Bureau," said the Major.

"You shouldn't talk like that, Mr. Meade," Elizabeth reproved him gently. An idea occurred to her. "Perhaps Aunt Mary could take her. She's not too old to take care of a baby, do you suppose, for a while?"

"Seem lak she could. I'll tote her down thar after while."

"Well," said Elizabeth quietly, "it seems that I need not measure out cornmeal for the farm families today."

The Major sat down on a stool and wiped his face. It was hot and sunny. He looked very tired, and Elizabeth's heart ached for him. Oh, my dear, my love, my husband, how can I help you? She went over to him and put her hand on his shoulder. He reached up and caught it and clung to it, like a child seeking reassurance.

Jackson came into the kitchen through the back door; Jackson, the butler, her mainstay. He looked unhappy; a frightened Dolly Ann followed him in.

"Marse Jon'than, I got to speak to you."

"All right, Jackson," Jonathan said wearily. "I expect I know what you want to say."

"Yassuh. You right, suh. Me and Dolly Ann, we jes' got to go, suh."

"All right, Jackson," the Major repeated. "You are free. You can go if you want to. I can't stop you, and I don't want to stop you if you want to go."

"I didn't think you would leave us, Jackson," Elizabeth said. "You and Dolly Ann."

"Fo'Gawd, Miss Lizze, we don't wanna go. Truf to tell, we kinda scairt, Miss Lizzie. We—we jes' bound to see how it feel to be free, come and go when and whar we wants to, nobody say nothing. We ain't never been nowhar, Miss Lizzie —meetin'house on Sunday, 'nother plantation for a wingding onc't in a while."

"I have never been anywhere much either, Jackson," said Elizabeth, tartly. "I have lived all my life in town and here at Fairview. Other plantations, a few trips to Richmond, over in the Valley, that's all I have ever been."

"But you could, Miss Lizzie," said Jackson. "You could ef you want to. Nobody gwine stop you ef you sez you gwine somewhar, to Wash'n'ton or mebbe even New York."

"You're quite right, Jackson," she replied. "I could. That makes a great deal of difference. I am just sorry to lose you. Where are you going?"

"In town fust. Don't know whar after that."

"Mebbe we come to see you sometimes." Dolly Ann spoke for the first time.

"I hope you will."

"I have nothing to give you, Jackson, to help you on your way," the Major said. "You know that."

"Yassuh, I knows how it is, Marse Jon'than." He paused for a moment. "I done told goo'bye to Miss Emily. Now I sez goo'bye to Lil'Miss."

"Goo'bye, Jackson," Janie said. "I'm sorry."

"Yassum, we's sorry too. Goo'bye Marse Jon'than, Miss Lizzie."

"Goo'bye, Miss Lizzie," Dolly Ann said.

"Goodbye," Elizabeth said. "And Dolly Ann—come back if you need to."

"Yassum."

They went out and Jackson closed the door carefully behind him. Nobody said anything. Elizabeth saw tears in Janie's eyes. She wanted to cry herself, and she had a strong suspicion that Mr. Meade did too. He left the kitchen and walked slowly down the long corridor to the back hall, and on into the house.

It was the next day that the men started coming down the road. Elizabeth came from the kitchen into the front hall, and saw that Janie was sitting on the porch steps. Poor little lonely girl, she thought. Now she has nobody at all to play with, except Baizy's Lucy. It came over her that there was no longer any need to say Baizy's Lucy. The little girl was now the only Lucy left on the place. Janie called to her.

"Mama, there are a lot of men coming down the road."

There was so little movement on the road these days that even one passerby was the cause of excitement. Elizabeth went out on the porch to see what Janie meant. Dust was rising from the road. It had rained several days ago, but now the dust was heavy again. It rose in little spurts, floated around and settled back on the road and on the bushes and undergrowth that lined the old snake fence. Standing where she was, Elizabeth could look down the driveway, between the cedar trees that edged it to the broad open space where the driveway ran into the road. Across this space a thin stream of men was straggling. Sometimes a single lonely figure trudged past. Sometimes they came in twos and threes, or in larger groups. A few of them rode horses, one man came by on a mule.

Elizabeth knew who they were. "They are the soldiers, Janie," she said. "General Lee's soldiers. They must have

31

finished paroling them. They are coming from Appomattox. Going home."

"They don't look like soldiers," Janie said.

"They don't, do they? The finest soldiers in the world, the best fighters in the world, but they don't look like it now."

She stood for a few moments watching the pathetic procession. "Poor things," she said. "If I just had something to give them."

Presently she turned and went back into the house. Mr. Meade was in the library and the door was closed. She hoped he had not seen the soldiers; it would only make him feel worse. He was lost and sunk in depression as it was. He had had to suspend publication of the newspaper. With no money, with most of the wires down, the railroads destroyed, the mails not moving, there was no way to publish a newspaper. Without the paper, with the plantation lying empty and deserted around him, with the Confederacy lost, Jonathan Meade was fighting a desperate battle against despair and utter futility. He had gone to town the day before and when he came back his face was grim.

"They are already there," he said, "the occupation troops. Blue uniforms are all over town. They have taken the Court House as their headquarters and they've set up a Freedmen's Bureau in Pace's Warehouse."

"Mr. Meade, honey," Elizabeth said, "it's going to be hard, nobody can deny that. It's going to be mighty hard, but we have just got to live through it. We have got to grit our teeth and stand it. Try not to fret yourself any more than you can help."

He stood looking at her, and slowly his face relaxed into a smile. Elizabeth knew that Jonathan was not a handsome man, by classic standards. He had the Meade blue eyes and the Meade length of limb, but his features were too rugged for beauty. They lacked the chiseled perfection of the old General's. However, to her he had always seemed a very charming gentleman, and she was convinced that no one had as sweet a smile as he.

"All right, Elizabeth," he said. "I will try not to fret myself any more than I can help."

Now she stood in the wide front hall of Fairview and gave herself a few moments of inaction to consider the situation that faced her. She had lived in this house all her married life; she had been its mistress for fifteen years ever since old

Mrs. Meade had died. The familiar rooms lay quietly around her, in their usual perfect order. Jackson and Dolly Ann had seen to that before they left. An alabaster bowl of japonica and forsythia stood on the pier table in the hall, reflected in the mirror behind it. The pair of inlaid tip-top tables standing against the wall on either side of the fanlighted doorway, the carved oak cathedral chair, the mahogany frame of the sofa, all shone burnished and dustless. The morning sun poured into the two parlors through the lace curtains on the east windows, with their blue velvet overdraperies, and glinted upon the small gold chairs, the blue and yellow brocaded sofas, the ormolu clock and side ornaments on the mantelpiece under their shining glass covers. Polished brass in the fireplaces, polished silver on the sideboard and serving table, polished floors and furniture, all was as it should be. This was her home, the center of her world, the ground in which her life had taken root. It was her function to keep it this way. How was she going to do it? It would soon be time for the usual spring cleaning, when the draperies were to be taken down, the rugs taken up, when every piece of china, every bit of woodwork was to be washed, every book dusted, everything that could be polished, polished until it shone. She thought of all the bedrooms upstairs, with their canopied four-poster beds and their fluted muslin curtains at the windows. The empty bedrooms. Spring and fall cleaning at Fairview had always taken a small army of servants. How was it going to be done now with only herself and Baizy? How was it going to be kept clean? And outdoors, the rose garden and the herb garden, the perennial borders and the cutting garden, and above all the vegetable garden. Dear Lord, how was it all going to be done? And Mr. Meade shut up in the library agonizing over a defunct newspaper, a deserted plantation, a lost cause and a lost world. The remnants of the Confederate Army straggling silently down the road outside, and she was going around talking about not fretting herself! She, who had built walls around whole areas of her consciousness, enclosing things she could not bear to think about, shutting off in sanctified ground the thought of her sons, her boys who were gone! Grit your teeth and stand it, she had said. Grit your teeth and close your mind and work your fingers to the bone!

Janie came running into the house. "Mama," she said, "there's a soldier out here who wants a drink of water."

Elizabeth sighed. "Well, water is one thing we have got. Run around to the back, Janie, and find Zeb. Tell him to dip a fresh bucket of water and bring it and a clean dipper out to the front porch."

The soldier was sitting on the bottom step of the front porch, in the shade. All Elizabeth could see of him was the back of an old butternut uniform and a battered hat, with most of the crown gone. Instead of going to the porch she turned and went out to the kitchen, where she went to Baizy's crock and took out a cold corn pone. With it in her hand she went back to the porch. The soldier stood up when he heard her coming and took off the old hat.

"Mawnin' ma'am," he said.

"Good morning," Elizabeth replied. "I'll have some cool water for you in a minute."

His uniform was ragged and there were no markings on it. His shoes were tied on with pieces of string. They stood looking at each other. Each knew what the other was thinking, but neither spoke. There was nothing to say. Finally Elizabeth broke the silence. "It is hot for April, isn't it?"

"Yes, ma'am, it shoah is."

"Have you far to go?"

"A right smart way, ma'am. Over near Cumberland Gap."

Zeb came around the side of the house with a bucket of water. Janie was following him. The soldier took a dripping dipper full and drank thirstily.

"U-m-m-m, that's good, ma'am. I was powerful thirsty." He wiped his mouth with the back of his hand.

"Are—are you hungry?" Elizabeth asked.

A strange look came over the man's face. "No mo'an usual, ma'am, I reckon. They gave us some rations two days ago."

"Could you eat this?" she asked, holding out the corn pone.

The soldier's face broke into a smile. "I'd be glad to try, ma'am," he said.

She could tell how hungry he was from the way he ate. When he had finished the pone, he drank another dipper of water.

"Thanky," he said. "Thanky kindly, ma'am, you and the little lady. That helps, that shoah helps." He turned to go.

"Goodbye," Janie said, and then added "sir" because he was one of General Lee's soldiers.

He smiled at her, put on his hat and started down the driveway, on his way west, to Cumberland Gap.

Elizabeth stood still on the porch after he had gone, thinking. "That gives me an idea, Janie. I expect most of them are thirsty. Zeb, go around to the back porch and get the old table that stands there, the little table, and another bucket of water and some gourds, and take them down to the road just outside the entrance. Janie, you come with me. At least we can give them water."

They walked down the driveway to the entrance, and when Zeb came with the table she had him put it on one side near the fence, in the shade of the trees, opposite the watering trough. He brought buckets of water and fresh gourds, and Elizabeth and Janie stood there and offered the soldiers water as they came down the road.

"Will you have a cool drink of water?" Elizabeth would say. Most of them accepted the water gratefully and silently. Very little was said. "It's hot for April"; "Yes, ma'am, I'll be glad to get home"; "Don't look like it rained much around here"; "Thanky, ma'am"; these were the things that were said.

These soldiers all looked alike. They all looked gray. They were sad-looking men, thin and tired and hot. Most of them were ragged. Their uniforms had been muddy, it had rained for days around Petersburg and on that last march to Appomattox. Now they were dusty. Most of their shoes were worn. Some had no shoes or boots; they plodded along in their bare feet on the dusty road. One man limped up to them in a pair of shiny black boots. He stood looking down at them sorrowfully as he drank his water.

"Took 'em fom a daid Yankee," he said. "Mighty fine boots, but they hurt so bad I cain't hardly wear 'em."

"Perhaps it would help if you took them off for a while and rested your feet," Mrs. Meade suggested.

"Might be. I'll try."

He sat down a little distance away, pulled off the boots and rubbed his feet. He had on no socks. Presently he stretched his legs out straight in front of him and began wiggling his toes. Some other time, Elizabeth thought, she might have laughed at the sight of the big, bare feet and wiggling toes, but today it was not funny.

A young officer rode up on horseback and dismounted at the watering trough.

"May I, ma'am?" he asked politely, as his horse started to drink.

"Of course," she replied, "and wouldn't you like a drink of cool water yourself?"

He came over to the table where she and Janie were standing. He was a nice-looking young man, obviously a gentleman. His uniform was faded and stained, but it had been brushed and pressed. There were lieutenant's bars on his shoulders. He wore black boots with spurs and held a wide-brimmed cavalry hat in his hand. A sword hung at his side. When he saw her look at the sword he laughed, and it was not a pleasant laugh.

"We have been allowed to keep our sidearms," he said. "A magnanimous gesture! Everything else is gone, but our officers may keep their horses and their sidearms."

"You will be glad to have the horse," she said. "There are not many left in Virginia."

"You're right. You certainly are right, ma'am. There aren't many left."

He was very young, but his voice sounded tired. He went over to the trough and pulled his horse's head out of the water and mounted him. Then he rode back to the table.

"This was very kind of you, ladies. Refreshment for man and beast. Thank you."

Elizabeth looked up at him, and there were tears in her eyes. She couldn't help it. For a moment the walls were breached, the memories were flooding through. Involuntarily, she reached her hand up to him.

"My son was a lieutenant too," she said. "A little younger than you, I reckon. He was killed at Petersburg in January."

A strange expression came over the young man's face. He reached down and took her hand and pressed it gently. "Don't weep for him, ma'am," he said. "Tears are for the living."

He bowed, put on his hat with a flourish, and rode off. It was quiet after he had gone. Nobody was coming down the road. Only the rustlings and twittering of birds disturbed the deep country silence. Occasionally a little breeze stirred the new leaves on the trees.

After a few minutes Elizabeth said: "Janie, I am going back to the house and tell Baizy to make some hot corn pones. With so few to feed now I think we can spare the meal, and I have got to do something for these poor men. You stay here and offer them the water. I'll send Zeb down to stay with you, and he will bring a fresh bucket."

She walked slowly back to the house and up the steps to the square front porch. Standing there between the fluted white columns, a slender woman whose beauty was beginning to fade, she looked back down the driveway between the cedar trees to the road. A group of soldiers was trudging past, and she watched the forlorn procession of silent, exhausted men, ragged, hungry, footsore and heartsick. She thought of the journey that lay ahead of each of them, of the ravaged homes many would find, of the struggle that faced them, and remembering the empty cabins down the hill, the empty barns and storerooms behind her, the empty fields around her, the empty rooms upstairs; remembering the swaggering blue-coated soldiers and the roistering Negroes in town, she was suddenly buffeted, submerged, by a rush of bitterness. A tidal wave of hatred swept over her. She was drowned in hatred, suffocated by it. She put her hands up to her throat and struggled to breathe through the hatred that filled her.

Hate was the comforter. Hate the conquerors, the destroyers! Hate them to your dying day and through death into eternity. Stiffen the backbone, strengthen the heart with hate; hold the head high in hate.

"God forgive me for these thoughts; oh, Lord, forgive me. I know Thy commandment to love our enemies and forgive those that trespass against us. I try to follow Thy ways, oh Lord, but this is too much. I can't do it. I can't. I am not one of Thy saints, Father in heaven, I am just an ordinary human being, and that's the way I feel. Forgive me and help me, Lord, but—that—is—the—way—I—feel."

With her small clenched fist she struck the railing of the porch repeatedly. Hate was the salt that would flavor the bread of poverty, the iron that would enter the soul. Hate was the bitter herb that would grow in the ruined gardens of the South from generation unto generation, amen. "I'm sorry, but that is the way it is, Lord, that is the way it is."

Presently she turned and went through the house to the kitchen, to measure out cornmeal and tell Baizy to bake some hot pones for General Lee's soldiers going down the road, going west from Appomattox.

5

Janie and her mother were in the back parlor, going over a new piece of music that Janie was to start on. General Lee might surrender, the Confederacy might die, sometimes Janie thought the skies might fall in, but she had to practice her music. There was no use telling Mama that she would never play well on the piano. "Yes, you will," Mama always said. "If you work at it you will learn to play—acceptably. Anyhow, I am not going to have a daughter of mine growing up without knowing something about music."

Emily was upstairs, as usual. She shut herself up in her room most of the time now, except when she came down for meals. Papa was in the library, waiting for Zeb to bring Black Prince from the stable. He was going to ride into town. Suddenly they heard the sound of wheels coming up the driveway, and horses' hooves. Mama and Janie looked at each other. Somebody was coming to see them.

"Go see who that is, Janie," Mama said.

Janie started out into the hall, but as she reached the doorway Emily came rushing down the stairway and ran through the hall like a whirlwind. A man was coming up the steps of the front porch, a man in a blue uniform. He and Emily met on the porch and to Janie's astonishment Emily ran right into his arms. They stood there hugging and kissing.

"Oh, Jerome, Jerome," Emily said. "I thought you weren't coming."

"Didn't you get my letter?"

"Oh, no, no. I haven't heard a word. I have been perfectly miserable. The mails aren't running."

"I was afraid of that. I came as soon as I could, sweet."

Mama had followed Janie out into the hall and Papa had come out of the library. All three of them stood in the hall looking at Emily in the arms of the Yankee officer. Over her shoulder he could see them, and he pushed her from him gently. Emily turned and saw them. Laughing and gay, she took the young man's hand and pulled him through the doorway.

"Mama, Papa, this is Jerome," she said. "Captain Jerome Tyson."

Papa bowed. Mama bent her head very slightly. Neither spoke.

Captain Tyson looked at Papa. "I am sure you know, Major Meade, that Miss Emily and I are engaged to be married."

"I have heard something to that effect," Papa said. His voice sounded strange. "I did not take it seriously."

"I can assure you, sir, that it is entirely serious. She and I agreed that we would not marry until the war was over. Now it is over, and I have come for her." He paused, but nobody said anything. "I have been ordered to Washington, and I must get there within three days. As no trains are running we must go by horse and buggy; unfortunately I cannot wait for us to be married here. My plan is to reach Charlottesville by nightfall. I understand that you have relatives there with whom Emily can stay, and we can be married there, if not tonight, then tomorrow morning. We can then continue the journey to Washington immediately."

Papa was not looking at him, he was looking at Emily. "Are you going with this man?" he asked.

The laugh had gone from Emily's face, but she did not hesitate. "Yes. Yes, I am, Papa."

"If you go, you can never come back."

"He doesn't mean that, Emily," Mama said. Her voice was hard, her whole body seemed to be hard and stiff. "This is your home, you can always come back—if you want to. But if you can leave us now, if you can go with this man, who has been killing your kinsmen and ravaging your country, if you can marry him and live among his people, I don't think you will ever want to come back."

Emily began to cry. "Oh, Mama, don't be so hard," she said. "He is no more responsible for this war than we are." She went over to her mother and put her head on her shoulder. "I love him, don't you understand?"

Mama did not move. She stood straight and rigid, giving no sign that she knew Emily was there.

"Go get your things, Emily," Captain Tyson said.

Emily straightened up and wiped her eyes. "Yes, I will, Jerome."

"Take only what you will need to get to Washington."

Emily went up the stairs, and the rest of them stood in the hall in silence. Janie was embarrassed. She had been conscious of many silences in the last week, heavy silences filled with unspoken things, but the things that were not said were sorrowful things. This was a terrible silence. Janie felt that the things not being said were angry, frightening things.

She could hear Zeb coming around the house from the stable with Black Prince. Captain Tyson's horse nickered in greeting. He was a beautiful bay horse, and he was pulling a pretty new buggy, very clean and shiny. Papa was looking at it through the door.

"Where did you steal that outfit?" he asked. "I have not seen a trap like that around here since Hunter's men came through."

A slow, brick red spread over Captain Tyson's face. Without a word he turned, crossed the porch and went down the steps to the buggy, where he stood with his back to the house.

Presently Papa went to the porch and called to Zeb: "I won't need Black Prince today, Zeb. Run him around the Field Road for exercise."

"Yas *suh*," Zeb said with a grin. There was nothing he liked as much as riding Black Prince.

When Emily came down the stairs she had changed from her cotton dress to her dark blue bombazine and she had on a straw bonnet tied under her chin with blue ribbons. She carried a reticule in her hand. Her eyes were bluer than the ribbons, but her face was pale and still showed traces of tears. She stood in the hall and looked at her father and mother.

"Goodbye," she said. "I'm sorry—sorry you feel like this and sorry to leave you, but I have to go. I love him, you see."

Nobody said anything. "Won't you tell me goodbye?"

Janie could not stand it any longer. She ran to Emily and put her arms around her. "I'll tell you goodbye, Emily. I am so sorry you are going away. I wish you wouldn't."

"Little Janie. Dear little Janie." Emily kissed her and stroked her hair. "Some day you will understand, honey."

When she reached the door she said: "Goodbye, Mama and Papa."

"Goodbye," they both said. They sounded as if they were speaking to a stranger.

Captain Tyson turned around when he heard Emily coming. He ran up the steps and took her reticule from her, and helped her into the buggy. Then he got in himself and snapped his whip. The beautiful bay horse and the shining buggy moved off around the circle in front of the house and down the driveway. The sounds grew fainter and fainter.

Mama sat down on the sofa and covered her face with her hands. Janie went over to her and Mama reached out and pulled her onto her lap and put her arms around her.

"Oh, Janie, Janie," she said. "My baby. You are all we have left. Four children and only one left." She rocked herself back and forth holding Janie as if she really were a baby and saying over and over again: "Four children. Four children."

Papa came and sat on the sofa beside her and put his arms around her. Janie felt so sorry for both of them that she cried on Mama's shoulder.

6

Jonathan Meade of Fairview, Major, C.S.A., rode slowly along the road going into town. He had no particular reason for going, no purpose to accomplish. It was Saturday afternoon, the fifteenth of April. It had been less than a week since the surrender. Except for the Yankees and the Negroes, the town stood closed, grim and silent. The *Herald* office was closed, the paper was not being published. The unaccustomed silence of the *Herald* building always depressed him, yet the habit of years drew him to it almost every day. He had no desire to meet any of his friends or associates. Too much unspoken tragedy hung in the air around them, and today the new bitterness of Emily's departure lay heavily upon him. A terrible restlessness seized him, however, when he sat quietly at Fairview; some sort of action was necessary.

The narrow country road the Major followed wound around the curves of rolling hills, between fields and stretches of woodland. For a while, as he rode, the fields and the woods belonged to him. Rail fences snaked along the edges of his fields, guarding them, but the fields, which should have showed the long straight furrows of the plow marching off toward the distant hills, lay fallow and untended. Tall pines showed dark in the woods against the new green of oak and chestnut, of poplar and gum, and the still bare branches of the ash trees. White dogwood blossoms lay like sifted light in the green gloom of the forest, and Judas trees were blooming on the slopes of the hills. All that nature could do to repair the ravages of man was being done.

The timber in the woods was valuable, and the woods needed cutting. He corrected the thought; the timber would be valuable as if there were anyone to cut it or anyone to buy it, or any way to move it to the lumber mill down by the river. The hewers of wood and the drawers of water had gone, the sawmill stood silent, the buyers were buying no longer. Stagnation lay heavy as fog around him, and yet this Piedmont countryside had been blessed. West of Richmond and the Tidewater, southwest of the blood-soaked fields of Spotsylvania, Fredericksburg, the Wilderness, east of the Shenandoah Valley with its mountain gaps and its long Valley Pike, this country had been spared the physical desolation of battle and marching armies. Except for Hunter's raid last summer it had not known the horror of invading troops. It was not battle-scarred. The desolation here came from attrition and forced neglect, from the gradual drawing off of men, of cattle and horses and food, the stoppage of trade and the breakdown of transportation, rail and river and canal. The land itself was unhurt. It spread out around him, dozing sleepily in the sun but stirring with fertility, young with spring, waiting for the plow and the seed, the axe and the saw.

Jonathan rode on beyond his own property, through the open country to the town, and down the long hill that led to its center, past the houses that sturdily climbed the steep slopes, where children played in the yards and life seemed normal to the outward eye. He turned at Twelfth Street and went to Main, and along Main to Tenth. There he turned right, down Tenth Street, down the hill, to Ally Martin's livery stable. That was where he always left Black Prince when he came to town. Ally was sitting on the sidewalk outside the wide entrance to the stable, in a rush-bottomed chair cocked back against the wall of the building.

"Evenin', Major," he said.

"Evenin', Ally. May I leave Black Prince here for a littte while?"

Ally nodded but did not move. "Take him on in. I let Jason go this afternoon, and I ain't got a boy. Cain't keep a boy any more, they won't work. Don't need one, and that's a fact. Funerals is all anybody hires horses for now. The dead cain't walk."

Jonathan led the horse into the dim interior and put him in a stall. There was plenty of room. Ally had only a few old carriage horses left.

"I didn't unsaddle him," he said, when he came back to the street. "I won't be long this afternoon."

"You heard the news?" Ally asked.

"What news?"

"Honest Abe's been shot."

"What?"

"Abraham Lincoln was shot last night. Assassinated. Died early this mawnin'."

Jonathan stared incredulously. "Man, are you sure? Is that a rumor, or is it true?"

"It's true, all right. Co'te House bell been tollin' all mawnin'. Them Yankees up there in the Co'te House is wailin' and gnashin' their teeth."

"Good God," Jonathan said. There was another chair on the sidewalk by the side of Ally's and he sat down.

"Blame us for it," Ally said gloomily. "Shoah's you bawn, they'll blame us for it."

"Who did it?"

"Crazy fool named Booth. An actor."

"Not Edwin Booth?"

Ally shook his head. "His brother, John. John Wilkes Booth."

"He's not a Confederate?"

"Naw, no connection with us. Father was an Englishman, they say, another actor. Whole family of actors. Lived first in New York and then in Maryland, when they wasn't actin' around the country. Don't make any difference, though. They'll blame it on us."

"Why did he do it?"

"Dunno. Didn't like Abe, I reckon. He ain't the only one, but it certainly is goin' to raise hell."

Jonathan stood up. "I would have said that the situation could not get any worse, but it seems I was mistaken."

He walked slowly back up the hill to Main Street and crossed to the opposite corner. Here the *Herald* office was housed in a two-story brick building facing Main Street. The composing room and the printing presses were on the first

44

floor, the city office and Jonathan's own office were on the second floor. The front door was closed and locked. Jonathan kept up the hill a short distance to a side entrance opening on Tenth Street, where a dark and narrow stairway led directly into the city room.

Tom Scott was there, sitting at his desk. Tom looked old, Jonathan thought. Well, he was; he must be well up in his sixties. He had been there when Jonathan bought the paper, more than twenty years ago, a printer in the composing room. Now he was the managing editor: Jonathan had given him that title when he went away at the beginning of the war. It was Tom who had kept the paper alive. Twenty years of age and a wide difference of background and culture separated the two men, but the close and congenial association of the years had wiped out these differences and forged a bond between them closer almost than family ties.

"Certainly am glad you came," Tom said. "I been thinkin' how was I going to get word to you. You've heard?"

Jonathan nodded. "Ally Martin told me." He sat down at an empty desk.

"You think it's bad?" Tom asked anxiously.

"Bad! I think it is tragic."

"You ain't wastin' any love on Mr. Abraham Lincoln, are you?"

"That's not the point," Jonathan Meade said. "I don't like murder, I don't want to see any man murdered, but what I'm thinking about is the effect it will have on the South. Say what you choose about Lincoln, feel as you will about him—and you know how I feel—but it's a fact that he was a strong man and he had the people of the North behind him. Without him that pack of wolves in Washington will tear us to pieces."

"I reckon you're right," Tom agreed. "I reckon you're dead right. How about Andy Johnson?"

"Does anybody know where Johnson stands? And wherever he stands, he is no match for Thaddeus Stevens." The thought of Thaddeus Stevens blackened an already dark world. "The deformed old hellcat," he said. "He will call his pack of Radicals together and they will make mincemeat out of the South."

He stood up and crossed to his own office, which opened off the city room at the front of the building. Here unaccustomed

45

orderliness confronted him. The piles of newspapers which usually spilled over the chairs and tables were gone. His desk was bare of the clutter which usually covered it, the long sheets of yellow paper on which he wrote his editorials, pencils, pens, newspaper clippings, scraps of paper. The wastebasket was empty. The place no longer looked like a newspaper office, and it made him feel ill at ease. Through the window looking to the west, sunlight streamed in a shaft of light down which dust floated lazily. He went to the window and stood looking along the cobblestoned street sloping precipitously down to the railroad tracks at the river's edge. The slow waters of the James, dyed red by the earth of its banks, moved on their leisurely way across Virginia to Richmond, to the Chesapeake Bay and the open sea. On the opposite bank the high bluffs showed the new green of April.

He turned to one of the front windows and looked down on Main Street. It was Saturday afternoon, but the street was almost empty. Most of the stores were closed. A few Negroes drifted by; most of them, he thought, would be down on River Street where the Freedman's Bureau was operating, or in the little streets off Twelfth where the Negroes flocking to the town were beginning to congregate. A group of Federal soldiers stood on the street, in front of the Holcombe House, talking; but the chairs lining the sidewalk in front of the hotel, under the awning, where leisurely gentlemen were wont to meet, were empty now. Silence lay like a blanket over the little town. It seemed to bask in sleepy peacefulness, but Jonathan knew that behind the closed doors of the small stores, the offices, the banks, the tobacco warehouses, the railroad station, the homes that climbed the steep hills behind him, there was no peace.

So Lee had surrendered and Lincoln was dead. Andrew Johnson was President of the United States and Jefferson Davis was running like a stag before the horns of the hunter. In Washington the Radical Republicans would be gathering like buzzards around the bier of the dead President, inwardly rejoicing. They had hated Lincoln. Now they would be mouthing sorrowful hypocrisies, and gathering their forces to grasp the new administration. And how was he, Jonathan Meade, going to get his crops in the ground? That was the immediate problem, the present desperate urgency. From all its journeying, his mind returned constantly to ask that question: how was he going to get the land plowed, the seeds sown, the tobacco seedlings transplanted? A workhorse or a mule! How was he going to get hold of a workhorse or a mule?

He went back into the city room. Tom was still sitting there, smoking his pipe, doing nothing.

"You better go on home, Tom," Jonathan said. "It don't do you any good just to sit there."

"It don't do me any good to go home, either," Tom said.

"I know. One place is about as bad as another." He wandered restlessly around the room.

"Pity you can't go to church tomorrow," Tom commented.

Jonathan was surprised. Tom knew they had not been able to come into town for church since Hunter's raid last summer.

"No way to get Elizabeth and the girls in town," he said. He had not told Tom about Emily. He could not bring himself to speak of it yet even to Tom. "We go to the Old Meeting House out there in the country whenever there's a preacher there, because we can walk to it. There isn't going to be a preacher tomorrow."

"I don't mean that," Tom said. "You couldn't go to church even if you could get in town."

"Why not?"

"Your church is going to be closed tomorrow. Mine ain't. I can go to church if I want to, but there ain't going to be any service at your church." For a moment a semblance of a smile crossed Tom's face.

"What are you talking about, Tom? Why isn't there going to be a service?"

"General Order No. 29," Tom said. The Major continued to look at him enquiringly. "You don't know about General Order No. 29? You ought to stay in town more, boy. Keep up with what's going on. I'll tell you about General Order No. 29, issued by the United States government. It says: 'In all churches where prayers have heretofore been offered for the so-called President of the Confederate States, a similar mark of respect is hereby ordered to be paid to the President of the United States.' That's what General Order No. 29 says, but your preacher, Reverend Henry Harrison, he says no."

Tom bent over and knocked the ashes from his pipe into the wastebasket. "It don't hurt us. Baptists don't have to pray for the President. Preacher says whatever comes into his

47

mind to say and if a prayer for the President of the United States don't happen to come into his mind, can't nobody blame him. But you Episcopalians, you got to pray by what is written in a book and the book says pray for the President. Only according to your preacher, his book says pray for the President of the Confederate States."

Tom chuckled. "Good for Henry Harrison," said Jonathan.

"He says the order of service is set by the General Assembly of the Episcopal Chuch of Virginia," Tom went on. "Maybe it ain't the General Assembly but whatever runs the church in Virginia, and he couldn't change it without their approval even if he wanted to, and he don't want to. The Yankee General says that don't mean a thing to him and the reverend gentleman will pray for the President of the United States. The reverend gentleman says he won't, so he's closed the church. There's a big sign on the front door of St. John's that says: 'No services will be held in this church on Sunday, April 16.' Episcopal churches all over Virginia are closing tomorrow, I hear." Tom banged his fist down on his desk. "There it is, Jonny. There it is. You can drag a horse to water but I'm damned if you can make him drink."

Jonathan, sitting on the edge of Tom's desk, was silent for a while. Then he too struck the desk with his clenched fist. "You're wrong, Tom," he said. "You're wrong. You can make him drink if you hold him there long enough, and we are going to have to drink. You might as well make up your mind to it. We are going to have to drink. Pretty soon we will all be praying for the President of the United States."

Looking at Tom across the desk, the Major saw a strange thing happen. Suddenly Tom's rugged, lined face began to work convulsively and tears came into his eyes. To hide them he put his big, gnarled hands over his face. To Jonathan Meade it was a shattering thing to see rawboned, hard-bitten, gallant old Tom Scott break up like that. He stood for a few moments with his hand on Tom's shoulders, and then he left him alone. He got his horse from Ally Martin's and rode home. The sun was sinking behind the mountains and the sky was colored with rose and gold as he went up the driveway.

7

On a day in the following week, when Major Meade went to his office he found not only Tom there, but young Leslie Vaughn. Leslie had been a reporter and copywriter on the *Herald* staff for the past two years, after he was invalided home from Fredericksburg, where he lost his left arm. Jonathan had a special feeling for him because of the arm, remembering how near he had come to the same loss.

"Mawnin', Major," Leslie said.

"Mawnin', Leslie," the Major said. "How are you?"

"I stopped by to see if anything was happening. If you don't start this paper again soon I am goin' to have to go up to Baltimore or maybe New York to get me some work."

"It wouldn't do you any good if I did start it, Les. You'd have to work for nothing. You know I haven't got any money."

"Well, having something to do would at least help to keep your mind off an empty stomach," Leslie said.

The Major looked at him sharply. He wondered if the boy really was hungry. "You'd better come out and help me plow my land," he said, only half joking. The thought came to him that if Leslie came out to Fairview he could at least get beans and cornbread to eat. Then he was sorry he had spoken, remembering the arm. To cover his slip he turned to Tom. "I've found a mule. Man over in Bedford County will let me hire him on credit. A farmer named John Foster. I'm going to begin plowing tomorrow."

49

Jonathan went on into his own office. Before he closed the door he said: "As soon as I have anything to go on I'll let you know, Les."

A few minutes later he heard Leslie go down the stairs. He felt sorry for him. He felt sorry for so many people, but what could he do? He sat at his desk and thought of his fields. The mule would be a great blessing. He was surprised that John Foster would let him use the animal on credit. He had had dealings with him before and knew him to be a hard man. Last fall, when he came home from the Army and found all his livestock gone, he had hired a mule from Foster to set out a field of winter wheat. The price had been exorbitant, even in Confederate money. The price they had agreed upon for future payment this time was also exorbitant, but Jonathan had to have a mule. It was a symbol, Jonathan reflected, a complete statement of the situation that faced him and all his class, the landed gentry of Virginia, that he should now be dependent upon a small farmer in Bedford County, whose acreage did not exceed one sixtieth of his own, for his most basic need; that he must accept whatever terms that unimportant countryman chose to offer him. John Foster had livestock; Hunter's men had not reached him. John Foster had money. Where he got it Jonathan did not know and he scorned him for having it, when all good Confederates would have turned their assets into Confederate bonds, now worthless. The livestock and the money put John Foster into a position of advantage and he was making the most of it. He was buying land, now dirt cheap all around him. He was coming up as others went down. Jonathan knew this was happening all over the state, all over the South. Wealth and importance had been built on sand, and the sands were shifting.

Tomorrow he would ride out into the country and get the mule. He would have preferred to wait a little while, his tobacco seedlings were not ready, but he was afraid he would miss his chance at John Foster's extra mule. He and Zeb would have to do the plowing and that made him smile ironically. He had never plowed a furrow in his life and Zeb had done little of it. He was a stableboy, not a field hand. He could not possibly put out the usual acreage in tobacco, not with only the two of them to work it, but he would cut down as little as he could. Tobacco meant money. The South Field, and the long level stretch down by the road, probably.

He would cut out the oats and barley. Without livestock they could get on without oats and barley. The winter wheat would give them some flour, if he could get it milled. Corn they must have. Corn and a vegetable garden just large enough for their own use. Later the fruit would come. The pears and the cherries were no problem. Though there were many pear and cherry trees on the place, the orchards were set in apples and peaches. He thought of the long rows of blossoming fruit trees stretching off to the low hills and up the slopes of the hills. By the grace of God, through no further effort of his own the fruit would ripen, barring a late frost. He must get it picked and sorted and packed and shipped.

Sitting in his quiet office, thinking of the ripening fruit and the fields of tasseled corn and the good smoke smell of curing tobacco hanging over the countryside next autumn, warmth ran through all the chilled arteries of his being. The land was the most satisfying thing in life, and he still had the land. John Foster might have cash, but he, Jonathan Meade, had land, and with God's help he would bring the land back to its own. He loved the newspaper, he was lost without it. It was child, his creation, but the land was life itself. His roots were in the earth. Earth and sun and rain, seed and harvest. The generations of his ancestors spoke in his blood.

Tom opened the door of his office. Tom's manners were casual. He never knocked. There was a scowl on his face.

"There's a—a person here to see you," he said.

A dapper young man came through the door into Jonathan's office. He was dressed in a blue uniform, very trim and new. He had a small black mustache. He walked with a swagger and he was smiling gaily.

"Good morning," he said. "Major Meade, I take it. My name is Jamison, Lieutenant Robert Jamison, and I come from General Curtis."

Jonathan was torn between an immediate violent dislike of the young man and his habitual manner of courtesy to a guest. Normally he would no more fail to rise in greeting a visitor to his office than to his home. Now the habit was broken; dislike won. He remained seated and bowed his head to acknowledge the introduction.

"The General has instructed me to tell you," the Lieutenant went on, "that he would like to see you in his office this after-

51

noon at two o'clock. His office is located in the Court House, you know, on the second floor."

It was borne in upon the Major that he, Jonathan Meade of Fairview, was being summoned by this young whippersnapper, in the name of the alien dictator who had taken possession of the Court House, to appear before him as a schoolboy might be summoned to the office of the headmaster. Murderous rage swept over him. He stood up. The Lieutenant stopped smiling when he saw his face.

"Tell your General," Major Meade said slowly, "that my office is located on the northeast corner of Main and Tenth Streets, and that the doors are open at all times through the day to those who have business to transact with me."

"But—but—sir—"

"That is my reply. Take it to your General."

The young man drew himself up very straight. He looked completely military now; the casual slouch was gone. "I will do so," he said, and turned and left the room.

Jonathan sat down. He could hear the Lieutenant's footsteps running down the stairs to the street. Tom came to the door.

"What's he want?"

"He came to tell me that his General wants to see me in his office at two o'clock this afternoon."

"You ain't goin', are you?"

"I am not going," Jonathan said. He took a deep breath. "Foolish of me, no doubt. I seemed to remember, Tom, that I'm the one who said we were going to have to learn to drink at the trough of the defeated."

Tom was prowling restlessly around the room. He came to a stop in front of Jonathan's desk.

"Listen to me, Jonny," he said. "I ain't been in the habit of killin' people, but I'm tellin' you, if I get through this thing without killin' one of them damned blue cockatoos that's struttin' around this town, swaggerin' and smilin' and orderin' people around, if I get through without killin' one of 'em, I'm goin' to be lucky, damned lucky."

That sobered Jonathan, because he knew Tom meant it. "Now you listen to me, Tom. You and I have both got tricky tempers. They sneak up behind us and take us by surprise. So we have to be careful, man, and watch out. There's no use

52

making a bad situation worse. It wouldn't do anybody any good for either of us to get hauled up before a military court, a Yankee military court."

"I know," Tom said. "You ain't tellin' me anything. All I'm sayin' is, I'm going to be lucky if I don't kill one of 'em."

He went back to the outer office, lighted his pipe and sat down. Jonathan wanted to go home, but he didn't like to retreat under fire, as it were. He did not know what repercussions there might be from his message to the General. He felt that he should stay where he was until he gave them time to take whatever steps they might want to take. He forced himself to wait. It was deadly sitting around the office with nothing to do. There were no newspapers to read, no editorials to write or copy to check, no coming and going of people. There was nothing to do but think, and look out of the windows at the quiet streets and the shining river under its green cliffs.

He did not have long to wait. Within the hour he heard footsteps coming up the stairs and again Tom appeared at the door.

"You got another visitor," he said.

This time it was a blue-uniformed colonel who entered, instead of the Lieutenant, and this time Jonathan rose to greet him, not because of the difference in rank but because of the difference in men. This was a grave, dignified man about his own age, who looked at him with direct, clear gray eyes.

"Major Meade, I am Colonel George Munger, from General Curtis' headquarters."

Jonathan bowed and motioned to a chair. "Won't you sit down, Colonel Munger."

The Colonel sat, facing Jonathan across his desk. There was a moment of silence while the two men appraised each other.

"It seems that you were offended by the General's summons earlier this morning," the Colonel then said.

"Let's say that I was taken by surprise," Jonathan replied. "This is a small community, Colonel Munger, a small world, no doubt, but we have our ways. I am not accustomed to being summoned like that, to appear at a specified time and place, by anyone."

The Colonel made a small impatient movement with his

53

hands. "But good God, man, this is no ordinary situation. It is a time of crisis. This is a military occupation, not a social gathering."

"We are learning that, Colonel," Jonathan said. "Perhaps we don't learn as rapidly as we should."

The Colonel drew off and approached the subject from another angle. "Even on the basis of military rank, few Generals call upon Majors."

Jonathan smiled. "Colonels also outrank Majors," he said. "I am being honored."

Colonel Munger's face showed a slight lessening of its stern rigidity. Jonathan thought he detected a glint of humor in the gray eyes.

"You have lost this war, Major Meade, militarily speaking," the other man said, "but I am finding that you have a weapon against which we are relatively powerless—the impenetrable wall of hostile courtesy with which you people have surrounded yourselves."

At this point the glint of the Colonel's eyes became more than a glint. For a moment Jonathan thought he was going to smile.

"Even your message to the General was polite—on the surface. The message took the General by surprise."

"I trust the young man delivered it—accurately."

"I think he did," Colonel Munger said. "Yes, I think he did. It sounded authentic. And on the basis of your invitation, the General sent me to see you. That took me by surprise. He is not always so forbearing. So, I will tell you what he wanted to discuss with you. You have learned that your newspaper, the *Daily Herald*, is the only paper published in this town and that it has a wide circulation throughout this area."

"That is correct."

"We have also learned that it has not been issued since the day of General Lee's surrender."

Jonathan nodded in agreement.

"The General would like to know what your plans are for resuming publication."

"I have no plans for resuming publication."

"You mean you are not going to publish the paper?"

"Not at present."

The Colonel frowned. "The General will be sorry to hear that."

"May I ask you, in all courtesy, Colonel Munger, what business it is of his whether I publish it or not?"

"And in all courtesy I will tell you, Major Meade. The General is the military commander of this district. All civil government has been suspended. He is the final authority here, the only authority. He is responsible for the peace and order of this region, the preservation of life and the orderly conduct of the processes of government. In order to accomplish this it is necessary that orders be promulgated and regulations set up. Various such orders and regulations have been issued, coming not only from his headquarters but also from Richmond and Washington."

"General Order No. 29, for instance," Jonathan said.

Again the brief gleam on the Colonel's face, gone in a moment. "General Order No. 29, and others," he said. "They will continue to be issued from time to time during this period of adjustment, which we all hope will be short. We are finding it difficult to inform the population in regard to them. Practically everybody professes complete ignorance of them. Ignorance of the law is of course no excuse, but it is unquestionably true that it is easier to enforce a regulation if people know it exists. We have set up a board outside the Court House on which all such matters are posted, and another one at the Freedman's Bureau, but they have done little good. The Negroes can't read them and the whites won't or don't. The Negroes, however, come to us, but not the white people. Your townspeople, Major Meade, have not flocked to the Court House since we have been there. It is our thought that an established newspaper, which they are accustomed to reading, would give us an acceptable channel of information to the people of this area."

The Colonel paused, and Jonathan nodded.

"Because of the breakdown of the usual means of communication, this town seems to be almost completely isolated. That is true of many Virginia communities, I understand. It must be remedied as soon as possible. Your people, Major, should know what is going on, especially in Washington, in their own interest and for their own protection."

"Yes," Jonathan agreed. "Yes, you are right." He rose and walked over to a window, thinking. When he came back to the desk he said: "Nevertheless, I am afraid my answer must still be negative, Colonel. I have no plans for publishing the *Herald* at present."

The Colonel's voice was cold when he asked: "Is that— merely stubbornness, Major Meade, or have you other reasons?"

"I have other reasons."

"At the risk of being charged with impertinence, I am going to ask what those reasons are."

Now it was Jonathan who made an impatient gesture. "For the most obvious reason in the world, man," he said. "Finances. I have no money to run a paper with, no money to pay employees."

"You were paying them up to ten days ago."

"I was paying them with Confederate money. I was buying paper and ink with Confederate money. I was accepting Confederate money in payment for advertising and the sale of papers."

"But had you no reserves of coin or securities or Federal currency? You must have seen what was coming."

"Every red copper cent that I possessed went to the Confederacy," Jonathan Meade said slowly. Sudden passion seized him. "And every drop of blood in my body, every resource of energy and intelligence, belonged to the Confederacy."

Shaken by this display of emotion, he stopped. Colonel Munger was looking at him gravely. There was silence for a few moments, then the Colonel sighed and stood up.

"There is no tragedy in history comparable to this damned fratricidal war," he said. "Very well, Major Meade, I will tell the General what you have said."

He turned toward the door. Jonathan stood watching him cross the room. He was conscious of no activity of his mind, of no logical thought, but by the time the Colonel had reached the door a resolution had welled up from somewhere in the depths of his being, a decision definite and firm.

"Tell your General, Colonel Munger," he said, "that I will publish the paper, some kind of a paper, as long as my present stock of newsprint and ink lasts. If by that time I have been able to get hold of some funds, either currency or credit, it will be continued. If not, it must again be discontinued."

Colonel Munger turned, with a smile on his face. "Thank

you, Major Meade. That is good news. I—appreciate your co-operation."

Then he did a curious thing; he drew himself up straight and saluted. It was an impulsive gesture. He could not have known how much it did to ease the pain in Jonathan Meade's heart.

That night, when he told Elizabeth about his decision to resume publication and about his interview with Colonel Munger he said: "The man was a gentleman, Elizabeth. He really was. I almost liked him."

Elizabeth was horrified. "Oh, Mr. Meade, you couldn't."

"Yes," he replied. "Yes, if he hadn't been a Yankee I think I would have liked him."

8

Jonathan and Tom Scott spent the afternoon following
Colonel Munger's visit making plans for the paper.

"It will have to be a one-page sheet at first," Jonathan said,
"printed on both sides. Get hold of Leslie, and Bob Haynes to
do the printing and old Andy Mapes to set type. I have been
worrying about him. Maybe we can sell enough papers, and
maybe even get some advertising in a little while, so I can
pay you all something. Not much, probably, but something
and that's better than nothing."

"Yes sir, I'll bet we can. And anyhow, Jonny, like Les said,
I'd ruther starve workin' on the paper than just sittin'
around."

Tom was in a state of joyful excitement, and Jonathan himself was filled with a new sense of hopefulness. Having made
the decision, it seemed to him entirely feasible to publish the
paper in a small way. He wondered why it had appeared so
impossible before. With a mule to plow the land at Fairview
and the paper going again, the shattered fragments of his life
were beginning to fit together into a recognizable pattern. Out
of the ashes of defeat and humiliation, out of the bitterness of
heart and spirit, one resolution was beginning to harden and
set within him. He would pull himself up out of the depths of
poverty and starvation which faced him. He would rebuild
his world, and he would rebuild it in the image and likeness

of the world that had been destroyed. Having lost one fight, he did not intend to lose another.

One afternoon not long after publication of the paper began, Jonathan was sitting at his desk writing an editorial. He was writing about the hope of spring, the bountifulness of nature, the fertility that lay in the good Piedmont earth and the necessity for getting it plowed and planted. Inwardly he laughed at himself. He, Editor Jonathan Meade, the political fire-eater, writing about the bountiful mother of all, Nature. Well, he would come back to politics later. Now Virginia was too crushed to care about politics. The problem now was to live, and Nature held the hope for food and life.

Les came in with some notices for publication from the Yankee headquarters. He was all bustling cheerfulness these days. He was a good reporter, and he scoured the town for news. "I'm gettin' mighty chummy with the Yankees," he would say with a laugh, "but they are the only people who know anything."

Jonathan looked at the notices. One of them set a slow excitement burning in him. It was an announcement that hereafter the Federal Quartermaster "would buy corn, oats, hay, etc., in the locality and would pay cash for them in order to obviate, to as great an extent as possible, the difficulty under which the community is laboring from the scarcity of money." Jonathan's barn was filled with hay. It was the only thing Hunter's men had not taken. When he had come home from the Army the irony of finding all that hay and no livestock to eat it had seemed bitter to him.

He finished his editorial and took the notices to Tom in the outer office.

"See that?" He pointed to the Quartermaster's announcement. Tom read it.

"You got hay?" he asked.

"I've got hay," Jonathan said.

He rode out to Fairview in deep thought. When he got there he went straight to one of the sheds behind the barn, and there he found what he was looking for. It was an old farm wagon he vaguely remembered seeing there, practically falling to pieces. It was so dilapidated that the Yankees had not bothered to take it. Major Meade could not imagine why it had not been thrown away long ago, but he thanked God that it had not been. He called Zeb. They pulled the wagon out into the open and went to work on it. They worked until it was dark and they began again at sunrise. Zeb was a pretty good carpenter. They sawed and nailed and reinforced and replanked, and mended the wheels, and greased the axle. Finally they stood off and looked at their handiwork.

"It looks like hell," the Major said, "but I believe it will hold together."

He and Zeb pulled the wagon around to the side of the barn under the big window in the hayloft, and Zeb went up into the loft and forked the sweet-smelling stuff into the wagon until it was full. Then Major Meade went to the stable and brought out Black Prince. The horse was the crux of the matter, he realized. Here was the problem. He backed Black Prince between the shafts of the wagon.

"Hitch him up, Zeb," he said.

He stood by the horse's head, and rubbed his nose and talked softly into his ear. When Black Prince felt the weight of the shafts and the tightness of the gear strap, he began to plunge and rear. Jonathan held on to the bit and stroked the shining black neck. He reached into his pocket and took out a lump of sugar. Elizabeth had a few left which she was cherishing for some unknown but possible future event, and he had taken one. The big horse quieted down when the sugar was offered to him in Jonathan's hand. He lifted his lips and daintily picked up the lump. It had been a long time since he had had one, Jonathan thought. Zeb worked quickly and efficiently. Jonathan continued to rub the soft nose and to speak reassuring, and when Zeb had finished the horse stood quietly. Jonathan was ready to go.

The whole family stood around watching him. Baizy looked disdainful. It always amused Jonathan to see the amount of scorn or disapproval she was able to express without saying a word. Janie and Lucy were merely curious, but Elizabeth's face was tragic.

"Don't look like that, my dear," he said. "There are worse things in the world than riding a patched-up hay wagon into town—including starvation."

"Of course, Mr. Meade," she said, trying to smile. "Of course there are, honey. But couldn't you let Zeb take it in?"

He shook his head. "Zeb has plenty to do here, and anyhow, I would have to go too to sell the hay."

He got up on the wagon and twitched the reins. Zeb went to Black Prince's head and pulled the bit gently. After a little prancing the horse moved off down the farm road. Jonathan waved to the watching group.

He drove very slowly. The load behind him swayed, the wagon creaked, and he was far from sure of Black Prince. The horse was restive, puzzled by the unaccustomed restriction of the wagon shafts and the unaccustomed load he was pulling, but he was obedient. Jonathan thanked fortune that he met nothing as he moved along the familiar road to town. Just before he reached the outskirts of the town he pulled off onto a side road that took him directly to the Fair Grounds, where the Federal troops were camped. The Quartermaster was using the cattle sheds as his storehouses. His office was set up in the little house back of the grandstand which was used by the managers of the Fair, and the judges. Jonathan drove his wagon into the grounds. When he came out the wagon was empty, and there were some Federal greenbacks in his wallet.

He drove down Twelfth Street, the wagon rattling over the cobblestones. Instead of turning into Main, as he usually did, he went a block farther and turned into River Street and drove to the back entrance of Ally Martin's livery stable, beyond Tenth, and into the courtyard. Ally would let him leave the wagon there, he knew.

Ally leaned up against the building and laughed when he saw Jonathan drive in.

"Lawd-a-mighty," he said, "where'd you get it from, the Ark?"

Jonathan climbed down from the wagon and grinned at Ally. "It's almost that old," he agreed.

"And Black Prince pullin' it." Ally couldn't stop laughing. "Well, suh, I never expected to see it."

"All the same," Jonathan said, "it got a load of hay to the Yankee Quartermaster."

Ally sobered immediately. "I saw 'bout that in the paper this mawnin'. Kinda thought I might sell my own hay. Make more from it than I get from these horses now."

"No, Ally," Jonathan said. "Don't do that, you'd be sorry later. Keep your hay and your horses. Things will get better in a little while." He thought for a moment. "I could give you a little something on account for all the credit you have let

61

me have." He took two one-dollar bills out of his wallet and offered them to Ally. "It's mighty little, but maybe it will help."

"Jumpin' Jehosaphat!," exclaimed Ally. He fingered the greenbacks. "Real money. Real honest-to-God money. Man, man, it will help, all right. It certainly will help. Thank you, Major."

"Thank you for the credit," Jonathan said.

The next day Major Meade repeated the trip to the Quartermaster, and for several days after that. He sold all the hay he could spare, remembering Black Prince and the mule. Each day the roll of bills in his wallet grew, and the time came when he rode out into Bedford to John Foster's farm and dickered with the farmer for the purchase of the mule. In the old days Jonathan Meade would have felt it belittling to his dignity to haggle with this man over a purchase price, but now he felt a new hardness growing in him. The face of dignity had changed. He knew that John Foster wanted cash as much as he wanted the mule, and he stood on that knowledge. In the end they reached a satisfactory agreement, and Jonathan paid for the mule in Federal greenbacks. He felt triumphant. On his way home he went by the marketplace and bought two frying chickens at old Jiminy Jones' stall. A few days ago Baizy had said to him plaintively: "Whyn't you git us some chickens, Marse Jon'than? I wants some fried chicken so bad I kin taste it." Baizy could always taste what she wanted to eat.

The old man rose to greet Jonathan as he approached. "Jiminy cricket, Major," he cried in his thin old voice. "I'm glad to see you. How are you? How're you gettin' on? I ain't seen you in a coon's age. You ain't been around here."

"I haven't been doing much buying, Jiminy," Jonathan said.

The old man cackled with laughter. "You and a lot of other people. It's been slow, boy, I'm tellin' you, it's been slow. Yas-suh, it certainly has been slow."

Jonathan wondered how old Jiminy was. He must be a hundred, he had a son who worked his farm out in the country, and the son was older than Methuselah. Jiminy had had a stall in the marketplace ever since anybody could remember, and it was rumored that over the years he had made a lot of money, though it was hard to believe, looking at him. It was also reported that he had not converted any of it into Confederate money or bonds during the war. The Major didn't like doing business with him, but he wanted two frying size chickens, and Jiminy had them.

That night they had a celebration at Fairview, a real feast. Baizy fried the chickens and they had dandelion greens the children had picked that day. After a long winter of dried beans the chicken and greens were wonderful.

"Nectar and ambrosia," Jonathan said, and they all laughed as if that was very funny. Baizy had also made a pudding, of cornmeal and blackberries, sweetened with sorghum. Jonathan had tasted better puddings, but the blackberries gave him an idea. He remembered seeing blackberries in the market that afternoon. This might be the source of another small dribble of cash into his growing fund.

"The berries are ripe, I see," he said. "Did you pick them, Janie?"

"Yes, sir. Me and Lucy picked them."

"Are there many of them?"

"Oh, yes, lots. Some huckleberries, too, and some little wild strawberries. We ate some and they were real sweet."

"Good. That's fine. Janie, tomorrow you and Lucy and Amos pick all the berries you can find. I believe we can sell them in the market."

The next afternoon Jonathan drove the old wagon into town with a load of berries and flowers. Elizabeth had taken branches of sweet-smelling syringa and clumps of purple and white lilacs and tied them together into bunches.

"I don't know whether anybody will want them or not," she said. "Most everybody has syringa and lilacs in their own yards, but we might as well try it."

Jonathan had sent word to old Aunt Mary that he wanted her to go into town with him. She was waiting for him in the back yard when he brought the wagon around, dressed in a clean calico dress with a bright bandanna tied around her head.

"How you 'spect me to git up thar, Marse Jon'than?" she asked. "I'se old."

"You are not old at all, Aunt Mary," Jonathan said. "Who said you were old? You just like to talk that way."

"I is old. I well remember the day you was bawn."

"That wasn't very long ago," he said. "What are you trying to do, make me feel old too?"

The wrinkled old face broke into a smile. "Ev'ybody was mighty glad to have a boy," she said. "All them gals."

Jonathan stood up on the wagon and pulled while Zeb hoisted Aunt Mary from the ground. She settled herself on the seat, with her skirt spread around her.

"What you want me to do, Marse Jon'than?" she asked as they drove off.

"I want you to sit in the marketplace and sell these berries and flowers to anybody who wants to buy them. Ten cents a bunch for the flowers, and fifteen cents a box for the berries. And Aunt Mary, don't you sell them for anything but money, you hear?"

She said nothing, but Jonathan knew she heard. At the marketplace, he picked out a shady spot and settled her in it, with the berries and flowers around her.

"Now remember, Aunt Mary," he said. "No snuff or bandannas or pipe tobacco or candy. Nothing but money, nickels and dimes and quarters."

"Gawn, Marse Jon'than," she said. "I hyeahed you."

The Major went to the office, wrote an editorial, looked over the news and talked to Tom and Leslie for a while. The paper was prospering in a small way. The people of the town had responded well to its renewal; all who could bought it. Some of the stores were opening and a few merchants brought in cards for publication, announcing their reopening and advertising such stocks as they had on hand. Little trickles of money were coming into the *Herald* office and were being divided among the four men on the staff. With one sheet a day, Jonathan figured he could make his newsprint last quite a while.

When he went back to the market for Aunt Mary he was pleased to see that all the flowers were gone, and most of the berries. The old woman was clutching a bandanna that rattled with coins.

"It looks as if you have been doing a good business," Jonathan said.

"Um-hmm. Folks is buyin' things all round heah."

A man came over to Jonathan. "Does this woman work for you?" he asked. He was a Yankee, but he did not have a uniform.

"If you can call it work."

"She is selling berries, isn't she?"

"Yes." Jonathan suddenly realized who the man was. "You are from the Freedmen's Bureau, aren't you?"

"Yes, I am. Have you got a contract with her?"

"No."

"Do you pay her wages?"

"No, I don't."

The man struck the palm of one hand with his clenched fist. "It seems to me it is about time you people realized that you have to have a contract with every freedman who works for you, and you have to pay him wages. We have been telling you that for weeks. You can't make these colored people work for you for nothing. There are severe penalties for doing it."

"Listen," Major Meade said. "This woman was born on my plantation and has lived there all her life. She was retired two years ago because she was too old to work. She lives on my property, eats my food and wears the clothes I provide for her. She doesn't do any work and I don't expect any work from her now. I'll go on feeding her and clothing her for the rest of her life, and nurse her when she is sick and bury her when she dies, but I won't make a contract with her because there is nothing to contract for. Now if that doesn't suit you, I'll just leave her right here and you can take care of her."

Aunt Mary had moved behind Jonathan so he stood between her and the strange man. She was staring at the man with frightened, hostile eyes. He stood hesitating, looking first at one then the other. Finally he gave an angry shrug of his shoulders.

"Oh, hell," he said. "I can't make you people out. All right, take her back where she came from, but don't let me see her in here again unless you have a contract with her."

On the way back to Fairview Jonathan was deep in thought. Gradually it was borne in upon him that Aunt Mary, sitting stiff and straight beside him, was offended.

"I had to say I would leave you with that man, Aunt Mary," he explained, "to keep him from arresting me for not having a contract with you. He comes from the Freedmen's Bureau, you know, and they have a new law about wages and contracts. I forgot about it when I took you in today. Of course I wouldn't have left you, but I had to tell him I would."

Aunt Mary said nothing, but Jonathan knew she was mollified. They drove the rest of the way in silence. Zeb helped the old woman out of the wagon when they drove into the barnyard, and Jonathan climbed down. She handed him the bandanna she was carrying in her hand. He untied it and poured the coins into a box, and then he gave her back her bandanna and with it two dimes and a nickel.

"Thank you, Aunt Mary," he said. "Now you can buy yourself something the next time you go to town."

She tied the coins into one end of the handkerchief. "I ain't goin' in town no mo'," she said firmly. "Naw *suh*, I ain't goin' neah 'at town."

With great dignity she walked away and went down the slope of the hill to her cabin. Jonathan stood looking at Zeb.

"You go to church, don't you, Zeb?" he asked.

"When they is a church. Ain't been no church for a while now."

"You are a good, God-fearing Christian man," Jonathan said. "I know that. I try to be a Christian too, and you know that I am not given to lying."

"Naw suh." Zeb was puzzled.

"But sometimes it's necessary. Sometimes it is just absolutely necessary. So what I want to tell you, Zeb, is this. If any of those Freedmen's Bureau people come poking around this place, and they ask you if you have a contract, you tell them yes, you have."

"Yassuh."

"And if they ask you where is the contract, you tell them to come and see me."

Zeb was beginning to smile. "Yassuh."

"And if they ask you how much I pay you, you tell them ten dollars a month."

Zeb was grinnly broadly now. "Yassuh, I tell 'um."

"And Zeb, when the tobacco crop comes in, that's what I will pay you."

Zeb jumped into the air and cracked his heels together. "Whee-e-e-e-e!" he yelled. "Yas *suh*."

9

In May a letter came from Emily. No one knew how it got there. The mails were still not running, but one day a man appeared in the *Herald* composing room, handed old Andy Mapes a letter, and disappeared. The letter was addressed to Miss Jane Peyton Meade. Andy took it upstairs and gave it to Tom Scott, and Tom gave it to Major Meade when he came to the office that afternoon. Jonathan recognized Emily's handwriting and was filled with a fever of desire to know what the letter contained. He had taken her going hard. Emily was his firstborn, and though he had loved his sons with the passion a man feels for the male descendants who will carry on the name and the tradition, the family had always said that Emily was the apple of his eye. He had found it almost impossible to speak of her betrayal at first until, nearly a week after she had gone, Elizabeth had insisted that he must tell the kinspeople.

"We can't keep it a secret, you know, Mr. Meade," she said, "and the longer we go without telling them the—the— funnier it looks."

So Jonathan had ridden into town one morning burdened with the unpleasant task of notifying the family that his daughter had shown herself to be so insensible to the loyalties expected of any good Virginian and to the standards of conduct that should have been ingrained in a Peyton and a

Meade, as to go off and marry an unknown Yankee soldier from New York.

He decided that he would take the news first to Jim and Hallie Peyton. He liked Jim Peyton, Elizabeth's brother, a quiet man with a sense of humor and some of Elizabeth's sparkle under the quietness. Jonathan had not seen him since he came home from Appomattox. He rode along the tree-shaded length of Jefferson Street to Sixth, where a big white frame house stood, surrounded by a white picket fence. Jim was sitting on the porch when Jonathan rode up, and he came down the path to meet him.

"Well, well, this is good," Jim said as they shook hands. "Glad to see you. I stopped by your office the other day to say howdy but you weren't there."

"Tom told me. Sorry to have missed you. I come to the office every afternoon but I usually work on the farm at Fairview during the mornings."

"Pretty hopeless proposition, isn't it? Who have you got to help you?"

"Only Zeb. Zeb and Baizy were the only ones who stayed. You should see me trying to plow a field."

"How are you, man? How is the arm?"

"Well, I've still got it," Jonathan replied. "There is that much to be said for it. It's a little stiff, not as good as it used to be."

"You were lucky. Mostly they chopped off the arms and legs when they were as bad as I hear yours was."

"Yes, I owe it to Bob Pierce. He said he thought he could save it, and he did. How are you?"

Jim looked thin and tired. "Oh, I'm all right. Never got nicked during the whole war, God knows why. So here I am."

"Here we are," Jonathan said. It was as near as they came to mentioning the end of the Confederacy. They were walking up to the path to the porch. "Is Hallie around? I'd like to speak to both of you."

Jim went into the front hall and called. Hallie's voice answered from the back of the house and in a minute she bustled out to the porch. Hallie bustled when she walked.

"Well, Jonathan, honey," she said. "I certainly am glad to see you, haven't seen you for a long time. How are you and how are Lizzie and the girls? Whyn't you come to see us sometimes?"

"Haven't been doing much visiting recently, Hallie. I came this morning to give you a piece of news. Emily has run off— well, I don't expect you could say run, she has gone off with the Yankee officer she met in Winchester when she went to visit Em and Murrell last year. I reckon you have heard about him."

"You mean she has married him?" Hallie asked.

A wry smile flashed across Jonathan's face for a moment. "It is to be hoped so. She went off with him a week ago."

To his amazement Hallie looked pleased. "Well, I declare," she said. "That's real romantic, I declare it is."

Jonathan had always thought that Hallie was a remarkably silly woman. He had never understood why Jim had married her, she was not even pretty. It was true, he conceded, that a certain amount of silliness could be allowed a pretty woman, but it was inexcusable in a plain one.

"That is not the way we feel about it. It is a great sorrow to both her mother and me."

"Well, I don't know," Hallie persisted. "When two young people fall in love and get married I think it's nice, and it *is* romantic, going off like that the minute the war is over. I'm sorry he's a Yankee, but you can't tell, maybe he comes from a good family somewhere up North and everything will be all right."

"What do you know about him, Jon?" Jim asked.

"I don't know a damned thing," Jonathan replied, and did not bother to apologize to Hallie. "His name is Jerome Tyson, he comes from New York, and he is a captain in Torbert's Cavalry Corps of Sheridan's army. We never spoke of it after Emily came home that time and told us about him. I didn't believe she would do it."

"Well, I'm not going to take it as a tragedy," Hallie said firmly. "I said the other day, if I hear of another tragedy I am going to scream and holler. I'm warning you, I'm just going to holler. I'm sick of tragedies. Emily may be very happy, if they are in love and he is a nice young man."

"Where have they gone?" Jim asked.

"They have gone to Washington. He has been ordered there, I don't know for how long."

"Well, at least she will have something to eat," Hallie said, "and that's more than we have."

Jonathan thought, as he and Jim walked back down the

69

path to the street, that was the first sensible thing Hallie had said.

"I am sorry about Emily," Jim told him. "I don't know, you can't tell about young people nowadays. They don't seem to have the same feeling, the same loyalties we have. Young Jim is talking about going to New York to live." They had reached the gate and stopped there. Jonathan could see that this was a matter that weighed heavily on Jim. "I hope he won't do it, I hate to think of a son of mine living in the north, but people have got to live, Jonathan. There's nothing to do here."

"Yes, people have got to live," Jonathan agreed. "How about you, Jim? How about the railroad?"

He had hesitated to ask that question. Before the war Jim Peyton had been Traffic Manager of the Western Division of the Southside Railroad. An old man named Raymond Allen had taken his place when he went into the Army. Jonathan wondered which of them would have the position now.

"They are working on it," Jim replied. "They'll get it patched up before long, I reckon. The bridges are the worst things. Most of the bridges are down and it takes time to build them. About me, I don't know yet. Things are still too confused and demoralized. I can't find out anything definite."

"Well, good luck." Jonathan knew how inadequate that was, but could think of nothing better to say.

"Give my love to Lizzie," Jim called.

Now some weeks later, riding home in the late afternoon with Emily's letter burning in his pocket, Jonathan reflected that one of the few satisfactory events he could bring to mind was the fact that Jim Peyton had been given his old position back.

When he reached Fairview Elizabeth and Janie came out on the porch to greet him, and he gave the envelope he was carrying to the little girl. Janie had never had a letter in her life, addressed to her personally, and she was awed by it. She stood holding it in her hand and looking at it until Jonathan said impatiently: "Go on, Janie, and open it. It is obviously from Emily, your mother and I want to know what she says."

Dear little Janie (Emily had written). I am writing to you instead of Mama or Papa because I don't know whether they want to hear from me or not. I deem it

70

only proper, however, that my family should know where I am and that I am very happy.

Jerome and I were married in Charlottesville the morning after we left home. We reached there after dark and I spent the night with the Prestons. Cousin Sarah did not invite Jerome to stay there so he spent the night at an inn. She wouldn't even go to the church to see me married, can you imagine? Cousin Frank was very polite, however, and though he and Jerome practically didn't speak a word to each other, he escorted me to the church and gave me away. We were married in old Christ Church, where Mr. Jefferson himself worshiped. It took us two more days of hard driving to reach Washington, stopping at Culpeper and Warrenton. We were glad to get here, I can tell you. At first we stayed at Willard's Hotel until we could find a place to live. Such elegance, my dear, you can't imagine. It puts our little Holcombe House to shame, but that is only natural, as Washington is a city and the nation's capital. It is crowded with people now, as you may believe, some riffraff but some very elegant. Lodgings are at a premium, but through family connections Jerome found us a big, pleasant room in a nice home on I Street. It is only a short walk for him to the War Office, where he is attached and will be until the fall, when he will leave the Army. We will then go to New York, where his family lives. He has a mother and father and two younger sisters, and I must confess, Janie, it scares me to think of meeting them.

The death of Mr. Lincoln—wasn't that awful?—of course threw a pall over the city, and it has been very quiet socially. Things are beginning to liven up now, and I am told that with the official mourning period for the President over there will be much entertaining. Jerome's family seems to be of some prominence and he knows a good many people, so I reckon we may expect some part in the gaiety. Oh, Janie, Jerome is wonderful, all I ever hoped for in a husband. He is so charming and handsome, all the ladies look at him when he comes into a room, and he is so kind and attentive and thoughtful, I would consider myself the luckiest girl in the world if it were not for this hateful war and all the feelings it has

71

aroused, and for the break with Mama and Papa. Perhaps time will heal the break. I can't talk to Jerome about it because he feels as strongly in his ways as they do in theirs. Isn't it awful, Janie, for people to hate each other so? You should hear the things they say about us Southerners, the things the papers print about us. We are all murderers and cutthroats and traitors, and inhuman and cruel, and we are just waiting to start another "rebellion," with what, I wonder? Sometimes it is hard for me to keep a straight face and a civil tongue, and I find it best not to read the papers, but when I think of Jerome none of this matters, and it is to be hoped that the hatreds will soon die, now that the war is over.

How are things there? Write to me, honey, my address is at the top of this letter, and tell me all the news. Give my love to Mama and Papa if they want it. I am sending this by a Federal officer, a friend of Jerome's, who is on his way to North Carolina.

Your loving sister,
Emily

Jonathan read the letter last. It was hard for him to wait patiently while Janie plodded her slow way through it and Elizabeth read it with concentrated attention. When it came to him he read swiftly, with the speed bred of years of newspaper reading, and bitterness against Emily rose up in him. Hitherto it had been held down by anxiety. Now his worry was assuaged; he could picture her "well and very happy," living in comfort, looking forward to gaiety, deeply in love with the enemy she had married, keeping a civil tongue in the midst of the detractors and slanderers of her people. He knew well what was being said about the South, in Congress and in the press.

When he had finished reading the letter he folded it, put it back in its envelope and gave it to Janie. No one said anything. Elizabeth sat staring out of the window. He wondered how she felt about it, but instinctively he shied away from speaking to her of Emily, for her own sake and for his own. The hurt was too deep for the passage of words.

"I can answer it, can't I?" Janie asked.

"If you want to," Jonathan replied, speaking carefully. Nothing would have induced him to write to Emily, nor would her mother, he knew; but Janie was only a child. She could not be expected to feel as they did, and he knew in his heart that, in spite of the bitterness, some contact with Emily would be a comfort both to himself and to Elizabeth. "When the mails start running again. You can't now, we have no Yankee friends to call upon to carry letters for us."

Janie took Emily's letter upstairs to her room and propped it up on the bureau in front of the mirror. She did that in order to be sure not to lose it before the time came to answer it, but also because it filled her with pride to remember that she had received a letter, addressed to herself with her full name, Miss Jane Peyton Meade.

10

In October a wonderful thing happened to Janie. Papa came home from town one day with a note for Mama from Mrs. Boyd, Katie Boyd, who was one of her best friends. Mrs. Boyd wrote that they were planning to drive over to the Tyler plantation, Meriden, on the Rivanna for the tournament that was going to be held next week, and couldn't Mrs. Meade and Janie go? She was going to take Martha and Mr. Boyd was going to ride over on horseback, so there would be room for the two of them in the carriage. Please say yes.

Mama read the note out loud and Janie was so excited that she jumped up and down. "How lovely," she cried. "We can go, can't we? Oh, Mama, can't we?"

"I am afraid not, honey," Mama said.

"Why not?" Papa asked.

"I am in mourning, Mr. Meade."

"What if you are," Papa demanded. "Mourning observances can be carried too far. This is not a ball or a reception or anything like that, it's just an outdoor gathering. You have been cut off here in the country for too long and you have worked too hard and I think you ought to go somewhere and have a pleasant time when you can. They haven't held a tournament since the year before the war. You will see a lot of your friends, and I expect that most of the people who will be there have lost someone in recent years."

"Why yes, I reckon that's true. I believe that certainly is true. You think it would be all right?"

"I most certainly do think so."

So it was settled, and Janie was enchanted. "What's a tournament like, Mama?"

"Oh, it's lovely. Knights on horseback ride and tilt, and the winner has the right to choose the Queen of Love and Beauty, and there is a ball at night when she is crowned—of course we won't stay for the ball."

"But there aren't any knights any more," Janie said.

"Oh, of course they are not real knights, they are just young men who are called knights for the occasion, and instead of tilting against each other and killing each other as they did in olden days, they tilt with their spears against iron rings held on posts all down the field. I can't describe it to you, Janie, you will have to see it for yourself, but it is a lovely sight."

"What will we wear?"

"Well, I'll wear my black silk, of course, and I think it will be cool enough for you to wear you new blue cashmere."

That was another excitement. Janie had three new dresses. Two of them were just ordinary daytime dresses, but the blue cashmere was special. She had never worn it and she could hardly wait to put it on. By the end of the summer she had had to have some new clothes, because she had grown and filled out so much that she couldn't wear the dresses she had.

That had been a strange, sad summer for Janie. She remembered it all her life. Through the years a word, a sudden sound, a fragrance, could take her back in memory to the lonely little girl whose world had collapsed around her. In other summers she had played, with Peyton and Sara Anne and the colored children, romped through the fields, climbed apple trees and fences, panted up the hill to the place where the trailing arbutus grew, almost running to keep up with Peyton; she had ridden her pony, driven into town to play with her cousins, paid calls with Mama. This summer she worked. The grownups were all too busy to have any time for her during the day, and at night they were all so tired they went to bed right after supper. Papa and Zeb got up at daybreak and worked in the fields until Papa rode into town to tend to the newspaper. Zeb kept on until sundown. Mama and Baizy worked the vegetable garden. Sometimes Amos helped them and sometimes he helped Zeb in the fields. Janie and Lucy made the beds and straightened and dusted the house and took care of the flower garden.

That was what Janie remembered most clearly of that summer, the flowers, the work in the garden. She developed a love for growing things that never left her. In later years it was said that Janie possessed a green thumb, she could grow anything. Her love of flowers and her uncanny knack with them she always traced to that faraway summer when she worked in the flower garden for the first time. The garden became her friend and companion. It took the place of the lost playmates. It gave her deep satisfaction to pull up the encroaching weeds, and the sight of a trim border stretching to the boxwood hedge enclosing the garden was full recompense for a long day's work. She loved the feel and the smell of the earth, the faint fragrance of box bushes warmed by the sun, the massed colors in the beds. All summer the soft sound of a mourning dove in the distance kept her company as she worked in the garden. The syringa and the lilacs passed; roses bloomed, and sweet william and little spicy pinks, and lemon verbena; hollyhocks stood straight and tall against the back fence and all along the row of empty Negro cabins. Honeysuckle covered the fences. No one had time to root it out now. Its fragrance filled the air. On a damp day the smell of the honeysuckle and the roses and the tall white lilies that grew against the side of the house was so heavy that it made Janie think of God, because it reminded her of what her mother had once said when she had asked about God.

"You can't see God, Janie," Mama had said, "any more than you can see a fresh breeze that blows in your face and stirs the leaves of the trees around you, but you can *feel* Him, just as you feel the breeze."

Janie felt that way about the heavy blended fragrances around her; you could not see them, but you could feel as well as smell them.

All summer she worked hard and she grew fast and she ate, as her mother said, "like a trooper."

"Not like a trooper in the Confederate Army," Papa said. "What that child consumes at one meal would have lasted one of them a week."

They had wonderful food during the summer months; corn

pudding and corn on the cob, butter beans and sun-ripened tomatoes, snaps cooked with fat meat, little green cabbages, cymlings and turnip salad. Occasionally they had a chicken and every now and then the Major brought some meat from town. They had battercakes and fried apples for breakfast, and batterbread for supper and sometimes hot biscuits. Peaches and pears and apples, of course, and when the watermelons were ripe Zeb would bring one up to the house and break it open in the back yard, and they would stand around eating it and trying to shoot the seeds at each other. In September when the persimmons ripened, Janie and Lucy would go out and pick a bucketful at a time.

Janie enjoyed all the good food. "I never saw such an appetite," her mother said. "I declare it does me good to see her eat. And she's growing like a green bay tree, Mr. Meade. What are we going to do about clothes for her?"

"We'll just have to get her some," the Major replied.

Day by day through the summer Jonathan Meade's store of coin and currency had grown. Every few days he drove the rickety old wagon into town filled with good things that came up out of the good earth at Fairview. He made no further effort to sell directly in the marketplace, but he made arrangements with old Jiminy Jones, and with Gordy Smith who kept the big grocery store on Main Street, and with the Yankee quartermaster, and between them he sold a lot of his vegetables and fruit. The fruit was the greatest problem. In other years he had shipped most of it on the big, flat-bottomed bateaux that plied the canal from Balcony Falls at the west to Richmond at the falls of the James. This summer the bateaux were not moving on the canal, the packet boats were not running on the river, the railroads were not running. From one end of Virginia to the other, there was no public transportation moving. His fruit had to be marketed in the locality. What could not be sold Mrs. Meade and Baizy dried. Perhaps he could sell the dried fruit in the winter.

Late in the summer Jonathan bought a secondhand wagon, from John Foster, who had a new one. "I declare, I don't know where that man gets his money," he said, "but he certainly is prospering. He's got a new wagon and he's buying land, too. You can get it cheap enough, heaven knows."

Although the wagon that Jonathan bought was not new, it was good and substantial. It would last a long time. Maybe when the tobacco crop came in he could buy a buggy. He smiled to himself at that. A cow, a horse, a buggy. Wages for Baizy and Zeb. Another field hand and wages for him. Some money in the bank, so that he could buy the things that could be had only with money. Clothes. Everybody needed clothes. Janie and Lucy were outgrowing everything they had. He was wearing the clothes he had had when he went into the Army four years ago. He was thinner now, and they hung on him. Elizabeth wore only black, of course, and as she had gone into mourning after the hard days began, she had almost nothing to wear. He could not get all this out of the tobacco money; not unless it was a very good crop and brought an unusually good price. Well, he would wait and see. One thing at a time. Now Janie had to have some clothes.

"The child can't go around in skirts up to her knees," he said.

When the day of the tournament came Janie put on the new cashmere dress. It was a soft shade of blue and it had a round white collar with lace on it. She wore her ruffled pantalettes; her hair was brushed until it shone, pulled straight back from her face and tied with a blue ribbon. She looked at herself in the mirror over her bureau and was secretly delighted. She thought she looked nice enough to go to a tournament. In preparation for the event she had gone into the library, to the row of Sir Walter Scott's novels, and taken down *Ivanhoe* and reread parts of it to refresh her memory of tournaments. Her head was filled with visions of knights in armor and prancing horses, and fair ladies dressed in silks and satins. The sound of trumpets and of steel slashing on steel rang in her ear. Janie had always been sorry that she could not have lived in times like that, and she was greatly excited at the thought of seeing such brave scenes re-enacted.

The Boyd carriage came for them early that morning, as it was a good distance to Meriden. Katie Boyd, Mama said, was one of the few people she knew who still had a carriage and horses. The two ladies were delighted to see each other, and Janie was pleased to see Martha, too. She was a quiet, timid little girl, and Janie had never liked her anything like as much as she did Sara Anne, but they used to play together frequently, and anyhow Martha was almost exactly her age and it was nice to be with someone your own age.

Mr. Boyd followed the carriage up the driveway on horseback. "You better come and join us, Jon," he said to the Major, who had come out to greet them.

"Wish I could, Ranny," Jonathan said, "but I'm pretty busy these days."

"I reckon you are. I hear the tobacco market is good this year. Thank God the Yankees smoke and chew."

Martha and Janie sat on the small seat, facing their mothers, with their backs to Andrew, the Boyd coachman. It was a beautiful day, sunny and crisp, but not too cool for comfort. Because of the autumn haze the mountains were pale blue, as if they were a long way off. The leaves of the trees shimmered in the sunlight. When the road permitted, the horses moved along at a good pace and the air blew fresh and sweet on their faces. The morning had nearly gone when they reached Meriden, but Mrs. Boyd said they needn't worry about time, because the tournament would not begin until the afternoon. In the old days they tilted in the morning too, but then there were so many more knights taking part.

They drove through the entrance gates of Meriden and up the driveway, but about halfway along they turned off on a side road that skirted some woods and ran across the meadows and took them to the tournament field, some distance away from the house. When the carriage stopped and Janie got out she stood speechless. Never in her life had she seen such a sight. People had come from all over, many people, and they were milling around and greeting each other like long-lost friends, which they were for the most part. Everybody was talking and laughing. They had come in every kind of conveyance imaginable, in carriages and buggies and wagons and carts. Several of the wagons looked almost as bad as the old one Papa had used in the summer. There were carriage horses and old workhorses and mules, and one funny-looking cart was drawn by an ox. People were laughing at that, and the driver was grinning good-naturedly. "Got us here," he said.

It was the tournament field that enchanted Janie. It was a long, level stretch, rectangular in shape, with a track running all around the outside of it, and down the center a broad, sawdust-covered course that split the field in two along its entire length. At intervals down one side of the course posts had been set in the ground with iron arms projecting over the course, and rings hanging from the arms. On top of each post

79

three-cornered pennants floated, blue and green and red and yellow. Larger pennants hung on poles at the four corners of the field, and at one end there was a brightly painted pavilion with little pennants around its roof. All the pennants fluttered in the breeze, and Janie thought she had never seen anything so gay and pretty.

Mr. Boyd went off to join Mr. Tyler and some of the other gentlemen who had gathered around the stable, and Mrs. Boyd led the way to the pavilion, where a great many ladies seemed to have gathered. Mrs. Tyler came to greet them as they approached. She was a tall, handsome woman. Janie did not remember ever having seen her before, but Mama seemed to know her well. The three ladies hugged and kissed each other.

"Gracious me, I'm so glad to see you," Mrs. Tyler said. "I'm so glad you could get here. Lizzie, honey, I have thought about you so much." She and Mama squeezed each other's hands.

Other ladies crowded around to speak to Mama and Mrs. Boyd. There was a great deal of kissing and laughing and exclaiming. Nobody paid much attention to Janie and Martha. Occasionally Mama would say to one of the ladies: "This is Janie, you know," and the lady would smile at Janie or comment on how tall she had grown, but for the most part she was left free to watch everything that was going on. She was especially interested in the young ladies, most of whom had gathered in the pavilion. It was disappointing to see that they were not dressed in satin and velvet. They were dressed like everybody else. The very young ones had on muslin and cotton dresses, though some of them wore bombazine like Emily's best dress, and Janie saw that a few had pretty, soft cashmeres like her own. There were almost all in pale colors, pink and blue and pale yellow or green, and to Janie's unaccustomed eyes they all looked lovely. The older ladies wore darker dresses, and a good many of them were in black silk, like Mama.

When they had finished eating their picnic lunch they sat for a little while in the warm October sunshine, surrounded by the movement and laughter and talk of people and the gay, bright fluttering of pennants. It all seemed wonderful to Janie.

Pretty soon there was a general stir, and people began collecting all around the edges of the field. Some of them went back to their own carriages and buggies to watch; some moved benches from the trestle tables to the end of the field on each side of the pavilion. The gentlemen came from the stable. Most of them gathered along the fences that lined the two long sides of the field or sat on the slopes that edged the fences. The benches inside the pavilion seemed to be filled mostly with the young ladies, though a few of the older ones sat at the back. Mrs. Tyler sat at one end, just under the canopy, and Janie and her mother and the Boyds sat on a bench at her side, just outside the pavilion.

Janie could see that something was happening way off at the far end of the field. She was so excited that she could hardly sit still. Every now and then she would bounce up and down.

"Sit still, honey," Mama said. "You are shaking the bench."

"I am so excited," Janie whispered. "Aren't you excited, Mama?"

Her mother smiled at her. "Yes, of course I am," she said, but somehow Janie did not think she was very much excited.

A man on horseback came trotting down the track on one side of the field, made the turn at the end and came to a stop in front of the pavilion. Janie saw that he was carrying a trumpet. First he bowed to the ladies and the two or three gentlemen in the pavilion, then he raised the trumpet to his lips and blew a long, thin peal, high and silvery. He turned around facing the field, and blew the call again. It was a wonderful sound, splitting the October air and carrying off over the fields to the mountains.

It was then that the knights came riding in, single file, at a walk, from the far end of the field. They came slowly and Janie almost held her breath in her eagerness to see them. When they rounded the turn and approached the pavilion she was shocked to see that they were not in armor. No shining chain mail, no helmets of steel. They wore riding coats or confederate uniforms. She was filled with disappointment. They weren't knights at all.

"Most of them are young officers," Mrs. Tyler told Mama, "who brought their horses home from the war."

The horsemen lined up in a row, facing the pavilion. Everybody clapped. The young ladies were all in a twitter. The trumpet blew again and a man stepped from the pavilion and faced the riders. He was a big man and he carried a big horn, through which he talked, and his big voice reached out over the field. He turned from one direction to another so everybody could hear him. He was Mr. Richardson Long, Mrs. Tyler whispered, president of the tournament.

"Ladies and gentlemen," the booming voice said. "It is my great privilege to welcome you here on this happy occasion in the name of the Piedmont Tournament Association and of our most gracious host and hostess, Mr. and Mrs. Daniel Thorne Tyler, who have made this splendid field available to us, as they have done for so many years in the past.

"This is a happy occasion, I say, because for us it marks the renewal of old ties, old customs and traditions, the coming together of friends and neighbors to celebrate after the tribulations of the last years. In this gathering of lovely ladies and gallant gentlemen, in this bevy of beauty behind me," he turned and bowed to the young ladies in the pavilion, who smiled and laughed, "in this array before me of brave young men, who have weathered the storms of battle and the dangers of a hundred bloody fields to return to their homes and take their part in rebuilding this old Commonwealth, this beloved land of our fathers, in these we see the hope and the promise of the future. This gathering symbolizes the coming of the rosy dawn of peace across the storm-tossed waters through which we have struggled for so long. The dark days are past, let us rejoice. We have met here today to see our friends, to renew old associations, to pledge our allegiance to the future, and—to enjoy ourselves. Forget the sorrows and tragedies, the destruction and devastation. Rejoice! Rejoice in the presence of these good people, in this good land, in God's good sunshine. And rejoice especially in the display of horsemanship, craftsmanship, skill and courage which these young knights will now spread before our enthralled eyes. May the best man win, and may he choose the loveliest lady as Queen of Love and Beauty."

The applause was cut short by the high, singing call of the trumpet. The man with the big voice now began introducing the knights. He called them each by name, with "sir" added: "Sir Robert Pendleton, of Accomac; Sir Julian Wade, of Orange; Sir Reverdy Morton, of Buchanan," and so on down the line. As each name was called the knight would raise his spear in greeting and his friends and relatives would yell.

When the introductions were finished the knights wheeled their horses so that they were in single file again, and at the sound of the trumpet they began to circle the field on the outside track. Three times they rode around it, first at a trot, then at a canter and finally a full gallop, pulling up at last just before reaching the pavilion. They rode beautifully. The fluid grace of motion was beautiful to see. A murmur of admiration rose from the people all around the field, and then a great burst of applause.

"They have had plenty of practice," Mrs. Tyler said. "Some of them were with Jeb Stuart, and some with Forrest, and some were in Floyd's Cavalry. They have ridden more than they have walked for four years."

Janie was feeling much better about the knights now. It was borne in upon her that it would not be possible to ride like that in armor. She remembered the pictures of armored knights on horseback, and how they had to be lifted up onto their horses, and how they sat there stiff and straight-legged. This was better; this was lovely. Each of the knights had selected some device to set himself apart from the others. Some of them wore colored sashes, each a different color. Some wore bright streamers flying from one arm, or colored armbands, or scarves around their hats. Only one had a plume. He wore a big cavalry hat with a black plume on it. Janie selected him as her favorite. She hoped he would win.

"Now," said Mrs. Boyd, "now the tournament is really going to begin. Isn't it exciting, Janie?"

"Oh, yes, ma'am," Janie said, bouncing up and down on the bench.

The trumpet sounded and the knight who was first in line rode up in front of the pavilion, saluted the ladies with his spear, wheeled and at a full gallop dashed down the course, his spear held up and out in front of him, aimed at the rings on the posts. It took skill and steadiness of arm and eye to put the spear through the ring and lift it off as the knight galloped by. When he had run the course he circled around the other side of the field and came back to the pavilion to await his turn again while the next knight tried his skill. They were to run the course four times, and the knight who captured the largest number of rings would be the winner, the King of the tournament, privileged to choose the Queen of Love and Beauty. One after another the knights galloped down the course. The pennants fluttered, the trumpet sounded its call each time a knight began his run. When one succeeded in taking a ring the people all yelled, sometimes they groaned when one failed.

It was all beautiful and exciting, but after a while Janie got restless sitting on the bench with Mama holding her so she could not bounce up and down. Presently, in an interval between runs, she said: "Mama, can I go down there and sit on the fence for a while?"

"Well—I reckon so," Mama said, "if you'll stay there. Don't go wandering off where I can't see you."

Janie jumped up. "Want to come, Martha?" she asked.

Martha shook her head. She would rather stay where she was, close to her mother and the other ladies. Martha was always timid. Janie crossed the grass in front of the pavilion and went over to the side of the field where the fence was. She found an open place where nobody was sitting and climbed up and sat on the top rail. This was wonderful. The riders passed right by her as they moved up to take their turns. She could see their faces now. She could bounce up and down on the fence and yell when a knight captured a ring.

After a while she realized that she was sitting next to a boy. She became aware of him because he kept looking at her so hard. She could feel his steady stare. When she glanced at him she saw that he was older than she was, but only a few years older, she thought. He was tall and slender and very dark; he stared at her with bright, black eyes. It embarrassed her a little, the way he looked at her, so she pretended that she did not know he was there. When a knight was running she forgot about him, but in between times she became more and more conscious of this strange, dark boy who kept his eyes fastened on her. Finally she could not keep from looking at him, and their eyes met. It was a long look, and when Janie turned her eyes away and glanced out at the field again, he spoke.

"When I grow up," he said, "I am going to ride in the tournament, and I am going to win. I'm going to be King of the tournament."

Obscurely, that irritated Janie; as Mama would have said "it put her back up."

84

"When I grow up," she replied, "I am going to be Queen of Love and Beauty."

They were silent for a few minutes. "I have a horse now," the boy said. "Have you?"

"No. I used to have a pony, but the Yankees took him."

"It is really my father's horse," he explained, "but he lets me ride him."

That was all they said, but the boy kept on looking at her. When the knights began the last run, Janie decided that she would go back to where the ladies were sitting. The tournament would be over soon and this boy made her feel uncomfortable. She slid down off the fence, and to her surprise he did too. She started across the grass toward the pavilion and he walked by her side. When she got almost to the benches at the side of the pavilion, however, he stopped. She turned to him, and again they stood looking at each other for what seemed to Janie a long time. Then she went on and he turned back to the fence.

When Janie reached the bench on which her mother sat she asked: "Mama, who is that boy going back over there?"

"I don't know," her mother said. "I was wondering who he was."

"His name is Calhoun," Mrs. Tyler said. "They are Valley people. His father is a Presbyterian minister over there, he has several small parishes."

"Not *the* Mr. Calhoun?" Mrs. Boyd asked.

"Yes, Katie," replied Mrs. Tyler. "That's exactly who he is." They both began to laugh.

"Who is Mr. Calhoun?" Mrs. Meade asked.

"Oh, Lizzie, you must have heard of him," Mrs. Tyler said. "He's the one who made that wonderful prayer."

"I haven't heard anything, Lulie," Mrs. Meade said. "I've been isolated out in the country for a year and a half. What prayer?"

"Well, it was last spring. It was right after the surrender, and the Yankee commander over there in the Valley ordered Mr. Calhoun to pray—it wasn't General Order No. 29 because Presbyterians don't have to pray for the President, and anyhow it wasn't the President he was to pray for, but just on general principles, I reckon, the commanding officer ordered him to pray for the Yankees, and this is what he prayed—we all nearly died laughing when we heard about it. He said: 'We beseech Thee, O Lord, to bless our enemies and remove them from our midst as soon as seemeth good in Thy sight.' " All the ladies laughed. "They arrested him and exiled him for it."

"Yes, they did, Lizzie," Mrs. Boyd said, when Mrs. Meade looked incredulous. "That's exactly what they did. They arrested him and sent him up to New York. But it was just too perfectly ridiculous. People have a sense of humor, even in New York, I reckon, and the Presbyterians up there got together and made a fuss about it, and they got him sent home. They took up a collection to pay his way back, because of course he didn't have a cent, and they sent him on back home."

Janie could see the Calhoun boy sitting on the fence. She could not help thinking about him, and she watched him now that a good distance separated her from those bright black eyes.

The knight with the black plume did not win the tournament, but Janie was consoled because the one who did was tall and handsome. He wore a Confederate uniform and a cavalry hat with a yellow scarf around it. The man with the big voice announced him as the victor and everybody clapped, and he rode up close to the pavilion and dismounted. A great quiet came over the whole field. The knight took off his hat and bowed to the ladies in the pavilion, then he pulled the yellow scarf off his hat, came forward and knelt before one of the young ladies on the front bench, offering her the scarf. A great yell went up, and the young lady, a pretty blond girl in a pale yellow dress, blushed all over her face. Then she laughed, took a brooch from her collar and pinned the yellow scarf to the front of her dress. The knight stood up and held out his hand to her, and she rose. The two moved forward a few steps and stood, bowing and laughing at the applause.

Janie was enchanted. It was the most romantic scene she could imagine; Ivanhoe could do no better. The Queen of Love and Beauty went back to the pavilion, the King of the tournament mounted his horse, and all the knights prepared to ride off the field. Before they moved, however, the trumpeter came forward, put the trumpet to his lips, and blew taps, long and slow. The crowd stood silent; the men took off their hats. Everybody knew what the long, mournful notes were saying.

People began leaving as soon as the tournament was over, and the road was crowded with homeward-bound vehicles. The young ladies and the knights, and a good many of the Tylers' friends were going to spend the night at Meriden and go to the ball that evening. Mrs. Boyd and Mrs. Meade said they must leave immediately, as they had a long way to go, but by the time they had said goodbye to everybody, and Mr. Boyd had gone back to the stable to see a colt of Mr. Tyler's, and they had said goodbye to Mrs. Tyler for the second time, the sun was sinking behind the mountains. Most of the crowd had gone by that time, and as the darkness settled over them they had the road to themselves.

Janie slept most of the way home, and she was so sleepy she hardly knew they got there. She remembered that Papa came out on the porch to meet them, everybody said they had a wonderful time, and Mama helped her take off her new blue dress, and her petticoats and pantalettes and put on her nightgown and get in bed. Her eyes were filled with the vision of knights on horseback, and the sound of trumpets rang in her ears. Back in her mind, never quite forgotten, was the memory of the tall, dark boy who had looked at her so hard.

11

Major Meade walked to and fro across the city room of the *Herald* office, slowly, holding in his hand a long sheet of proof sent up from the composing room downstairs. Tom Scott sat with his feet on a desk, smoking his pipe; Leslie Vaughn sat at his desk, supporting his head with his one hand. In the two years that had passed since the end of the war he had lost the ebullience that had characterized him. He looked older and tireder. Jim Peyton stood at one window, silently looking down at Tenth Street, and Randolph Boyd wandered restlessly around, occasionally sitting down at an empty desk.

It was a blustery early March day, cloudy and chill. A fire burned in the big stove in one corner of the room. Its small crackling sound was incongruously cheerful.

Presently Tom Scott broke the silence. Taking his pipe out of his mouth he said: "I'm just tellin' you, Jonny, you better be careful or you'll find yourself in jail and the paper suspended. All you got to do is remember the Richmond *Examiner* and Petersberg *News* and all the other papers that have been suspended."

"I am not likely to forget them," Jonathan said, "but they can't put the President of the United States in jail, much as they might like to. All I'm doing is quoting him. Any paper in the country has a right to quote the President's veto message."

"Papers in the South ain't got any rights," Tom replied. "You know that well as I do."

"I am going to print it just the same," Jonathan said stubbornly.

"Well, I hope they don't haul you off to prison in Fortress Monroe, like they did John Mitchell of the *Examiner*."

"And Jeff Davis," said Jim Peyton with bitterness in his voice. "Remember him? You might see him if they take you to Fortress Monroe."

"Two years," Ranny Boyd said. "Nearly two years, and they've still got him shut up in that prison without trial. Why in hell don't they try him?"

"They can't," Jim said. "They haven't got any case against him, not any more than they have against eight million other Southerners, except that the eight million elected him as their President."

Again there was silence in the room. Jonathan sat down at a desk and began reading the proof of the President's veto message. The sound of slow footsteps came up the stairway from the side entrance on Tenth Street, and Dabney Wilcox came in, a thin cadaverous-looking man with shrewd, dark eyes, who had been one of Jonathan's closest friends from boyhood, and who had married his sister Kate. Jonathan greeted him with a motion of his hand.

Dabney stood looking at the group of silent men. "What's the news?" he asked.

"Passed over the President's veto," Jonathan answered. "Passed by both Houses of Congress without discussion, debate or consideration of the veto message. The Military Reconstruction Act is now Law."

Leslie Vaughn stood up and struck the desk with his clenched fist. "Damn it to hell," he said. He ran his fingers through his thick brown hair and his hand was trembling. "We haven't even got a name any more. We are not Virginia. We are not a state, we're a territory. We are a conquered province. Military District No. I. Military District No. I," he repeated, his voice rising. Then he sat down and again supported his head with his right hand.

Dabney Wilcox crossed the room and leaned against a corner of the desk where Jonathan sat.

"Listen to what the President says, Dabney. Listen to what

89

Andrew Johnson, Southerner turned Yankee, Democrat turned Republican, hater of all landowners and so-called 'Southern aristocrats,'—listen to what he says about this hellish bill."

Jonathan read aloud: "Such a power has not been wielded by any monarch in England for more than five hundred years. In all that time no people who spoke the English language have borne such servitude. It reduces the whole population of ten states—all persons of every color, sex and condition, and every stranger within their limits—to the most abject and degrading slavery. No master ever had a control so absolute over his slaves as this bill gives the military officers over both white and colored persons."

"Ain't that a pretty lot of words?" asked Tom, banging his pipe against the wastebasket.

"Well, you'll have to admit that old Andy has tried," Dabney said. "He has tried to carry out a policy of moderation toward the South."

"And he'll probably get impeached for his trouble," Jim Peyton said.

Jonathan, remembering the day of Lincoln's death, when he and Tom Scott had discussed the prospect of Andrew Johnson's Presidency, repeated himself now. "He is no match for Thaddeus Stevens," he said. Stevens in the House, Sumner in the Senate, Stanton in the Cabinet. The three S's, speak their names with a hiss! "He is no match for those jackals in Washington."

"It ain't just Washington," Tom said. "You know that, you read the Northern papers."

"Yes, I know," Jonathan agreed.

Ranny Boyd moved toward the stairs. "Well, I reckon I'd better be getting along. I just stopped by to find out what had happened." He went slowly down the steps and out into the chill March twilight.

Leslie Vaughn stood up to go. "Whyn't you wait and go home with me, Les?" Tom said casually. "The old lady'll give us some supper."

Leslie shook his head. "Thanks, Tom, but not tonight. Some other time."

Jonathan and Tom watched him anxiously as he went out.

"He's taken to drinkin'," Tom explained to the other two men.

"I know," Dabney said. "I have seen him around. It's a pity, he is a nice young man. Some people can't stand up against adversity."

Jonathan gave a short laugh. "Our esteemed brother-in-law Tim Ashby, for instance," he said. "Taking the Ironclad Oath!"

"Well, I don't know," Dabney said. "What could he do? Ashby Hall was at stake. If you were behind in your taxes and were going to lose Fairview, how do you know you wouldn't take the Ironclad if you could get away with it?"

"All right," Jonathan said wearily. "Maybe I would have. It is hard to know what a man will do if he is pushed hard enough. All the same, Tim Ashby makes me sick, sitting on the porch with his feet on the railing while Josie and the girls work themselves to death trying to keep that place going."

"Yes, he is a lazy hound," Dabney agreed.

"Speaking of the Ironclad," Jim Peyton said, "did you know that Elias Webber has taken it and been given a position in the Internal Revenue Office?"

Jonathan stared at him. "Elias Webber? How could he take the Ironclad?"

"Same way a lot of the others have done—perjure themselves, swear they not only never fought for the Confederacy but never gave aid or comfort to anybody connected with the Confederacy."

"It's the only way they can make a living, I reckon, some of them," Dabney said. "It is hard to get any work unless you ask for a pardon and take the Ironclad. Elias Webber's tobacco business went to pieces during the war and went out completely when they took over his warehouse as a hospital. He has been at rock bottom for the last two years."

"So have a lot of other people," Jonathan said. "And Webber was a ranting secessionist. When we were fighting against secession he was hollering for it, and all during the war he went around talking about what he was doing for the Cause and how much tobacco he was sending to the boys in the Army."

"Well, he has forgotten all that now," said Jim Peyton. "Now he has always been a good Union man, and as a reward for his loyalty he is going to get a nice, comfortable salary from the Federal Government."

"The low-down skunk," Jonathan said.

91

Dabney Wilcox looked at him. "You're too bitter, Jon. It don't do you any good."

"No, it don't do me any good, but how in God's name can you help it?"

Jim Peyton stood up. "Well, I'm going home," he said. "Coming, Dabney?"

"I am supposed to go by your house for Elizabeth, Dabney," Jonathan said. "She has been with Kate this afternoon. Wait until I finish this proof and I'll get the buggy and drive there."

2

Jonathan and Elizabeth Meade drove home in silence through the March twilight. It was cold, and Elizabeth was bundled up in her cloak, seemingly sunk into it with her head lowered against the wind. She ought to have a carriage, Jonathan thought, leaning over to tuck the lap robe more tightly around their knees. A carriage was an impossible dream, of course. He had bought the buggy secondhand from Ally Martin when the tobacco crop came in the first year after the war, and it had seemed beautiful to them at that time. It was a good buggy and Ally had done his best with new paint. Just as the first fresh vegetables that came to them after the long winter of dried beans had tasted like fare for the heavenly hosts, so the sturdy, newly painted little buggy had looked like a golden chariot. Once more the family could get into town, once more they could drive to church on Sunday mornings, with Janie squeezed tightly between Jonathan and Elizabeth on the narrow seat.

Now these things were established and accepted, and the larger requirements of normal existence were pressing in upon him with insistent demands. Jonathan often felt that in the two years' fight that lay behind him he had made little headway; sometimes it seemed to him that he had in fact lost ground. To be sure he had held on to Fairview and he had kept the paper going. He had paid his *Herald* staff, little enough, but something. They could exist. His family and servants had been fed and clothed; he had eked out small wages for Baizy and Zeb, and for Jake and Susie too, who had turned up one morning that first autumn with the request that they be allowed to return to the plantation. The bare necessities of life had been supplied, but that was all. It was a touch-and-go, hand-to-mouth existence. No security had been built, no prosperity was in sight. Everywhere, at Fairview, in the newspaper office, in the streets of the town, the homes and yards and gardens, the slow inroads of poverty were making themselves progressively evident. Shabbiness covered his world, a corroding shabbiness that destroyed grace and beauty, deadened the color and weakened the fabric of life. Not only was the drabness eating inot the physical structure, it was corroding the spirit, the moral fiber of his society, as witness Leslie Vaughn and Timothy Ashby. As witness himself.

Although he knew himself not to be a deeply introspective man, he had always been aware of his own purposes and motivations, conscious of his own characteristics. He held a certain picture of himself, changing and moderating with the changing years, but basically the same, projecting the same personality. As a young man he had thought of himself as quite a dashing fellow, not handsome but possessing charm and gaiety, inspiring comradeship with men and having a way with the ladies. Almost too dashing, in fact, at one period in his life, while attending the University, earning for himself the pained disapproval of his strait-laced mother and even the impatience of his more lenient father. That time had passed. He had married Elizabeth Peyton, bought the local newspaper and settled down as a solid citizen, genial, courteous, well-intentioned to man and beast, having a proper reverence for God, not above the failings and sins of humanity, but not willfully sinful and sinning only within the limit of a gentleman's code. Always a gentleman, always honorable. Endurance and courage had been the qualities called for during the war, and he had been able to call them up within himself sufficiently to make a creditable record, supported by a passionate attachment to the cause of the Confederacy.

This was the picture of himself with which he had lived all his adult life. Against its familiar outlines he found it difficult to recognize the man he now felt himself to be, depressed, bitter, filled with helpless frustration and smoldering rage. It had been bad enough before, but now this new outrage had come upon them, this damnable Reconstruction Act, begotten in the perverted brain of the old hellcat, Thaddeus Stevens,

93

passed by a servile Congress and applauded by a vengeful nation, humiliating to the spirit, searing to the soul, destroying all hope. It almost frightened Jonathan to feel the murderous emotions he had been experiencing all day. "It don't do you any good," Dabney Wilcox had said. Jonathan knew it not only did him no good but that it was actually poisoning his life, corroding the inner man, to allow himself to dwell on these destructive emotions. Yet so strong were his feelings that he made no effort to turn away from them. He had no desire to overcome them. The only consolation he had, the only recompense he could find for the degrading situation into which the South was being forced, for the loss of dignity and manhood, was the luxury of bitterness toward the perpetrators of the outrage.

"Mr. Meade," Elizabeth said, breaking the silence that had held them since they had left the Wilcox home, "something has got to be done about Josie and the Ashby girls."

Jonathan had known for a long time that something ought to be done about Josie and the Ashby girls, but he felt that this was a poor time to discuss the matter. He turned in revulsion from a consideration of other people's problems. He had never been rude to Elizabeth in his life, however, so he forced himself to say: "Something certainly ought to be done, my dear, but what? What can we do?"

She did not answer his question but said instead: "Kate and I were talking about it this afternoon, and it is just terrible, Mr. Meade. Those girls are growing up out there without any education or accomplishments at all. Josie is too busy to teach them and Tim is too-good-for-nothing. They all work terribly hard, of course, and still hardly have enough to eat, and no proper clothes. Mary and Helen are old enough now to be young ladies and they have no life at all. Kate says that every now and then they come into town to spend the night with her and go to a party and it just breaks her heart to see how they look. The few things they have to wear are three and four years old and of course they have grown up since then. The dresses have been let out and let down and washed and turned, and they are pathetic. They have no party slippers and each of them has only one halfway decent pair of shoes, and when they come into town, do you know what they do, Mr. Meade? Kate says they wear old farm shoes to walk in and carry their good shoes until they get to the colored Baptist church just on the edge of town, you know, and then they go behind the church into the bushes and put on their good shoes and hide the old ones until they come back the next day. Isn't that awful, Mr. Meade? Your own nieces! Can you imagine what your mother would have said to that?"

Jonathan was silent. He could very well imagine what his mother would have said. The plight of the Ashby girls was deplorable. He resented it with his whole being, but it was merely part of a totally deplorable situation, one more count against a world which had become unfit for decent people to live in.

Elizabeth went on: "Kate said she couldn't stand it any longer, so last week she bought some sprigged muslin and she is going to make each of them a party dress. Mary and Helen, I mean of course—the three younger girls are still just children, though I reckon Maggie must be going on to fifteen. That's nice of Kate, isn't it, Mr. Meade?"

"Very nice," Jonathan replied.

"She says that maybe she can manage to get them some party slippers too. You know, Mr. Meade, Dabney Wilcox is doing right well with his real estate business. Who in the world would be buying land nowadays?"

"The buzzards—the carpetbaggers and scalawags. Some of our own people too, who have managed to sell their plantations for cash and have come to town to live. Some of the country people, small farmers, men like John Foster. I don't know where they get the money, but a big change is taking place in Virginia, Elizabeth. The big landowners are being squeezed out."

Elizabeth was silent for a few moments and then, with a slight hesitation, she said: "That's what I think the Ashbys should do."

"What?"

"Sell Ashby Hall and come to town to live."

"Sell Ashby Hall," exclaimed Jonathan startled. "Good God, Elizabeth, that's what they are all fighting against. That's why Tim took the Ironclad Oath."

"I know, but I don't think holding on to Ashby Hall is the most important thing in the world, when they haven't got any way to keep it up. I think the lives of the girls are more important. After all, they haven't got any sons to inherit the place."

Elizabeth suddenly stopped speaking and sat quietly, sunk once more into her cloak. A sort of grim silence hung between them, and Jonathan knew that they were both facing the bleak fact that they too had no sons to inherit Fairview.

Black Prince plodded slowly on, head down, as if he shared in a universal gloom. The fire had gone out of him; he was accustomed to the shafts and gear straps now, to the weight of the buggy. In the gathering darkness they came to the familiar snake fence edging the Fairview fields. Some of the rails were down; the tendrils of winter-blighted honeysuckle clung to many of them. Soon they would be covered with green leaves and rich-cream blossoms, fragrant and destructive. For four generations honeysuckle had not been allowed to grow on Fairview fences. For two years it had grown where it chose; gradually it would pull down the fences.

When they reached the entrance driveway Jonathan was conscious of the paint scaling off the gateposts with their carved wooden pineapples. Undergrowth was blurring the clean outlines of the trunks of the cedar trees bordering the driveway, and he knew that when spring came in a few weeks the wide front lawn, once so velvety, would be covered with crabgrass and weeds. The house was dark, except for a light in the kitchen. Kerosene cost money, it must be preserved. The dreariness of the wintry night, the neglected lawns and fences, the dark house, was all of a piece with the bitter depression, the futility and hopelessness which filled his mind, cut out of the same cloth, part of the same pattern.

As the buggy approached the house Jonathan saw a light coming along the windowed corridor connecting the kitchen with the house, and by the time they drove up to the front steps Zeb had come out of the kitchen to take Black Prince, and the front door was opened by Janie, who ran out to meet them, with Susie standing in the doorway holding a lighted lamp.

"Oh, Mama, Papa," Janie cried. "I'm so glad you've come. "You're late. Baizy has made Sally Lunn for supper."

She hugged her mother and held up her face to her father to be kissed. He bent down and kissed her, and then stood looking at this child of his, his one link with the future. He put his hand under her chin and lifted her face. A sweet little face, with clear blue eyes—the Meade eyes, he thought with some satisfaction—a pretty mouth and a firm chin. A little too serious, a little too conscious of her responsibility as the only remaining child of the family, a little too quiet, perhaps, as a result of her loneliness. A child should remain a child as long as possible, God knew the time was short enough.

For a moment, before they turned and went into the house to the warmth of the fire in the library and the lighted lamps, shutting the door against the blustery night and, for at least a partial and temporary surcease, the depressing, the degrading, the impossible reality, Jonathan felt the old resentment against that other daughter, the disloyal one, so happy in her treachery, living in comfort, indeed even in luxury as he gathered from her letters to Janie, among the enemies of her people, the promulgators of the evil.

12

One day in June of that black year, Major Meade sat at his desk with a sheet of yellow foolscap in front of him and a pen in his hand. He had been sitting there for an hour and the sheet of paper was still unmarked. Twice Andy Mapes had come up for the editorial for next morning's paper, and twice Jonathan had reported that it was not ready. It was not often that he was at a loss for subject matter or words for his editorials, but today the only thoughts that came to him were not publishable; not in Military District No. I, in the year 1867.

He tried to concentrate. He wanted to be done with the job and go home; he wanted to leave the office and to leave the town behind. He wanted to breathe the cleaner air of Fairview, where there was no Yankee military, no Radical Republicans, no Elias Webber. Feeling was high in the town, he knew, tension hung in the very air. If there was going to be trouble he did not want to witness it, he did not want to be involved in it.

The Radical Republicans were going to hold a meeting that night, in Masonic Hall. They were going to stage a torchlight procession down Main Street. Elias Webber was going to preside; resolutions were to be passed endorsing the military government, endorsing Reconstruction, endorsing the recent call for a constitutional convention to be held in Richmond in the autumn, a convention to which no former Confederate might be a delegate, for which no former Confederate might vote. Jonathan Meade knew the order of procedure for tonight's meeting because it had been sent to him for publication in the *Herald* that morning. He had not published it, and an indignant Elias Webber had come to his office to protest. Jonathan had told him to go to hell. Flatly, specifically and with much satisfaction he had told Elias Webber to get out of his office, and go to hell. Red-faced and furious, Mr. Webber had complied with the first request. Of the fulfillment of the second Jonathan had no doubts. He knew he was walking on eggshells in doing this. Elias Webber was the darling of the present military government, a formerly respectable member of the community now become a willing tool for their hands. He had decided, however, that there was a limit to caution. Come what might, he would not publish the order of procedure for the scum and riff-raff who called themselves the Radical Republicans.

From the street outside came the sound of voices raised in song, and Jonathan recognized the words of Inness Randolph's jingle, which was then being sung from one end of the South to the other. Major Inness Randolph, formerly of Jeb Stuart's Cavalry, had fired one last futile but intensely irritating—to the Yankees—round of verbal buckshot at the enemy. His little popgun had been picked up with glee by the entire South.

> *Three hundred thousand Yankees*
> *Is stiff in Southern dust;*
> *We got three hundred thousand*
> *Before they conquered us.*

Jonathan went over to the window and looked down on Main Street. The singers were standing directly under him, he could see only the tops of their heads. A group of men across the street in front of Wright's Emporium began to sing, with broad grins on their faces. Jonathan knew none of them. They were rough-looking men; he thought they might be workers in Ranny Boyd's iron foundry, or railroad men, or they might be bargemen from the canal. Some of the bateaux were running though canal traffic had never come back fully since the war. Their voices came up to him:

> *I can't take up my musket*
> *And fight 'em now, no more*

> But I ain't a goin' to love 'em,
> Now that is certain sure.
> And I don't want no pardon
> For what I was and am;
> I won't be reconstructed
> And I don't give a damn.

A Yankee soldier came running along Main Street from the direction of Eleventh. Soldiers had been patrolling the streets all afternoon to prevent trouble. At sight of him the singers disappeared. Jonathan was filled with a mixture of amusement and disgust at the speed with which they melted into the nearby buildings, or walked singly down the street, looking innocent. By the time the patrol reached the corner, filled with the almost apoplectic rage the song aroused in the occupation troops, he faced an empty street. A burst of raucous laughter came out of a second floor window of the building across Tenth Street from the *Herald* office, occupied by the Life Insurance Company of Virginia. The soldier looked up angrily. Jonathan could see the figures standing in the window across from him, but he doubted that the patrol could. He looked at the sign on the building. "I'm surprised they haven't made them change that sign to 'Life Insurance Company of Military District No. I,'" he told himself bitterly.

He stood at the window for a few minutes longer, then he turned back to his desk with a resolve taken. The sight of those men, adults, Virginians, once free men, running like mischievous boys at the approach of a Yankee patrol had lost its amusing aspect; disgust had taken over. He would no longer be a party to such servility. He would say what he chose to say in his own newspaper. "And I don't give a damn." He hummed the last line of Inness Randolph's verse and sat down to write his editorial, giving himself for the first time the exquisite pleasure of expressing his opinion of the Radical Republicans, and of all carpetbaggers, scalawags, mugwumps, turncoats, blood-suckers, jackals, panderers and parasites. In closing he wrote:

> Among the scarcely recognizable forms of humanity which now infest this community, circling around us like buzzards seeking their prey, is one who dwelt among us for many years in normal human guise, showing no sign

of the cloven hoof, or the horns and tail of the minions of Satan. Mr. Elias Webber, who now leads the rabble, was once one of us. He was a ranting war man all during the war, and boasted how much he did for the gallant Confederates. All that is gone, erased from the record, surely forgotten by Mr. Webber. Some there may be who would say that he is a creature of most astute intelligence; certainly he knows a good thing when he sees it. He has now taken the Ironclad Oath as the recipient of a fat Federal office and lives on lamb and green peas every day. Bully for our old Democratic friend Webber.

When he had finished Jonathan took the editorial downstairs to patient old Andy Mapes, got his horse from Ally Martin's and rode home, feeling happier than he had for many months.

The editorial appeared in the *Herald* the next morning. Tom Scott read it and chortled. "Sort of sound like yourself again, Jonny," he said. "The damn bastards!" Nevertheless he looked at Jonathan anxiously. "Hope they don't put you in jail."

Later in the morning Leslie Vaughn came in. Poor Les! He kept himself going during the day, and he was still a good reporter, but Jonathan knew that he drank heavily at night. He was getting a name in the town as a drinker.

"They don't like it, Major," he said. "They don't like it at all."

"Who doesn't like it?" asked Jonathan.

"The Yankees. I stopped by the Court House on my way here this morning. They are pretty mad. But most specially the Webbers don't like it."

"I shouldn't think they would. I didn't do it to please them."

"There is talk about what the Webber boys say they are going to do to you. Elias Webber's two sons have been going around town saying they are going to shoot you. I don't like it."

"Talk," said Jonathan. "Just talk."

However the Yankees and the Webbers might feel about the editorial, as the day went on Major Meade realized that in general the town rejoiced. All day people came by the office to tell him so. Friends stopped him as he walked down the street to congratulate him. Some shook his hand in silence. Many men did not trust themselves to speak in those days. Jonathan took the paper home and showed the editorial to Elizabeth. She read it in silence and smiled at him when she finished, but he knew that she was worried.

The next morning Major and Mrs. Meade and Janie were having breakfast in the dining room when they heard the sound of a horse coming up the driveway at a gallop. They looked at each other and Major Meade rose and went to the front of the house. Mrs. Meade and Janie followed. Tom Scott was running up the steps to the porch. He took off his hat when he saw Mrs. Meade, but he spoke to Jonathan.

"Listen, Jonny, I come to tell you—" he said, and paused. He looked hot and excited, and he sounded almost breathless. Tom was not used to riding galloping horses. "You know those two Webber boys, sons of old man Webber?"

"Yes, I know them."

"Well, they're layin' for you. They are standin' on the corner right across the street from the office, and they got guns in their hands. I come to tell you, you better get to the office another way this morning. Come down Tenth and in the side entrance instead of coming up across Main Street."

"Now, Tom," Jonathan said, "you know me better than that. You know I am not going to be intimidated and made to go skulking around back entrances by a couple of young braggarts."

"For God's sake, boy, this ain't any time for bold, brave words. Ain't any use getting shot if you can help it. I tell you those men are standing right there on the steps of the Presbyterian Church. They say they're goin' to shoot you, and damned if I don't believe they will."

Elizabeth was looking at him despairingly. Her face was white.

"Listen, Elizabeth and Tom. If those men intend to shoot me, going in the side entrance this morning won't do any good. They will have plenty of other opportunities. I can't go into hiding, you know. I'll go to the office the same way I have gone every day for twenty-two years, but I will take my pistol with me. If there is any trouble I'll defend myself."

Tom sighed. "You're a damn fool, Jonny, but I love you."

"You are the best friend a man ever had, Tom," Jonathan

said. "Thank you for warning me. I'll be prepared. You go on back to the office, and I will be there in a little while."

"I'll be watchin' out for you," Tom said.

Major Meade went back to the dining room and finished his coffee.

"Do you suppose, Mr. Meade," Elizabeth asked, "that they will try to shoot you?"

"I don't think so, Elizabeth. Even under military government there is supposed to be some law in this community. I think it is just talk."

"Mr. Meade," she said, "don't go. I can't stand any more."

"Elizabeth, honey, what would you have me do? I can't hide out here in the country until those men get tired looking for me. If they really are looking for me they can shoot tomorrow just as well as today."

"Couldn't you notify—the authorities?"

The Major laughed shortly. "And get arrested myself, probably, for disturbing the peace."

He went into the library and took his pistol from the desk drawer. When Zeb brought Black Prince around Mrs. Meade and Janie went out to the porch with him. He put his arms around Elizabeth and kissed her. "Now don't worry, honey. I've been shot at before, you know. Anyhow, I think this is just bluster."

Janie ran to him and hugged him. He lifted her up and kissed her. After he had mounted he waved to them. "I'll be home as usual this evening," he said. They stood on the porch watching him ride down the driveway.

Jonathan rode slowly into town. He was in no hurry to get there. In spite of his assurance to Elizabeth he thought it entirely probable that the Webbers were in earnest. To himself he admitted that they had a right to be angry. His editorial was insulting; he had meant it to be insulting. He could not imagine that a man who had so flagrantly aligned himself with the lowest elements in the community, who had so publicly renounced his natural loyalties, could have the capacity for feeling insult at a statement of these facts, but assuming that he had, or assuming that his sons had, they surely had justification.

The familiar road lay in front of him, dappled with shade where the woods were, sunny and hot where it went by the open fields. His life was bounded by that road, from Fairview to town, from the town back to Fairview. He could not remember a time when this had not been true. As a small child sitting in the carriage with his mother and sisters, as a growing boy on his pony, later on the riding horse his father had given him when he was fifteen years old. His years at the University and his years in the Confederate Army had marked the only breaks in the continuity of the part this stretch of country road had played in his life. He wondered if he was riding it now for the last time, and trying to examine his own heart and mind candidly, he admitted the existence of the old fear, the fear he had always felt when he rode into battle, knowing the presence of the enemy, knowing the imminent possibility of death. Many times he had asked himself if all men felt that fear. He knew that some of the bravest did, that some of the war's notable heroes had fought fear with deeds of reckless gallantry. Well, he had gone through the war without showing fear, and had come out alive; he would at least 'go through this brush with danger without showing fear.

He rode down the steep hill and into the town, going along Twelfth to River Street instead of turning at Main as he usually did. This would allow him to come up the hill on foot after he had left Black Prince at Ally Martin's, instead of riding past the Presbyterian Church on horseback to go down the hill to the livery stable. He allowed himself this deviation from custom because he sometimes took that route by choice, and because he did not want to make himself a more obvious target than necessary. As he came up Tenth Street from River to the stable entrance in the middle of the block Jason appeared to take the horse, and Ally got up out of his chair and stood looking, anxiously at Jonathan.

"Them Webber boys been standin' up on the corner waitin' for you," he said.

"I know, Tom Scott rode out this morning to tell me."

"I don't see 'em now, I don't know where they're gone, but I reckon they're up there. Listen, Major, whyn't you go round the block instead of straight up to Main. Whyn't you go down River to Ninth and up Ninth to Market and across to Tenth so's you could come down Tenth to your office without crossin' the corner at Main?"

"Would you?" Jonathan asked.

"You bet I would," Ally said. "I ain't any hero."

"Neither am I, but I can't see what good it would do. If I get to my office without meeting them what's to keep them from shooting me when I come out? And if not today, what about tomorrow? If they are really trying to get me I'd better meet them soon than late. It is not a pleasant prospect to live with from day to day."

"I reckon you're right. Well, I'll be comin' along behind you, and I've got a gun."

"Don't do that, Ally," Jonathan said. "You keep out of this. This is my business and I would hate for you to get mixed up in any trouble on account of me."

"Unh-hunh," Ally grunted.

Jonathan started up the steep hill to the corner of Main and Tenth, where the *Herald* office stood directly across the street from Wright's Emporium and diagonally across from the Presbyterian Church. As he approached the church he reached into his pocket and took out his pistol, continuing up the hill holding it straight down in his right hand. He still saw no sign of the Webber brothers, but the back of his neck was tingling with the familiar prescience of danger, as if his hair was trying to stand on end. When he was far enough up the hill to get a view on Main Street and the slope of Tenth as it continued its way up to Market, he saw that Andy Mapes and Bob Haynes were standing on the sidewalk in front of the composing room entrance and that Tom and Leslie Vaughn were waiting at the side entrance. They started down the hill at sight of him, and at that moment a man ran out of the Presbyterian Church, yelling something at him as he came. That was where they had been, Jonathan thought, hiding in the vestibule of the church. A shot rang out and he heard the tinkling of glass as it crashed through a side window in the basement of Wright's Emporium. He stood still and carefully aimed his pistol, but as he pulled the trigger the Webber man ducked behind a stone pillar carved with the name of the church and holding a gold-lettered placard giving the hours of services, which stood in the grass plot in front of the building. Suddenly another man emerged from the dim interior of the church vestibule and fired at Jonathan from the steps. The bullet whizzed harmlessly past him and buried itself in the brick foundation of the Emporium. As Jonathan prepared to fire at the man on the steps, he could hear Ally Martin's running footsteps behind him, and could see Tom and Les running toward him across Main Street. At that moment the first Webber brother leaned out from behind the stone pillar and fired at Jonathan.

Slowly Major Meade's arm dropped and the pistol fell from it. He was conscious of a shattering sensation in his head, sending a shock through his entire body, depriving him of strength or motion. He was conscious of other shots, and of running footsteps and shouts. He was conscious of lying stretched out on the stone pavement, and this surprised him because he did not remember falling. Voices were all around him.

"He ain't dead," one said, "but I reckon he's hurt bad."

"My God, it's his eye," another said. "The bullet went right through it."

Somebody was feeling his heart. "The heartbeat is strong. Run get Dr. Pierce, fast as you can."

The voices were getting farther and farther away. The sunny day was blotted out, darkness settled over Jonathan. He was cold. The stone pavement was cold and hard. As he slipped into unconsciousness he saw Elizabeth's white face as it had looked that morning. "I can't stand any more, Mr. Meade," she had said.

Part II

13

Miss Bessie Mason stood at the front window of her up-stairs classroom and watched the procession of young females come through her gate, up the perennial-bordered walk and into the house. It was the opening day of school and, as they had done for the past twenty-five years, most of the daughters of good families in the town and surrounding countryside were converging upon the old Mason house, where Miss Bessie ran her School for Girls and Young Ladies.

In carriages and buggies they came, but mostly on foot, the younger ones accompanied by nurses or parents or in groups. Some of them were new and entered timidly, most of them knew each other well. The sunny September morning was filled with gay greetings, giggles, shrill screams and moans of pretended distress at having to return to school. They were all gathering in the wide center hall downstairs and on the verandah that stretched across the back of the house. Presently Miss Bessie would go down, make an impressive entrance, impressively welcome the girls and young ladies to a new school year, and sort them out into classes, the little ones downstairs under the direction of Miss Georgianna Wingfield, the intermediate girls in Mrs. Preston Davis' classroom across the hall, and the older girls in this room, presided over by Miss Bessie herself.

Miss Bessie Mason was a tall, impressive-looking woman, handsome in a forbidding way, surrounded by an aura of refined accomplishments. She was the supreme arbiter in matters of culture and erudition in the town, fields which for the most part the gentlemen left to the ladies and the ladies referred to Miss Bessie. The basis for this eminence was that she was widely traveled. In a society many of whose members had never been beyond the limits of the Commonwealth of Virginia, having no need and little desire to do so, and few of whom had ever crossed an ocean, Miss Bessie's travels set her apart. Her familiarity with foreign places, her knowledge of foreign ways, shed a luster upon her and gave authority to her opinions. She was the very heart of the Philharmonic Society, for had she not heard the great orchestras of Europe? Her criticism was final for young ladies aspiring to the arts of watercolor painting or china decoration, for had she not visited the fabulous museums of Paris and Vienna? Her taste in dress and interior decoration was accepted with respect by the ladies, because she had actually seen Queen Victoria and been to Buckingham Palace and Windsor Castle.

The Honorable Stuart Corbin Mason, Miss Bessie's father, had been a man of wide interests and discriminating tastes. He had taken the Grand Tour in his youth, at a time when the custom was dying out among the well-to-do families of Virginia, and he had so far departed from the ways of his people as to marry an English girl. He had brought her to the town as a bride when he came there to practice law back in 1820. His legal activities were limited; his profession was never an important part of his life, but as a man of substance, of education and wide experience, he became the town's most outstanding citizen. When he decided that he would like to go to Congress, the people of the district had sent him there, and kept him in Washington until his death.

As a child Miss Bessie frequently visited her relatives in England. She spent weeks at a time in London, she traveled extensively on the Continent, and as the capstone of her glamorous experiences, she went to school in Paris. For two winters she was finished and polished in the French capital. After her mother's death and toward the end of her father's life the foreign travels ceased, but Miss Bessie still spent much time with him in Washington. When the Honorable Mr. Mason was gathered to his fathers, his daughter discovered that, in order to maintain the style of living to which he felt entitled he had exhausted not only his entire patrimony,

109

but the store of indulgent credit the community had been willing to grant him. He was deeply in debt. Penniless and humiliated by her father's indebtedness, Miss Bessie was confronted with the choices which faced any impecunious and unattached gentlewoman of the period; she could open a school for young ladies, she could turn her father's house into a boardinghouse, or she could descend upon the family of some reluctant relative and remain there in a state of helpless dependency. Miss Bessie chose the young ladies.

It was a decision which met with general approval. Nothing could be more suitable, in the opinion of the townspeople than for Miss Bessie Mason to shed the light of her accomplishments upon the young femininity of the town. No one could be better fitted for the task. This was an appraisal of her abilities which Miss Bessie herself did not share. After years of experience, from the pinnacle of her authority, she could smile at the memory of the abject terror she had felt when first confronted by the bland young faces of her charges. It was all very well to have visited the capitals of Europe, to have acquired in Paris an adequate French accent and a proper knowledge of ladylike deportment, but what about facts? What about organized courses, methods of instruction, ways to fill the interminable hours of the school day? During those first years all Miss Bessie hoped for was to keep two jumps ahead of her pupils. She studied her lessons with an earnestness and a concentration they never equaled. Gradually she learned her way through the forests of fact, she evolved a teaching technique. To her own complete surprise she discovered that she was a good teacher. Having learned her lessons she could impart the information to young minds. She could even inspire interest in some of them, the most promising. She was an excellent disciplinarian; there was no foolishness about her classes. The forbidding manner was largely a product of those years, now it had become a habit.

Looking out of the upstairs window, Miss Bessie saw Laura Ashby coming into the house. That pleased her. She was glad that Josie Ashby had finally taken things into her own hands, sold Ashby Hall and opened up a boardinghouse in town. It was too late to do much about educating the older girls, but Laura and Nancy at least could be brought up as young ladies should be. Kate Wilcox was paying for her niece's schooling this year, but the boardinghouse was doing very well, most of the unattached young men in town were taking their meals there, and Josie said she would be able to send Laura to school herself next year, and Nancy too.

Sara Anne Williams, Maria Lacy and Antonia Hunter came through the gate. The other two went on into the house, but Sara Anne lingered outside, evidently waiting for someone. Sara Anne Williams was one of Miss Bessie's favorites, being to her mind the prettiest girl in the school. For all her prickly exterior, Miss Bessie had a soft spot in her heart for beauty. She rejoiced in all the pretty young faces confronting her year after year. Sara Anne was not a very good student, but she was so lovely to look at, and so gay and good-natured, that Miss Bessie didn't think it mattered much. With beauty and a happy heart, she felt that the Lord would have been sort of gilding the lily if He had added brains too.

A buggy drove up to the gate, and Miss Bessie recognized Major Meade and his daughter, and knew why Sara Anne was lingering. She and Janie Meade were dear friends. Poor Major Meade, with his lined face and the black patch over his right eye. He had had a hard time. Elizabeth Meade had come to see her a while ago about entering Janie.

"I wish we could have sent her sooner," she said. "She will be sixteen years old next month, and that is late to be starting to school. We have been distressed about it, but we couldn't help it, Bessie. You know that. Things have been—difficult."

"Of course, Lizzie. Difficult for everybody but specially for you."

"Mr. Meade is very hopeful now that the Yankees have gone and Virginia is a state once more. Even if we did have to ratify the Fourteenth Amendment to get in, he thinks it will be worth it."

"Yes, and with a decent man in the Governor's Mansion."

"But don't you think it's ironic, Bessie, that we should rejoice over having a governor who is a carpetbagger from New York, a Republican and a former colonel in the Yankee Army? Still, he is a Conservative Republican, and more or less respectable, as you say—not an Underwood or a Hunnicutt."

Miss Bessie smiled a stiff little smile. "There will be other elections, Lizzie, other governors and other congresses. We will get our own back in time."

The two ladies looked at each other. Then Lizzie Meade

111

spoke hesitantly: "I have taught Janie as well as I could. I think you will find that she can keep up with the other girls. She has a quick mind."

"I'm sure she will be all right, Lizzie. You must be a good teacher. I remember how well Emily did in school." Miss Bessie did not know whether or not Emily's name was mentioned in the family, but having brought it up she asked a question she had been wanting to ask. "How is Emily, Lizzie? How is she getting on?"

"She is very well." Mrs. Meade spoke stiffly. "She seems to be—happy. She has two children now, a little girl and a younger boy."

"That's nice. I am glad to hear some news of her, I was always fond of Emily."

Now Miss Bessie stood watching the little group on the sidewalk outside the gate, Major Meade, Janie and Sara Anne. She did not remember seeing Janie Meade since she was a little girl. She was tall now, taller than Sara Anne, slender and sweet-looking. Presently the Major patted her shoulder, got back into the buggy and drove off. The two girls came on into the house.

The incoming stream was petering out, soon only one or two late stragglers could be seen coming down the street. The grandfather's clock on the stair landing began to whir. It played its little piece of music and then struck nine slow and solemn notes. Miss Bessie smoothed her hair, fluffed out the lace at her throat, and majestically descended the stairs.

14

Janie sat on the railing of the front porch at Sara Anne Williams' house. It was lined with boys and girls; others sat on the porch swing and the chairs, and some of the boys sat on the floor. Tom Gordon was playing his banjo, and they were all singing a rollicking song, swaying in unison from side to side in time with the music.

It was a Friday night, and though it was late September the darkness was still warm and flower-scented. Janie was spending the night with Sara Anne. She had been doing this for years from time to time, but tonight was different. It was like a party. She felt very shy among all these lively young people, who seemed to know each other so well and to have so much to say to each other. Sara Anne was completely at home among them. She laughed and sang and twinkled her merry eyes at the boys and knew exactly what to say when they joked with her. Janie was tongue-tied, especially with the boys. Up to that time boys had been merely playmates, with whom she had frolicked and ridden. This was a new relationship. It was as if she and her friends were young ladies with their beaux, and though the thought surprised her, she realized that was only right and proper. After all, she would be sixteen years old next week. She was now one of the young ladies of Miss Bessie Mason's School for Girls and Young Ladies, and a part of the crowd of boys and girls who met, Sara Anne said, almost every Friday night at each others' houses.

A boy was sitting on each side of Janie on the porch railing. She glanced timidly at them. One was Corbin Pratt, whom she remembered as a child. The other was a good-looking boy with a shock of yellow hair, whom she did not know. Presently the yellow-haired boy nudged her with his elbow.

"Come on and sing, Miss Janie," he said.

She was thrilled. It was the first time a young man had ever called her Miss Janie. She did not know the words of the song, but she began to hum the tune, and gradually she picked up the words. When they finished he said: "You've got a pretty voice."

Janie smiled at him, but she still could think of nothing to say. It made no difference then because they began to sing another song, but she wondered if she would always be timid and shy with young men. She reminded herself of Martha Boyd, who never had anything to say, and that surprised her.

After a while they went into the house and danced. They did a Virginia Reel and then Sara Anne started a cakewalk. Janie had never danced a cakewalk, but she followed the other girls and did what they did. They pranced and bent and twisted, threw back their heads and waved their arms. Tom's banjo went faster and faster, and they all cavorted until they were breathless and leaned up against the walls and the furniture laughing. Mrs. Williams came in with pitchers of lemonade, and then she sat down at the piano and began to play waltzes. This was what Janie liked best. She danced with the nice, unknown boy, and with Corbin Pratt, and with Young Ranny Boyd and Tom Gordon, who could dance now that Mrs. Williams was doing the playing. With the music and the dancing it was not necessary to talk, and she got on very well.

Janie enjoyed her new school. When Miss Bessie took her into the little office at the end of the upstairs hall and questioned her in regard to her store of knowledge, she was delighted to find that under her mother's schooling she was well up with the other girls in most subjects and ahead of them in history. Only in geography was she lacking. Miss Bessie appeared horrified to discover that she knew little of the world and could not name any of the capitals of Europe except

London and Paris. She assigned Janie to Mrs. Davis' geography class in the intermediate girls' room. In her own class under Miss Bessie she was to study English literature and composition, European history, French, general science and drawing. Janie soon began to feel at home in Miss Bessie's classrooms. Having never studied with anyone else or recited in public, she had no previous measure of comparison, and she had not known how well she would do in school. It pleased her to find that she had no trouble keeping up with the other girls, and in fact surpassing most of them in her ability to learn quickly.

Friday nights were the big occasions for the girls and boys of her age. After that first time at Sara Anne's Janie stayed in town frequently, going back to Fairview with the Major the next day at dinnertime. Occasionally somebody gave a real party, with Old Tom Walker's fiddles or even the Italian Orchestra that played for the Cotillion Club and the grown-up parties, but for the most part they gathered informally and sang and danced to music of their own making, banjo, accordion or piano.

The next time she stayed with her cousins, Martha and Susan Wilcox, and the crowd met at Jennie Lee Davis' house. Janie and the Wilcox girls and several others in the neighborhood went there together in a group, but when they were ready to leave the yellow-haired boy asked Janie if he might take her home. She knew his name now, it was Johnny Russell. She was excited at the idea of being escorted home by a young man. It was only three or four blocks to the Wilcox house. They walked slowly down the street, kicking up the leaves that had fallen from the trees, and talking. Now that they were alone together Janie had no trouble finding conversation. It was dark between the street lights on the corners, and the flagstone sidewalk was rough, so Johnny offered her his arm. Arm in arm they strolled along, and Janie enjoyed the walk very much. I've got a beau, she kept thinking, and the thought delighted her. It was going to be wonderful to be a young lady. She was sorry when they reached the house.

2

The great excitement that spring was Emily's visit. After seven years Elizabeth and Jonathan Meade had finally

115

worked themselves up to a reconciliation with her. Their first bitterness had mellowed but it had not died, and it was a hard decision to make. Emily and Janie had corresponded with each other from time to time ever since Emily's first letter had come, and Elizabeth herself had written to her daughter when the Major was shot, feeling that she should know of the tragedy. They had exchanged letters occasionally after that, but the stiffly polite notes did little to break down the barrier that separated them. To Elizabeth it seemed against nature to be separated by resentment and ill will from her own child, and as time went by the feeling grew that it was wrong to maintain that strained relationship, regardless of provocation. She knew that the first step must come from them, but for many months she and the Major had hesitated. That winter they had made their decision, and she had written asking Emily to come home for a visit.

She came on a Saturday in April. Major Meade hired a carriage from Ally Martin to meet her at the depot, as it was impossible for Emily and the children and her baggage to get into the buggy. Elizabeth put on her black silk dress that morning, and Janie her Sunday dress, which was made in the new fashion, with a draped skirt without hoops or crinoline. They both wore their hair as ladies had been doing for years, parted in the middle and drawn down smoothly on each side of the face with a big knot on the nape of the neck. From the fashion notes that came out in the *Herald* each week they knew that this was old-fashioned. Frizzes and "waterfalls" and other elaborate ways of dressing the hair were now in style, but most of the ladies of the town still clung to the old way.

Baizy and Lucy and Susie all had on clean calico dresses and white aprons, and as the time approached for the carriage to reach Fairview, Zeb and Jake and Amos came up to the house and hung around waiting for Emily to arrive. When they heard the sound of wheels on the driveway they all ran to the front of the house. The carriage drove up to the porch and the Major emerged and helped Emily out. Then he lifted the two children out. Emily and her mother rushed to each other.

"Oh, Mama, Mama," Emily cried. "I am so glad to see you." They clung to each other and there were tears in the eyes of both. Then Emily turned to Janie.

"And Janie! Mercy me, you've grown up. You are a real young lady." She kissed her and held her off to look at her. "And a pretty one, too."

"So are you," Janie said shyly, looking at her sister with admiring eyes.

In spite of her newly grown-up airs and graces, Elizabeth thought, Janie was still very shy with people she did not know well, and Emily seemed almost a stranger now. She looked very elegant and stylish, in a brown silk traveling dress, elaborately draped, and long brown silk gloves. Sure enough, there were frizzed bangs across her forehead. Her hair was arranged in long curls, and the curls were pulled up to the top of her head and caught there hanging down the back to the collar of her dress in a loose cluster which bobbed when she moved. She had on a brown straw bonnet, cut high in the back to show the curls, and projecting out in front, with a scooped effect, farther than any bonnet Elizabeth had ever seen. It was lined with pale blue silk, framing Emily's face prettily.

Elizabeth turned to make the acquaintance of the children. She had been almost as excited about seeing them as she was about having Emily back again. "Our own grandchildren, Mr. Meade," she had said, "and we have never laid eyes on them."

Mathilda, who was almost six, was a pale, thin little girl with light brown hair and brown eyes. Little Jerome was four. He looked sturdier, and he had Emily's blue eyes. They were both very solemn. They shook hands politely and allowed themselves to be kissed, but they said nothing and they showed no animation.

I reckon they are scared, Elizabeth thought. This is all strange to them.

Dinner was a cheerful meal that day, everybody was happy at the reunion. Elizabeth watched this daughter of hers. Emily had developed and matured. She was a poised and self-confident woman now. She talked interestingly of her life in New York. The family at Fairview had known from her letters that her husband's family was well-to-do; the Tysons, father and son, were stockbrockers on Wall Street, but they had not realized the extent of the Tyson prosperity.

"The family is really quite wealthy, Mama," Emily said. "That was a surprise to me. I didn't know about them when I

117

married Jerome, I didn't know what to expect. It was—well, it was sort of exciting to find out how rich they are."

It was wonderful to have Emily back, to forget the old bitterness and to assume the normal position of a mother with a married daughter living in a distant city. For the most part the visit went off very well. The relatives and Emily's old friends in town were all glad to see her, and several parties were given for her. Everybody thought she looked wonderfully well and they all admired her clothes and her stylish appearance. She had beautiful clothes, and lots of them. It was not all pleasant, however; there were difficult spots and thorny subjects that must be avoided.

One afternoon the three ladies were all sitting upstairs in the big front bedroom sewing. Elizabeth made some pleasant remark about how nice it was for them all to be together at home like that, and then she said: "The next time you come, Emily, you must bring—your husband."

She could not bring herself to call him Jerome; Emily could not know what it cost her to make the suggestion. His name had been mentioned only occasionally by Emily herself. The others had carefully skirted around him in all their talk, and had tried to avoid all mention of the war, or politics or any of the unpleasant subjects which might have caused tension between them. The conviction had been growing in her mind, however, that a good marriage, such as Emily evidently had, based upon love and mutual satisfaction, must be accepted and respected.

There was a little pause before Emily replied, and then she said: "I don't believe he will ever come here, Mama. He can't forgive Papa for asking him where he stole his horse and buggy."

Janie, whose first adoring admiration of Emily had recently shown some signs of dissolving, flared up at this.

"Well, I don't know why he should mind that," she said. "Heaven knows they took all the horses and buggies they could find."

"That was during the war," Emily said. "It was part of the tactics of war, to impoverish the South so that the people couldn't fight any longer. It was done to help win the war, just as the battles were fought; but when Papa said that to Jerome the war was over. It was a matter of personal honor."

"Oh, fiddlesticks!" Janie exclaimed rudely. "What did people's silver services and family portraits and rugs and velvet hangings have to do with winning the war? What did my pony have to do with winning the war, or our carriages, for that matter? They just took what they wanted when they could get it."

A flush spread over Emily's face, and she got up and left the room.

"Oh, Mama, I'm sorry," Janie said. "I didn't mean to say that. I've tried real hard to keep away from the war, but I declare, all this self-righteousness and superiority makes me mad. She is so stuck-up."

Elizabeth could understand how Janie felt. There was a tinge of arrogance in Emily's manner which was not pleasing, and she was not only self-confident, but self-assertive. She obviously, and quite naturally, enjoyed her wealth and position, and she described her home, her friends, her glittering social activities with a satisfaction verging upon smugness. Everything about her new life was perfect, and she seemed to have adopted its ways with the zeal of a convert. Elizabeth tried to be understanding but sometimes she had to watch her quick temper to keep from flaring up. Emily saw her former surroundings through different eyes now. The town was such a funny, hilly little place, it amused the visitor from New York. The house at Fairview needed painting. The blue velvet over-draperies at the parlor windows were shabby, didn't Mama think she should get new ones? The back yard was all cluttered up, one of the men ought to keep it neat. The honeysuckle ought to be pulled off the snake fence, one of the rails was down at the entrance. It was so distressing for Aunt Josie to run a boardinghouse, couldn't something be done about it?

In spite of these small difficulties, which could be put down to the normal frictions of family life, Emily's visit was for the most part a happy one. Much of the time she was sweet and natural, she seemed to enjoy herself, and Elizabeth was deeply grateful for the restored family unity.

On Saturday just before Emily returned to New York, Sara Anne came out to Fairview with the Major at dinnertime to spend the afternoon and night with Janie. Emily was planning to leave on Monday and she had begun her packing. Her clothes were spread all around her room. Janie and Sara Anne appeared at the door.

"Emily," Janie said, "before you get all packed up, show Sara Anne your dresses."

"You don't mind, do you, Miss Emily," Sara Anne said. "I would just love to see all your pretty things."

"Why of course, Sara Anne. I'm glad to show them to you. Come on in."

Sara Anne admired everything, the dresses, the dainty underclothes, the dressing gowns. At Emily's insistence she tried on bonnets and draped herself in shawls, and preened in front of the mirror, looking charming. Among Emily's possessions were two party dresses, over which the girls were ecstatic.

"Oh, my, Miss Emily," Sara Anne cried, "I never saw anything so lovely. You must look like a queen in those dresses."

Emily stood looking at the two girls. "I wonder how you and Janie would look in them," she said.

"Oh, like princesses, at least, wouldn't we, Janie. Maybe when we are married ladies we will have dresses like that."

"I think it would be nice for you to have them now," Emily said, "without waiting to be married ladies. Try them on."

The girls stared at her. "You don't mean—?" Sara Anne said.

"I mean I'd like to give them to you, if you can wear them. Come on, try them on and see. You try the yellow dress, Sara Anne, you are dark. Janie, you take the pink one."

The girls were tremulous with joy as they took off their cotton dresses and slipped the shining folds of the party dresses over their heads. Emily hooked them up the back. The yellow dress fitted Sara Anne as if it had been made for her; she and Emily were about the same height and size.

"It's perfect," Emily said, "and you look lovely in it. You will take all the young men by storm."

"Oh, Miss Emily, I just don't know what to say. I never thought I would have anything so perfectly beautiful."

The pink moire dress was a little too large for Janie. She was slimmer than Emily, and slightly taller.

"You are such a slender little thing, Janie, you must put on a few pounds," Emily said. "But this can easily be taken in, here at the side seams, and it is very becoming to you."

The girls just could not believe it. They walked around the room and postured before the mirror and shook themselves to make the rich silks rustle. Emily enjoyed it all.

"Come on, let's go show them to Mama," she said. Then she paused. "You don't suppose she will mind my giving you a dress do you, Janie?"

Janie was horrified at the idea. "Oh, no, Emily, she couldn't. She just simply couldn't."

Mrs. Meade offered no objection. "It is very kind of you, Emily," she said. "The girls won't know themselves in dresses like that."

Janie forgave Emily for everything. Her sister was sweet and generous, she decided. You could excuse her for putting on a few airs, and she supposed it was natural for her to accept her husband's point of view in regard to the necessities of war. Even without the dresses, however, she would have been sorry to see Emily leave. It had been wonderful having her here. She had always been fond of Emily, and she much preferred having people in the house, and comings and goings, to the quiet and emptiness of closed rooms. She had grown fond of the children, too. In spite of Emily's protests, they had enjoyed the pleasures of the country and had become livelier and noisier since they came.

"I don't know what I will do with them when I get them home," Emily said.

They were all sorry to see her go, and there was much talk of her next visit. Jerome's name was not mentioned again, however.

15

All that summer the pink dress hung in Janie's wardrobe; there was no occasion elegant enough to wear it. In October, however, on Janie's seventeenth birthday, Mrs. Meade gave her the big party she had had on her mind for several years, feeling that Janie had accepted so much hospitality that something must be done in return. It was the first time in ten years there had been a real party in the house, and everybody was excited about it.

The Major was glad to see gaiety come back to Fairview. Hospitality had been the keystone of his lost world. To him the quiet house, the years devoid of visitors and entertaining, meant only one thing, poverty. Poverty was the deadly enemy; all his energies were bent on overcoming it. Every return to the old ways was a triumph. It would be good, he told himself, to stand once more in his own doorway and greet his guests; good to see Elizabeth, smiling and cordial, managing the party with her usual quiet efficiency. Good also to see his young daughter moving among her friends in her own home, pretty and gay, as a Meade daughter should be.

"I don't know whether we can afford it or not, Elizabeth," he had said when she first spoke of it. "It depends upon the tobacco this year. It looks good now, and I think it will be all right. Let's do it, and let's do it well, as we would have in the old days."

"I certainly will, Mr. Meade," Elizabeth had replied. "I

have waited a long time for this, and I am going to do it up brown."

Elizabeth was very happy in the preparations for the party. It was to be a big one; she invited all the young people in Janie's crowd, and she stretched the age limit up and down to include as many of the sons and daughters of her friends as she could. She also invited some of the mothers and fathers, good friends of hers and the Major's, and all the aunts and uncles. The Tylers were going to drive over from Meriden for the party and spend the night. Their only remaining unmarried daughter, Ginny, was too young, but they had a son, Raiford, who was just the right age, and he was coming with them. Families were coming from several nearer plantations, but they preferred to drive back home that night.

Old Tom Walker with his fiddle, his violoncellist and two banjoists were engaged to furnish the music. The rugs were taken up in the parlors and the hall, and the floors polished until they shone. All the leaves were put in the dining room table and the best lace tablecloth was used. An alabaster bowl of pink roses and pink and purple asters stood in the center of the table, between the tall branched candelabra. The house was filled with flowers, asters and chrysanthemums and late roses. Lamps were lighted in the dining room, the library and the hall, but only candles were used in the parlors. There were dozens of them, in the crystal chandeliers and the sconces around the walls, and on the mantelpieces and the piano. All the furniture was taken out of the parlors except the piano and sofas and gilt chairs against the wall.

Janie thought it all looked lovely, in spite of Emily's remarks about the shabbiness of the hangings at the parlor windows. People were too used to shabby furniture to pay any attention to the worn spots. She herself was in a state of happy excitement. She was thrilled at her role of hostess. It was a new and delightful experience for her. In addition to its other excitements, the party gave her a chance to wear the pink moire dress. Her mother had taken it in for her and it now fitted perfectly. For her seventeenth birthday Mrs. Meade gave Janie a seed pearl necklace which had been her own mother's. It was made of twisted strands of tiny seed pearls from which hung three round medallions of larger pearls. The combination of birthday party, pink dress and pearl necklace lifted Janie into an ecstasy of happiness. When she put on the dress and clasped the necklace around her throat, she stood looking at herself gravely in the mirror, and she was enchanted by the elegance of her appearance. She wore frizzed bangs now, but she had not been able to work herself up to the loose curls that Emily had worn. Her hair was lifted up, instead of being drawn down over the ears as in the old fashion, and caught into a huge, shining knot at the back.

I look fashionable, she thought joyfully. I look like a stylish young lady.

As she started downstairs, relishing the rustle of her silk dress, Tom Walker's fiddle started up in the back parlor. The other instruments would not be played until the dancing began, but Tom was to play his fiddle all during supper. The sound of the singing strings completed Janie's joy. It played on her exultant emotions as Tom's bow was playing on the strings. This perfect moment surrounded her like an iridescent bubble. This was the way to live, she told herself, the way she would like always to live. Music, lights, flowers, the rustle and sheen of silks, friends arriving at an open doorway. Romance hanging in the air like a tangible presence. Not yet, she thought, not quiet yet, but soon. A little more time to enjoy the flavor, the fragrance of this heady wine of youth, and then romance would descend from above, where it hung now with a faint, rosy glow, and blind her expectant eyes with its brightness.

Her father was standing at the foot of the stairs watching her come down. When she reached the hall he bowed to her, formally. "I am glad to greet a grown-up young lady," he said, "and a lovely one."

Janie was overcome by such a compliment from the Major. "Oh, Papa, thank you. It's the dress, Emily's dress. Isn't it beautiful?"

"I wasn't speaking of the dress," the Major said.

Mrs. Meade came into the hall. "Oh, you're all dressed, aren't you, honey. Come here and let me see you."

Janie went over and stood in front of her. Mrs. Meade turned her all around and then she said: "It's very nice. Perhaps a little elaborate for a young girl, but very pretty, and you look sweet in it, honey."

The company began to arrive. Carriages came up the drive in a steady stream. Everybody who had a carriage used it and invited friends to drive out with them. Some of the young men in town went together and hired carriages from Ally Martin, or buggies to bring their girls out alone. When the vehicles were emptied they were driven around to the barn where the horses were hitched. It was warm enough for the front door to be left open, and the Major stood in the doorway to greet the guests as they arrived. When the ladies had gone upstairs to leave their capes and shawls, and the gentlemen had put their hats on racks in the back hall, they went into the front parlor where Mrs. Meade and Janie stood. Soon the music of Old Tom's fiddle was almost drowned out by the sound of voices.

Sara Anne came with Carey Morgan, wearing the yellow dress. Its soft folds and draperies shimmered over its yellow taffeta foundation. She had a yellow and a red rose caught in her brown hair at one side. She winked at Janie as she greeted her hostesses, and stroked the yellow dress with loving fingers.

"Doesn't Sara Anne look lovely, Mama?" Janie asked.

"Yes, she is certainly a very pretty girl," Mrs. Meade replied. "She's an arrant little flirt, but I must say she flirts charmingly. If I were a young man I expect I would be doing just what they are doing." She was looking at the group that had immediately gathered around Sara Anne.

When everybody had arrived, and the greetings had been exchanged, and Tom had given up trying to make his fiddle heard, they all trouped into the dining room, going around the table in a long line and coming back with laden plates. There was Virginia ham and chicken salad and scalloped oysters, brandied peaches, Sally Lunn and beaten biscuits and little hot rolls. The older people went into the library or stayed in the dining room, the young ones sat on the sofas in the parlors and the hall and on the stairs all the way up to the first landing. Some of them went out onto the front porch to sit, and the side porch overlooking the garden. Old Tom Walker wandered around playing his fiddle, going from one room to another, stopping at one group and moving on to the next. For dessert they had Baizy's wonderful rum cake. Mrs. Meade had wanted to have ice cream, but it was hard to serve ice cream to that many people.

When supper was over the music and the dancing began. The fiddle, the cello, the banjos tuned up and broke into gay music. Tom was an expert at calling the dances, his voice could be heard all over the house. "Honor yo' pardners," "ladies to the right," "swing yo' pardners," "do-shay-do."

The mothers and fathers watched the dancing for a while, then gradually the gentlemen gathered in the library, the ladies in the dining room. "They *will* separate," Elizabeth complained. "They always do, at our age." Perhaps it was just as well. The ladies were being served Madeira wine that had been the old General's. The gentlemen, she knew, were imbibing stronger spirits. For the young people she had mixed a nice fruit punch. The big silver punch bowl stood on a table at the back of the hall, under the arch of the stairway. The coachmen who had driven the carriages out from town, and the Fairview servants, congregated outside and watched the dancing through the windows. They had had their own party supper in the kitchen. It was all just as it had been in the old days. Tomorrow would come, but tonight they had the past back again.

Janie floated through the evening in a haze of happiness. Everything about the party seemed perfect to her, even the weather. It was a warm, soft night, and a great yellow harvest moon shone down on the strolling couples. Mindful of her responsibilities, she kept an eye on her guests, and everybody seemed to be having a good time. There were more than enough young men, and no wallflowers. Even Martha Boyd, who was sometimes a problem, had a partner for every dance. Janie herself had a whirl. The young men clamored to dance with her. They were just being polite, she told herself, they had to dance with her because it was her party. Whatever the reason, it was thrilling to find herself surrounded by young gentlemen begging to dance with her and arguing with each other over their right to a fair share of Miss Janie's time. She felt important and pampered, and she reveled in it.

At midnight the musicians played "Home, Sweet Home" and the guests began to leave. Gradually the carriages drove away. Janie stood out on the porch and waved goodbye to them all. Only the Tylers were left. Mr. Tyler and Raiford were talking to Major Meade in the library. Janie liked young Raiford Tyler; he had been very attentive to her all evening. She turned and went into the hall. Mrs. Meade and Mrs. Tyler were standing there, looking around helplessly. The house seemed quiet and empty, with an after-the-party emptiness. The rooms looked bare and disheveled.

"Doesn't a house look awful after a party is over?" Mrs. Meade asked. "Let's just blow out the candles and turn out the lamps and go to bed. We'll tackle the mess tomorrow."

Janie kissed her mother goodnight. "Thank you, Mama. It just simply couldn't have been lovelier."

16

The autumn after Janie graduated from Miss Bessie Mason's School for Girls and Young Ladies, Major Meade bought a barouche and another horse. Black Prince was getting old, but the Major still rode him into town when he went alone, so for the most part the new equipage was at the disposal of Mrs. Meade and Janie.

Janie was now a full-fledged young lady, educated and prepared for life. She could name the capitals of Europe and she knew the kings of England from the Norman Conquest to Queen Victoria. She was reasonably well acquainted with the Victorian novelists and the British poets. She had a smattering of the French language, could sing sweetly and played the piano somewhat less than adequately. She was an accomplished needlewoman, and she could make Sally Lunn, hot biscuits, and what even Baizy admitted were good layer cakes. She had never been more than thirty miles away from Fairview, and the United States outside of the South was as unknown to her as Russia and more inimical. Life stretched ahead of her in enchanted vistas, all leading to the dim, still vague, figure of the man who would come, soon now surely, trailing clouds of romance and eternal devotion.

In the meantime Janie was prepared to enjoy herself in her new leisure and freedom. She and her mother now took part in all the social activities of the town. More and more also their friends could come out to Fairview, a good many of the families having their own carriages and buggies again. Some of the young men had horses and could ride out to call on Janie. Mrs. Meade rejoined the Philharmonic Society, of which she used to be an active member. Janie belonged to a sewing circle. Once a week the girls met at each other's houses and spent the afternoon sewing and embroidering.

One June day, a year after Janie's graduation, she went into town to attend a meeting of the circle at Antonia Hunter's house, and to spend the night with Sara Anne. It was hot and sunny, but there was a breeze stirring and Toni's big black parlor was pleasantly cool. The girls had much to talk about. The June cotillion had taken place the week before, and that was good for a lot of conversation. Some of them were excited about a new man who had come to town. He was taking his meals at Aunt Josie Ashby's.

"I declare, he is the handsomest young man I ever saw in my life," said Linda Richardson. "Oh, Laura, you are so lucky. You always meet them first."

"As far as he is concerned it doesn't do any good," Laura said. "He doesn't pay any of us the least bit of attention. He just comes and eats his meals and goes away."

"He's like that with everybody," Maria Lacy said. "The other night when we were all going on the picnic to the Island, you know, Dick Partridge asked him to go with us and he declined, and when Corbin Pratt asked him if he would be interested in joining the Cotillion Club he said no thanks, he was too busy for such things."

"It's such a waste," Linda sighed. "A handsome young man like that shutting himself off by himself."

"What's his name?" Janie asked.

"It's Avery Calhoun," Laura said.

Janie almost choked on her lemonade. "Oh!" she cried.

They all looked at her inquiringly. "Is he tall and dark?" she asked.

Laura nodded. "He is real tall and very dark. Do you know him?"

"I don't reckon so," Janie said slowly, "but I met a boy once—I don't know what his first name was but his last name was Calhoun, and he was tall and dark. I just wondered if it was the same person. Of course," she added hastily, "it was years ago, we were just children. He came from somewhere up in the Valley."

129

"This one came here from Big Lick, but he could have come from the Valley before that."

"He looks as if he had come straight out of the pages of a book," said Linda dreamily. "King Arthur's Round Table or something like that."

A slow excitement was mounting in Janie. Eight years had passed since the tournament at Meriden, but she had never forgotten the black-eyed boy sitting on the fence, with the bright pennants fluttering in the October sunshine and the sound of trumpets in the air. That was a day set apart from all other days, a scene taken, as Linda said, straight out of the pages of a book. A fairy tale, it had always seemed to her, a shining unreality that lifted the imagination and stirred the heart to expectant joy. It's fairylike quality, its unreality, though realized, yet held intimations of beauties that could be real. That bright scene was a prism reflecting light and shedding color on the real world around her. If this was the tall, dark boy grown to manhood, if he was here in this town and could be seen and talked to, it might be that some of the luster and the color would again be reflected upon the present reality.

"Has he come here to live?" she asked.

"Yes, he's with the new railroad," Laura said. "The Virginia and Durham, you know, that's just been completed. It runs from here all down through North Carolina. The main office has been opened here, and he is the freight, or the assistant freight, manager, or something like that."

All that evening at Sara Anne's excitement worked in Janie. She couldn't keep her mind off the afternoon's conversation. She felt convinced that the Avery Calhoun of her cousins' enthusiasm was the same person as the strange boy who had looked at her so hard that day at Meriden. Several young gentlemen came to call on the girls that night; Carey Morgan, one of Sara Anne's many beaux and certainly the most devoted, and Corbin Pratt, and Johnny Russell, just home from the University. Johnny was still Janie's most attentive beau. He wrote her regularly from Charlottesville, dashing letters filled with compliments and sentimental protestations. When he was at home he gave her a great rush. With him that evening was Raiford Tyler of Meriden, who had come to Janie's seventeenth birthday party. He was Johnny's best friend at the University, and he too had been very attentive to Janie.

130

He had taken to stopping by in the town to visit Johnny on all his trips between Meriden and Charlottesville, and sometimes when he was at home he rode over to Fairview to call on her. The two young men maintained an elaborate rivalry for Miss Janie's time and attention. Janie knew very well, however, that there was nothing serious in Raiford's gallantries. One of the basic points in her code of ethics in dealing with young men was that you never took them seriously unless they themselves were serious. Compliments and gallantries were to be expected. Any gentleman who did not pay compliments to a lady, regardless of her age or the degree of her charms, was a boor, and certainly any reasonably pleasing young lady had a right to expect them from the young men around her. They were among the enchantments of young ladyhood, a part of civilized social intercourse. No matter how extravagant the protestations, however, they were never to be taken seriously if uttered with a smile, with humor in eyes or voice. If a gentleman wanted to be taken seriously he had only to be serious about it. Janie, therefore, knew in what category to place each of these young men. Johnny was serious, Raiford was not. She accepted the attentions of each on those terms, and enjoyed them both. She was glad to see them both that evening.

The young people sat out on the front porch in the warm darkness. The lamps in the parlor shed a glow through the windows, and the air was sweet with honeysuckle. All evening, during the talk and the laughter, the snatches of song, and the raillery and joking, Janie kept thinking about Avery Calhoun. How was she to find out whether or not he was the strange boy of her memory? He had been there two weeks, Laura said, and he had made no effort to see her. Silly, she told herself. He probably didn't even know what her name was. He had probably forgotten all about her anyhow during these past eight years. Probably he was used to tournaments, and certainly he had met dozens of girls since that time. The thought depressed her unreasonably. Anyhow, she decided, she could find out about him by having dinner at Aunt Josie's some day; she would invite herself there soon.

There was to be a barn dance out at the old Cabell place two days later, and they were trying to persuade Raiford Tyler to stay over for it.

"I won't stay unless I can take Miss Janie to it," Raiford said.

"Well, you can't take her because she is going with me," replied Johnny.

"No, I'm not," Janie said. "I am going with Ranny Boyd. He asked me a long time ago."

To save her life she could not keep a note of deprecation out of her voice. Ranny Boyd, like his sister Martha, was not a popular member of the group. They were both pale and solemn, without humor or social charm. Ranny had attached himself to Janie and, to her dismay, he was serious about it. He fell over himself asking her to go to parties and dances with him, and sometimes she felt impelled to accept his invitations. After all, a barn dance was only a barn dance; it was not important like a cotillion or a ball. It did seem too bad, however, that she should have to go with dull old Ranny when she might have gone with either Raiford or Johnny.

"Oh, blast!" Raiford said. "It's not fair, when I am here for such a short time. Well, then, I won't stay unless I can have every third dance. How about it, Miss Janie, will you dance every third dance with me?"

Janie giggled happily. "I'm not making promises," she said. "You'll just have to take your chances."

"That's right, Jan-ie," Sara Anne said. "Don't you let them tie you down."

"That's Miss Sara Anne's motto," said Carey Morgan gloomily. "She won't let you tie her down for a minute, about anything."

"Mer-cy, no," Sara Anne said. "Not yet. Not until I'm ready to be tied down for good."

"When that time comes, I hope you will let me know."

"Well, I certainly will, Carey. I'll certainly an-nounce my intentions—when I have any."

Sara Anne was like that. She could afford to be high-handed with her beaux because she had so many of them. Everybody knew that Carey Morgan had never looked at another girl since he and Sara Anne were children. In the end, Raiford agreed to stay for the barn dance. Janie knew he had meant to all along.

The next morning Janie walked downtown from Sara Anne's house on Sycamore Street to Main to meet her mother. Mrs. Meade was coming in town to do some shopping, and she and Janie were going to pick up the Major and drive back to Fairview for dinner. She went down Sixth Street, from Sycamore to Jefferson, and from Jefferson to Market. The street was so steep that you had to hold yourself back as you walked. Ridges had been chiseled in the stone pavement to give people a foothold and keep them from slipping. From Market to Main it was not so steep, but Janie was still watching her step as she walked along in her long skirts and her good shoes. When she reached the corner of Main Street she looked up. A young man was standing on the opposite corner, and as she started to cross the street he turned and looked directly at her. Her heart began pounding furiously. She would have recognized him anywhere; even without the conversation of yesterday she would have known him immediately. There was a quality about him that set him apart. As she reached the sidewalk on which he was standing he took off his hat with a sweeping gesture and bowed to her.

"Miss Meade, this is an unexpected pleasure," he said. "I am Avery Calhoun. Do you remember me?"

Triumph flashed through Janie's mind. He had not forgotten; he had remembered her all these years. "Why, yes, Mr. Calhoun," she said in a small voice, because she felt quite breathless. "I remember that day at Meriden very well."

Avery Calhoun was immaculately dressed in a white linen suit and a wide-brimmed Panama hat. His thick black hair waved slightly; he wore the merest suggestion of sideburns. His skin looked very white in contrast to the dark hair and brows. His brilliant black eyes, widely spaced between thick black lashes, were looking at her just as they had looked at the little girl on the fence at Meriden.

"I hoped you did," he said. "I have never forgotten it. It is wonderful to meet you like this. I have been wondering how I could approach you. I have come here to live, you know."

"Why, have you really, Mr. Calhoun," Janie said hypocritically. "How nice! I hope you will like it here. We think it is a pleasant place to live."

"I'm sure it is. I have been wanting to ask if I could call on you."

Janie was feeling even more breathless. Because of that, or

133

for some other reason, she retreated far off into the distance. "My mother and I will be glad to welcome you at Fairview, Mr. Calhoun," she said.

He bowed again. "I will give myself that pleasure soon," he said.

Janie smiled at him and moved off down the street, hating herself. Why in the world had she been so prim and prissy with him, so formal and sticklish? Why had she brought her mother into it, as if seeking protection behind parental chaperonage? She had sounded like—like some of the young ladies in Jane Austen's books, instead of being natural in the casual, easy-going manner of her usual custom. Probably he would not come to see her now that she had acted so standoffish. I wouldn't, she thought, if anybody talked to me like that.

He did, however. He rode out to Fairview to call the next afternoon. Janie had not expected him to come so soon, even if he came at all. She was sitting upstairs in her mother's big front bedroom, sewing, when she heard the sound of a horse's hooves coming up the driveway. She went to the window to find out who it was, and saw Avery Calhoun ride up to the house, hitch his horse, and come up the porch steps. He was riding a splendid black horse, and he was dressed in an elegant gray riding suit with red facings. He looked even more spectacular than he had in his white linen suit the day before. Later, Janie was to learn that he had worked and saved for years to buy the horse and the riding clothes, but now she was filled with a mixture of consternation and pleasure. Mr. Avery Calhoun was no ordinary young man. He was almost overpowering, and here she was, in a blue gingham morning dress, certainly not the costume she would have chosen for his first call. The doorbell tinkled in the dining room, and Janie knew it was also tinkling in the kitchen. She ran into her room with the idea of changing her dress, but when she heard Lucy coming to answer the doorbell she decided there would be no time, so she went out into the hall and hung over the railing of the stairwell to hear what was being said.

"Good evenin', suh," Lucy said politely.

"Good evening. Are Mrs. Meade and Miss Meade at home?"

"Yassuh, they's heah. Don' know what Miss Lizzie is, but Miss Janie, she's upstairs. Won't you come in, suh."

"Will you tell them that Mr. Avery Calhoun is calling."

"Yassuh."

Lucy left him in the front parlor and started up the stairs. Janie ran back into her room and smoothed her hair and powdered her nose.

"Gent'mun to see you," Lucy told her, coming to the door. "Sez he's Mr. Avey Calhoun."

"Oh, Lucy, look at me," wailed Janie. "I'm not properly dressed."

"You looks prutty," Lucy said consolingly. "Ain't nuthin' the matter with what you got on."

"Well, it will have to do," Janie said, running a comb through her bangs. "If you see Mama, tell her to come to the parlor."

There it was again, she thought. I really must be afraid of him, I keep dragging Mama into this. As she went down the stairs she resolved firmly to be natural and easy with him, as she would with any other young man. The minute she entered the room with him, however, she was conscious of the same curious restraint. It reminded her of the way she had felt when she first encountered boys in the role of beaux. She felt shy and tongue-tied. He rose as she came in and they shook hands.

"I told you I was coming soon," he said. "I hope this is not too soon."

"Certainly not too soon, Mr. Calhoun," Janie assured him. "I am glad to see you." She sat on the blue brocade sofa and he sat beside her. The blue velvet hangings had been taken down for the summer, but the room looked pretty with white lace curtains. "I hope you had no trouble finding Fairview."

"No, I knew how to get here. I have ridden out here before, but I lacked the courage to come in."

Janie was surprised. "Does it take so much courage to call at Fairview?" she asked.

He smiled slightly. "Yes, it did until I met you yesterday. I didn't know whether or not you remembered me, you see, and I thought I would have a hard time explaining myself if I was a total stranger to you. It has been a long time since that day at the tournament. Even then, you remember, we were not properly introduced."

Janie laughed. "How did you know my name?"

"I asked, until I found out. How did you know mine?"

"I asked too. Mrs. Tyler knew who you were. She told us about your father and his prayer for the Yankees."

Janie thought that was funny and laughed at the recollection, but Avery did not laugh.

"All the years of my father's laboring in the vineyard of the Lord," he said, somberly, "failed to make as much impression on his people as that one prayer."

He sounded prissy too, Jane thought, perhaps they had that effect on each other. She tried to change the subject.

"In spite of the time it has been, we had no trouble recognizing each other."

"I would have known you anywhere," he said, "even though in the meantime the pretty little girl has grown into a very lovely young lady."

"You pay pretty compliments, Mr. Calhoun."

"I am not in the habit of paying compliments, Miss Meade. I only speak the truth."

Janie would have felt at home with that statement if he had smiled when he said it, but there was no humor in his face or voice. Its absence left her at a loss. My, but he's solemn, she thought. He takes everything you say so seriously. She would have to pick her way carefully through the conversational quickstands if she hoped to keep the talk in a light vein. She tried again.

"How does it happen that you have come here to live, Mr. Calhoun?" she asked, as if she did not know.

"I have a position with the Virginia and Durham Railroad," he replied. "For a number of years I have worked for the Southside Railroad in Big Lick, and when this new line opened offices here I was fortunate enough to get the position of assistant freight manager. It is a fine opening for a young man, but I have much to learn."

"You probably know my uncle, Mr. Jim Peyton, who is in charge of the Southside offices here."

"Oh, yes. I admire Mr. Peyton very much, he has been a big help to me."

Mrs. Meade came into the back parlor from the garden, with a big basket of roses in her hands. Mr. Calhoun rose.

"Mama, this is Mr. Avery Calhoun," Janie said. "He has come to call on us."

Mrs. Meade smiled at Avery. Janie knew that she had no idea who he was.

"How do you do, Mr. Calhoun. Just let me put these flowers down, I'll be right back."

"May I take them for you?" Avery asked.

"No, I'll just call Lucy to put them in water."

Janie's instinct had been right, she was glad to have her mother with them in the parlor. Mrs. Meade kept the conversation going with ease, and when the young man rose to go she invited him to stay for supper.

"Thank you very much, Mrs. Meade. That is very kind of you, but unfortunately I have work to do tonight."

They went out to the porch with him and watched him mount and ride off down the driveway.

"Well," said Mrs. Meade, "who is that strange young man?"

"Isn't he handsome, Mama? Doesn't he look wonderful on horseback?"

Mrs. Meade looked at Janie sharply. "Yes, he is certainly handsome. He is a remarkably good-looking young man, and a very striking figure on horseback, but—"

"But what?" Janie asked.

"I don't know," her mother replied. "He seems a little strange to me, so solemn and sort of—intense."

That was it, Janie thought. Mama had put her finger on it, on the quality that set him apart. He was intense. You could feel it in the way he looked at you, the way his black eyes bored into you. She explained about the boy at the tournament long ago.

"Oh, yes, I remember," Mrs. Meade said. "You sat on the fence with a boy and he walked back to the pavilion with you. Lulie Tyler told us about his father and his prayer."

"I mentioned that this afternoon, but he didn't seem to think it was funny."

"I expect the young man is without a sense of humor," Mrs. Meade said.

After that Avery Calhoun called at Fairview frequently, and Janie began to get over her constraint with him. He was always grave, he would have no dealing with chitchat or light conversation; there was, as Mama said, no humor in him, but she discovered that he talked very well about serious matters in which he was interested. He was interested in railroads and their beneficent effect upon the country and the South's need for them; in the shipments of tobacco and the volume of

137

freight loadings, and the industrial development of Virginia. He was deeply interested in the Bible and could quote long passages to illustrate his ideas. He and Janie agreed completely as to the relative merits of Mr. Dickens and Sir Walter Scott, but they differed in regard to the poets, expecially Mr. Tennyson, whom Janie greatly admired. Avery had no use for poets, but on the other hand he liked the words of Mr. Thomas Carlyle, which she found to be excessively dull, not to say incomprehensible.

As the weeks went by Janie thought a great deal about young Mr. Calhoun and looked upon him with mixed emotions. He stirred her as none of her other friends had done, and yet she was not sure that she liked him. Her heart always beat faster at sight of him; she blushed when his name was mentioned. She was very self-conscious about him, and had not mentioned him to any of her friends, not even Sara Anne. She did not mean it to be a secret, but for some reason she could not bring herself to speak of him. He came to see her two or three times a week, but she never saw him anywhere else. He was never a part of the groups that gathered on each other's front porches, nor did he come to the picnics and barn dances and hayrides which took the place in the summer of the more formal entertainments of the winter. She spoke to him of it once, several weeks after his first visit.

"Why is it, Mr. Calhoun," she asked, "that I never see you in town, at any of the parties?"

"I don't care for social gatherings, Miss Meade," he said, "and as you know, I am very busy."

"Oh, but Mr. Calhoun! That's not right, really it isn't. You can't work all the time, and some pleasure is necessary."

"I find my pleasure in other ways," he said firmly.

Janie had to leave it at that. She grew more and more self-conscious, however, about the apparent secrecy surrounding her friendship with him. She was glad when it ended. One evening she and Sara Anne were walking along Market Street on their way to Sara Anne's house from a tea party they had attended when she saw Avery coming toward them. She was filled with embarrassment and she knew she was blushing. Sara Anne was looking at Avery and did not notice. She nudged Janie.

"The young Apollo," she whispered. "Isn't he divine?"

Avery took off his hat with a flourish and bowed. "Good evening, Miss Meade."

"Good evening, Mr. Calhoun." Sara Anne was staring at her now. "Miss Williams, this is Mr. Avery Calhoun."

"This is a pleasure, Miss Williams," Avery said. "Miss Meade speaks of you often. You have a most ardent admirer in her."

For once in her life Sara Anne was practically speechless. "Thank you," she said in a small voice.

There was an awkward pause. Janie broke it by smiling at Avery and walking on. When they were out of earshot of Avery, Sara Anne turned on her.

"Jan-ie Meade," she exclaimed indignantly. "You know him. And you have never said a word about it."

Janie tried to sound natural. "I told you I thought he was a boy I met a long time ago."

"He has been to *see* you." Sara Anne made it sound like an accusation.

"Yes, he has been to call at Fairview."

"And you never told me. Why didn't you tell me you knew him?"

"I don't know, Sara Anne. It just never came up."

"Nev-er came up! Why Janie Meade, I wouldn't have expected such deception from you. And you're blushing."

Janie knew she was blushing, and she knew too that she had no real explanation of her reticence in regard to Avery. She could not have told herself why she had not mentioned him to the girls.

The word spread rapidly, and Janie was subjected to much teasing. The girls were indignant.

"Why the idea," said Toni Hunter. "When every girl in town has been dying to meet him."

"Why don't you blame Laura?" Janie asked. "She knows him, too."

"He has never been to call on *me*," Laura said.

"Why don't you bring him to some of the parties?" asked Linda Richardson. "You never have."

"He won't come," Janie said. "He doesn't like parties. He is shy." She added that in self-defense, but she did not really think that Avery was shy. The girls did not believe it either.

"Shy, my foot!" Linda said. "She is just holding him for herself."

"I am not," Janie said furiously. "He just says he doesn't like social gatherings. He was very firm about it when I asked him."

After that Janie made up her mind that she was going to get Avery Calhoun to mix with the crowd, if only occasionally. She brought up the subject again.

"It doesn't seem natural, Mr. Calhoun," she said, "for you never to associate with any of the young people in town. It sort of—sets you apart. They think you are standoffish. If you are going to live here you ought to be a part of things. It wouldn't take much of your time to join us every now and then, and it would—please me."

Avery gave a courtly little bow. "I am at your service, Miss Meade," he said. "If it will please you I will most certainly do it."

That was the beginning of Avery's mingling with the group of young people who were Janie's friends. As it turned out, however, it was a small beginning. Occasionally he joined them on somebody's porch in the summer twilight; occasionally he escorted Janie to a party. Watching him in these surroundings, Janie had to admit that he did not belong there. Handsome as he was, courtly of manner, graceful of movement and gesture, completely self-possessed and obviously not shy, he yet did not fit into the inconsequential talk, the easygoing banter with which her friends amused themselves. Avery always gave her the impression of being a long way off in mind and spirit; and not only that, not only detached from the chitchat and casual laughter but, she reluctantly thought, in his own opinion a long way above them. This casual assumption of superiority irritated her; it also intrigued and interested her.

One afternoon in late August, when the tobacco was ripening in the fields and the apple orchard was heavy with fruit, Jane and Avery walked up the hill behind Fairview to the place where the trailing arbutus grew. There was no arbutus there now, of course, but it was a sweet spot and Janie had a sentimental attachment for it. It always reminded her of the happy time of her early childhood when she and Peyton roamed the countryside together. They strolled down the long, straight aisles of the orchard, between the laden trees, and across the West Field. When they came to the weathered snake fence separating the West Field from the

Creek Field, Janie was, for a moment, confronted with a problem. In the old days, and even now if she had been alone, she would have climbed the fence without giving it a thought, but that was obviously impossible in the presence of a gentleman. She paused, staring at the fence in perplexity, until she realized by lifting off the top rail she could easily step up onto the second rail, with due modesty even in her long skirts, and with Avery's assistance step down on the other side. He, however, had other ideas, and he quickly took charge of the situation. Without a word, he picked Janie up in his arms, held her there for a moment, and leaning over the fence, set her down gently on the other side. Then he climbed over himself.

Janie was filled with confusion. She knew that he had done it deliberately, instead of taking the easier, more prosaic method of getting her over the fence, so that he might hold her in his arms for a moment. Every motion he had made was a caress. Her heart pounded, she was as breathless as if she had already climbed the hill almost running to keep up with Peyton's sturdy boy's figure ahead of her. She was familiar with these sensations, but now she was conscious also of a surge of feeling which was new to her. The strength of his arms around her, the roughness of his coat against her cheek, the nearness of his face to hers, the gentleness of his touch, these things sang through her consciousness like the long-drawn-out notes of a banjo string. She could not bring herself to look at him; she could not speak. She stood still where he had put her, until by the pressure of his hand on her arm he urged her to move again. They walked across the field toward the creek in silence. Avery did not mind silences, she knew. To him they seemed natural, but with him she had always felt that every pause must be quickly filled with conversation. She searched her mind desperately for something to say, but as always in moments of strain she was speechless. She was still too shaken by emotion and embarrassment for easy words to come.

They began to climb the lower stretches of the hill, walking slowly along the bank of the swift little stream. Its murmur sounded in their ears, and as the silence continued, a strange thing happened to Janie. She began to feel at home with it. It became a companionable silence; it drew them together, instead of separating them, as awkward pauses had seemed to do in the past. By the time they reached the spring which gushed out of the rocks and ran down to join the stream, it was easy for Janie to begin pointing out all the small landmarks of her affection. Easy, too, to tell him about Peyton and her childhood efforts to keep up with him. They passed the level stretch where the woods thinned out and the arbutus grew in the spring, and went on to the top of the hill. There they sat on a flat outcropping of rock, and looked at the countryside spread out below them in all directions, forests and fields, jumbled hills and distant mountains. Strange, Janie thought, how distance made familiar things look unfamiliar, or was it height that gave them anonymity? The roof and chimneys of Fairview, seen through the trees, might have been those of any house. There was no individuality to the well-known fields, the much traveled road to town looked merely like a gash cut between the trees. This was a wide and beautiful but unknown land they looked upon, filled with the romance of strangeness.

Avery drew a deep breath. "This country," he said, "is God's country. I do believe it, Miss Meade."

Janie laughed. "I feel that way too, but when you come right down to it, Mr. Calhoun, neither of us has ever seen any other country."

"You're right, we haven't, have we? I'd like to travel and see the world, but never to live anywhere out of sight of the Blue Ridge Mountains."

Having mentioned Peyton, Janie was reminded of how little she knew about this man at her side. "Have you any brothers or sisters, Mr. Calhoun," she asked. "You have spoken only of your mother and father."

"My parents had three other children," Avery said. "One sister, older than I, lived to be five, the others died in infancy."

"Oh, I'm so sorry. How terrible for your mother."

"Yes, life has been sad for her, I'm afraid. Things were hard and rough in the remote country in which we lived. We had none of the comforts or conveniences of modern living. Even before the war it was a struggle, and during the war years we often lacked even the bare necessities."

"I know," Janie said. "I remember all during the last year of the war we didn't have anything to eat but cornbread and dried beans and fruit."

"Frequently we didn't have even that. We had only what the parishioners gave us, and they had little to give." He looked at Janie, his dark eyes somber. "That is why I have not followed my father's calling. I had hoped to be a minister of the Gospel too, and sometimes my conscience hurts me for having turned away from that path, but I tell you, Miss Janie, when you have lived without knowing where your next meal is coming from, when you and your family have faced actual hunger, it does make a mark on you."

Janie hardly noticed what he had said. Her attention was focused on his use of her name. This was the first time he had called her anything but Miss Meade, and the more familiar Miss Janie sounded sweet to her ears. She wondered if he was conscious of the change, or if he had spoken unthinkingly. As Avery continued she had her answer, for he soon repeated the name.

"That was when I made up my mind that I would see to it that neither I nor those I loved would ever have to face that situation again. I hope I am not too worldly, Miss Janie, but I do not intend to spend my life in poverty. I mean to get ahead." There was hard determination in his voice. She could understand now his intense preoccupation with his business, the hours of study and extra work that he put in at night. "The times call for men of action, of vision and industry. Virginia needs them. I figure that it is possible to serve the Lord in whatever calling I may follow, and that I can also serve the State and myself in my present work."

Now he would be off on his favorite subject, Janie thought, and she was well content. It was pleasant to sit in the sunshine on the breeze-swept rock at the top of the world and listen to Avery talk about the spreading of railroads like a network through the South, opening up idle lands, creating industries by which men could earn their living, building prosperity on a firmer foundation than the old system had known. Such talk stirred Janie's own imagination, and she could understand a young man's urge to play his part in a new world of progress and opportunity.

To her surprise, however, he did not go on with the subject. Instead he said: "There is going to be a tournament again this year at Meriden, you know."

"Yes, they are held every year, I think. Mrs. Tyler always

143

says why don't we drive over for them, but I have never been to one since that time. Have you?"

"No, but I am going this time. I am going to ride in the tournament."

"Why I declare, Mr. Calhoun, are you really? Isn't that exciting? Of course you should, with that beautiful horse, and you ride so well, too. I remember you said that when you grew up you were going to win and be King of the tournament."

"And I remember you said that when you grew up you were going to be Queen of Love and Beauty."

"Of course we were just children," Janie said hastily, to cover her confusion.

"But we are not children now, Miss Janie," Avery said, looking at her with his intense black eyes. He allowed a pause to elapse before he went on. "That is another resolution I made long ago, to own a horse, to ride well, and to compete in a tournament with you watching in the pavilion. I have worked hard and planned for a long time to carry out that resolution. I hope you will make it possible by coming to the tournament."

The implications of this statement astounded Janie. He seemed to be saying that she had been included in his plans ever since that childhood meeting long ago. It was hard to believe, but there was a purposefulness about this young man which was convincing.

"Will you come, Miss Janie?" he asked.

"Why yes, Mr. Calhoun," she said. "I expect it can be arranged, and I would love to see you ride."

Avery stood up with a swift movement, stretching his arms out as if in triumph. "Thank you, Miss Janie," he said. He held out his hand to pull her up, and they started back to Fairview. They went slowly down the hill and across the fields, and this time they walked in silence. Janie felt no need for conversation. All the forces of her mind and heart were occupied with the new emotions that were surging through her and the new worlds opening up before her.

17

Janie and Sara Anne sat in the pavilion at Meriden. The tournament was about to begin, and for Sara Anne it was a new experience; she had never been to a tournament before. She was filled with excitement and little sparkles of merriment shone in her eyes. Raiford Tyler had asked her to come. She had spent the night at Fairview with Janie, and the girls had driven over that morning with Major and Mrs. Meade. To Janie it was like a well-remembered tale, and in her bemused eyes it was still a fairy tale. It was all just as it had been eight years ago, the green stretches of the field, the fluttering pennants, the sunshine and the crowds. The gay little pavilion was filled with chattering ladies, young and old. Their dresses were brighter and gayer now, and they had come in proper carriages and buggies. Some of the carriages were shabby, to be sure, but there were no oxcarts or farm wagons now, no mules or work horses. The big difference to Janie between this tournament and the other unforgotten one was that now she was one of the young ladies in the pavilion, and Avery Calhoun was riding in the tournament.

She could see the knights gathering at the far end of the field. When the lovely, long notes of the trumpet called them to enter, she watched for Avery's appearance with fascinated attention. The knights rode in slowly, in single file, looking straight ahead. Avery was fourth in line, on his splendid horse, in his gray riding clothes. He wore a wide-brimmed gray hat, and dark red streamers on his arm to match the facings of his riding coat. When he reached the turn and started down the track toward the pavilion, his horse began to rear and prance. Janie knew Avery was making him do that for the effect; Midnight was spirited, but he was beautifully trained and obedient. She smiled a little to herself, sensing that Avery was playing the part to the last fine touch for her benefit.

The knights lined up in front of the pavilion. The trumpet sounded and Mr. Richardson Long, president of the Piedmont Tournament Association, stepped forward to open the tournament and to welcome the crowds. The same Mr. Richardson Long, but considerably bigger now. Mr. Long had put on weight in the intervening years; even his voice sounded bigger. Again he spoke of lovely ladies and gallant gentlemen, of bevies of beauties and brave young men. Again he introduced the knights, who saluted with their lances. When the trumpet sounded the knights began circling the field, slowly at first, then faster and faster. Janie watched Avery and was proud of him. He rode beautifully and he cut a dashing figure, there was no doubt about that. She knew it from the evidence of her eyes and the pounding of her heart, but she also knew from the excited murmurings of the other young ladies around her when he rode by.

On the first run Avery captured three rings. So did a young man named Martin Fry. Raiford Tyler took two, as did a number of others. Between the courses the pavilion buzzed with talk and laughter. Martha Boyd was there, looking pale and prim. She came to the tournament almost every year, and had driven over that morning with Mr. and Mrs. Boyd. Ranny had come too, but was not riding in the tournament. Toni Hunter was here; she was talking with a group of girls from Orange, where her grandparents lived and she often visited. Janie knew some of the other girls, from neighboring plantations, but many of them were unknown to her. She sat quietly, with no desire to talk. She was filled with an unaccustomed detachment, withdrawn into her own private world, where she was acutely conscious of every detail of the scene around her, drawing it into herself, absorbing sound and color and movement.

On the second course Martin Fry took the lead; at the end

of the third he and Avery were again tied, and Raiford was left far behind. Sara Anne sighed.

"I knew he couldn't win," she said. "He told me he didn't have a chance, but I am sort of sorry. He is sweet, Jan-ie."

"Yes, isn't he," Janie agreed absently. She was not thinking of Raiford Tyler at that moment.

The tie was maintained in the fourth run, but in the fifth, as Sir Martin Fry approached the first ring, his horse stumbled, and he was shaken out of the tense, poised position which he had assumed, lance raised to slip through the ring. Before he could collect himself he had passed the post. A long, low cry spread over the field. The crowd was like that; they yelled and clapped when a knight succeeded in lifting a ring, and they wailed and moaned when he failed. The young man apparently was badly shaken by the incident. He missed the next ring also, and ended the run with only one point to his credit. Avery, on the other hand, went through the run with a skill which was almost clocklike in its precision—the run, the raised lance, the aim, the lifted ring and the run again. He took all three rings again on that course.

Sara Anne pinched Janie in her excitement. "He's going to win, lov-ey, I do believe he's going to win," she said.

Janie believed it also. She realized she had felt all along that Avery would win. She knew a dawning confidence that whatever Avery Calhoun set himself to do, he would do.

He did win; when the last course had been run, Avery was well ahead. The crowds roared, the trumpet sounded a call for the knights to line up in front of the pavilion. To Janie the roar and the call of the trumpet seemed far off and muted. Inwardly she had taken flight, she was retreating in disorder from this noisy scene and the unaccustomed prominence which she knew was coming.

When the knights were lined up Mr. Long stepped forward in front of the pavilion.

"Ladies and gentlemen," his big voice boomed through the big horn, "the tournament has been fought, the course has been run, the best knight has won. We gladly pay homage to his horsemanship, to the strength of his arm and the sureness of his eye. By skill and sportsmanship, in an open field and a fair contest, Sir Avery Calhoun has won the highest score, and I am happy to proclaim him King of this tournament.

Upon him now falls the happy privilege of designating the young lady of his choice as the Queen of Love and Beauty."

Midnight advanced several paces in front of the line of knights. Avery took off his hat and bowed; to deafening applause he dismounted and shook hands with Mr. Long. All around Janie in the pavilion the young ladies were twittering and giggling. Sara Anne was so excited that she was bouncing up and down, much as Janie had done as a child at that other tournament, but Janie sat motionless, staring at Avery as if she were hypnotized. He walked slowly toward the pavilion; when he was almost there he stopped and took the dark red streamers from his arm, then came on to where Janie was sitting. He stood there for a moment, looking down at her, then sank on one knee in front of her and offered her the streamers. A great roar went up from the people all around the field. The ladies in the pavilion exclaimed and murmured and clapped.

Janie wished the earth would open up and swallow her. Every eye in all that crowd was focused on her, and for a moment she felt a trembling panic. What should she do, how should she behave in this bright glare of public attention? Then out of the deep well of memory she drew the picture of that other young lady who had been chosen Queen of Love and Beauty, and with the recollection came courage and poise. She threw back her head and laughed gaily, waving the red streamers in her hand; then she fastened them around her own arm. Avery held out his hand to her, and she rose and went out with him into the open space in front of the pavilion. Together they stood, laughing and bowing into the applauding crowds. Presently Avery escorted her back to her seat, and remounted Midnight; the trumpet sounded and the knights rode off the field, with Avery at their head. The tournament was over. Janie did not notice that this time taps was not played at its conclusion. The trumpeter ended with the notes of a gay little tarantella.

People crowded around Janie, congratulating her. The girls hugged her, the ladies and gentlemen smiled at her. Mrs. Tyler kissed her.

"I'm so pleased, Janie," she said. "I declare to goodness, it's wonderful having you as Queen of Love and Beauty. Your young man certainly made a splendid knight, and you behaved so well, honey. You should be proud of her, Lizzie."

"I am," said Mrs. Meade, kissing her. "I certainly am proud of you, precious. You didn't look a bit scared."

"Well, I was," Janie confessed. "I was scared nearly to death."

Janie and Sara Anne were going to stay at Meriden that night to go to the ball, but Major and Mrs. Meade were going back to Fairview immediately. Raiford was to bring the girls home the next day. Janie went with her mother and father to the barouche and kissed them goodbye.

"I am impressed with the importance of being the father of a Queen of Love and Beauty," said the Major, patting her arm. "I am not accustomed to such distinction. Congratulations to my little girl."

Janie laughed. "Of course it is Mr. Calhoun who should be congratulated. I didn't do a thing but just sit there."

The Major's face broke into a smile. "I expect you had already done your work," he said, "or the young man would not have chosen you."

When they had gone Janie went to the house and up to the room she was sharing with Sara Anne. It was a small room at the back of the house, but it had the advantage of housing only the two of them. The big rooms were filled with cots and trundle beds for all the young people who were staying for the ball. Mrs. Tyler said she thought they would like the small room better. It had a pretty single four-poster bed, and a cot had been set up in the corner opposite. When Janie went in Sara Anne was already there. She was sitting on the side of the cot, in a ruffled white dotted swiss dressing gown, with her brown hair hanging around her shoulders.

"Come in, your majesty," she said. "Come in and make yourself at home."

"Oh, Sara Anne, let me take the cot. I don't mind sleeping on it a bit, I declare I don't."

"Mercy, no, you're the Queen of Love and Beauty. You couldn't poss-i-bly sleep on a cot."

Janie laughed. She was pulling her dress off over her head.

"And you're the luckiest girl in the world," Sara Anne went on, "in the—whole—wide—world. He is div-ine. He is just perfect-ly divine, and he's all yours. I am green with envy. The green-eyed monster is gnawing at my vitals."

"Silly!" Janie said. "You, with every young man in four counties at your feet!"

"Not Avery Calhoun. Not Mr. Avery Calhoun."

"Well, you might spare me one beau," Janie said, brushing her hair.

"Don't be so modest, Jan-ie," Sara Anne told her. "You've got plenty of beaux, you're not suffering."

Janie had a new dress for the ball, and so had Sara Anne. It was time, they agreed. All during the past year, to all the cotillions and dances and evening receptions, they had worn Emily's gift dresses and their own graduation frocks. These had had hard wear and showed it. It was exciting to have new dresses. Janie's was blue mousseline de soie over blue taffeta, made with a basque and a much draped skirt. She and her mother had been working on it for weeks. Sara Anne's was pink. When the girls were dressed they admired each other.

"Blue is your color, Janie," Sara Anne said. "It certainly is your color. It goes with your eyes." They stood together looking into the mirror. Sara Anne began to laugh. Her cheeks were pink and her brown eyes were full of merriment. "You know what I think? Just between ourselves, in the bosom of this room and to go no further, I think we look mighty pretty."

They laughed at each other in the mirror, then for sheer joy they began to dance. They did a little dos-a-dos, circling each other back to back, retreating, advancing, and circling again, laughing and swaying to the music of their own youth. It ended with Sara Anne cakewalking to the door, head thrown back, knees thrust forward, prancing and waving her arms, while Janie laughed as if she would never stop.

With her hand on the doorknob Sara Anne said: "Let's slay 'em tonight, lov-ey. Let's just mow 'em down."

Out in the hall the girls stopped laughing, straightened up into ladylike poses and demurely descended the stairway to the wide front hall, where the young gentlemen were waiting for them.

For Janie the tournament ball that night was an end and a beginning. It so definitely marked a place in her life that, looking back on it in later years, she felt as if a line had been drawn across a page of the record. It reminded her of the deep path cut through the trees by the road into town, which she and Avery had seen from the hilltop that late summer afternoon when he had asked her to come to the tournament.

Such and such things, thoughts, feelings, ideas, hopes and fears, lay on one side, such and such on the other. Yet the details of the shining occasion were always vague in her mind. The only image that stood out clearly was Avery himself, the figure of Avery, the thought of Avery, the presence of Avery. From the moment he made his way to her through the crowd of young gentlemen in the hall at Meriden and she put her hand on his arm to lead the procession into supper, until Old Tom Walker and his orchestra had played "Home, Sweet Home" for the third time and then resolutely put away their instruments, he filled her consciousness so completely that everything not centered in Avery faded into a shadowy, shifting background.

Meriden was one of the few plantation houses west of the Tidewater and its neighboring counties which possessed a ballroom, a long paneled room extending from one of the wings of the big house. The wide oak boards of the floor shone like old gold. Dozens of candles hung in crystal chandeliers. At one end there was a little musicians' gallery, and on it was grouped Old Tom Walker's full orchestra, fiddles, banjos, and violoncellos. Tom himself, however, wandered around the dance floor, playing his fiddle in every corner.

On the steps of the gallery Avery crowned Janie Queen of Love and Beauty, with a wreath of flowers presented by Mr. Richardson Long, with appropriate eloquence. Janie hardly heard him, she was so busy trying not to look self-conscious and to behave as she thought a queen should. Avery and Janie led the opening figure, expertly called by Tom. Janie danced every waltz with Avery, and he danced only the waltzes. In between, he stood against the wall, a tall, dark figure, with the other extra young men, or went out through the french windows to walk in the dark garden, while Janie went through all the gay motions. She danced with the other clamoring young men; she marched and curtsied, swung and twirled, advanced and retreated. She made inconsequential remarks to her partners and laughed at theirs. It was all an empty show, almost automatic, meaning nothing. It was only when the orchestra struck up the music of a waltz and Avery moved toward her to claim the dance that she came alive. The prescribed twelve inches apart, with his arm around her waist, his hand pressing lightly against her back, they circled and turned and glided across the shining floor to the strains of "The Blue Danube," or "Tales of the Vienna Woods," or "Wiener Blut." Janie thought of her seventeenth birthday party, and she felt as if she were looking back from a distant place upon a different self. That had been the promise, this was the reality. That had been a frail loveliness, this was a strong and heady enchantment. All during the past weeks, since the afternoon of her walk with Avery, she had been asking herself the question: Am I in love, is this the right, the foreordained man for whose arrival I have been waiting? Always, in answer, doubts and questions had arisen, his intense seriousness, his strange detachment, his difference from all the other young men of her world. Now there was no longer any question; she knew. I'm in love, I'm in love. The words rang like a refrain through her mind and her body; the orchestra played them, her feet danced them. Waves of exultant emotion swept over her, drowning doubts and questions.

Through the golden haze that surrounded her, Janie gradually became conscious of the fact that Avery was dancing with no one but herself. The realization embarrassed her, and she spoke to him about it.

"You should dance with some of the other young ladies, Mr. Calhoun," she said. "It's quite—noticeable."

"I am not fond of dancing, Miss Janie," he replied. "Except with you. I am here tonight only because of you."

Sweet words, but Janie persisted. "It makes us a little conspicuous."

Unaccustomed humor showed in Avery's face. "I think we are a little conspicuous anyhow. If you will notice, a good many people seem to be watching us."

Janie had not noticed. Now she looked around the room and was startled to see that what Avery said was true. People were watching them. Some of the older ladies and gentlemen, sitting on the little chairs around the walls of the ballroom, were smiling at them. Some of the extra young men, waiting for the end of the dance to seek partners for the next one, were grinning. Heavens, was it so plain, she asked herself. Were her feelings so clearly written on her face, for all the world to see? Had Avery seen? She felt herself blushing at the thought, and that was strange, because she realized, suddenly, that she did not mind if he had. She did not care who saw.

"You should at least dance with Ginny Tyler," she said.

Ginny, the last of the Tyler children and the only unmarried daughter, was very young. She had been allowed to come to the ball because it happened on her fifteenth birthday. She was having a whirl. All the young men were dancing with her and she was obviously loving it.

Avery looked at Janie in surprise. "You're right. You certainly are right, Miss Janie. I was forgetting my manners."

He claimed Ginny for the next dance, which was a Virginia Reel, and later he led Mrs. Tyler onto the floor, to lead a cotillion figure. Except for those two gestures of courtesy, however, he danced with no one but Janie.

When the ball was over, when the musicians simply would not play any longer, the party began to break up. Most of the girls were going to spend the night; some of the young men were staying and some were leaving. Avery was going immediately.

"You are not going to ride home tonight, are you?" Janie asked.

He shook his head. "No. My mother is staying with her sister near here, at Big Island. I am going to pay her a little visit. I will be back in two days. May I see you then?"

"Yes. Oh yes."

"Goodbye, Miss Janie."

"Goodbye—and thank you. It has been wonderful."

They stood looking at each other. It required a real physical effort for Janie to turn her eyes away from him. Two days without seeing Avery stretched interminably before her. When he had gone she made her way through the crowded hall, saying goodnight and goodbye to the young people who still stood around talking and laughing, and ran upstairs to her room. She undressed quickly, hanging her pretty blue dress up carefully in the wardrobe, and went to bed, where she lay staring with unseeing eyes into the darkness. When, later, Sara Anne came in and lighted the lamp, she pretended she was asleep. She was in no mood for talk and the usual after-the-dance confidences, even with Sara Anne.

The next day Raiford Tyler drove the two girls home. Janie was very quiet all during the long ride, and they teased her a little.

"My heart's in the Highlands, my heart is not here," hummed Raiford, and Janie only smiled at him. Her heart was too deeply committed to bother with denials.

153

Raiford and Sara Anne were gay. She giggled and batted her eyelashes at him and teased, and before they reached Fairview Janie realized that Raiford's affections were now centered upon Sara Anne, and seriously, or she missed her guess. He looked at her friend as he had never looked at her, and though he smiled and laughed when he paid his compliments, there were times when there was no smile in either voice or eyes. Janie wondered how she would have felt if this had happened several weeks ago. Would she have been jealous of Sara Anne for taking a beau away from her, even one who was not serious? Now there was no room in her consciousness for jealousy. She watched the developing romance with a sort of condescending approval, as of one detached from all this in time and space. It seemed to her a pleasant thing for Raiford Tyler to be in love with Sara Anne Williams.

The next two days were arid and profitless to Janie. Her unaccustomed quietness did not go unnoticed at home; she knew her mother was looking at her with questioning eyes. She attended to her household chores, she sewed and she read. At least she sat with a book in her hand and occasionally she read a page or two, but she knew little of their contents. Her mind refused to detach itself from the thought of Avery. His image filled the world. Everything hung in suspension, awaiting his arrival.

He came late in the afternoon of the second day. She was upstairs when she heard his horse coming up the driveway. She did not go to the front window to see who it was because she knew it was Avery. She did not run to the bureau to smooth her hair and powder her nose. Such details were unimportant. She crossed the hall and went down the stairs, meeting Lucy coming up to tell her that Avery was there. He was standing by the fireplace when she entered the parlor. For a moment they looked at each other, and then without a word Janie went into his arms. She had left words far behind her. There was no language to express the happiness she felt.

18

Janie Calhoun took a deep breath and pulled the laces of her corset tighter. She was dressing to go to Sara Anne's wedding, and she was very happy about it. It was exciting enough in itself. She had kept her various beaux dangling on the hook long enough, and besides Sara Anne was now twenty-one years old. In addition to her pleasure at seeing her friend married and settled down, and so evidently happy about it, Janie was filled with excitement over the wedding itself, because she and Avery were going together, not only to the ceremony at the church but to the reception afterwards. It was one of the few times since they were married that they had appeared together at any social gathering. Janie sighed. Avery hated parties so much, he was so set against every kind of festivity, so completely uninterested in other people. Then she resolutely pushed out of her mind the nagging worry that always came to her when she thought of Avery's attitude and temperament.

There had been other reasons why they had not taken much part in social life during these two years; getting settled in their little house, the new responsibilities that had come to her as a young matron with a household on her hands, the coming of the baby. It could not all be charged to Avery's detachment, and as time went on, she told herself, he would certainly change, especially now that he was doing so well in his work and had been promoted to the position of

Division Freight Manager of the Virginia and Durham Railroad.

Her pretty dress lay spread out on the bed. It was one of her trousseau dresses, a light brown silk shot with blue, and there was a brown bonnet lined with blue silk to go with it. She slipped the dress over her head and went to the mirror above the bureau to see if its soft folds had disarranged her hair. She stood for a few moments looking at herself. I don't look any older, she thought. I really don't believe I do, and the extra few pounds are becoming.

She went out into the hall and leaning over the railing called softly, so as not to wake up the baby: "Vicky." When Vicky appeared she said; "Come here and hook me up, will you."

"Yassum." Vicky came into the bedroom. She was a nice girl and a good baby nurse. Janie had engaged her before the baby came because, though young, she had had experience with children. When she had first come to be interviewed and Janie had asked her name, she was disconcerted by the reply.

"My name is Virgin Mary Queen Victoria," the girl had said, pronouncing each word carefully and correctly.

"What do people call you?"

"I laks to be called Virgin Mary," was the dismaying reply.

"Well, I expect we had better call you Virgie," Janie had said. "Isn't that what most people call you?"

"Yassum, that's what they calls me, but it ain't my name. I don't lak to be called outa my name."

Janie understood about the tyranny of names. Her mother hated the name of Lizzie so much that she had refused to give either of her daughters her own pretty name of Elizabeth, and she herself much preferred Jane to Janie. She searched her mind for some solution.

"Perhaps you would rather be called Vicky," she said. "That's a nice name."

The girl had brightened. "Yassum, thas a right nice name. Better'n Virgie."

So Vicky it was, and she was a great comfort to Janie. She had known very little about cooking when she first came, and Janie herself knew very little. A family could not live on cakes and biscuits and Sally Lunn, so Baizy's help had frequently been called upon. Now Vicky was becoming a good cook, and she was fine with the baby.

156

Janie took another deep breath and squeezed in her waist with her two hands while Vicky pulled with her young strength and carefully hooked her up the back. The dress was all right when it was fastened. It did not look too small and it fitted her prettily.

"Now, Vicky, when the baby wakes up give him his bottle. It's all ready in the kitchen, but be sure to warm it."

"Yassum."

"And then take him out for a little ride in his carriage. And oh, Vicky, do be careful."

Vicky giggled. "Yassum, I will. I done tuk keer of babies befo', Miz Calhoun."

"I know you have," Janie said, "but you see, I haven't, Vicky, and I'm still a little nervous about it."

"You'll learn," Vicky said comfortingly. Janie remembered that was what Baizy used to say. "Ne'mind, little gal, you'll learn," Baizy used to tell her.

Well, she was learning. When you were little you thought you would know all there was to know by the time you were grown, and then when you were grown you found that you had just started. What good did the kings of England do her now? Vistas of new things to be learned opened before you all the time, every time any change came in your life. Perhaps you had to go on learning, one thing after another, as long as you lived. A new thought came to her. Perhaps when you were older, when you were really old and nothing much was happening to you, learning new things would be what made life interesting. Standing in front of the mirror, giving her hair a final pat, she wondered whether you ever reached the place where there was nothing new to learn.

"Hand me my bonnet, will you, Vicky," she said.

Janie tied the ribbons of the bonnet under her chin and then, going to the chest, she took out the crowning glory of this outfit, her blue velvet shawl and matching reticule. Hearing the opening of the front door, she ran downstairs to meet Avery.

"I'm so glad you've come," she said. "I have finished dressing so you can have the room to yourself. Vicky, take some hot water up for Mr. Calhoun."

"Yassum." Vicky disappeared through the dining room into the kitchen.

Avery kissed her. "You look very pretty," he said.

157

He was sweet about paying compliments. "Thank you, darling. Your clothes are laid out. I'll wait for you down here."

Waiting for Avery, she wandered around the parlor, straightening a candle on the mantelpiece, fluffing a pillow on the sofa, moving an ornament on the teakwood whatnot. The little room looked cozy and cheerful, with the sun coming in through the bay window at the front and a coal fire glowing in the grate. A big bowl of the last yellow chrysanthemums from the back yard stood in the center of the table.

Janie would not have admitted it, but she was still a little disappointed that Sara Anne was marrying Carey Morgan. Not that there was anything against him. He was a nice young man; she and Sara Anne had known him all their lives. He was pleasant and cheerful and good-looking enough, she supposed, though to her eyes nobody seemed very good looking compared with Avery. Carey was tall and blond and he undoubtedly had charm, and he and Sara Anne were in love with each other, so Janie was sure that everything was as it should be. All the same, Sara Anne could have married Raiford Tyler, and she thought that would have been so much nicer. When her friend had first confided to her, in deepest confidence, that Raiford had asked her to marry him, Janie had been delighted.

"Oh, darling, it would be ideal," she said. "Raiford is so nice and the Tylers are so well-to-do, and you could live at Meriden."

"I know, Janie, it would be wonderful." Sara Anne wandered aimlessly around the room. "The only trouble is—I don't seem to want to marry Raiford."

Janie, with her then new sensitivity to the emotions of the heart, had understood and sympathized. Now she knew that the reason Sara Anne had not wanted to marry Raiford was that she had wanted to marry Carey.

"I have always meant to marry him, when the time came," Sara Anne had said. "Ever since I can remember."

"I wish I had known it," Carey had replied. "If I am old before my time, it will be your fault, Sara Anne, for keeping me in suspense so long."

Raiford had been crushed when he learned that Sara Anne really was going to marry Carey, and Janie felt sorry for him, though she did not think there was much use wasting sympathy on young men whose girls chose some other man. They certainly seemed to find it easy to console themselves. Johnny Russell had married Antonia Hunter less than a year after his heart had been broken by Janie's marriage to Avery; and Ranny Boyd, to everyone's surprise, had recently brought home a bride from Baltimore.

Avery came downstairs and, as always, Janie felt proud of him. He looked very dashing in his black frock coat and high, starched white collar. They walked down Jefferson Street and up a block to Madison, where St. John's Church stood on the corner. A good many people were seated in the church but the wedding party had not yet arrived. Janie went down the aisle on the arm of Corbin Pratt, who was one of the ushers, with Avery coming behind, and he took them way up to the front on the bride's side and ushered them into a pew in which Major and Mrs. Meade already sat. Janie squeezed her father's hand and reached over him to pat her mother on the arm. She saw Mrs. Meade every few days, but she did not see the Major so often now and she missed him. She always had a sad feeling about leaving them alone out there at Fairview. They had wanted the young couple to live with them, but it would have been too inconvenient for Avery, and Janie herself, secretly had wanted to live in town, where everything was so comfortably near and she could run in on her friends during the day and they could come to see her.

Mr. Thomas Saunders was playing the organ. The music made a soft background for the rustlings and whisperings around her. Janie sat quietly, relaxed, glad to be in St. John's again. She always felt as if she were coming home when she entered the church. It was not her church now. Avery was a Presbyterian, of course, so Janie had become one too.

"A wife should follow her husband," Avery had said, and she and her parents had agreed with him. It was a small sacrifice, she felt, to make for Avery.

She liked her new church; it was smaller and simpler than St. John's, but she admired the pastor, the Reverend Mr. Arthur Hammond, and the people had been very cordial to her. All the same, she missed this church, in which she had been baptized and confirmed and married, and to which she had come almost every Sunday of her life. She missed the vested choir, and the stone columns and vaulted arches going up and up into the high beamed gables. When she was a child she used to follow the soaring lines of the carved arches with

159

her eyes during the sermon and try to figure how you could climb up to the top of them, and having done so, how you could get down again. She missed the great stained glass window behind the altar, depicting the Transfiguration of Christ, and more than anything she missed the Book of Common Prayer and the ordered precision of the service. Mr. Hammond was a good preacher and she felt sure his prayers reached God as effectively as those in the Episcopal prayer book, but his words lacked the beautiful cadences of Bishop Cranmer's sixteenth century language, which lifted you up in spirit by its power and rhythm, even when you were not quite sure what it meant.

The music of the organ increased in volume and Janie knew that the wedding party was gathering in the vestibule. Sara Anne's mother, and her grandparents, old Mr. and Mrs. Lewis, were ushered into the pew just in front of the one in which they sat. The church became quiet, with the hush of anticipation, and in a few moments the strains of Mendelssohn's wedding march soared up through the vaulted arches. Carey came out from the vestry with Jimmy Hardesty, his best man, and the ushers proceeded with slow solemnity down the center aisle and took their places on each side of the chancel. They were followed by the bridesmaids and finally Sara Anne on her father's arm.

It was a pretty wedding and Sara Anne made a beautiful bride. Janie's eyes were misty by the time all the words had been spoken and the young couple turned and came back down the aisle together, smiling radiantly. She always cried at weddings; not her own, she had been too scared to cry, but other people's. Avery frequently accused her of sentimentality. "You're very sentimental, Janie," he would say, and Janie would reply: "And why not? What's more important than sentiment?"

The bride and groom were getting into a carriage when they came out of the church. Everybody was standing around smiling and talking. Major and Mrs. Meade, and Janie and Avery strolled down the street to the Lewis house, going slowly so the wedding party would have time to get there before they did. Lamps were lighted in the big, old house where Janie had stayed so many times; November afternoons were short. Fires burned in all the fireplaces, the rooms were filled with flowers, and everything looked very gay. Sara

Anne and Carey, Mr. and Mrs. Williams and Mr. and Mrs. Morgan stood in the receiving line. This was supposed to be a small reception, but it seemed to Janie that all her friends were there. It was fun to see them all gathered together for such a pleasant event. Janie moved from one group to another, and somewhere she lost Avery. She did not see him anywhere around, and she supposed that he had gathered with some of the men, probably in Mr. Lewis' library at the back of the house. Perhaps he and Uncle Jim Peyton were talking railroads, she saw Aunt Hallie across the room. Miss Bessie Mason was there, majestic in a beaded black silk dress and bonnet. Janie had grown very fond of Miss Bessie since she had graduated from school. Her house was just a block from Miss Bessie's house, and sometimes in the afternoons after school was over she stopped by to see her former schoolmistress. Miss Bessie had tea in her own sitting room every afternoon, and Janie enjoyed going there. She would never have dreamed when she was in school that this imposing person could be so friendly and so easy to talk to.

She stopped to speak to Antonia and Johnny Russell. Antonia was one of her best friends and she had always liked Johnny more than most people, even though she had not fallen in love with him. Ranny Boyd was there too, with his funny little colorless wife; and Martha Boyd was there, pale and prim as usual, but very elegantly dressed in the latest fashion. Mr. Boyd was making a lot of money with his ironworks, and the Boyd ladies, including young Ranny's wife, were dressing up "fit to kill," as Mrs. Meade said. Try as she would, Janie had never really liked Martha Boyd, but for the sake of family friendship and old association, she forced herself to be cordial to her. She stopped now to speak to her.

"Sara Anne makes a lovely bride, doesn't she?" she said, making the most obvious comment at a wedding because she always found it hard to think of anything to say to Martha.

"Very pretty," Martha replied, in her little clipped voice. Her offhand manner implied that it was a matter of no importance how Sara Anne looked. That was the trouble with Martha, Janie thought, she was a snippy little thing. It was not just that she lacked either beauty or charm, but she also lacked sweetness. She was plain, downright stuck-up, and it irritated Janie. She did not think Martha had anything to be stuck-up about, except her father's prosperity.

In loyalty to her friend she said: "She and Carey certainly make a handsome couple."

"Yes," Martha agreed. A little smile came over her face. "I'm glad she finally gave up trying to catch Raiford Tyler."

Janie stared at her unbelievingly. Martha Boyd must know perfectly well that Raiford had tried his best to marry Sara Anne. In her indignation she started to say; "Why, she could have had him any time she wanted in the last two years," but changed her mind. She would not argue about a thing like that with a person like Martha Boyd. Especially not at Sara Anne's wedding. She looked coldly at Martha and moved away.

The dining room table was loaded with good things to eat, and a three-tiered wedding cake stood at one end. When the receiving line broke up, Sara Anne and Carey came into the dining room and cut the cake together. Then came what Miss Bessie called the *pièce de résistance* of the reception. Tall, napkin-wrapped bottles were brought in, and they were told that they were to drink the health of the bride and groom in champagne. Everybody crowded into the dining room and there was a cheerful popping of corks and gurgling of wine being poured, and they all lifted their glasses to the laughing young couple, wishing them happiness and prosperity.

This was old Mr. Lewis' contribution to the festivities. He had, it seemed, strong feelings about the importance of champagne at weddings. He stood now beaming with pleasure at his gesture of hospitality.

"A wedding without champagne," he said, "may be legal, but it certainly lacks the traditional gaiety and sparkle that a wedding should have."

"Well," whispered Antonia Russell to Janie, "I am glad he concedes the legality, because I certainly didn't have any champagne at my wedding."

Janie laughed. "Neither did I. I have never even tasted champagne but once or twice before in my life."

She stood in a group of friends, sipping the bubbling liquid and thinking it delicious, when she saw Avery come into the room. She lifted her hand to show where she was, and pulled a little away from the group, waiting for him to make his way through the crowd. When he came up to her she was surprised at the expression on his face.

"I am told," he said, and his voice was hard, "that it is wine you have in that glass."

"Yes, champagne, to drink the health of the bride and groom."

"Put it down," he said, peremptorily.

Janie stared at him.

"I said put it down," he repeated, "and we will leave here immediately."

When Avery was angry his mouth took on a pinched look. She saw that he was angry now. Slowly a hardness rose up in her, to match his hardness. Placing her wineglass on the sideboard she said:

"I will put the glass down, and if you want to we will leave as soon as we can without being conspicuous, but we will not make a scene and we will not do anything to spoil Sara Anne's wedding reception."

For a long moment they stood looking at each other as if they were antagonists, as if there were no love, no shared life between them, and then Avery turned and made his way out of the room. Janie leaned up against the wall for support; she found that she was trembling uncontrollably. Mrs. Meade pushed through the crowd to speak to her.

"We have got to leave now, honey," she said. "Your father wants to stop by the news office before we go home. I'm coming in town tomorrow to have dinner with Lucy, and I'll stop by to see you and the precious baby. How is he?"

"He's fine," Janie answered, trying to sound natural. She could not bear for her mother to know that there was any trouble between herself and Avery, any break in her first idyllic happiness. "Vicky is taking care of him, but I expect we had better go too."

"You look mighty sweet in that dress."

"Thank you, Mama."

"I like to see you all dressed up and enjoying yourself. You don't do it often enough."

That was as near as her mother ever came to commenting on a situation which was, Janie knew, a matter of concern to the family. She smiled at Mrs. Meade.

"I'm pretty busy," she said. "Be sure to come by tomorrow."

"I will."

Janie waited a few minutes after her mother left, and then went to find Sara Anne. She and Carey were in the front parlor, surrounded by a chattering group of friends.

"Darling," she called when she saw Janie.

"You look perfectly beautiful, Sara Anne," Janie said, "and it has been a lovely wedding."

"Thank you, lov-ey."

"I have got to go now. Vicky is taking care of the baby." Janie put her arms around Sara Anne and the two girls clung to each other for a few moments. "I hope you will be very, very happy," Janie said, with her lips against Sara Anne's soft cheek.

"Oh, I will. I know I will, Jan-ie."

If ever anyone was cut out for happiness, Janie thought, it was Sara Anne, radiant in her white satin wedding dress, her lovely face framed by the frothy folds of her veil. Anything else would be unthinkable, and yet her own heavy heart told her that happiness was elusive, impermanent, insecure. It could not be firmly grasped, it could not be counted upon.

She went out into the hall to look for Avery. He was not there, but she saw Christopher Peyton. Janie was fond of this tall young cousin.

"Find Avery for me, will you, Chris," she said, "and tell him that I'm ready."

He grinned at her. "He is out on the front porch. I just saw him there. Taking the evening air, alone. He certainly does like his solitude, doesn't he?"

This was another indication of how strange her family found the aloof young man she had married. To the big, informal, convivial family connection, uncles and aunts, great uncles and aunts, in-laws, cousins to the third and fourth generation, Avery Calhoun was incomprehensible.

Janie smiled at Christopher, ignoring his remark. "All right, thanks. I'll get my wrap."

When she came downstairs in her blue velvet shawl she went straight through the hall to the porch. Avery was there. He joined her in silence, and in silence they walked the few blocks to their house.

Inside, Avery picked up the paper and settled himself in front of the fire in the parlor. Janie went to find Vicky and the baby. They were in the kitchen, where Vicky was beginning to prepare supper. The baby was in his basket on the kitchen table, kicking and crowing. She picked him up in her arms and held him close. The warm little body comforted her, so soft, so full of life, so infinitely precious.

"Been good as gold," Vicky said. "He's a real good lil' baby, Miz Calhoun. Don't hardly ever squall."

"He's a wonderful baby," Janie said. "A wonderful, beautiful, perfect baby."

Vicky giggled, and Janie held the baby off to look at him. At ten months of age he was ridiculously like Avery. Suddenly it frightened her to see this tiny replica of the angry man in the parlor. Dear Lord, she prayed silently, don't let him be like that. Don't let him be angry. Give him a loving nature, fill him with human kindness. The baby reached out a fat, grasping hand and caught the blue and brown silk bow on the shoulder of her dress. He smiled a wide, toothless grin, making happy, crooning little noises and kicking his blue-booteed feet triumphantly. Janie's heart was comforted. She put him back in his basket, then stood irresolutely for a few minutes, looking out of the kitchen window. The tiny little row house which she and Avery had rented since their marriage, so small that at first it had seemed to Janie, accustomed to the spaciousness of Fairview, like a doll's house, had a tiny, board-fence-enclosed back yard, which she had made into a pretty little garden. It was brown and sere now, as gardens must be in November, but it would be gay again with color in spring and summer.

What must she do about Avery? She had learned to dread the bleak silences which descended upon them when Avery was displeased. Usually she rode out the silence by ignoring it. She behaved as naturally as she could, made inconsequential remarks as they occurred to her, and gradually he returned from the dark place of his anger. This time she did not feel inclined to ignore the situation. Some of the hardness which had risen in her at the reception still remained. To quarrel with Avery was unthinkable, but surely something must be said, some notice must be taken of this, to her, unreasonable attitude.

She went into the parlor and sat in the rocking chair on the other side of the fireplace. Avery went on reading the paper.

"I'm sorry you were displeased, Avery," Janie said, "but honestly, honey, I don't understand you."

He lowered the newspaper. "I don't think it should be so

hard to understand. You know how much I dislike frivolity. A wedding is a solemn thing, sanctified before the Lord. All that chitter-chatter and giggling and gossiping—and then to see you all, including my wife, standing there guzzling wine —" He left the sentence unfinished.

"Nobody was guzzling, Avery," Janie said. "We had one glass of champagne to drink the health of the bride and groom. It's traditional at weddings, you know. Jesus Himself turned water into wine at the marriage in Cana."

Janie always hesitated to use the Bible as authority in talking to Avery because he knew it so much better than she did. He could quote a dozen passages to prove his points. She felt on secure ground, however, in mentioning the miracle of the wine. He made no reply and she went on.

"It wasn't champagne, but we had wine punch at our own wedding, you know, Avery."

There was a pause before Avery spoke. "No, I did not know," he said. "I didn't drink any of it, but if I had known I could not have done anything about it. A man can't leave his own wedding, and I am not responsible for the actions of your parents. But I am responsible to the Lord for the customs and habits of my own household, my own wife."

Janie's spirit rose up in protest. "You are not responsible to the Lord for me, Avery," she said, more sharply than she had ever spoken to him. "I have my own dealings with the Lord, and I'm responsible for my own soul."

Avery crushed the newspaper in his hand, and stood up. "The Calhouns have always been a God-fearing, God-serving family," he said, stormily, "walking in the ways of the Lord and hearkening to His voice. You are now a Calhoun. There will be no drinking of wine or spirits in this family." He flung the paper down in his chair and stalked from the room.

Janie lay awake a long time that night, thinking. Avery was her husband. She loved him, he loved her. She knew that. Their love was the one sure foundation of their marriage. For the rest she was wandering on strange and uncertain ground. His temperament and attitudes, his ideas of right and wrong, of human relationships to God and to man, were all alien to her. To Avery gaiety was a sin; to her gaiety and happiness, where they could be found, were as natural and as much a part of life as sunshine. He spoke of the servants of God; she had been taught by her mother to speak of God's children.

There was something Biblical about Avery, something patriarchal. Abraham, Isaac and Jacob, communing with their God and transmitting to their people the direct commands of a wrathful and jealous Jehovah. A God of vengeance, or a God of love? Staring into the darkness, with Avery asleep beside her, it seemed to Janie that was the choice which faced her, and dependent upon that choice hung her marriage. She had no intention of accepting his God, but she could force herself to the outward acceptance of his way of worshiping God. Her husband, her beautiful baby, the dignity of her marriage, were worth the sacrifice. There must be no more angry words, no more wounding incidents of Avery, in protest, pacing the front porch alone in chill darkness or flinging down his newspaper and stalking from the room in righteous wrath. If, to the glory of God, Avery felt it necessary to live an austere, withdrawn, inflexible kind of life, she would try, with the help of her more loving God, to lead it with him, in quietness and peace.

19

When little Elizabeth, Janie's second child, was born a year later, Avery's mother came to stay with them for a time, to take charge of the household until Janie could be up and around again. Janie would have preferred to have her own mother with her, but Avery suggested the arrangement, and she had always had a slightly guilty feeling about the elder Mrs. Calhoun. She found it hard to get close to her, and as they saw each other only occasionally for short periods, she was conscious of a constraint between them which she did not want but had not known how to overcome. Her feeling in regard to her mother-in-law was usually expressed in the phrase "poor Mrs. Calhoun," so worn and washed-out did she seem to Janie, who felt pity for her but no affection. Afterwards, she was always grateful for this visit because, seeing her intimately day by day, she found in the quiet woman who moved so efficiently around the little house not only sterling qualities of character, which she had not doubted were there, but also a charm compounded of serenity, wisdom and an unexpected touch of humor. Poor lamb, Janie thought, she must have had a hard time holding on to a sense of humor, living with the Reverend Strachan Calhoun. Certainly she had not transmitted the quality to her son.

In the time immediately following Elizabeth's birth Janie was filled with a deep contentment. She lay in the big four-poster bed, which her mother had given her from a guest room at Fairview, and contemplated her world with satisfaction. She felt very close to Avery in those days. He was so delighted, and so awestruck, by the miracle of the children. He adored little Avery, and now this tiny bit of femininity who was his daughter fascinated him. He would stand for minutes at a time looking down at her in her basket, occasionally rubbing a finger against the soft little cheek or touching a tiny hand.

"She will be like you," he said one day.

"I don't believe so, Avery," Janie replied. "Of course you can't tell a thing in the world about them at this age, but that little fuzz of hair is dark, and I think her eyes are going to be dark."

Avery shook his head. "No, I want her to be like you," he said, as if that settled the matter.

Janie knew he was paying her a compliment, so she said, "Thank you, darling."

Several days later, when he came home from his office late in the afternoon, he had a small, square package in his hand, which he handed to Janie almost shyly. When she opened it she found an oval-shaped moonstone brooch pinned to the white satin cushion of the little jeweler's box. The cloudy fire of the moonstone was picked up and heightened by an edging of diamond chips.

"Oh, Avery," she cried, "how lovely. How perfectly lovely. I have never had anything so pretty."

Janie was pleased and touched. The brooch was charming, and she knew it must have cost more than Avery could afford. He had probably given the matter much thought, and she sensed that the gift and the moment were important to him. She could not keep out of the back of her mind, however, a little amusement that Avery, who so hated frivolity, should have given her anything as frivolous as a piece of jewelry.

"It is only a token," he said, bending down to kiss her, "but given with love."

"And received with love," she said, pressing her face close to his. "Thank you, darling."

At times like this Janie felt that there was nothing she would not do for Avery, no sacrifice she would not make for him and her two beautiful children.

Mrs. Meade came almost every day to see Janie and the baby. The grandchildren were a great joy to her. She had protested against naming the baby Elizabeth.

"They will call her Lizzie," she warned. "As sure as you're born, they'll call her Lizzie."

"No, they won't, Mama," Janie said. "I'll see to that. All Elizabeths are not called Lizzie, and I want to name her for you."

"That's mighty sweet of you, honey, but I just want to say that if anybody calls her Lizzie they'll have me to reckon with."

The Major also came frequently. Janie rejoiced to see how much pleasure he took in his grandchildren. She knew that in them he saw the continuity for which he had been struggling. The old order would be renewed in these new lives. Fairview would go on, occupied by his descendants as it had been by his ancestors, unfortunately with a different name, but still the Meade blood and the Meade tradition. Sitting in her room with Elizabeth in his arms and little Avery playing on the floor, her father looked happier than she had seen him in years.

During the peaceful days following Elizabeth's birth, the aunts and uncles and cousins all came to call on Janie and see and admire the new baby. Miss Bessie Mason came, and then to Janie's pleasure she repeated her visit several times. She and Mrs. Calhoun liked each other, and they enjoyed having a cup of tea in front of the fire in the late afternoon, and talking. Janie was glad for her mother-in-law to have this companionship. Sara Anne dropped in often, and Antonia Russell, and Maria Lacy, who was now Mrs. Corbin Pratt. Janie was always glad to see them, and she learned the news of the town from them. This was true, in fact, even when she was up and around, for her life now was pretty well centered in her relatives and these few close friends.

One afternoon in early December, when Janie was sitting up in a rocking chair by the sunny front windows of her bedroom, Sara Anne came to see her. The house was quiet. Mrs. Calhoun had stepped out to mail a letter to her husband and had said she thought she would stop by to see Miss Bessie. Little Avery was playing in the kitchen with Vicky, and the baby was asleep. Janie had been pretending to read the paper, but in reality she was merely sitting, relaxed, savoring her contentment.

She heard the front door open downstairs and then Sara Anne's voice calling:

"Ja-a-n-ie."

"Hello," she called back. "Come on up."

Sara Anne ran up the stairs and breezed into the bedroom, bringing a feeling of cold, fresh air with her. Her cheeks were pink, and her eyes were bright with excitement. She kissed Janie and held her cold hands against her neck to make her squeal, crooned over the baby for a moment, and took off her coat. Then she said: "I've got news for you, honey. I can't wait to tell you."

"What is it?"

"You won't believe it. You simply won't believe it, but it's true. Hon-est-ly it is."

"Go on and tell me."

Sara Anne drew up a chair close to Janie. "Raiford Tyler—now hold your breath—Raiford Tyler and Martha Boyd are going to get married."

Janie stared incredulously at Sara Anne. "I don't believe it."

"They are, they certainly are. Mrs. Boyd is giving a tea tomorrow and they are going to announce it."

"How do you know?"

Sara Anne giggled. "Mrs. Boyd told Mama this morning, in strictest confidence. Mama just couldn't help telling me, and I can't keep from telling you, in strictest confidence."

"But Sara Anne," Janie protested, "why? Why would Raiford marry Martha Boyd?"

"Mon-ey, lov-ey. M-on-ey."

"Oh, no." Janie looked so shocked that Sara Anne laughed.

"People do, you know, Jan-ie. People do marry for money."

"But not Raiford," Janie said. "And the Tylers don't need money."

"Well, I don't know. It takes a lot to keep up a place like Meriden, and you don't make money on a plantation now the way you used to. I reckon the Boyds are getting to be real downright rich, with the ironworks, and now Mr. Boyd has built a plow factory. I reckon the Tylers wouldn't mind having some of that money. Of course I'm just guessing. He may be mad-ly in love with her."

"Shucks," Janie said. "How could a person like Raiford be madly in love with that prissy little thing? How could anybody be madly in love with Martha Boyd?"

Sara Anne laughed. "Aren't we mean? Two mean lil' old cats, that's what we are."

Janie remembered Martha Boyd's remark at Sara Anne's wedding reception: "I'm glad she finally gave up trying to catch Raiford Tyler." All the meanness was not on one side, she reflected. Martha must have had this in mind even then.

"Well, I think it is awful for Raiford," she said, "and it just kills me to think of Martha at Meriden."

"I know," Sara Anne said sorrowfully. "She doesn't belong there any more than a jaybird."

"And you could have had Meriden."

"But then I couldn't have had Carey, lovey. Meriden couldn't make up to me for Carey. Nothing could."

Sara Anne seemed to be radiantly happy. She and Carey were living at Aunt Josie Ashby's boardinghouse. They could not yet afford a house of their own, not even a tiny one like Janie's. Carey was in the insurance business. He was an agent for John Price & Son, and though he was said to be a good insurance man there was not much money in the business unless you had your own agency. That was what they were working toward, an agency for Carey. In the meantime they had taken one of Aunt Josie's big front rooms. There were more rooms to rent in the Ashby house now that all the girls were married except Nancy. Laura Ashby and her new husband also boarded there, and the big, lively household was fun, Sara Anne said.

Sure enough, the next day the announcement of the engagement of Miss Martha Hall Boyd to Mr. Raiford Tyler was made, as Sara Anne had said it would. It created quite a stir; everybody Janie saw for days following the announcement marveled at this unexpected romance, if romance it was.

2

One morning at breakfast, when Janie was well enough to come downstairs and have her meals with the family in the dining room, she sat looking with affection at the elder Mrs. Calhoun, realizing what a help she had been, marketing and planning the meals and supervising Vicky and taking charge of little Avery. It came over her that something should be done for her entertainment. Aunt Kate, Aunt Lucy and Aunt

172

Hallie had each invited her to dinner, and Mama had taken her out to Fairview several times, but it was a measure of how completely the Calhouns had slipped out of the life of the town that none of the older ladies outside of the family had come to call on Mrs. Calhoun, nor had she been invited anywhere.

Janie smiled at her mother-in-law. "It is so nice having you here, ma'am. You have been such a comfort, but I'm afraid you must be having a mighty stupid time."

"Oh, no, Janie," Mrs. Calhoun protested. "I enjoy being here very much with my children. Don't you worry about me."

"You ought to take your mother for a drive, Avery," Janie said.

Avery still owned Midnight, and rode him whenever he could take the time from his work. He had no buggy, but he could always rent one from Ally Martin.

"Would you like that, Mother?" he asked.

"Why yes, Avery. It is not necessary, of course, but I always enjoy a drive. I should think Janie could go too."

Avery looked at Janie in surprise, as if the idea of taking her for a drive had not occurred to him before. "Yes, I'm sure she could," he said. "All right then, we will go driving on Sunday afternoon."

He finished drinking his coffee and stood up to go to his office. Bending to kiss Janie goodbye, he said: "My mother does not need entertainment, Janie. Her life is centered in her family and her church, and that's where she finds her happiness. She walks in the ways of the Lord, and she knows from whence comes her strength."

It was said pleasantly, with affectionate admiration for his mother, but Janie sensed reproof in it. The remark was so typical of Avery's attitude that it cut like a flash of light through the peaceful haze of her contentment. Across the table, Mrs. Calhoun was looking at her, and meeting her eyes, Janie saw in them an expression of compassionate understanding.

"The Calhouns are good men, Janie," Mrs. Calhoun said softly after Avery had left. "Good and godly men, but they are hard to live with."

Now Janie was filled with compassion for this quiet woman; not the pity she had felt for poor Mrs. Calhoun because of her poverty-worn life and the death of her babies one by one, but compassion for the struggle of heart and spirit she must have gone through in this family of self-righteous, godly and humorless men before she achieved the quietness, before she knew, as Avery said, from whence came her strength.

She realized that she could talk about Avery to Avery's mother. She had wanted to talk to someone ever since the first idyllic months of her marriage. She would not mention her problems to her friends, and she had not been able to bring herself to speak of them to her own mother. Her parents, she knew, had had doubts and reservations about Avery from the first. They had begged her to wait, to hold off for a while until she knew him better, but she, to whom the God-sent rightness of her marriage to Avery had seemed self-evident, would not hear of delay. She had never regretted it for a moment, but she wished she had been better prepared for the unexpected exigencies of conflicting personalities and alien concepts.

"Avery *is* a good man," she said, "and I love him very much, but Mrs. Calhoun, ma'am, I just don't understand him."

"I have been trying to understand Avery all his life," Avery's mother said. "It's not easy, even for me, who has had a lot more experience with the Calhoun point of view than you have, little Janie."

"He is so contradictory. He likes display, really he does, ma'am. You know, he dresses so fashionably, and that beautiful horse, and his elegant riding clothes. He knows people look at him when he goes riding and when he walks down the aisle in church on Sunday. He wants to succeed and he talks about having a big house when we can afford it, and yet he behaves as if it is wrong to enjoy life at all. You must be solemn and serious and sort of—ingrown, all the time. Laughter is frivolous, and it's a sin for people to get together and have a good time, and music and dancing and gaiety are instruments of the devil."

The older woman nodded. "I think you have put your finger on it, Janie. Avery is contradictory. He is torn—pulled to pieces by the conflict between his conscience and his ambition."

She paused for a few moments, and Janie waited. "I don't know, of course, honey. How can anyone know what goes on in the heart and mind of another person, even your own child? But this is what I think is the trouble with Avery. He comes from a line of Scotch-Irish Calvinists, stern men, who worshiped a stern God. Theirs was a hard religion. They took it hard, and they had to fight for it. Because of it they left Scotland and went to Ireland, and they left Ireland and came to this country, first to Pennsylvania and then on down the Valley of Virginia."

Abraham wandering from Ur of the Chaldees through the deserts of Arabia to the well of Hebron.

"Avery's father and his grandfather and his great-grandfather were all ministers of the gospel, laborers in the vineyards of the Lord, as they were fond of saying. It was taken for granted that Avery would follow in their footsteps. He was brought up for that calling. But there was this difference, Janie. His forebears were willing to accept the life that went with the calling. Poverty and isolation; small parishes in remote places; little contact with the outside world. Little contact even of the mind, for there was never any money for books or publications or travel. Avery couldn't bring himself to accept that life. He hated it. All during his childhood he hated it."

Vicky came into the dining room with hot coffee but neither woman paid any attention to her, so she went back to the kitchen.

"Avery has a driving ambition. He wants position in the world, and prominence and success. He wants to be somebody. He loves beautiful things, and, as you say, he likes display. And he has an unshakable determination. When he goes after something he goes after it with an almost frightening concentration and intensity. It was that way about you, my dear. From the time he saw you at that tournament when you were a little girl he made up his mind he was going to marry you. It was soon after that that he said he would not go into the ministry. It hurt his father terribly, but he stuck to it. He saved his money for years to buy that horse and the riding clothes. He rode and he practiced for years. He got a job in Big Lick, but he waited and he watched until there was a chance to come here, to the town where you lived, and he began to court you as soon as he got here and he married you. You must always remember, honey, that he loves you very much."

"Yes," Jane said. "I know that."

"Now he is concentrating on success in his business, and he'll get it, Janie. He will probably end by being an important figure in the railroad world. You'll have that big house he talks about. But the trouble is, the generations of his ancestors rise up in him, his conscience won't let him rest because he turned away from the ministry. He told me once that he knew he had betrayed the Lord. So he tries to make it up to the Lord by holding out against worldly pleasures. He won't give up his ambitions, but he won't let himself enjoy the things his ambitions bring him."

Janie sat in silence, considering her mother-in-law's words. She understood the force of a driving determination. She had seen it working in her father and in some of the men she knew in the town, among her relatives and friends of the family; but with them it was a simple and direct concentration upon the accomplishment of a purpose, the focusing of energy and willpower, of mind and heart, upon one desired end. Their property, their civilization, their world had been shattered, broken into small pieces; they would put them together again, as nearly as possible as they had been before. For them there was no agonized conflict of motives, no bitter battle of conscience.

"I was glad when Avery refused to go into the ministry," Mrs. Calhoun went on. "I would not have said so then, either to Avery or his father; I wouldn't say so now to anybody but you, Janie, but I was glad. I wanted something better for Avery. I was born and brought up a Presbyterian, but not a Scotch-Irish Calvinistic Calhoun Presbyterian. I learned to accept it long ago, but I have never been at home in my husband's world. I wanted a broader life for Avery, a wider view of both God and his fellow man. I was very happy when you and he were married. I thought that with a happy-hearted girl like you, against the background of your family and your traditions, he might expand and open out."

She paused for a moment. "I am sorry to see that it hasn't worked that way."

"No, it hasn't worked that way," Janie said sadly. "I have

tried, Mrs. Calhoun, but I reckon I just don't know how. It's like bumping my head against a stone wall."

The older woman rose and came over and put her hand on Janie's shoulder. "I know, my dear, I know how it is. But you are both very young still. Maybe time and prosperity, and his children growing up around him, will mellow him. Don't give up, honey, keep on trying. I think he is worth it."

"Yes'm," Janie said. "I'll keep on trying."

"And remember, Janie, strength comes, if you pray for it."

When Mrs. Calhoun left to go back to her home Janie embraced her with real affection.

"Please come back soon," she said. "It has been wonderful to have you here, you've been such a help."

Though it was true that Mrs. Calhoun had comforted Janie by her sympathy, and had given her a better understanding of Avery's nature, she could not say that this understanding helped her to live with Avery in peace and happiness, or to cope with his moods and his rigidities. It was all very well, she thought, to know that he was torn by inner conflict, but she still could find no basis for understanding why the conflict existed. Depths of human complexities, dark vistas of mental and spiritual turmoil opened up before her, which she had not known existed. She must have a very simple and uncomplicated nature, she thought, because these conflicting currents were incomprehensible to her. As the months went by, she was deeply troubled to realize that a certain resistance was building up in her, a lack of sympathy for all this self-created inner travail of Avery's, which seemed so unnecessary. She had to watch herself constantly to keep from taking issue with him. I am just not wise enough to deal with Avery, she told herself. Wisdom and understanding she must strive for and, if she could not achieve these, at least the strength that Mrs. Calhoun had said would come with prayer.

20

Janie wandered restlessly around the house. She went up-stairs, where everything was in order. She came back down-stairs to the parlor. She ought to call Vicky and talk about the meals, she must go to market that morning; she ought to sit down and cut out the new little dresses she was planning to make for Elizabeth. She had promised to go over and sew with Sara Anne that afternoon, and the dresses must be ready to work on. Sara Anne was expecting a baby, and things were not going well. She hardly ever went out of the house now and everybody was worried about her. Janie could settle to none of these things. She was miserable, just perfectly misera-ble.

She and Avery had quarreled last night, and it was the worst quarrel they had ever had. Looking back on it, Janie was filled with bitterness. Usually, after any disagreement with Avery, she was contrite, but she felt no such emotion now. She felt only anger and rebellion.

I have tried so hard, she thought. I have given in to Avery about everything, I have tried to do what he wants and to live the way he wants to live. It's just no use, I run into a stone wall all the time.

There was an acrid smell in the air. Janie stood still and sniffed. Then she went into the dining room and called: "Vicky, is anything burning back there?"

"Naw'm," Vicky called back. "Ain't anything burnin' but the stove."

As she returned to the parlor the newly installed fire siren in the Court House tower began to sound. Its shrill wailing cut through her. Oh, Lord, that meant there was a fire somewhere, and Avery would be there, in the midst of it. He was a member of the town's Volunteer Fire Brigade, and Janie knew that, regardless of the urgencies of his office, he would drop whatever he was doing at the first sound of the siren, and run up the hill to the firehouse. She had always encouraged his interest in the Brigade. It was his only activity outside of his work and his family, and she had hoped that the Monday evening fire drills and rescue practices would bring him into closer touch with the young men of the town. She was frightened, however, whenever there was a real fire and she was glad that the City Council had decided that the town must have a regular, paid fire department. Nothing brought Avery into closer touch with people, and it would be good not to have to worry about him every time the fire siren sounded. A Fire Chief had been engaged and was already in town building up a professional company. At that moment Janie wished fervently that the new company had taken over.

Through the front windows she could see that a haze of smoke was rising from somewhere downtown, down the hill, on Main or Market Street; cinders, ashes, tiny particles of smoke were beginning to float through the air. Mindful of her clean lace curtains she closed the sashes of the bay window. She stood there now, watching the sky, filled with a growing uneasiness that overlaid but did not cover the deep unhappiness she had felt all morning. The siren had stopped and the silence was worse than the shrill wail had been. The sound of the siren had suggested action, firemen dashing to their posts, equipment being hauled into position. The silence was asking a tense question. It spoke only of suspense.

Smoke was billowing up in great gusts now, heavy and black. The dark pall suited her mood. The rolling billows of black smoke reminded her of Avery. No, that was not right. The smoke came from fire, and there was no fire in the black rage that had possessed him since their quarrel last night. It was a cold rage. It came over Janie in a flash of illumination that all Avery's intensities were cold. They were the intensity of wind, not fire.

It was ironic, she thought, that their quarrel had been about the Volunteer Brigade, or rather, about the Firemen's

179

Ball. She ought to have known better than to bring up the subject, but the annual subscription ball given by the Brigade was going to be a special occasion this year. It was going out of existence, this would be its final fling. The outgoing volunteers were trying to raise enough money to present the incoming professionals with new uniforms, and everybody was being urged to attend the ball. They were bringing a real orchestra from Richmond, and the young ladies of the town with their escorts were going to dance a minuet in colonial costumes. Janie wanted to go very much, she hungered for the sound and the color of gaiety and for contact with her friends, but more important than that, she knew there would be real resentment against a member of the Brigade who did not support this final event. She made up her mind to speak to Avery about it.

They were sitting on the back porch, overlooking the little garden, in the early June darkness. "I really think we ought to go to the ball this year, Avery," Janie said. "It will be the Volunteers' last party, and all the members should be there."

"Now Janie," Avery said with patient reproof, as if he were speaking to one of the children, "don't let's go over that ground again. You know I am not going to the ball."

Janie started to protest, but a weariness came over her. What was the use, you couldn't change Avery no matter what. She gave a little shrug of resignation and said: "Well, we ought at least to buy tickets to show our interest and support."

"I have no interest in this thing."

"But why not, Avery? You have been a member of the Firemen's Brigade ever since you came here to live. It is as much your Brigade and your town as anybody's."

"I meant I have no interest in the ball. Of course I am interested in the Brigade. I would make a contribution if they want to raise money, but a ball is a silly and frivolous way to do it, and I will have no part in it."

The impatience which Janie increasingly had to struggle against rose up in her. "Oh, Avery, don't be like that," she said. "People like to enjoy themselves. A little pleasure every now and then is a part of life. You know that most people would rather go to a ball than just hand out some money."

"Light-minded people would, and it is a fact, Janie, that

you are a light-minded woman. I don't blame you," he went on before she could speak. "It's the way you have been brought up. Your parents are light-minded people, your relatives and friends are. You come from a light-minded world."

"Avery Calhoun, don't you dare say that. You know all the tragedies that have happened in our family and how wonderfully Mama and Papa have borne up under them. You know how hard they have worked and struggled, and have gone on trusting in the goodness of the Lord. Light-minded indeed!"

"I thought I could change you," Avery went on as if she had not spoken. "I thought that with maturity and responsibility you would settle down and see the light, and be willing to accept a good Christian way of life."

"And I thought I could change you, Avery," Janie said quietly. "I thought that as time went on and you associated with all the good people around us you would see a Christian life doesn't mean being solemn and hard and rigid, and that you can worship God with happiness in your heart instead of gloominess."

"True happiness comes from harkening to the voice of the Lord and walking in His ways, not from silly little worldly fripperies."

"How do you know so much better than anybody else what the Lord wants?" Janie demanded. She realized that the argument was getting out of hand and they were saying wounding things to each other, but she could not stop. All the worries and suppressed rebellions of the five years of their marriage were urging her on. "Does God speak to you privately? Does He deliver His commands to you personally? Are you Abraham or Isaac or Jacob? Are you Moses on Mount Sinai?"

Avery stood up. Lamplight from the dining room filtered onto the porch through net window curtains. He raised both hands above his head, and in the dim light his figure looked abnormally tall. With his upraised hands he did indeed resemble a prophet of the Old Testament.

"Yes," he said. "God speaks to me, in the still, small voice of conscience, as He does to any who will listen to Him. But you—you and all your kind—close your ears and refuse to hear His voice and turn away from His commands."

Janie rose and faced him. "No, my conscience speaks to me

181

too, but it delivers a different message. My conscience speaks of love and kindness and friendliness to people, and laughter to soften the edge of problems and difficulties."

"Your conscience speaks of worldly pleasure and the beguilements of the Devil," Avery said.

He moved past her and went into the house, and she could hear his footsteps going upstairs. Janie sank back into her chair and covered her face with her hands. For a few moments she rocked back and forth. "I have tried not to say these things. I have tried not to say them, and now they have been said. Things that have been said can't be unsaid. Now we know, we know."

Presently she got up and went into the house. She locked the door to the porch and put out the dining room lamp, and went upstairs, stopping to look into the little room where the children slept. When she went into the front bedroom the lamp was burning but Avery was in bed. He neither moved nor spoke. In silence she undressed and got into the big four-poster. In silence they rose in the morning, ate breakfast, and in the same black silence Avery left the house. Now he was down there in the midst of the smoke, fighting the fire.

Suddenly Janie heard a sound from down the hill, a dull roar muffled by distance, and huge plumes of smoke shot up into the air. The smoke was filled with great tongues of flame that shot up and then died. A strong wind from the west tore the smoke into shreds, into wisps and plumes and fantastically waving streamers. Sparks died into ashes, and the wind picked up the ashes and carried them off in tortured swirls, to drift finally down upon the housetops and the yards and the streets all over town.

Turning from the window, Janie saw Vicky standing in the parlor doorway, her eyes big with fright. "Mighty big fire, Miz Calhoun," she said.

"Yes, something terrible must be happening, Vicky. I am going to find out what it is. Run upstairs and get my bonnet from the shelf in the wardrobe, will you?"

With her bonnet on she went to the door, then turned back. "Stay with the children, Vicky. Keep them right with you, and I'll be back in a few minutes."

Outside, the June day was hot. The air was thick with soot and wind-blown ashes; the smell of the smoke stung her nostrils. Janie went down the steep hill that was Tenth Street, walking rapidly, bracing herself against the slope, past Sycamore Street and on to Market. As she went the smoke grew worse, she began to hear sounds coming up the hill, a roar and a terrifying sizzling and sputtering of flames, the voices of men. People were hanging out of windows watching. When she got near the intersection of Tenth and Market Streets she found herself blocked by masses of people, filling the cobblestoned stretches of the street, held back by members of the Home Guard stationed at intervals. The west sidewalk of Tenth Street was not blocked off, and though it was packed with people, she began a determined inching forward until she reached the intersection and saw a terrifying sight in front of her.

The entire block, the square between Ninth and Tenth, Main and Market Streets, was on fire. Here, at the Tenth Street end of the block, most of the buildings had fallen into tangled masses of flaming debris. Further down the block toward Ninth Street the walls of buildings still stood, starkly silhouetted against the flames that poured through roofs and out of windows. The firemen were all down at that end now. The streams of water from their hoses seemed to have little effect upon the fire except to make the terrible sizzling sound she had first heard, and to send up clouds of steam through the smoke. She could not recognize any of the firemen at that distance, but she could see them moving about and she knew that Avery was among them.

Janie continued her slow way through the crowd, pushing and edging along the narrow sidewalk. She wanted to get to the corner of Tenth and Main; she could see that little of the *Herald* building stood, but she wanted to know exactly what the situation was. Inwardly she was crying out in pity for her father. Poor, poor Papa, it wasn't fair. He had stood enough, this was too much. Too much. As she went she could see activity on the roofs of the buildings on the four streets facing the burning inner core of the square, figures of men moving around purposefully, and she realized that bucket brigades had been organized. They were pouring water on the rooftops to prevent the spread of the fire. The entire front of Wright's Emporium on the corner opposite the *Herald* building was covered with wet blankets hung from the windows. The worst of the fire had passed that point now, and the westerly wind was carrying the sparks in the opposite direction.

Finally she reached the corner of Main Street. Opposite her the two side walls of the *Herald* stood, gaunt memorials to the soundness of the building. It was one of the oldest in town, and these two walls were made of stone. The roof, the front and back walls and all the interior of the building were gone. Somewhere under the smoking ruins must lie the printing presses and other machinery, the books, the records, all the equipment of a newspaper office, accumulated over the years. Gone, wiped out, in an hour. She did not see her father, and a sudden terrible thought came to her. Where was he? Where had he been while the building was burning?

She turned to a pleasant-faced woman standing next to her. "Has anyone been—injured?" she asked.

The woman shook her head. "No, thank God." Then she added: "Not yet."

"What happened, how did it start?"

A man standing in the crowd, so close that his elbow was jammed into Janie's back, answered her. "Started in Jones Brothers hardware store next door to the *Herald*. They kept a lot of oil stored in the basement, in barrels. Clerk went down there this morning and when he couldn't find what he wanted he lighted a flare—just a piece of paper, and the crazy fool dropped it on the floor where some oil had been spilled. The whole place went up, just like that." He snapped his fingers. "Burned so fast the people in the store had a hard time getting out themselves, couldn't save a piece of stock, or the books or anything."

"Was anything saved from the *Herald* office?" Janie asked.

"Old files, complete files of the *Herald* going back to 1816. They got them out, but that's about all."

Another man in the crowd was looking at Janie curiously. "Ain't you Major Meade's daughter?" he asked. He was a big man. He looked like a gentleman.

"Yes," Janie said. "Yes, I am." They all looked at her pityingly.

The talkative man shook his head. "Terrible thing! Mighty bad! That clerk ought to be shot."

Down the street another building fell, a slow, majestic caving in of walls and roof, a crashing of bricks and timbers, and a great spurt of flames into the murky sky. Janie stood there watching, overcome by the demoniac power, the terrible fascination of fire. She felt rooted to the spot, glued there, unable to take her eyes off the terrible destruction as the great monster ate its way through building after building. She forgot Vicky and the children at home, she forgot to worry about Avery, all her consciousness was centered on the leaping flames, the rolling black smoke, and the crashing fall of buildings.

Presently someone cried excitedly: "The wind has died down. The wind ain't blowin' any more."

It was true, the wind had died down. A murmur spread all around Janie. "It's a Lord's blessing. Without the wind they can hold it to this one block."

Later it went into the record that the only thing that saved the downtown section of the town was the dying down of the wind. "Thank God," people said. "Thank the Lord."

The last building on Ninth Street fell in. Now the entire block was a smoking, flickering mass of rubble and debris. Only the two blackened walls of the *Herald* office were left standing. The firemen began working their way back down the block toward Tenth Street, sending streams of water from the hoses into the tangled masses. The frantic activity on the rooftops of the neighboring houses had ceased. People began to relax; some of them went away but most of them stayed watching, fascinated, the final throes of the great fire.

After a while, as the firemen drew nearer, Janie recognized Avery, and felt weak with relief. There he was, wet, dirty, bedraggled, but safe. She saw that though he had on the blue coat of the fireman's uniform, and the tall, visored fireman's hat, he apparently had not had time to put on the red trousers which were the most distinctive feature of the Brigade's uniform. His high boots were worn over the trousers of his suit. They were covered with soot and dripping with water, as he was manning the nozzle position on one of the hoses. Some of the firemen had on complete uniforms, but some wore only the hat and boots.

A tall man in full uniform was moving around among the firemen, giving directions. Janie wondered who he was. Soon the man who seemed to know all about the fire told her.

"That's Chief Bertram," he said. "John Bertram, the new Fire Chief. He comes from Baltimore. This is a hell of a way for him to begin, beggin' your pardon, ma'am."

When the Fire Chief got almost to the corner of Tenth Street he stopped and stared up at the stark walls of the *Herald* building. Janie, looking at them again, saw something she had not seen before. At the top of the wall on the street side some of the stones had fallen out, leaving an irregular gap, and a split had developed in the wall, beginning about the middle of this gap and running back toward what had been the rear of the building. Chief Bertram was staring at the split. Several other men came up to him, and they stood looking. One of them was Uncle Jim Peyton. Janie was glad to see him. He would know about Papa, if she could reach him. I ought to go home, she thought. Vicky will be scared, but I must find out something about Papa. Uncle Jim was just across the street, but she could not get to him. The Home Guard wouldn't let her, in the first place, and she would make herself terribly conspicuous if she tried to leave the massed spectators and join the men in front of the *Herald* office. Avery was over there too. She saw him put his hose down and some of the other firemen began reeling it in. Their work was just about finished. The devastated block lay smoldering in the hot June sunshine, but there were no more flames to be seen. Avery was trying to wipe some of the grime and dirt from his face and hands with a handkerchief.

The group of men across the street seemed to come to an agreement. The Fire Chief moved away, giving directions to some of the firemen. The members of the Home Guard, who had relaxed their vigilance and had begun to move away, came back and began pushing the crowds back.

"What's it all about?" the big man next to her asked.

A tall young militiaman answered. "They're going to pull the wall down. It is liable to fall at any time, and it might fall out on the street. They are going to pull it the other way, so it will fall inside, in the space between the walls, but some of the stones might come this way. You'll all have to move back."

Two firemen ran up with a ladder, followed by two policemen. Several members of the Firemen's Brigade were talking to the Fire Chief, arguing and waving their arms. They seemed to be pretty mad. Mr. Bertram kept shaking his head stubbornly.

Again the Home Guard explained: "Fire Chief won't let the volunteers go up the ladder. It's dangerous business. He wants the policemen to do it because they are professionals. The firemen don't like it."

Finally, with angry gestures, the firemen stood aside, and the two policemen picked up the firemen's ladder and placed it with great care against the front facing of the wall. Slowly and cautiously they began to climb, carrying between them an anchorlike piece of iron with a rope attached.

"It's a hook and ladder anchor," somebody said. "What they goin' to do with it?"

There was no answer and they all stood watching in silence. The people farther up the hill, who could not see what was going on, began to press forward, and again the members of the Home Guard had to hold them back. To save her life Janie could not make herself leave. I'll go in a minute, she kept thinking, as soon as I see what is going to happen.

The Chief of Police had joined the Fire Chief on the sidewalk, and the two officials, surrounded by a group of men which included many of the firemen, stood quietly looking up at the policemen as they climbed the ladder step by step. The crowd watched in silence. Up on Market Street Janie could hear the movement of people and the sound of voices, but here, on the corner of Main and Tenth, there was neither movement nor sound.

At the top of the wall a piece of the cornice which had held the ceiling in Major Meade's office was still in place. When the first policeman on the ladder had reached that point, with his head and shoulders above the wall, the second man released the iron into his hands, and with infinite care he fitted a fluke of the anchor in the cornice, on the inside of the wall. Janie could feel the tension in the group of waiting men. Gradually the policeman released the weight of the anchor, so there would be no sudden jerk, and when it hung in place, with the rope dangling from it, the two men began a cautious descent. As their feet touched the pavement and they lifted the ladder from the wall, a cheer went up from the crowd.

Now the Fire Chief picked up the rope and holding it lax in his hands, he and all the men around him began to move back and away from the doomed wall. It was a long rope, and they went to its full length before the Chief, with the help of several others, began to pull, gradually increasing the tension on it. The split in the stones widened, and with a dull roar the wall fell, away from the street, into the space which had been the *Herald* office. Gusts of smoke and ashes rose in the air so that people had to turn their faces away, and Janie covered her nose and mouth with a handkerchief. As the atmosphere cleared she saw that only a few feet of the outer wall of the building remained.

Now I must go, she told herself. There was a general milling around. Many people were leaving now, and she realized that it was going to be slow work going back up the hill. It was then that she heard a cry from the men still standing across the street.

"Oh, Lord, the fire has started up again," said the woman next to her.

It was true. The fall of stones had stirred up the smoldering rubble, and flames were licking through the debris and creeping back up the hill. A wail went up from the watchers. Several members of the Volunteer Brigade moved closer and stood watching the leaping flames, among them Avery.

Janie had stepped down off the curbing and turned to make her way up the hill. Looking back she saw Avery standing there; he seemed to be looking directly at her. With his dirty face, his tousled hair, his sodden clothes, he seemed to her to be somehow softened, vulnerable, disarming. Her heart melted, her anger left her. She loved him. In spite of his harsh rigidities, in spite of their different worlds, she loved him. She must not let their differences ruin their lives; she must learn, she must try harder. She lifted her hand in a gesture of greeting and smiled at him.

There was no response from Avery. Was he looking at her or merely in her direction? Did he see her, or was she lost in the crowd? Suddenly he sprang into action. Looking at the spreading flames he called: "Come on, boys, this is our job. Let's put it out," and jumped into the tangled mass. Several of the firemen followed him.

"Oh, no, no, no," Janie kept saying, and she realized in surprise that she was speaking out loud. The big man was looking at her. Her words were seconded by Chief Bertram. When he saw the men in the burning area he rushed up and began yelling at them: "Come out of there, you crazy fools. Come out." Some of the other firemen started to go in and he turned on them. "Keep away, keep away. Are you all crazy?" Then speaking more calmly to the men who were fighting the

188

fire, he said: "That fire has nowhere to go. It won't do any harm. Get out of there, you'll kill yourselves."

One of the Volunteers, young Wally Thompson, grinned and waved jauntily at the Chief. Avery neither looked up nor spoke. He was bending over, shifting rocks and loose rubble onto the creeping flames, trying to smother them. Janie was filled with fear.

Why does he have to do this? she thought. Why, why? He's acting, he's just acting before all these people. I've always said he likes display. Underneath, however, deeper than words, lay the thought, maybe he was still angry. Maybe he was still so mad he just didn't care. And again the question, had he seen her. Was he punishing her?

The five men were strung out in a line, facing the standing wall which had separated the *Herald* office from Jones Brothers hardware store, stamping and beating the flames, covering them with debris, pushing them toward the wall, which would cut off their progress. Chief Bertram was getting more and more agitated. He was yelling: "For God's sake, get away from that wall. Keep away from the wall."

Suddenly other voices picked up the warning; a chorus went up. "Watch out for the wall. Get away, get away."

There was an urgency in the voices which reached the firemen. Several of them stopped their work and stood still. Avery straightened up and looked around at the calling voices. That was the way Janie saw him, standing on a pile of rubble in his dirty blue fireman's coat, his face streaked with soot, looking over his shoulder at the men on the sidewalk.

It was at that moment that the wall fell. It began at the bottom, near the ground, where the firemen were stamping on the flames and shifting the stones. Watching from across the street, it seemed to Janie that the entire wall disintegrated in one movement. In one incredibly long moment the wall, which had been solid, became a mass of separate stones, hurtling down from above, crashing down upon the men who stood there. In one unbearable moment the space where five men had stood became a great pile of fallen stones and mortar, sending up clouds of smoke and ashes.

A long moan went up from the crowd, a curious sound which did not seem to come from human throats. It was followed by utter silence. The watchers stood immobile, frozen by horror, rooted to the cobblestone streets and the stone-paved sidewalks. Janie had never known such silence. It lasted only a moment, then the scene broke into yelling, screaming confusion. Men rushed from all directions upon the smoking ruins. With their bare hands they scratched and tore at the stones, the crumbling mortar, the bricks that had faced the other side of the wall. Those who could not reach the pile milled around aimlessly, shouting unintelligible directions. Only Chief Bertram, who had been so agitated, was now quietly, coldly calm.

"It's no use, men," he called. "Nothing could live under that."

Nothing could live under that. The words kept echoing in Janie's mind. Nothing could live—nothing—nothing. The world wavered in front of her eyes, the ghastly scene blurred, she was afraid she was going to faint. She made a motion with her hands, and the big man who had been standing next to her all during the fire put out his arms to catch her. Janie leaned up against him for support and closed her eyes.

When she opened them the world was steadier. Across the street, in the milling crowd in front of the *Herald* office, she saw her father. She did not know where he came from, where he had been, but she knew she must reach him. She took a deep breath and summoned all her strength.

"Thank you," she said to the man.

"Ma'am," he said. He had kind eyes and he looked worried.

She paid no attention to him and started across the street. There was no question now of being held back by the Home Guard or by the fear of being conspicuous. The Home Guard were working on the pile of stones, all order had departed from the street. Nobody paid any attention to her as she made her unsteady way to where her father stood, and caught his arm.

"Good God, Janie," he said when he saw her. "What are you doing here?"

Major Meade was covered with ashes and soot. One sleeve of his coat had been cut away; under it his arm was bandaged. His hair was wet and streaked with grime, his face was gray with ashes and with horror. The black patch was gone and his eyelid drooped over the empty socket. He looked so desperate, so unutterably pathetic, that Janie felt she could not bear it. She put her arms around his neck and sobbed on his shoulder.

"Oh, Papa, Papa," was all she could say. The Major could not know that the tears were for him. She had not reached tears for Avery. They would come later.

Uncle Jim Peyton ran up to them, staring unbelievingly at Janie. "How did she get here?" he asked.

"I don't know," Major Meade said, "but take her home, Jim. Get her away from here. I'll send for her mother, but in the meantime get Hallie or somebody to stay with her."

Janie went with Uncle Jim. Her legs felt weak and in spite of the heat she was shivering all over. He had to put his arm around her to help her as they slowly climbed the hill, past Market and Sycamore Streets to Jefferson. When they reached the little house he led her into the parlor, calling for Vicky. She ran in from the kitchen, wiping her hands on her apron.

"Law', Mist' Peyton, I been so scairt," she said.

Uncle Jim motioned to her to be quiet. Janie was sitting on the sofa, and as she seemed to be incapable of motion herself, he lifted her feet and stretched her out on its length.

"Get me some whiskey, Vicky," he said.

"We ain't got no whiskey."

"Well then, some wine."

"Ain't any sperits of any kind in this house," Vicky said firmly.

Uncle Jim stood still for a moment. "Damn all Puritans," he said with feeling. He moved toward the door. "Make some tea, Vicky. Hot and strong. Where are the children?"

"Upstairs takin' their nap."

"Keep them there. Don't let them come in here, and keep Mrs. Calhoun where she is. I'll be back in a few minutes. And make that tea, Vicky."

"Yassuh."

Janie lay quietly on the sofa, with her eyes closed. She felt dazed, her mind was not functioning properly. Bits and scraps of ideas floated through it. It was silly to be so cold in June. She could not remember what she had told Vicky to have for dinner. Why were the children so quiet? Maybe she had better get Vicky to light a fire, she couldn't stop shivering. She mustn't catch cold. Poor Papa, what had happened to his arm? Where had Uncle Jim gone?

He came back soon carrying a bottle, and with him was Miss Bessie Mason. Miss Bessie came over to the sofa where Janie was lying and took off Janie's bonnet, which nobody had thought of doing. Then she took off her shoes and rubbed her feet. Vicky came in with the tea.

"Get me a blanket or a quilt, please, Vicky," Miss Bessie said.

Uncle Jim poured some of the steaming, almost black tea into a cup and filled it up with whiskey from the bottle.

"Give her this, Miss Bessie," he said. "It will help her. Her mother will come as soon as we can get word to her. If you can't stay I'll send for Hallie."

"I can stay as long as I am needed," Miss Bessie replied. She knelt down by the sofa and put her arm under Janie, lifting her up so she could drink the tea.

I ought not to drink it, Janie kept thinking. It's whiskey and Avery would not approve. He would hate for me to drink whiskey.

She had never had whiskey before except in eggnog at Christmas and New Year's. Ladies had wine but not strong drink, except in eggnog. Avery didn't think good Christians ever had it, and it had been a long time since she had had any eggnog. She ought not to drink the tea. She kept on drinking it, however. She finished the cup. The warmth of the tea and the strength of the whiskey spread through her body like a beneficence. The shivering stopped. When Vicky came with a blanket Miss Bessie wrapped it around her. She opened her eyes and the room was blurred, so she closed them again quickly. Uncle Jim was leaving; his voice and Miss Bessie's sounded far off. She began to sink deep into drowsiness, and soon she was asleep.

21

Darkness and terror. And smoke. Janie moved and the terror left her when she felt Mama's cool hand on her forehead and heard Mama's voice say, "Darling, I am glad you've waked up." She went out into the hall and came back with a lighted lamp, and the darkness went away. The smoke was still there, the smell of smoke was everywhere, acrid in the nostrils. Janie was lying in her own bed, her big four-poster bed in her own room, alone. She was alone because Avery was dead. Avery was lying under a pile of great stones down on Main Street. Nothing could live under that. She could see Avery's face as it was turned toward her the moment before he jumped back into the smoldering debris. She could see his unseeing eyes looking at her, through her, past her. She gave a cry and sat up in the bed. Mama came and put her arms around her.

"Oh, Mama, Mama, I failed him," she cried. "I failed him."

"Hush, honey, don't say that. That's foolish, Janie. Don't say it."

She did say it, though, over and over again in the first days after Avery's death. Later she went on saying it to herself.

"You are just being morbid, Janie," Mama said. "This is a terrible thing, a tragic thing, and my heart aches for you, but it is not reasonable to blame yourself. It is not sensible. You had nothing to do with it."

"I sent him to his death with anger in his heart," Janie said.

"Avery had an angry heart. I am sorry to say that, but he did, Janie. You know he did. He seemed to be angry with the world."

The Calhouns came, of course. Mrs. Calhoun—poor Mrs. Calhoun, childless now—passed over her own grief and tried to console Janie.

"He needn't have jumped back into the fire," Janie told her. "The others wouldn't if he hadn't. He was angry with me. He looked straight at me and jumped in."

"Whatever it was between you, my dear," Mrs. Calhoun said, "whatever the impulse that made him do that, you can be sure it came from his own nature. We make our own lives, you know."

Dully Janie wondered how Mrs. Calhoun could believe that. How could anyone as good and kind as Mrs. Calhoun have made for herself the sort of life she had had to live? By marrying Mr. Calhoun, she supposed, but where was the justice of it? Mr. Calhoun, of course, saw in Avery's death the punishing hand of God, to which all must submit for the sins and sorrows of the world. Janie herself was not capable of consecutive thought, she could only feel, and she felt to the depths of her being that the tragedy was her fault. Avery was her husband, her responsibility, and she had failed him or he would not have expressed his anger in that foolhardy gesture. She lived in a half-world of misery and gray shadows. Nothing was real except the anger there had been between Avery and herself. The words they had spoken to each other in anger burned across her mind.

It was Mrs. Calhoun who had to explain to little Avery that his father had gone to God and would not be back. It was Mrs. Meade who had to make the decisions about Janie and the children and carry them out. There was nothing to do but give up the little house and move them back to Fairview. Avery had left a small life insurance policy, that was all Janie had.

Janie grieved over parting with Vicky, she was such a comfort. Vicky did not want to live in the country, however, and anyhow Janie could not afford to keep her. There was no need for her, Baizy and Susie were at Fairview, and Susie was a good children's nurse. Mrs. Meade and Vicky and Zeb packed Janie's wedding presents, her small supply of silver and china and glassware. A moving van came and men carried out the furniture, the big four-poster bed and the chest of drawers that Mrs. Calhoun had given her—she wouldn't take it back, though Janie would not need it at Fairview—and the sofa and chairs and whatnot in the parlor. Mrs. Meade arranged to sell the dining room furniture to Mr. Minnick's secondhand store, and that gave Janie the money to pay for the moving without borrowing on the life insurance money. Ally Martin sent a carriage to take the little family to Fairview, he wouldn't let them pay for it, and Janie said goodbye to Vicky and watched the bags and reticules and toys and small parcels being taken out and packed into the carriage. When Mrs. Meade and the children and Susie, who had come in to help, had gone out and were waiting for her to come, Janie lingered in the tiny hall and looked around at what had been her home, hers, Mrs. Avery Calhoun, to manage and to run for her husband and her children, where she had failed. It looked dirty now, though certainly she and Vicky had kept it clean. Dirty and dingy and forlorn. She leaned up against the wall and cried for a few moments, then she straightened up, lowered the long, black, crape-bordered veil over her face, and went out and got into the carriage and drove to Fairview.

She did not go back into her old room. Mrs. Meade thought it would be better for her to take the back guest room so that little Avery could have the adjoining small guest room. Her four-poster had come out of this room and now it was put back into its place. Janie took off her little widow's bonnet of black crape, put her clothes away in the big chest, and hung her one black dress in the wardrobe. After a while she would have to do something about getting some mourning clothes. Now it did not matter, because she never went anywhere, not even to church on Sunday. She sat in her room for the most part, looking out of the window, thinking. "It's a fact, Janie, that you are a light-minded woman," Avery had said. Had she been a light-minded woman? "Your conscience speaks of worldly pleasures and the beguilements of the Devil," Avery had said, and she had said to him, "How do you know so much better than anybody else what the Lord wants? Are you Moses on Mount Sinai?" Had he known? Was he right, did God demand fear and austerity and gloom? Had she been wrong in clinging to a loving God? She had not tried to believe in Avery's God but she had tried to live according to his belief. Over and over again she came back to that, she had tried. She had given up her friends and her parties and her little gaieties. Would God judge her by her efforts or by her failure? Was Avery's death a punishment, as Mr. Strachan Calhoun believed, and if so a punishment of whom for what? Surely if God had wanted to punish her He would have done so directly, not by taking Avery. After all, it was Avery who had died, in the prime of his young manhood, with all his life before him. But it was because of her that he had died. She could not get around that. There was her guilt, that Avery would not have gone back into the fire, taking four other men with him, if he had not been angry with her. Perhaps he might not have done it if he had not seen her standing there, watching him. If she had not argued with Avery about the Fireman's Ball, if she had not set herself up against him, if she had yielded and kept silence, as she had promised herself a thousand times to do, if she had stayed at home when the fire started, perhaps the tragedy would not have happened. If—if—if! And where did God come into this?

These were the thoughts that Janie lived with day and night. In the life of Fairview she felt like a ghost and acted like one, she knew. From the depths of her misery she realized that she must be a very gloomy person to have around, but she met the thought with indifference. Everybody was kind to her. Her mother tried to draw her out in little ways, by telling her bits of news, urging her to go to church on Sunday or to take walks through the summer-flowering countryside. Janie refused all overtures.

"I know it's the shock," Elizabeth Meade said gently. "I know you are suffering from shock, but you must try to pull yourself out of it, honey, for your children's sake."

The children loved being in the country. Elizabeth played placidly in the kitchen with Baizy and Susie, or out in the yard with Susie to watch over her. Little Avery spent most of his time around the farm with Zeb and Amos and Jake. He rode the farm wagon and watched the milking of the cow and made a great thing of helping with the feeding of the chickens and the pigs. Janie knew the men would take care of him. She knew also that Avery was puzzled by the change in his mother, and that she ought to make an effort to be more like her old self. Later she would, she told herself.

One day about a month after her return to Fairview, Elizabeth Meade came into Janie's room, where she was sitting listlessly looking out of the window.

"I am sorry to tell you this, Janie," Elizabeth said, "but I think you ought to know. Sara Anne has had her baby. She had a very bad time, and the baby died. It was a little girl. Sara Anne almost did, but now she is going to be all right."

Janie was shocked out of her apathy. "Oh, Mama, how terrible. I'm sorry. Poor Sara Anne."

"I thought perhaps," her mother said tentatively, "you might like to go to see her."

The idea of going out of the house, into town, horrified Janie. For a moment she was on the point of saying that she could not possibly do it. Then she realized that of course she could and she must. Her darling Sara Anne. She had almost forgotten that the baby was coming.

"Yes," she said. "Yes, I would like to go this afternoon."

So she put on her black dress and her little crape cap with its long, enveloping veil, and Zeb drove the two ladies to the Lewis house on Sycamore Street. Sara Anne had gone back there to have her baby. It seemed strange to Janie to be outdoors driving down the familiar road, where the woods were deep and green and the fields rich with growing corn and tobacco. Janie raised her veil while they were in the country but put it down again when they got into town. She felt so sorry for Sara Anne. She had not seen her since Avery's death. Sara Anne had not been able to go anywhere during the last months. She had written to Janie but had not come. Poor dear. She realized that for the first time since the fire she was thinking of somebody besides herself.

Mrs. Williams met them in the hall. She kissed them both. "So sweet of you to come, Janie, honey," she said.

Old Mrs. Lewis was lying down and Elizabeth Meade insisted that she should not be disturbed. Mrs. Williams looked very tired.

"Yes, it's been bad," she told them. "We are terribly distressed about the baby, a darling little girl, perfectly formed, Lizzie, but she just didn't live. Couldn't stand the pressure, I reckon. Anyhow, Sara Anne is going to be all right, and that's the important thing."

They went upstairs. As they approached Sara Anne's room Janie saw her mother reach out a hand to hold Mrs. Williams back. She went into the darkened room alone. Sara Anne was lying motionless in bed, her eyes closed; she opened them as Janie entered. Janie was shocked to see how white and drawn she looked, how drained of life and vitality. She went swiftly across the room, and as she went she reached up impatiently and took the pins out of her widow's cap, letting it fall to the floor with the veil making a pool around it. She knelt by the bed, putting her arms around Sara Anne and her face against hers. Their tears wet each other's cheeks. Neither said anything. There was nothing to say, and no need for spoken words. The words that came to Janie's mind were "Though I walk through the valley of the shadow of death." In their different ways they both knew that valley now. She did not finish the verse. "I will fear no evil" had no place in her heart.

Later when she went back to Fairview and little Avery ran to meet her she held him close. At least I have my children, she thought.

As the fall came on, Janie began going to church on Sunday. Swathed in her widow's weeds she sat in the pew with her parents and tried to feel the presence of God. People spoke to her in the hushed voices of sympathy. Then they would drive back to Fairview. Sometimes some of the aunts and uncles or the cousins came for Sunday dinner. Several times during the fall Sara Anne came to spend the day with Janie. She was all right now; outwardly she seemed her old self. Janie knew that inwardly she could not be. She knew how greatly the baby had been wanted, she knew the shadow of fear that hung over Sara Anne that she could not have other children. But the merriment had come back to the warm brown eyes, the sweetness and gaiety were there. Sometimes also Toni Russell or Maria Pratt came to see her. Mama was trying to draw her out, she realized.

On sunny autumn days she went walking through the gaily colored countryside, in the woods where the maples flamed against the dark green fir trees and the pines, taking the children to play in the leaves, or walking down the aisles of the apple orchard between the fruit-laden trees while the men picked and crated the apples. One day she went through the orchard and across the West Field to the stream and started to climb the hill to the place where the trailing arbutus grew in the spring, but soon turned back. The memories were too strong. She could not go there yet.

One great source of unhappiness for Janie was her financial situation. Her father was having such a hard time and here she was back on his hands, and not only herself but her two children. She must do something to earn a living, but what could she do? She didn't know enough to teach, and her whole being revolted at the thought of trying to run a boardinghouse. Aunt Josie had made a success of that venture, but she had been so much older when she began it, she had struggled for years with that big estate in the country, she knew so much more about cooking and housekeeping, and she had had the five girls to help her. Janie knew she could not do it, but what else was there for an almost penniless widow to do? She spoke of it once to her father, shyly, with difficulty. The Major was hurt.

"I am sorry that you should feel that way, Janie," he said. "Certainly you know that Fairview is your home. You are all we have, everything here is yours, and your children's. Emily doesn't need it and wouldn't want it, nor would I want her to have it. Whatever there is is yours."

Janie knew that was true and she tried to accept it. Avery's insurance money would provide cash for a while, for the things that had to be bought. Growing children needed clothes. Mrs. Meade selected materials for her in town, and all that winter Janie worked on little dresses for Elizabeth and little-boy suits for Avery. She also made herself a black calico dress for house wear and a black mull dress for church and company when the warm weather came.

Major Meade had insurance on the *Herald* building and the equipment, and when the rubble and the debris of the great fire had been cleared away and the business houses on the four sides of the ruined block began to rebuild so that the life of the town could go on, he too built, a good two-and-a-half story brick building much like the old *Herald* office, but with a little more space, a little more conveniently arranged. The insurance money covered the building, and he was proud of it and took pleasure in it. With such a building up-to-date equipment was necessary. This was expensive, the Major did not have the money. He had to go into debt to buy the printing presses and machines for a well-equipped newspaper office. He had never been in debt before in his life and it had a curiously depressing effect upon him.

One morning in the spring Janie came through the dining room from the kitchen. She had had her breakfast earlier with the children; Major Meade had finished his and had ridden into town. Elizabeth Meade still sat at the table, and Janie was horrified to see that her mother was crying. She could not remember seeing Mama cry since the day General Lee surrendered. "Darling, what's the matter?" she asked.

Elizabeth Meade wiped her eyes. "Oh, Janie, I'm sorry. I didn't want you to see me like this."

"But what is it, honey?"

"I am so worried about your father. He is not well, Janie, and he is so depressed and worried himself. Things are not going well with the paper, and he simply can't bear being in debt. I don't know what it is, I don't know why the paper shouldn't be getting along all right now that he has the new building and the new printing presses, but something has gone out of him, Janie. He has had to stand too much. This last blow has taken the life out of him, and he doesn't seem to be able to cope with things. There is talk of starting a rival newspaper in town, and that would just kill him, Janie." The tears began to flow again. "With your tragedy and all his worries, I don't know, this is such a gloomy household, we are all so unhappy, I don't know how to help either of you. I reckon it's just the same with me as it is with him, Janie, I expect we are just getting old."

Janie felt as if she could not bear it. She put her arms around her mother.

"I am so sorry, honey," she said. "I didn't realize—I have been so selfish."

"Grief *is* selfish," Elizabeth Meade said.

Janie straightened up, and then she said something that surprised her greatly. She said: "It's not grief, it is guilt."

Her mother looked at her. "I am glad you realize that. I have thought so for a long time."

Janie was so taken aback at her own words that she stood for a few moments thinking about them.

"There is grief of course, Mama," she said, speaking carefully. "I loved Avery. In spite of our differences I loved him. I miss him very much, and the failure of our marriage is a great sorrow to me, but you can live with grief. It is the guilt that seems so terrible to me."

"You can live with guilt too, Janie," her mother said. "Very few people get through life without knowing guilt in their secret hearts. Remember that, my dear. We all have our failures and our burdens to live with."

All right, Janie thought, I will have to learn to live with mine. After that she began to make an effort. She had been brought up on the assumption that one of the duties of a lady was to make things pleasant for those around her. No matter what she might be feeling herself it was her responsibility to maintain the social graces and oil the machinery of living, and make her family happy, especially the gentlemen. It was part of the code that was ingrained in her, inherited from generations back, and yet she had forgotten it in the dark months of her widowhood. She knew this was one of the reasons her mother was so upset; this was a gloomy household and she could do nothing to lift the gloom.

Now Janie joined her mother in the effort to cheer the Major. She noticed how gray and tired he looked, that he sat at the table at mealtime in almost complete silence, that at night when he usually read he would hold a newspaper or a book in front of him while gazing off into space. She tried to think of small items of conversation that would interest him. One evening she proposed that they have a game of backgammon, and the Major really seemed to enjoy that. She began trying to spruce up for supper in the evening, as she always used to do, but here she ran into a problem. She had so few mourning clothes, and she did not feel that she could afford to buy others. The insurance money must be made to last as long as possible for the children. As the hot weather came on her one black silk dress was too heavy, she did not want to wear the black mull she had made for herself just sitting around the house, and certainly she could not spruce up in the black calico she wore every day. She consulted her mother about it.

"I certainly think you could afford to get yourself another dress, Janie," Mrs. Meade said, "and you ought to, you certainly do need it. But even so you wouldn't want to sit it out here at home with just me and Mr. Meade. When we are alone here in the country, I don't see any reason why you shouldn't wear some of the dresses you had before—even if they are not mourning."

So Janie went to the chest where she had put her clothes when she came back to Fairview and got out several of her summer dresses, a blue-and-white checked gingham for morning wear so she would not always have to put on the black calico, and a white dotted swiss, a lavender-sprigged muslin, and a pale blue voile. With these she could change her dress for supper, and brush her hair until it shone and put on a touch of rouge, and look like her old self. I am doing it for Papa, she told herself, and for little Avery, who loved to see his mother looking pretty, but she admitted that it also made her feel better. It was easier not to feel despondent when you took some pains with your appearance.

June passed and Janie faced the fact that it had been a year since Avery died and she still could not think of him nor of that awful day without the dull ache of guilt "in her secret heart" as Mama had said. Try as she would, play with the children, talk to Sara Anne, dress up, play backgammon with Papa, read the papers in the effort to get interested once more in what went on in the world, she still always came back to the uselessness of the deaths of those five men and the part she had played in that waste.

One evening in July, Janie came downstairs after having put the children to bed. Glancing into the dining room she saw that supper was not ready so she kept on along the hall intending to sit on the front porch for a while. As she passed the library door she saw that Papa was sitting in there with a strange man. They both rose as she went by and Papa called to her. She was horrified. Here she was, in the presence of a stranger, not in mourning. She had on her white dotted swiss. Thank goodness, she thought, white is the next thing to mourning black, but even so she was deeply embarrassed. Why hadn't somebody told her that they had company? There was nothing to do but go into the library. Papa said:

"Janie, I want you to meet a friend of mine. This is Mr. Darby, Henry Forbes Darby. This is my daughter, Henry; Mrs. Calhoun."

The stranger came forward to greet her and Janie raised her eyes to his for the first time. She was startled to see that he looked familiar, and with a rush of memory she knew that this was the big, kind man who had stood next to her during the fire, who had caught and kept her from falling when the stone wall fell and she heard the Fire Chief say "Nothing could live under that." She had never seen him before nor had she since, and now here he was in Papa's library, smiling down at her, a tall man with unruly brown hair and humorous gray eyes and features that were too rugged to be handsome, and Papa spoke of him as a friend and called him Henry.

He put out his big hand and she put hers in it. "This is a pleasure, Mrs. Calhoun," he said. "I am mighty glad to meet you."

"How do you do," Janie said in a small voice. She wondered if he remembered, if he recognized her.

"We were just finishing our toddies, Janie," the Major said. "Suppose we go out on the porch until supper is ready."

Janie turned and moved toward the front door, but both Mama and Susie appeared to say that supper was ready now, so they went into the dining room. The Major and Mr. Darby did most of the talking during supper, though Mrs. Meade entered in at times. Janie said almost nothing. She had been so quiet for the last year, so hidden behind her black veil that it was hard to come out and make pleasant conversation. She felt as she had in her young girlhood, when she was always shy with strangers.

The two men talked about public affairs. The country seemed to have recovered completely from the panic of 1873 and the ensuing depression. Things were booming in the North and certainly this town was growing and prospering. It had always been a prosperous town, the Major said, until the war came. The administration of President Hayes had turned out better than anyone could have expected, certainly for the South. You had to credit Hayes with that, he had withdrawn the Yankee troops from the Southern states and with the crumbling of the rotten carpetbagger governments the South had finally recovered control of its own affairs. Surely now it would be able to recover its old prosperity.

"The South must always remember that of Hayes," the Major said.

"That's what some of the Republican politicians hold against him," Mr. Darby said. "He ain't popular with his own party. I don't reckon they'll nominate him again."

"He is too honest for the Republicans," the Major replied. "Even though he stole the election from Sam Tilden, he has turned out to be an honest executive. I don't suppose you can say that he stole the election, that was the *New York Times* and the Republican satraps, but certainly he took advantage of the steal."

"He don't deserve to be re-elected," said Mr. Darby, "but when you come right down to it I can't think of any other Republican I'd rather have, and after 1876 I don't reckon there is any use thinking we can get a Democrat."

Mr. Darby had a nice deep voice and a nice friendly smile, but he used the most awful grammar. Janie didn't mind

203

"ain'ts" and "he don'ts," lots of people used them, it was good old English, Papa said, but Mr. Darby did not hesitate to use double negatives and singular verbs with plural nouns and adverbs where adjectives ought to be and all kinds of mistakes. Except for that he certainly seemed to be a gentleman, his manners were perfect, he was well dressed and well groomed, and he knew a great deal, being well versed in politics and finances and Victorian literature and the Latin classics.

After supper they sat out on the porch, and Janie felt less self-conscious there, with fireflies pinpricking the summer darkness and the air sweet with the fragrance of honeysuckle and garden pinks. Flashes of heat lightning cut across the western sky, and after a while Mr. Darby said it looked as if a storm was coming up and he had better start for town. When Amos had brought his horse around and he had ridden off after many protestations of pleasure and gratitude for an evening spent in such pleasant company, Mrs. Meade asked the Major about him.

"Henry Forbes Darby," he said. "A fine man, I have known him for years. He lives over in Lexington, he's a lawyer but he runs a weekly newspaper on the side. That's how I came to know him."

"He seems to be a very pleasant person," Mrs. Meade said.

"I never heard such grammar," Janie put in.

The Major laughed. "He knows better. It's just an affectation, he says juries like it."

"We are not a jury," Janie replied. "I think he ought to do better when he is talking to ladies."

There I go being prissy, she thought. I always do that when I am on the defensive, but why should I be on the defensive with this man? She asked herself that question and knew immediately the answer; because he had seen her at the most terrible moment of her life. He, of all the people in the world, had looked at her with his kind gray eyes at the exact moment when she had realized what Avery had done and what she had done through Avery.

Two weeks later Mr. Darby again came to supper, but this time the Major announced in advance that he was coming, so Janie was properly clothed in her black mull mourning dress. The two men rode out from town in the late afternoon. The Major called for toddies to be brought to the library, and they shut themselves up in there with the door closed and stayed so long that finally Mrs. Meade sent Susie to knock on the door and say that supper was ready. After all, something was owed to smothered chicken, broiled tomatoes and batter-bread, with sillabub for dessert.

It was after they had finished supper and were settling themselves on the front porch that the Major said: "Henry, I think we might tell the ladies our news, don't you?"

"It's up to you, Major," Mr. Darby said.

"I am selling the *Herald* to Henry Darby," Major Meade said. "We have just been going over the papers, we will sign them in Allen Purcell's office tomorrow morning. I think the time has come, Elizabeth."

The glow had faded from the sky behind the mountains and twilight was settling over the fields, but it was not yet dark enough to hide the expression on Mrs. Meade's face. Janie herself felt as if she had been slapped. Papa without the *Herald!* She wondered why he had chosen to tell them in the presence of Mr. Darby, where they must be formal and polite and not speak what they felt. Probably that was why he did it, he thought the stranger's presence would break the edge of the blow a little.

There was a silence which drew out into awkwardness. The Major broke it. "There are others who would like to get control of the paper. I am glad to have it go to a gentleman, one who is a native Virginian and a good Democrat."

"Thank you, Major," Mr. Darby said. "I can promise you that I will try to keep the *Herald* up to the standard you have set for it."

"You will do much better," Major Meade said.

Then they tried to talk of other things, but the conversation was heavy. Nobody really cared about the single tax or whom the Democrats might nominate for the Presidency next year, and even the iniquities of the Readjusters and the prospects of the tobacco crop in the fall did not hold their usual interest. Mr. Darby left early. When he said goodnight he took Mrs. Meade's hand and looked down at her.

"I hope you don't hold it against me, ma'am, that I am buying the paper," he said.

"If it is what Mr. Meade wants I am grateful to you," she said.

He took Janie's hand too. "Goodnight, little lady," he said.

."The next time I come I hope to see that boy of yours." He and little Avery had taken a great liking to each other. Janie was not sure she was pleased. She had mixed feelings about this big man who seemed to be injecting himself into their lives.

They watched him ride off and still sat in silence. It was dark now, there was no moon. Presently Elizabeth Meade said: "Was it necessary, Mr. Meade?"

The Major sighed. "I think so, Elizabeth." There was a pause and then he tried to explain. "The town is growing, the population has doubled since the war. It needs an up-to-date newspaper, and I don't seem to be able to give it to them. I am in debt and I lost a lot of advertising with the makeshift paper I had to get out after the fire, and my best people have died, good old Tom Scott and Andy Mapes, and Les Vaughn is not worth a tinker's damn, the new ones I got down there are not as good, and I'm not as good, Elizabeth. I am tired. The truth is I'm getting old."

Elizabeth got up and went and sat on the arm of his rocking chair and put her hand on his shoulder. The Major went on.

"Things are bad in the state, politically, I mean. Billy Mahone and the Readjuster-Republicans are tying this state up as tight as a bale of hay. I just don't understand—" the Major paused to consider the problem, "—I don't understand how a man who fought so gallantly and loyally for four years in the Confederate Army as General Billy Mahone did could so deliberately betray the good name of his state and his people as he is now doing."

"He is a person of no background," Elizabeth said. "His father was a tavernkeeper."

"Well, he was a good soldier. A good campaigner. He's shrewd and he's smart. We beat him in the gubernatorial election last year but he is going to run for the Senate next year and he is gathering around him every corrupt element in Virginia. With the help of Yankee railroad money and the venality of our own people—we have to admit it, Elizabeth."

"Some of our own people, Mr. Meade," Elizabeth said.

"Yes, some of our own people. He has got the Readjusters, and some of them are respectable people—though essentially dishonest, I am convinced, or they would not advocate dishonoring Virginia's just debts,—and the Republicans and the

Negroes and what's left of the carpetbaggers and all the scalawags. It's a potent combination. They've got their eyes on this town and on my newspaper. What they would like to do is to push me into selling out to them, some of the better element of the Readjusters have approached me. Of course I would never do it voluntarily, but the debt is hanging over my head. My creditors might push me over the edge. Henry Darby is a lot younger than I am, and he is a fighter. The paper will be safe with him, I'm sure. He will take over the debt and he is giving me a good price for the paper. I can put the money into Fairview. That's the important thing, Elizabeth, this plantation of ours."

She put her arm around his shoulders. "I think you are exactly right, Mr. Meade," she said. "You are very wise and I am so glad you have made this decision."

"We are fortunate to have a man like Henry Darby come along at the right time," the Major said. "It seems he has had it on his mind to branch out with a real newspaper for some time. He likes it better than lawyering."

When the papers were signed and the *Herald* actually turned over to Mr. Darby and the Major was no longer required to go into town each day, the Fairview ladies had thought he would be lost and disconsolate.

"I dread it," Elizabeth Meade said to Janie. "I can't remember a time when that newspaper office hasn't been a part of his life. What will he do?"

What he did was to turn with new enthusiasm to the management of the farm, and it became apparent to them that that was where his real love lay, in the wide fields of Fairview, in corn and tobacco and apples, in wheat and oats, in cabbages and watermelons and chick-peas and all the things that came up from the good rich soil.

There were heavy snows that winter, and with the Major no longer riding into town each day sometimes they felt very cut off from the world. What they missed more than anything else was the newspaper. In good weather Major Meade would go in twice a week and come home with all the back numbers and they would catch up on the news. Mr. Darby also rode out frequently, bringing the papers and talking over his plans for the paper with Major Meade. As the months went by he came more and more often. During the spring he came every Sunday afternoon, riding out with the Sunday papers and bringing small presents for the children. Little Avery would hear him coming and run down the driveway to meet him, and Mr. Darby would reach down and pull him up on the horse in front of him, and they would ride triumphantly up to the front porch. Sometimes Mr. Darby would ride around the circle several times for Avery's pleasure, or go around to the back of the house to the stable and barn, with the little boy bouncing up and down with excitement and pummeling the horse's neck in glee.

"Henry's lonely," Major Meade explained. "He lost his own little boy as well as his wife in the scarlet fever epidemic of '72."

Mrs. Meade felt very sorry for him, and she began asking him to Fairview for Sunday dinner. All during the spring Mr. Darby could be expected every Sunday, and after he had discussed politics with the Major and they had each expressed their opinion of Billy Mahone and the Readjusters and the Republicans, he and Janie and the children would go walking. They walked through the woods and the fields, and down the old road to the river, and through the orchard, and one afternoon Janie found herself leading them up the hill to the place where the training arbutus grew. She knelt down and parted the rough leaves and buried her face in the hidden, fragrant blossoms. She picked a spray, and when she started to get up from her knees he reached down and pulled her up, and took the spray from her hand and put it in his own buttonhole.

"Thank you, ma'am," he said, though she hadn't done a thing about it, and she knew that she blushed.

They sat down on the pine needles in the sunny glade while the children played in the woods, and the spring that flowed out of the rocks on the other side of the stream made soft purling sounds as it ran down to join the stream.

"Ain't there a piece of poetry about 'a day in spring'?" Mr. Darby asked.

Janie laughed at him. "I reckon there are a lot of pieces of poetry about a day in spring," she said.

"I mean one that begins that way. I ain't much on poetry, I know more Latin and law than poetry, but it seems like I got something running in my head about 'what is so fine as a day in spring.'"

"Mr. Darby, why do you talk like that?" Janie asked, to her own great surprise. "You know better, don't you?"

He smiled at her. "I'll tell you, Mrs. Calhoun, it's sort of like putting on carpet slippers when you come home tired at night. Nice and easy, you know, and comfortable. I began it because juries up there in the hills where I was practicing law when I was real young don't like fancy talk. A city lawyer talking real good grammar wouldn't have a chance. Now it's gotten to be a habit. Yes, ma'am, I know better. I went to the Webb School in Tennessee when I was a boy, and if they don't teach you grammar there they put a dunce cap on you and send you home. I can talk real good when I want to."

Again Janie laughed. "You needn't tell me, Mr. Darby, that it is any easier to say 'real good' than it is to say 'real well.'"

This time he put back his head and laughed. He had a nice, chuckling laugh. "You got me there, ma'am, you certainly have got me there."

He went on using bad grammar, however, just the same.

2

Janie sat in the kitchen while the children were having their supper. Mama had not come downstairs yet and Papa and Mr. Darby were having toddies in the library. When the children finished Susie would take them upstairs and get them ready for bed, and she would go in and greet the gentlemen. She would go up to hear the children's prayers and say goodnight to them, and come down when supper was served. That was all right. It was after supper that worried her.

She knew with absolute conviction that the time had come for her to make a decision. She could not hold Mr. Darby off any longer. She had seen it coming for some time. She had been frightened last Sunday when he was here and she had felt it in the air and seen it in his eyes. He just wasn't going to wait any longer. She had managed to keep the children with her every minute, however, and after a while he had accepted it and said nothing. Tonight would be different. If she could just stay on the porch with Mama and Papa it would be all right, but she knew it would not be like that. Henry Darby would suggest strolling in the garden, or walking over to sit on the fence of the West Field to watch the sunset or something like that. And there she would be. What was she going to do?

When she had first realized what Mr. Darby's intentions

were she had been shocked. Surely he should realize that a widow whose husband had been killed in such tragic circumstances would have no thought of another marriage. It was not—she searched for a word—well, seemly, it was certainly lacking in respect for the dead, for him to show his feelings so clearly. That had been months ago, last summer really, and all this time she had been trying to pretend that she did not see, and trying to prevent the situation from coming to a head.

Little Avery was gulping his food as fast as he could. "Kin I go speak to Mr. Darby when I'm th'ough?" he asked.

"Don't talk with your mouth full, Avery," Janie said. "Yes, drink your milk and you can go in and say goodnight to Mr. Darby."

Avery slid down off his chair, picked up his mug of milk and drank it without stopping for breath. Then he started for the door.

"Stay only a minute, darling, and then go on upstairs. I don't want to have to call you, Avery," she said to his departing back.

"Yassum."

She could hear his footsteps running down the long corridor to the back hall. Elizabeth was dawdling with her supper. She had so little appetite it worried Janie sometimes, and yet she seemed to be healthy.

"Go on and finish your grits, honey. Susie is waiting for you."

When Susie had led the little girl upstairs Janie still lingered in the kitchen. She stood at the window and looked over the quiet fields. Baizy was putting the finishing touches to supper and the smell of Sally Lunn came from the oven.

"Seem lak Mr. Darby's a real nice man," Baizy commented.

"Yes, he's very nice," Janie agreed.

"Seem lak he hangin' round mo'n mo' all'e time."

"He and Papa are great friends,' Janie explained, "and then he is very fond of little Avery."

"Humph! 'At ain't the only reason," Baizy said cryptically.

Janie pretended she had not heard. She realized, of course, that everybody on the place knew, just as she knew, why Mr. Darby hung around more and more all the time, but nobody had ever spoken of it. It had now been three years—one month short of three years—since Avery had died. Just this spring she had gone into light mourning. She still wore black when she went into town, and she still wore her little widow's cap, but with a short veil at the back instead of the previous long, enveloping veil. Here at home she had worn white and lavender all during the spring. She was beginning to achieve a sense of peace, to learn that you could, as Mama had said, live with guilt. It was still there, but now she could push it into the background. It no longer struck her like a blow between the eyes every time she thought of Avery and of the life she had hoped to live. She had seen the life that she could live stretching ahead of her, quiet, peaceful, centered around the children and the activities of Fairview; and then here came this big old Henry Darby, with his nice voice and his chuckling laugh and his kindness and his bad grammar and his obviously amorous intentions toward her, and upset the whole picture. How could she let herself become emotionally involved with another man, how could she relinquish her hard-earned peace and give her life over to another marriage with all its problems and difficulties and unknown and unexpected possibilities? And yet how could she let Henry Darby go?

Presently she turned and walked slowly down the kitchen corridor into the house. The evening went exactly as she had known it would. At supper the gentlemen told the ladies about the opening of the new dry goods store in town. Wright's Emporium had merged with Garrett's Ladies Shop, and they had built a splendid new store, to be called Garrett's and Wright's. It was the most elegant store in town, Mr. Darby said, and the display of dress goods, notions, draperies and carpets would certainly delight any lady. He had brought out a copy of that morning's *Herald* to show them, as it had a full description of the store.

A shoe factory had recently been opened in the town, and that was encouraging. There were no two ways about it, this town was prospering, but it was disappointing that the state as a whole was not faring better. Richmond to the east with its tobacco industry, Danville to the west with its new textile industry, and this town with its long-established raw tobacco trade and its diversified industries, were the three bright spots. Otherwise the state was lagging. The census of 1880 was disturbing, so many more people had left Virginia in the last decade than had come into it.

211

"We are losing some of our best brains to the North," Mr. Darby said. "Our rosy dreams of the 'New South' don't seem to be working out anywhere in the Southern states. What's the matter with us, Major, why ain't we taking hold?"

"The burden of the Negro, the destruction of our agriculture, and the lack of capital," the Major said. "Especially the lack of capital. When Northern capital does come into the South it comes to enslave, not to prosper, to draw off the profits for the enrichment of the North."

"And to subvert our legislatures," Mr. Darby said, "as witness the election of Billy Mahone to the Senate with Northern railroad money."

The talk always came around to Billy Mahone and the Readjusters. When they went out onto the porch after supper Janie took her seat in a rocking chair next to her mother but, as she had expected, she was not allowed to stay there long. Mr. Darby leaned against a white column, smoking his pipe. When he had finished he knocked out the ashes and put the pipe in its case. The sunset had gone but there was still light in the sky. He turned to Janie.

"Come on, Miss Janie," he said. "Let's go see how the Jacqueminot rose is getting along." He had given Janie a Jacqueminot rosebush the summer before.

He held out his hand to pull her up from her chair. Now what could she do? She could not say: "No, Mr. Darby, I don't want to walk in the garden with you." So she put her hand in his and he pulled her up, and put her hand through his arm. Arm in arm they went down the steps and around the house, and along the perennial-bordered path to the rose garden, and through it to the trellis at the end where the Jacqueminot rose was getting along very well, as they both knew it was. They strolled through the roses and around the box hedge to the grape arbor separating the garden from the cutting garden. By that time the daylight had faded and a silver moon was coming up in the sky and the air was full of the damp, sweet smells of the May evening. Henry Darby leaned up against the frame of the arbor and looked at Janie.

"I think this is as good a time and place as any for me to speak what's on my mind," he said. His voice was soft and deep. It caressed her with its softness. "You know I love you, nobody could've missed seeing that, but I want to make it formal and official. I love you very much, Miss Janie, and I'm hoping you'll marry me as soon as possible."

So there she was. "Oh, Mr. Darby," she said, "I—I couldn't."

"And why not, ma'am?"

Janie tried to speak with dignity. "I have been through a tragedy, Mr. Darby. I am just beginning to get myself together again. I—I am not ready—I just couldn't—"

"It's been three years," he said. "Three years is a long time, and time heals. I know that. I been waiting for two years to speak to you, I don't want to wait any longer, Janie."

"You don't understand, Mr. Darby."

"Oh, yes, I do. I understand real well." He smiled at her. "I hope you notice I said real well that time. I know you been blaming yourself for your husband's death, and feeling guilty about it. Well, let me tell you something, young lady, you don't know nothing about guilt. Let me tell you what happened to me. I had a wife, a lovely young lady, we'd been married only four years, and a little son, Henry Forbes Darby, Jr., just two and a half years old he was, and as sweet a little fellow as you ever hope to see. And I went up to Staunton to try a case one time, it took two or three days, and when the case was finished I let myself be persuaded to go on a little hunting trip with some of the boys up in the mountains. So I sent word by a friend who was going on down the Valley, and went up into the mountains and shot a deer and a lot of rabbits and had a good time, and when I went home four days later I found my wife and baby dead of scarlet fever. Now how do you reckon I felt? How many nights do you reckon I walked the floor thinking that if I hadn't gone hunting I might had saved them. I don't know how, they had kin and friends and the doctor and all, but just the same I wasn't there and I ought to have been there and if I had been there I might've done something. I know all about it, Janie, you can't tell me anything about feeling guilty toward the dead. But I know too that the living have got to go on living. Life makes demands on you and you got to stand up and face it as long as there is breath in you. It don't do any good to go on glooming around and cutting yourself off from the world."

Janie could not think of anything to say.

"I don't know why you should feel guilty about your hus-

213

band, but that ain't the point. The point is, if you do feel guilty you got to work it out yourself and make your own peace and go on living, and make as good a thing as you can out of the rest of your life. You'll have to excuse me, ma'am, I'm going to say something I reckon I ought not to say, but it ought to be said, and that is, I been watching you mighty closely these last two years, and I think it's more a sense of duty that is holding you back than anything else. I don't think you owe any more duty to the past, it's time to turn to the future."

He reached out and put a hand on each of her shoulders. To her surprise the hands were shaking, until they clasped themselves firmly around her shoulders.

"You are still a young woman, Janie, you got a lot of life ahead of you. I'm older than you are but not enough older to make too much difference. We have both known tragedy and we have both felt guilt and that is a bond between us, but I think the time has come to forget all that and make a life for ourselves."

He drew her to him and put his arms around her.

"No, no, Mr. Darby. No, you must not—you have no right, Mr. Darby—"

"That's what I'm asking for, Janie-girl, the right. I am a man and you are a woman and we love each other. Oh yes, we do," he said as she started to protest. "You know how I feel and you—" He paused and laughed his chuckling laugh. "Well now, look at you!"

Janie had put her head on his shoulder, with her cheek pressed against his coat, and she kept it there. She could feel the pounding of his heart. Nothing had ever felt so good as the strength of that shoulder and the triphammer beating of that heart. She stood there without moving or saying anything. Henry's arms tightened around her. He bent down and kissed the side of her forehead, which was all he could reach, and she knew that her heart had found its resting place.

Part III

22

Janie and Henry Darby stood on the front porch of Fairview and watched the children go down the driveway on their way to school. Jonathan's thirteen-year-old boy's figure was clad in a new blue serge suit, the tight trousers coming just to his knees. He walked with a little swagger. Jane wore a new blue jumper dress over a white blouse with frilled ruffles at the neck and wrists. Both children wore long black stockings and black shoes. Each carried a lunch box and two nickels for carfare into town and back.

The coming of the electric streetcars to Fairview was the most exciting thing that had happened to the family in a long time. The city had been working on the line for two years, to everybody's inconvenience, but just two days ago it had opened up and the cars had begun coming past Fairview. There had been a ceremony in town, at the point where the new tracks branched off from the old line, with the Mayor and the City Council taking part. Henry had been there. At Fairview Janie and the children and all the colored people on the place had gone down to the road to watch the first car come by, and had waved and yelled at the waving crowd which had ridden out just for the fun of being on the streetcar's maiden trip to Greenway. Now on the opening day of school the children were going to ride on the streetcar for the first time. It had rattled past Fairview on its way out ten minutes ago. It would have reached the end of the line and would be coming back in a few minutes.

"Do you suppose they will be all right?" Janie asked anxiously.

Henry laughed and put his arm around her. "What you think can happen to them, honeybunch? All they got to do is get on the streetcar and get off right in front of the school."

"I know, but they look so little. And they have always been driven to school before, with somebody to see that they get there safely."

"The conductor will see that they get there safely. That car will be filled with children by the time they get to the school."

The streetcar came dashing down the road, swaying with momentum under its overhead trolley, clanging its bell as it came. It slowed and stopped in front of the Fairview gate, and the two small figures standing there turned and waved, then disappeared into the maw of this shining new conveyance, painted dark green with a buff colored band below the windows. The conductor pulled the bell cord twice, and the car moved forward on its way, rattling and clanging, into town.

"It wouldn't be any trouble to send them in the carriage," Janie said in a small voice.

Henry squeezed her and shook her gently. "Old stick-in-the-mud. Don't let's change anything, that's what you say. It's going to be grand to have the carline come past Fairview. You'll get used to it, honey, it's just because this is the first time."

He kissed her and then went to the edge of the porch and yelled with his powerful voice: "Amos, saddle Jasper and bring him around. I'll be ready in about ten minutes."

"Yassuh," came a faint voice from the other side of the kitchen.

"Old stick-in-the-mud," said Janie. "You keep on riding horseback into town when you have a streetcar right at your front door."

Henry put back his head and laughed. "You got me there, sugar, you certainly got me there. The thing is I ain't opposed to progress, I just like to ride horseback."

They went back into the dining room for Henry to finish his coffee. Elizabeth had come down. She was sitting at the table, clad in a pale blue challis dressing gown which swept the floor around her chair. It fitted her young figure snugly in

217

front; the fullness was provided by a broad box pleat in the back, running from the collar to the hem.

"Good morning, Mama. Good morning, Pa." To the Calhoun children their own father was Papa, Henry was Pa.

Elizabeth's cool little voice had a brittle quality. Where she got her clipped enunciation no one knew. "From her Scotch ancestors," Henry said, with one of his big laughs. She was a grown-up young lady now, having graduated from school in June, and she claimed the privilege of coming down to breakfast after the younger children had finished.

Henry drank his coffee, kissed Janie and Elizabeth and crossed the dining room to the hall door. "See you at dinnertime." Then he grinned at Janie. "Maybe I'll come out on the streetcar."

When he had gone Janie turned to her daughter. "Did you have a good time last night, darling?"

"Yes, Mama, it was a nice dance."

Janie wondered if that was going to be the end of the conversation. She knew better than to press Elizabeth for details. If there was anything she wanted to tell, she would tell it, unemotionally, in her small, clipped voice. If there was nothing she cared to say, all the king's horses and all the king's men could not get her to talk. This strange young daughter of hers, as remote as if she dwelt on another planet, as impersonal as the Dresden china shepherdess on the whatnot in the parlor! How could you get close to her, how penetrate that cool outer shell?

Elizabeth was a problem, and that was a fact. Not, heaven knew, because of anything she did or didn't do that was wrong. To all outward seeming she was a perfect daughter, a proper and dutiful young lady. She did many things well. She had always been near the top of her class at school, she rode well, danced well, sewed beautifully, played the piano better than Janie ever could. Whatever she was given to do she did with detached competence, without apparent enthusiasm, interest or excitement. She had no close friends, no spend-the-night-with, confide-in friends among the girls, and few beaux. None, really, when you came right down to it, because the young men who occasionally invited her to go to dances or on picnics or hayrides, were Avery's friends, not his sister's beaux. Remembering her own girlhood, Janie could not bear to have Elizabeth miss that brief and lovely interval, the iri-

218

descent bubble of youth, so easily pricked, so quickly gone.

"I am glad you enjoyed it," she said now, realizing perfectly that Elizabeth had said only that it was a nice dance, not that she had enjoyed it. As there was no reply to this she went on, trying to capture Elizabeth's interest. "We must begin to make some plans for your birthday dance in November." Elizabeth had had other birthday parties before, of course, but this was to be a really big affair, in recognition of her young ladyhood. "Would you rather have it here at Fairview or at Calisthenics Hall in town?"

Elizabeth did not answer for a few minutes, then she said: "I don't want a dance, please, Mama."

"Oh, darling, why not? Your nineteenth birthday! We've planned it for so long." Elizabeth said nothing. "I wish you were a little more interested in things and in people, honey. Most young girls would be crazy about having a dance. I don't see why you should be so different. It is natural for a girl to have some gaiety and pleasure."

Janie stopped suddenly, filled with consternation. A memory came to her through the years in between. She saw herself sitting with Avery on the little back porch of the tiny house on Sycamore Street in June darkness, the light of the lamp in the dining room coming softly through the lace curtains at the window. She heard herself saying: "Oh, don't be like that, Avery. People like to enjoy themselves, a little pleasure once in a while is a part of life." Good lord, history was repeating itself. Janie sat in silence.

Elizabeth was buttering a biscuit. With her eyes focused on her plate she said: "Mama, I have something to tell you. I am going to be married. I am going to marry Hugh Ames."

Janie felt as if she had been flattened, as if the breath had been knocked out of her body. She stared at Elizabeth.

"Why—why, honey," she stammered. "Married! To Hugh Ames?"

Hugh Ames was the young man who had taken her to the cotillion last night. Janie remembered him vaguely as a boy; he had come to the house occasionally in recent years—with Avery, she thought. The idea of romance between him and Elizabeth had never occurred to her; there were a dozen young men the family knew better.

"But darling, you hardly know him."

Elizabeth smiled. "I've known him all my life."

"But so slightly, you can't have known him well, he has hardly ever been to the house."

"Oftener than you've noticed, Mama, with Avery's friends. His family is poor, you know, they have no horses. Now he can come because of the streetcars, but for a long time he had no way to get here except when he came with other boys. I was in high school with him for two years before he went to Washington and Lee. We saw each other every day." She laughed. "That's why I begged to be allowed to go to public school even before Miss Bessie Mason closed her school. I think we have always known that we were going to marry each other."

"And you never said a word about it," her mother commented wonderingly.

"There wasn't anything to say until we were old enough, and he was in a position to get married. Last night we decided the time had come."

"Isn't he still in college?"

Elizabeth shook her head. "He is not going back. He has been offered a position in Mr. Fosdick's shoe factory. That's why we can get married."

Dear heavens, could you imagine anything duller than a position in Mr. Fosdick's shoe factory, Janie thought. The mental picture she carried of Hugh Ames, although vague as to details, depicted in general outline a heavy, unhumorous young man, awkward in movement and slow in speech. A dull young man in a dull position.

"Oh, darling," she said. "You are so young. Couldn't you wait a while?"

"I am no younger than you were when you married my father," Elizabeth replied.

True, true, and that was the point. How could she tell Avery's daughter how little she had known of Avery's real personality when she married him, how warn her of the vast unpreparedness of the young? Perhaps, however, Elizabeth knew and understood this large young man she was planning to marry; or perhaps there was little to know or understand, no twists of personality or tortures of conscience to deal with. Perhaps this was the secret of Elizabeth's remoteness, that an absorbing love had come into her life so early as to make other relationships seem unimportant. It was hard to believe, however. Elizabeth was calmly eating hot biscuits and strawberry preserves, as detached in her manner as usual, showing none of the excitement, the thrills, the protestations of joy and happiness which might be expected of a young lady newly engaged to be married.

Piercing screams suddenly sounded, approaching from the direction of the kitchen. Janie was undisturbed; she knew that the sounds indicated joy, not distress. Henrietta, her youngest, dashed into the dining room and threw herself into her mother's lap, exploding with shrill laughter.

"I pulled Fwisk's tail and he licked me all over," she screamed.

"Don't yell so, darling," Janie said. "You will wake up brother Avery."

Henrietta stared at her in surprise. "Ain't he waked up yet?" she asked.

"No. He was out late last night and this is his last morning at home, before he goes back to the University. We wouldn't want to wake him up, would we?"

The little girl considered the matter for a moment and shook her head. She slipped out of Janie's lap; with a finger to her lips to indicate quiet, she tiptoed with exaggerated caution out of the room. A moment later Janie heard her calling the dog outdoors. The present Frisk was a collie puppy given to Henrietta by her father on her sixth birthday.

Janie returned to a consideration of Elizabeth. "Well, I don't know what to say. If that's what you want, darling—"

"That is what I want, Mama," Elizabeth said placidly. "So instead of a dance you can give me a wedding."

She had finished her breakfast now and stood up. Janie went over to her and kissed her. "You still seem like a little girl to me, honey, and it is strange to think of your getting married. I suppose all mothers feel that way." She was taller than her daughter; pressing her cheek against the dark hair she said: "I hope you will be very happy, darling."

"Thank you, Mama." Polite and poised, Elizabeth crossed the dining room to the hall and started upstairs. Pausing on the landing she leaned over the railing and said to her mother: "I wanted you to know, Mama, but please don't say anything about this. Hugh wants to come out tomorrow to speak to you and Pa."

Janie lingered in the hall. She was shaken, both by Elizabeth's announcement and the manner of it. Presently she went into the front parlor and stood looking at a portrait of her mother hanging there. It had always hung on the stair landing until Janie moved it into the parlor after Mama's death two years ago. It was not good art, Janie suspected, but it was a charming representation of Elizabeth Meade, dressed in a full-skirted yellow gown, in her early maturity, before the wearing of black silk had become habitual with her.

"You couldn't tell me anything when I wanted to marry Avery, could you, honey?" Janie said to the portrait, "and now I can't tell Elizabeth anything. But you knew that I was vulnerable, and I don't believe Elizabeth is. I don't believe she is going to be hurt by life, whatever happens."

The morning sunshine poured through the east windows and the two parlors glowed. They had been redecorated three years before, for the first time in thirty-five years, and it was a source of deep satisfaction to Janie to remember the pleasure it had given her mother. Mama loved these rooms, and hated their shabbiness. Chinese rugs in cream and soft blues now covered the floors; the blue velvet overdraperies had given place to yellow brocaded hangings. All the sofas had been reupholstered in tufted blue satin and the seats of the small gilt chairs in the yellow brocade of the draperies. Mama's dress in the portrait went beautifully with the new decorations, and Janie wished she had thought to hang the portrait in the parlor while Mama was there to see it.

When she went back into the hall she met Avery coming downstairs.

"Did Henrietta wake you up?" she asked.

"Naturally. Henrietta would wake up the dead." He said it with a smile, and when Avery smiled his whole face smiled. When Avery laughed, the sound was so infectious that nobody could resist it. In fact, nobody could resist Avery under any circumstances, in Janie's opinion. Like the golden parlors in the morning sunshine, Janie glowed in the presence of her son.

She adored all her children; she would, she told herself, have died by inches for any of them. She would have denied indignantly any hint of favoritism, but she knew deep within herself that nothing in all the fullness of her life meant to her what this splendid son meant, her firstborn. So like his father in outward appearance that he startled her sometimes, he was unlike him in every characteristic of mind and heart and

222

spirit. Outgoing and friendly, happy-hearted, generous, charming, good! Avery was good with a special kind or goodness that sometimes humbled Janie. Avery was perfect. You are just a silly, doting mother, she frequently told herself. Nobody is perfect. No matter how many times she said it, however, she knew perfectly well that she could find no imperfections.

He kissed her good morning. "It certainly is time I was waked up. I've slept like a top. Do you suppose Baizy would give me some breakfast?"

"Baizy would give you the world on a silver platter if she could, and you know it."

Avery laughed. "Right now I would rather have some ham and biscuits and coffee, or anything Baizy happens to have handy."

"Suppose you go out and see what Baizy happens to have handy, and then you had better get at your packing. I'll help you when you are ready."

Janie went upstairs, where Ella was bustling around making beds, sweeping and dusting. Her room was in order. The big front room which had always been Mama's and Papa's was now hers and Henry's. Like the front parlor beneath it was flooded with morning sunshine. Janie wandered around, straightening small objects that needed no straightening, pausing to look at herself in the mirror without really seeing herself. The house was very quiet with the children at school. She felt aimless; she would give Baizy time to fix Avery's breakfast before going out to the kitchen to talk over the day's meals. Avery's clothes were laundered and pressed and spread out in the guest room. There was nothing to do for him until he was ready to pack. She sat down in a rocking chair by the front window and absent-mindedly picked up a dress she was making for Henrietta. She began whipping on lace with a speed born of long practice.

Elizabeth's marriage would change her plans. Janie had wanted to give her a happy year, of parties and pretty clothes and gaiety. She had thought that after the first of the year they might even go on a trip to New York. They had a standing invitation to visit Emily, but Janie thought it would be more fun to stay at a hotel. They would go to the theater and dine in restaurants. Janie had wanted to see Elizabeth warm up, her eyes sparkle and her cheeks flush with excitement. A vain dream, perhaps, but she would have liked to try. It was going to be a gay winter, and just out of mourning for Mama and with a young lady daughter, Janie had looked forward to it happily. There would be much entertaining, there would be plays and concerts at the new Opera House; Janie had been planning several parties for Elizabeth. Now there would be only the one big event, the wedding, to prepare for. She would lose Elizabeth before she had ever had the warm mother-daughter relationship she yearned for.

Henrietta was yelling again, but this time outdoors. Janie went to the window and watched the little girl and the puppy playing in the yard, under the copper beech, scampering and rolling over each other on the grass. Frisk's tail was wagging furiously, and at every opportunity he licked Henrietta's face with moist affection while she screamed joyfully. Janie smiled at the absurd little figure. Henrietta was the only one of her children who was homely. "Just plain homely," she said, but Henry always denied it.

"She ain't pretty," he would say, "but she's cute. She's got something, you wait and see."

"She certainly has, sir," Avery once said, in reply to Henry's statement. "She's got cast iron lungs and steel vocal cords."

Certainly Henrietta's noise-making facilities were phenomenal. Janie sighed; something would have to be done about that voice before she grew up.

2

That evening after supper, when Henrietta had been put to bed and Jonathan and Jane were doing their lessons, Janie and Henry sat in the library. It was warm enough to sit out on the porch, but Henry wanted to show her a copy of that morning's *Herald*. The paper had made a survey of the business situation of the town, and he was proud of the *Herald* for having done it and proud of the town for what the survey showed. The front page, except for the advertisements around the edges, was given over to an article headed "Qualifications of This City to Become a Manufacturing Centre." He read items from the article to Janie while she embroidered a bureau scarf. She was thinking more of all the sewing and embroidering that would have to be done to get Elizabeth's trousseau ready than she was of what Henry was reading, but she enjoyed his pride and excitement. She wanted to tell him the news about Elizabeth, but did not feel that she could in view of Elizabeth's request.

"This city has an admirably managed system of public schools, embracing 10 schoolhouses, 65 teachers and over 3000 pupils," Henry read. "It supports a large wholesale trade, with 71 houses and aggregate sales for last year of $12,362,116. We got twenty-four churches, and listen to this, honeybunch, 51 manufacturing enterprises, employing 2779 hands, doing an annual business of $4,765,411 and paying annual wages of $794,601. That's a heap of money, sugar, I'm tellin' you, that's a heap of money."

Henry went on picking out bits of information from the long article. "We still got a big tobacco business, though we ain't ever equaled what we sold in 1890, before the depression set in. We got four railroads, goin' all over the state and down into North Carolina and west as far as Ohio. We got five and six-tenths miles of electric streetcar lines now and a new one, goin' over on Emerald Hill, has been chartered. I tell you, Janie-girl, this town is prosperin'."

"That's nice," Janie said placidly. The new prosperity was reflected in the newspaper and was making itself felt in the life of Fairview. For the first time in her life, except in the early childhood she hardly remembered, poverty was not a daily companion. There was enough money now to redecorate the house and rebuild the fences, to hire Ella, the new housemaid, and a new farmhand, to get the children a pony and keep the grass of the front yard cut. Enough money to buy some pretty clothes and give some parties and perhaps go to New York. Enough to give Elizabeth a proper wedding, if she insisted on getting married.

"Yessuh, it's prosperin', and it's growin'," Henry said. "And it's growin' this way. The town is comin' out toward Fairview, Janie."

Now Janie understood Henry's purpose; it was not the first time this discussion had taken place. She put down her embroidery. "Oh, Henry, don't ask me to sell the Fairview land."

Henry hitched his chair over toward Janie. "Now listen, sweetie pie, now you just listen to me. I know how you hate to talk about this, but we got to talk about it. We just got to talk about it. We just got to face some facts. There ain't any sense in sittin' out here and refusin' to face facts. Thirty years ago, just after the war, this town had seven thousand people in it. Now we got twenty-five thousand, includin' the suburbs, that is, and the suburbs will soon be part of the town. All the new people, they got to have somewhere to go. They are spreadin' out all around, but the well-to-do ones, the ones with the most money to spend, are comin' out this way. You know that, you see it every time you go in town. Well now, here's the way it is. Somewhere back, your grampa, or maybe it was your great-grampa, sold off the land on the other side of the road, between the road and the river, all except the strip leading to the old wharf."

"It was Great-Grandpa. Grandpa didn't approve of it, Papa said."

"Well, anyhow, it was sold, and people are buildin' all along there; they're goin' to come out to Fairview on that side of the road no matter what. There ain't anything you can do about that. And what I want you to be thinkin' about, Janie, is what you goin' to be doin' sittin' here with all this land spread out around you and the town goin' on out past you. Why do you think the city built the streetcar line all the way out to Greenway, and is goin' to build a park and a bandstand and a dancing pavilion at Greenway? Because that's where the town is goin', honeybunch, that's where the town is goin'. What you goin' to do with all this land? You know you can't farm all of it; some of it ain't been touched since the war. You know your pa wore himself out, just about, tryin' to keep it the way it used to be, and all he could manage to do was hold on to it and pay his taxes and scrimp out a mighty poor livin'."

Janie was silent, remembering Papa's tired, lined face, his grim determination, the burned-out energy, the struggles and tragedies that put him in his grave at the age of sixty.

"That's the reason," she said in a low voice. "Because he worked so hard, worked and struggled and fought to keep Fairview and build up the old life again. He left it to me, in trust, as his father left it to him, so it would go on from one generation to the next. Just when we get so we can keep it properly and live the way he wanted us to live, you want me to sell it."

"That ain't true, Janie," Henry remonstrated. "You know I

don't want you to sell Fairview. I just want you to sell some of the land, land you don't use and ain't got any need for."

"It's all a part of Fairview."

Henry began walking back and forth across the library floor in front of the fireplace. He always paced the floor like this when he was doing what Janie called "fixing to make a speech."

"The world is changin', Janie-girl," he said. "The world is changin' fast, and it seems mighty silly to me to sit here like old King Canute with the waves comin' up around your feet and refusin' to move." He was silent for a few moments, standing with his hands in his pockets staring unseeingly at the portrait of Great-Grandpa Marshall Meade which hung over the mantelpiece. Then he began walking again. "When our people first came to this country, Janie, they set about building up a system, a way of living, that was just as much like the one they left behind in England as they could make it, granting a great, untouched wilderness and granting slavery. That's what we had in Virginia before the war, the English manorial system, an agricultural civilization, big estates, a landed gentry; all our ideas and customs, the way we talked and the way we thought, transplanted from English country life. There's not a part of the United States as much like England as the Commonwealth of Virginia."

It was a funny thing about Henry, Janie thought, that when he was "making a speech" and his mind was absorbed in what he was saying, he used better grammar than in his casual talk.

"Well, then the war came and wrecked it all, leveled it to the ground, destroyed our system and our wealth. So what did we do? We set about building it right back up again, as much like the old way as we could make it, granting physical destruction and poverty, and granting the abolition of slavery. And we have come mighty near doing it, I want to tell you, mighty near. I don't mean physically, we haven't got the big plantations and the slaves, we are poor and shabby as all get-out, we haven't recovered the beauty of the old way, but all our ideas, our customs and traditions, our ways of doing things, our ways of living and of wanting to live. Our feelings. Everything we do and think and feel comes straight down from the old way. We've got landed gentry all around

227

who don't own a foot of land. Take me for instance. I never owned a piece of land in my life except the *Herald* office. This is all yours, not mine."

"It is ours," said Janie.

Henry smiled at her, but went on talking. "And yet there is nothing in the world that would be so completely satisfying to me, to any man of our class, as to stand on my own land and look around at my own broad acres, fertile fields with growing crops, orchards, meadows with cattle grazing, and say to myself: This is mine, my earth, from which I draw life and sustenance. Oh, there is a calling for the land in the blood of all of us, Janie; don't think I don't know it. That's why the war was such a deeply personal thing to us, it was our own special land that was being fought on, our good earth, our forests and rivers and mountains. I know how you feel, I know how your father felt."

Henry was walking faster and faster, from the front windows to the back wall of the library. Janie could see that he was deeply moved, and so was she. She had no answer for his passion.

"People say we live in the past, but they've got it wrong. We don't live in the past," Henry said, "we've just brought the past along with us and made it the present. That's all right, up to a point. We can keep a lot of it, but we have got to learn what we can keep and what we must give up. The old system is gone, so what should we do? Build a new one, if we got any sense. Build a new one and put into it all the good things we can hold on to from the old one, and let the rest go. You can't fight against time and tide, Janie. This is an industrial age. It is industry that has made it possible for England to build up a great empire, it's industry that is making the North boom with a wealth nobody ever thought of two generations ago, it's industry that's making this town grow. You just got to face it, wealth has gone out of the land."

"That's what I don't understand," Janie said. "Why? Land has been the basis of wealth since the beginning of time. People still have to eat, and feed their cattle and wear clothes. They still smoke and chew tobacco. Certainly wealth hasn't gone out of tobacco."

"Well," Henry said, "a lot of people wouldn't agree with me, I reckon, but as far as this region is concerned I think it has, just about."

228

"Oh, Henry, why do you say such a thing?" Janie said with impatience.

"Because this country grows dark-leaf tobacco, honey. Over in the southwestern tip of Virginia and down in North Carolina the land grows bright-leaf tobacco. Nothing you can do about it, the land does it, and bright-leaf tobacco is what people are beginning to want. This town has been a tobacco center for a hundred years, but mark my words, Janie, the center is shifting. Bristol sold more tobacco than we did the last two years."

Janie picked up her embroidery and took a few stitches, but found that her hand was shaking. She could not argue with Henry about this, he knew so much more than she did. He was probably right, but she could not bear the thought of selling any part of Fairview and she resented Henry's logic. His family had lost their land right after the war, he couldn't know what Fairview meant to her. He had stopped pacing the floor and was leaning against the mantelpiece now, looking down at her.

"The Tylers can keep on running Meriden in the old way," he said, "and living the way they used to live, but it's not because Meriden is making money, it's because they got the Boyd money behind them. We can keep on living here for a while longer with this idle land around us, and fix the place up some, but it's not because Fairview is making money but because the paper is. Remember that, Janie, the money is coming from the paper, not Fairview."

"Money isn't everything," Janie said, realizing how prissy she sounded.

"No, it ain't everything." Henry had reverted to his normal language. "There's lots of other important things, but there ain't any use pretendin' that it ain't important. Poverty ain't a nice thing to live with, and when it's the poverty of a whole region it's bad. What I say is, there ain't any use bein' poor if you don't have to be. If we lived off somewhere in the country, with nothin' happenin' near us, we could piece out a livin' on the land, I reckon. Not a very good one, with five children to think of, but enough to keep body and soul together. But with a town growin' up all around us and property values boomin' so fast you can't keep up with them, it just don't make sense to sit out here with a lot of useless land and hold on to it for no reason except that little Janie

229

Meade's ancestors patented it a hundred and twenty-five years ago and she wants to say that what her ancestors left her she has kept."

Henry had never spoken to her like that, and she looked at him in surprise. Meeting his gray eyes she realized how strongly he felt about this. The good-natured humor which usually lighted his face was gone.

"Leavin' out the money, it makes us look silly, Janie."

"What do you want me to do?" Janie asked in a low voice.

Henry came over to her quickly, pulled up a chair and leaned forward, his face alight with interest. "I'll tell you what I want you to do, sugar," he said. "I want you to sell a strip of Fairview land nearest to town, about thirty acres of it, I think, good level land with trees and a view of the mountains. Real estate people been after me for a long time about that passel of land, especially your cousin Allen Wilcox. People want to build on it. We'll sell that right away and then we won't sell any more for a while. We'll go slow about it, because real estate values are going up all the time. We'll see what happens when that strip gets built up, and when more people want to come out here we'll sell some more. It ain't just the road frontage either, Janie, it's all the way back. First thing you know they'll be cutting side streets back from the main road."

Henry could not know how his words hurt her. The thought of streets being cut through Fairview fields back to her beautiful hills was like a pain in Janie's heart.

"We'll sell off the land bit by bit as it is wanted, but we'll keep plenty of it here around the house, the barn and stable and orchard, and fields for the animals to graze, and plenty of room for a big vegetable garden, and all the land along the creek back to the spring on the hill. As far as livin' is concerned you won't know the difference, Janie, but as we sell off the land we can stop fighting to make money out of farming on a big scale. We can just farm for ourselves, and what we get for the land we'll invest for you in stocks and bonds, and the money'll come rollin' in without your liftin' a finger. Let the Yankees work for you, honeybunch, while you sit in a rockin' chair and sew a fine seam."

Henry laughed and Janie tried to smile but was nearer to tears. In his absorbed interest Henry did not notice.

"It's goin' to be a fine broad street comin' out here, Janie," he went on, "lined with trees and with big, pretty houses all along it, and the streetcar line connectin' it up with downtown. It's goin' to be a fine, prosperous town, where people can get work and make money and live nicely. You can see it already, not just the new building but people paintin' their houses and fences, and plantin' gardens and cleaning up their back yards again. It's in the air, sugar, there's a new feelin' in the air."

Still Janie said nothing, and her silence finally penetrated Henry's absorption. He came to her and put his hand on her shoulder. "I know it's hard for you at first, sweetie, but you ain't goin' to be sorry when you get used to the idea, honestly, I don't think you're goin' to be sorry. I don't know anybody would enjoy bein' rich, well, at least real well-to-do, any more than you. And anyhow, Janie, I don't see what else we can do. It's just one of those things that's bound to happen."

"I keep thinking of Papa," Janie said.

"I don't know how the Major would'a felt about it. He couldn't see anything but the land, he might'a felt just the way you do. I reckon he would, but there's one thing I do know, Janie, and that is that Miss Lizzie wouldn't feel that way. Miss Lizzie would agree with me all the way. She'd say sell the land like a shot."

Janie knew that was true. She could hear her mother saying: "I am tired of being poor. I am tired of the South's being poor. I am tired of everything I look at being shabby and rundown. I want to see us get back up to the top, where we belong. I am in favor of everything that might bring prosperity back to us."

She had said that when the city first began fixing to build the streetcar line out to Greenway, and wanted to buy a strip of land the entire way across the road frontage of Fairview, from one end of the property to the other, so that the road could be widened into a broad thoroughfare with plenty of space on each side of the car tracks. Janie had hesitated at that, but Mama had been very firm. "By all means sell the strip," she had said. "The fences are all down anyhow, it would be a relief to see them cleared away. Take the money and build new fences."

"All right, Henry," Janie said. "We will sell the land, just as you say."

23

Elizabeth was married in December, and her mother felt that the wedding was all a girl could wish for; a candle-lighted church ceremony, a big reception at Fairview—possible now with the streetcar running right by the house—a three-piece orchestra playing soft music, flowers, lights, a splendid pink-and-white wedding cake, and champagne punch.

Janie struggled with her conscience in regard to the punch. The thought of Avery came to her constantly as she planned the wedding. This was Avery's daughter who was being married, and Avery would not have approved of champagne punch. Since the day of his death Janie herself had never touched wine or whiskey, not even eggnog at Christmas. It was an atonement that she offered to Avery's memory, an assuagement of the feeling of guilt she had never been able to overcome. Elizabeth, however, wanted a wedding with all the fixings. She had her father's love of display uncomplicated by his sense of sin at its use. She wanted champagne punch; Henry took it for granted that they would serve it, happy in the fact that they could now afford it. Janie herself wanted champagne punch. Not having been able to give Elizabeth the thing she most wanted to give, and to receive in return—close, warm, loving companionship and mutuality of interests—she was determined to give her all the outward things a daughter might want on her wedding day. She could find no other way to show her love and her yearning hopes for this child's happiness.

After the first shock of surprise, Janie had become reconciled to Elizabeth's marriage. Perhaps this was the answer to the problem she presented. Probably her own dreams of shared gaiety were empty and vain, and Elizabeth had a better sense of the real values of life than she. Perhaps as a young matron she would develop more warmth of mind and heart than she had in her untouched girlhood. If there was nothing to recommend Hugh Ames as a son-in-law, there was nothing against him either. His family, although never important or distinguished, were gentlepeople. She knew his mother slightly and she remembered that Mama had known his grandmother, who was a Preston, when they were girls. The family was poor, but that was a common heritage, not to be held against them. Hugh himself, as she came to know him, confirmed her original impression of being a dull young man, heavy in body and mind. Henry made inquiries, however, and learned nothing to his disadvantage, he had a reputation for industry, his manners were good, and he seemed to be devoted to Elizabeth. She, on her part, went through the weeks before the wedding in a state of placid satisfaction.

Janie enjoyed all the bustle and preparation for the wedding and the making of Elizabeth's trousseau. She engaged Jennie Miranda, the town's best sewing woman, for weeks and turned the small guest room into a temporary sewing room. Elizabeth wanted a new wedding dress, having no interest in the gown carefully folded away in the cedar chest in the attic in which her mother and her grandmother had been married. Yards of lustrous white satin were bought and turned into a modish dress with a long gored skirt flaring into a voluminous train, a tight-waisted basque with high collar and enormous leg-of-mutton sleeves. The trousseau included two daytime dresses, two silk afternoon dresses, two evening dresses, a brown broadcloth suit made by the ladies' tailor in town, two pretty new dressing gowns for house wear in the morning, a pink silk dressing sacque—and the underclothes. A dozen of everything a bride must have, and yards and yards of lace and embroidery ruffling must be whipped onto the fine cambric and lawn petticoats, drawers, chemises, corset covers and nightgowns. Janie and Elizabeth, Jennie Miranda and Susie all rolled and whipped endlessly, and Henry complained good-naturedly that you could not walk across the floor of any of the upstairs rooms without getting tangled up in ruffles.

The house was in a swivet for weeks, but when the day of the wedding came, Janie knew that every detail had been attended to, every arrangement made. The church, the flowers, the minister, the organist, the house, the refreshments. The presents spread out in the library, Elizabeth's new clothes packed in her new trunk, her brown going-away suit and huge brown velvet hat ready to be put on, her valise packed —they were going to Richmond for a few days' honeymoon. Baizy and Susie and the caterer's man waiting in the kitchen, old Zeb, dressed in new blue livery, ready to open the door to the guests when they came from the church. Amos, also in new blue livery, with the carriage at the front door. Everything in order, everything perfect. She wished Mama could have been here to see her namesake's wedding. This was the kind of wedding Mama had had, the kind she would have liked to give Janie when she married Avery. She wished her mother could know that they were now back where they belonged, not at the top certainly, far from it, but back where they could do things properly, where the old traditions and the old ways could be observed.

The family and the servants gathered in the hall to wait for Elizabeth to come down. Henry, wriggling his chin uncomfortably in his high dress collar, looked around him in dismay. He was, Janie knew, nervous at the prospect of walking down the aisle with Elizabeth and giving her away.

"Holy mackerel, sugar," he said. "We got two more daughters. We gonna have to go through all this when they get married?"

Janie laughed. "I wouldn't worry about that now if I were you. You've got a long time before you'll have to do this again."

She was looking at the little girls, standing solemn and quiet in their stiff taffeta dresses, even Henrietta awed into silence by the impressiveness of the event. Avery, home for the wedding, came down the stairs, incredibly handsome in his formal dress clothes, and then Elizabeth came, with Susie holding her train to keep it from touching the polished steps.

White was not becoming to Elizabeth, it made her look sallow, so Janie had introduced her to the secret beauty aid of the Meade ladies for two generations, Dorine's Liquid Rouge, imported from Paris, bought in secret and always kept hidden in top bureau drawers. Before coming downstairs Janie had touched Elizabeth's cheeks into delicate color, and now in the gleaming satin, her face framed by the old rose point veil that had been Mama's, she looked positively pretty. Everybody told her so, and she smiled at them and said "Thank you" in her small cool voice, and allowed Avery to throw her mother's blue velvet cape around her and help get herself and her train and her leg-of-mutton sleeves into the Fairview carriage. It was going to take two carriages to carry all the family to the church. Janie and Henry went with Elizabeth, and Avery, Jonathan and the little girls went in a rented livery stable carriage.

In the church Janie was surprised to realize how unexcited and unemotional she felt. Perhaps it was catching, or perhaps she had used up whatever emotions she had felt about Elizabeth's marriage. Now she felt relaxed, inwardly quiet, free to enjoy, as she always enjoyed, the candlelit beauty of the church, the music, the ordered cadences. As the ceremony proceeded and every detail clicked into place as it should, she felt a detached satisfaction.

It was when she was back at Fairview, receiving the guests in the front parlor, that emotion returned to her, and she began to feel happy and gay. Gay and thankful. All her blessings rose up in front of her and paraded through her mind. She was thankful that Elizabeth had the husband of her choice and the kind of wedding she wanted; thankful for Henry standing so solidly beside her, and for her darling children, for this house, for these gracious rooms, filled with candlelight and firelight and flowers and people. Thankful for the people, the friends of a lifetime, of several generations, in fact; all kinds of people, old and young, good and bad, some ugly, some funny, some charming, but all familiar, all bone and sinew of her world, and therefore held in tolerant affection. Mrs. Jim Wetherlow, who was as crazy as a Juney-bug and hopped down the street like a child playing hopscotch to keep from stepping on the cracks in the sidewalk; Miss Milly Durham, who refused to grow up and kept on wearing the bobbing curls on each side of her face and the crinolined skirts of her youth; the three pretty Hunt sisters who had the reputation of being "fast" and did not get married in spite of

235

having more beaux than any girls in town; Mr. Alan Thomas, a revolting old man with a straggly white mustache and moist red lips, who claimed the privilege of age to kiss all the very young girls (he had tried it on Elizabeth once but only once). Martha Boyd Tyler, as pale and prissy as ever, but beautifully and stylishly dressed, as she always was, and Raiford Tyler—poor Raiford, who was getting fat and had pouches under his eyes, it was rumored that he drank too much. And all the dear ones, Sara Anne, lovely and charming as usual but still wearing the old brown silk dress which had been her party costume for so long, it was too bad that Carey Morgan never seemed able to make a go of things. Old Mrs. Calhoun had come for Elizabeth's wedding, of course. Janie rejoiced in the peace and comfort that had come to her since Mr. Calhoun's death, living as she did with her sister on the farm near Big Island. Miss Bessie Mason, old now and frail, but still majestic in black velvet, was there; Antonia and Johnny Russell, happy and prosperous; Maria and Corbin Pratt, not so happy or prosperous; Aunt Josie, who no longer ran a boardinghouse, and Mrs. John Embrey, who did, and with whom Elizabeth and Hugh were going to board for a while. Four of the five Ashby girls were there with their husbands—Helen had married a man who lived in Chicago, of all places; and Christopher Peyton, who lived in Richmond now, brought his wife and oldest daughter, Ginger, back to town for the wedding. It was a shame that all the Peyton children lived in other cities so that Uncle Jim, with Aunt Hallie gone, was by himself in the white frame house on Sycamore Street. All the cousins and the aunts and uncles were there—Aunt Kate had gone to the wedding but had not come to the reception because she was in mourning for Uncle Dabney—and the young people, Elizabeth's friends, Avery's friends, Hugh's friends, his roommate at the University, who was best man at the wedding; it was a gay crowd, the house was full, the music of the orchestra was almost drowned by the laughter and talk, the movement and gaiety.

Janie loved it all, and when Elizabeth had changed into her tailor-made suit and the young couple had gone off to the depot in the livery stable carriage, accompanied by a hilarious group of young people, including Avery, and the last guest had gone, and Susie had taken the little girls off to bed, practically asleep on their feet, and Mrs. Calhoun had gone upstairs and Jonathan had gone out to the kitchen to see what he could find to eat, she sank happily down on one of the tufted sofas and stretched her tired feet in front of her.

"Wasn't it lovely, Henry?" she said. "It was a beautiful wedding, wasn't it, darling, and everything went off like clockwork. Elizabeth was pleased, she really was. She thanked us very sweetly, didn't you think so?"

"She ought to have been pleased, you've nearly worked yourself to death over it."

"Oh, no, I've enjoyed it, it's been fun, really. I know it has cost us a lot. We can use some of the money from the sale of the land if it is too bad," she added anxiously.

"No we won't," Henry said firmly. "That money is going to be invested. I can manage the wedding all right. But you know what, sugar, I say let's encourage the little girls to run off and get married when they grow up."

"Oh, Henry, aren't you ashamed of yourself," Janie said, laughing. "I think it is wonderful to look forward to two more weddings. At intervals, of course."

"Lo-o-o-n-g intervals," Henry said, taking off his white tie and opening the high collar.

2

Young Avery Calhoun lifted his valise onto the back platform of the streetcar and swung himself up after it. He was lucky. The first car coming to the depot after his train got in was marked *Greenway*, which meant that it went by Fairview. Stowing the valise under the seat, he settled himself for the ride. He was taking the family by surprise; they expected him tomorrow, not today. There would be explanations, and he did not know himself exactly why, that morning, he had suddenly decided to come home on the noonday train. He was still in the mood of exaltation which had filled him ever since his talk with the Bishop yesterday. He had wanted to get away from the University, from his roommate and his friends and his classes; to think, to plan and to dream. He wanted, he realized, to tell his mother about his plans. He had been so shy about this dream of his, so hesitant to mention it, feeling presumptuous at the thought that he might be one of those called by God to His special service, that he had kept his ambition locked in his own mind. It was certainly

237

time he was beginning to talk about it, with only two more months before his graduation, and everybody asking him what he was going to do when he left the University. Especially Pa, who wanted him to come onto the *Herald* staff, and if not that, to study to be a lawyer. He knew that he was going to be pressed to make a decision over this Easter holiday. Now that he had talked to the Bishop he felt prepared to announce his hopes. He wanted to tell Mama first, and he hoped she would be at home so he could talk to her before Pa got home from the office.

The motorman sounded his bell and started the slow climb up the hill to Main Street. The conductor collected Avery's nickel. Other passengers got on as the car rattled along Main and again slowed to a crawl as it pulled up the long, steep slope leading out of town. What used to be out of town, rather, it was certainly building up fast now. New houses were all around, with stretches of open country in between them. They passed the beginnings of a big house being put up further out than the others, and Avery grinned to himself. This was a part of the Fairview land Mama had sold last fall, and it was the Buford Joneses who were building there. He and Pa had laughed about it, and had felt sorry for Mama at the same time, because she really minded. It was bad enough to have sold the land, she said, but to have old Jiminy Jones' grandson build on it was more than she could stand. Mama never could forget old Jiminy, and you could hardly blame her. Avery remembered the old man when he was a little boy and Mama would take him to the marketplace with her, a dirty old man with a tobacco-stained white beard and a high cracked voice.

"Jiminy cricket, Miss Janie," he would say, "that's a fine little man you got there with you." And he would give Avery an apple or a pear or a bunch of grapes, and Mama would say "Thank you very much, Mr. Jones, that's real kind of you," and take the fruit away from Avery, because old Jiminy's hands were so dirty that everything he touched had to be washed or peeled or cooked before Mama would let you eat it.

When Jiminy died it was discovered that he had more money than most people in town had. He had never known what to do with money and so, over the untold years he had run the stall in the marketplace, he had just put it in the bank and left it there. His son Robert, who always lived out on the farm in Nelson County, was like his father, but his grandson, Buford, was different. Buford knew what to do with money. He put it to work; he invested his own and other people's money and now he had a very prosperous brokerage firm in town, and had gone heavily into the opening up of the new coalfields in West Virginia, which was proving a fine investment for a good many of the businessmen of the community. Buford Jones was rich, richer than anybody in town, probably, except Ranny Boyd.

The car rattled on into the open country now. The only house that had been put up farther out than the Jones' new place was "Young Ranny" Boyd's. "Young Ranny" was in his middle forties, but as he was obviously younger than his father he was still given that appellation. He had built on the opposite side of the road, a fashionable new white frame house with a veranda running around three sides and gables and turrets and cupolas and a lot of elaborately carved fretwork. Very elegant, probably, but not as nice as the old, solidly built brick houses with columned porches.

Avery rang the bell as they approached the Fairview entrance, and the car ground to a noisy stop. With his valise in his hand he walked slowly up the driveway. There had been a time when he had thought this cedar-lined avenue, marked morning and afternoon by the straight black shadows of the trees, was interminably long, stretching endlessly from the road to the house, a breathless run for short legs. Now the legs were long and the distance seemed short. Some of the avenue had been taken away when the road was widened, of course, but the real difference in perspective, he knew, lay in the difference between the eyes of a child and the eyes of a man. "When I became a man I put away childish things," he quoted to himself, and his heart lifted with joy at the thought that the time had now really come for him to put away childish things.

He saw no one when he entered the house and went upstairs. Leaving his valise in his room, he crossed the hall to his mother's room, tiptoeing in case she should be asleep. He was disappointed to find no one there. He went downstairs and, hearing sounds in the back yard, he went out there to find the little girls, who swarmed over him with squeals of joy. Henrietta wrapped herself around his right leg and he had to pull her loose to kiss her. He fished from his pocket the small paper bags filled with a mixture of lemon and peppermint drops which he always brought them when he came home, and in the relative quiet which descended upon them he went into the kitchen to greet Baizy, who was gratifyingly glad to see him.

"Where's Mama?" he asked.

"She gone in town to church, Mist' Avery." Avery had not quite got used to being called mister by Baizy. "Good Friday, it is." Of course, Avery had forgotten, in his own preoccupation.

Baizy was getting old. She was almost thin; the voluminous bosom and broad hips were gone, her face sagged. She ought to let Mama get someone to help her in the kitchen but she wouldn't do it. Susie could do the laundry and act as the children's nurse; Ella could clean the house and wait on the table, but nobody could cook but Baizy. He knew it would be that way as long as she could stand on her two feet.

"How are Lucy and the children?" he asked politely.

"They's fine, Mist' Avery, just fine."

"How many children has she got now?"

Baizy laughed. "She just got seven, she ain't had any mo' in the last few years. She got fo' boys and three gals. And you know sump'n, Mist' Avery." Diffident pride lighted up the old face. "Them chillun goes to school, they kin read and write real good. They got schools for cullud chillun now."

"Of course," Avery said. "They've got public schools for everybody now, and everybody is supposed to go to school."

He wandered restlessly around the kitchen. "You hongry, Mist' Avery?" Baizy asked.

"Well, not to say really hungry, but open to suggestion. What have you got?"

Baizy went to the cake box and lifted out a chocolate layer cake. "What you think about this?"

"I think it couldn't be better."

He was eating the cake when he heard the carriage coming up the driveway. It paused for a moment at the front steps and then came around the house on its way to the stable. Through the window Avery could see Amos in the still-new blue livery which had been bought for Elizabeth's wedding. As he crammed the last morsel of cake into his mouth his mother hurried into the kitchen. He was filled with the surge

240

of deep affection he always felt when he saw her, so pretty, so warm and loving. She was dressed to kill, in her favorite shade of blue silk, ruffled, beribboned and draped, and a blue velvet hat with ostrich tips curling around her face. Long black kid gloves covered the tight sleeves almost up to the point where they burst into leg o' mutton fullness.

"Precious," she said, "Susie just told me you were here. What on earth—why didn't you let us know? How did you get out here?"

Avery laughed and put his arms around her. "I am a big boy now, Mama. I came on the streetcar."

"I am so glad to see you, honey. You look well, and I do believe, Avery, that you are still growing. You look taller and taller all the time, and oh, darling, you are so handsome. Isn't he beautiful, Baizy?"

"He sho' is," said Baizy.

"My dears," Avery protested, "you must learn to control yourselves. Suppose you said something like that before any of my colleagues at the University, my life would be ruined."

"We've got better sense," Janie said, "but we can say it to each other. Come on, let's go in the house and talk. I want to hear about everything."

They went down the long corridor and through the door into the front hall. Janie stopped at the pier table to take off her hat, lifting the long hatpins out of it carefully. She smoothed her piled-up, still shining hair in front of the mirror, and then they went into the library, Janie keeping up a running fire of questions: Had the train been on time? Had he come straight out from town? He hadn't seen Henry? Had he seen the children? How long could he stay? Were any of his friends going to visit him over the Easter recess? How did he happen to come today when he had said he could not leave the University until tomorrow?

"Well, I just decided to this morning. I only missed one class, it didn't make much difference. I wanted to come, so I just decided to. Mama—" She had sat down in one of the armchairs by the fireplace. Avery lifted a straight chair and sat down beside her, "Mama, I've got something to tell you."

A startled expression came over his mother's face. "Oh, Avery," she said, "don't tell me you are going to get married too."

This was so remote from anything in his mind that Avery

241

himself was startled. "For heaven's sake, Mama, what an idea. What put that into your head? Of course I am not getting married."

"Well, thank goodness. Elizabeth's marriage was enough of a shock, it would have been just too much for you to do it too right now. All right, darling, go on."

She smiled at him sweetly, interested as always in what he had to say. Avery felt deflated. For a moment his immense piece of news seemed to have shrunken.

"It's just that I have decided—I know what I want to do when I graduate from the University."

"Oh, I'm so glad, honey. I certainly am glad. I knew you would have to make up your mind soon, but I didn't want to say anything until you did. Is it the paper, or do you want to be a lawyer?"

"No. No, it's not either one." He found that he could not sit still. He rose and stood looking down at his mother. "Mama, I am going into the Church, into the ministry. I am going to be a minister." Triumph was in his voice, and now the words came in a rush. "I have always wanted to, all my life, more than anything else. It's in the blood, I reckon, all those generations of Calhoun ministers. But I didn't know, I wasn't sure—" He hesitated. It was hard for him to express in words his veneration for the high calling he was choosing, the sense of his own inadequacies, his feeling of presumption in aspiring to the ministry. "Well, I didn't know whether they would want me, whether I could measure up to it. But yesterday I talked to the Bishop. He confirmed a class at Christ Church last Sunday and stayed in Charlottesville for a while. I wanted to talk to him, I thought this was my chance to find out. I asked Dr. Stanard to arrange it and he did. We had the most wonderful talk, I don't know how long, nearly all afternoon, I reckon. He's a grand old man, Mama, a saint, one of the chosen. I can't tell you how splendid it was to talk to somebody like that. He asked me all sorts of questions, we talked and talked. I've been—well, I've been in the clouds ever since. That's why I came home, I couldn't face Old Fuddledy and his Roman Civilization this morning, and I wanted to tell you right away. The Bishop said he thought I should go into the ministry. He said—" Avery stumbled over this, but he felt that his mother should know how encouraging the

242

Bishop had been, "he said that he thought they would be fortunate to have me in the Church."

The Bishop had, in fact, said a great deal more than that. "It is a rare pleasure," he said, "to meet a young man who so evidently has a vocation to the ministry and who combines dedication to the service of God with a—personality, shall I say, which I feel sure will guarantee spiritual leadership of a high order. You ask my advice and I say unhesitatingly that you belong in the Church, and the Church is fortunate to have you."

Avery had been so intent on his news and on the joy the Bishop's words had given him that he had not noticed his mother's reaction. Now, waiting for her to reply, he was surprised to find her looking at him silently, the blue eyes troubled, the small face drained of the affection, the understanding, the gentle humor which he had always known from her.

"Aren't you pleased, Mama?" he asked as she continued to say nothing. "I thought you would be pleased."

"I—I am surprised, Avery, very much surprised."

"I shouldn't think you would be. The Calhoun men have been ministers for generations. Grandmother says that even my father wanted to be, though in the end he didn't."

"They—they were different," Mama said, as if she was speaking with difficulty. Then with a rush, "Oh, Avery, you are so different from them, from your father and grandfather. You are outgoing and friendly and gay and happy, I just can't see you in the ministry."

This was a point of view which meant nothing to Avery. He struggled to express his feelings. "I can think of no happier calling," he said, "than to take the word of God to my fellow men."

He stood looking down at her, puzzled and hurt. He had not expected Pa to like his decision, but it had not occurred to him that Mama would not. He sensed that she was going through an inner struggle, but it was over in a few moments. She rose and came to him.

"If that is the way you feel about it, darling," she said, "of course, of course you must do it. If that is where your happiness lies I wouldn't have you do anything else."

She reached up and kissed him, and he put his arms

243

around her. They stood quietly, but for the first time in his life Avery felt a barrier between them. He spoke of something that troubled him.

"Pa won't like it."

"He will be disappointed, he hoped you would come on the paper."

"It will mean three more years before I can earn anything, before I can make a living, and there will be expenses, of course. Do you think we can manage, will Pa mind?"

She pushed away from him and now the warmth had returned to her face.

"Oh darling, of course not, you know he won't mind. It would have been the same if you studied law, and he was prepared for that. The paper is doing real well now, and Pa is always generous. You know that. Besides, I have some money of my own now, and what's mine is yours, darling. Always." She paused. "We'll tell Pa tonight, but not until after supper."

"All right," Avery said. The need to be alone came over him again. "You'd better go and take your nap. I am going for a walk."

He went out the front door and stood on the porch for a moment, undecided. He did not know where the children were, and he could not face them now. There was silence in the back yard, and he thought it probable that Susie had taken them upstairs to dress for the afternoon, but he was not going to take a chance on it. He avoided the back yard by circling around the old copper beech, skirting the flower garden and the cutting garden, and climbing the fence into the orchard. Spring was late that year and the trees were just coming to life. Avery walked down the long, straight aisles of the budding fruit trees, climbed the fence into the West Field and crossed it to the creek, making its busy, noisy way down the hill to the distant river. He followed the creek up the hill. This was his favorite walk. His mother had brought him here many times when he was a small boy, and had told him how as a child she used to come here with her brother Peyton, who had died so young and so tragically because he was taken ill when the Wilderness fighting was going on and all the doctors were desperately working against the tide of wounded and dying men, so that no one could be found to minister to Peyton or tell them what was wrong with him.

As he climbed the hill Avery was conscious of the chattering stream, the new life of the woods, the smell of pine needles warmed by the sun, but his thoughts were concentrated upon his talk with his mother. Mama was not pleased at his decision to go into the ministry. He had not expected this and it hurt him. It was a thing so greatly desired by himself, so splendid a way of life, so noble a calling, that he could think of no basis for disapproval. What did she want for him? Wealth, power? Surely not, Mama was not grasping or greedy, but if not, what?"

He came to the place where the water purled out of the rocks and tumbled down to join the stream, and stood for a few moments watching and listening to the rush of clear, cold water. He came to the place where the trailing arbutus grew and getting down on his knees he parted the rusty leaves and found, as he knew he would find, the pale, fragile beauty of the blossoms. He buried his head in them and inhaled the fragrance, then closed the leaves back over the blossoms and went on to the top of the hill, to the topmost rock, and stood there looking out over the countryside, high above it, forests and fields and hills, the roofs and chimneys of Fairview through the trees, the long gash of the road, broken now by the poles of the streetcar line, the blue mountains to the west, dark against the sunset sky. Old mountains, gentle, beloved mountains, cradling, serene, weathered and softened by time. Standing there on the rock-tipped hilltop in the golden glory of the sinking sun, remote, alone and yet never alone, the kingdoms of the spirit lay spread out before him, God in His infinitude, man in the likeness of God. He closed his eyes and gave himself up to the wave of exaltation that swept over him, forgetting his mother, forgetting even the Bishop and his words. It was this, and not the words of the Bishop, that made him know where his life lay, this communion with God, this oneness with all God's creation, this joy that welled up in him like the waters of the spring coming through the rocks. "Behold upon the mountains the feet of Him that bringeth good tidings, that publisheth peace," he quoted to himself.

Presently he started down the hill in the early twilight. Darkness had settled over the world by the time he reached the yard and saw the lamplight shining through the windows of Fairview.

3

Janie was deeply shaken by Avery's announcement. After the first shock she tried not to let him see it, but she knew that he had seen, and that for the first time a shadow had fallen over the complete oneness of understanding and affection which had always been the basis of their relationship. She must try to make it up to him. Her spirit was still in rebellion, however; to save her life she could not accept the picture of Avery in the black clerical garb or the dour clerical aspect that she associated with the ministry. It was so different a life from what she had wanted for him. That brought her up sharply. What had she wanted, what did she want, for this beloved son? Wealth, importance, fame? Yes, she would like these things for him, but as accompaniments, not as the prime objectives of his life. What did she wish for him above everything else? The answer to that was clear. Happiness. She wanted him to have a happy life. But happiness was a result, not a cause. What was the basis of happiness? A satisfying profession, a happy marriage to a pretty girl of good family, charming children, a successful career bringing recognition and a measure of material prosperity, many, many friends. These were the items making up the picture, heretofore unformed, of life as she would wish it for Avery.

But were these things not possible in the ministry? It was days before she got around to asking herself that question, days of inner probing and unaccustomed introspection. Henry had taken the news quietly. He was polite about it, but Janie knew he was not only disappointed at Avery's decision, he was repelled by it. Henry was a good man, a good, kind man, but he was not religious. He accepted God as the ruler of the universe without giving the matter much thought. He went to church on Sundays because that was part of the pattern of life he lived by, but Janie knew that neither church nor the concept of God had ever touched him deeply nor penetrated into his inner life. All men of religion, call them ministers, rectors, pastors, preachers or priests, were "parsons" to him, living in a world apart, viewed with respect slightly tinged with a certain skeptical scorn. The idea that a handsome, spirited young man, possessing intelligence and charm, holding his future in the hollow of his hand, would deliberately choose to leave the world of men and affairs and dwell in that separate realm was incomprehensible to him.

Henry had always made a point, however, of not interfering in the lives of his stepchildren. He had tried to be helpful, a strong staff to lean upon, as counselor and friend, and he held on to that role now, as Janie had known he would. If young Avery Calhoun, having reached the age of twenty-one, standing on his own feet and able to make his own decisions, wanted to be a parson, and if that decision met with his mother's approval, he would do what he could to help him on his way.

The decision did not meet with Janie's approval, but she knew, with a sure knowledge that swept aside her inner revolt, that this was a thing in which she must not interfere. This was Avery's life, a reaching out of his deepest self; she would only lose him if she did not go with him along his chosen way. So the necessary steps were taken, consultations held, letters written, application made for admission to the Seminary the following autumn. When Avery went back to the University he glowed with a warmth of happiness which penetrated even the incomprehension of his family.

After he had gone Janie found herself deeply troubled, not, now that she had accepted the decision, so much by it as by her reaction to it. Until this time she had lived by her instincts and her code, instincts ingrained in her, no doubt, by generations of adherence to the code. She had accepted, without question, the edicts of her time, her place, her family; the existence of God, the moralities of her forebears, their beliefs, attitudes, customs. Now for the first time in her life she felt the need to probe, to analyze, to question. What were the values she lived by? What had she made out of the raw material of her life? What kind of person was she, what kind of mother was she? You are a middle-aged woman, Janie Darby, she told herself. You've got grown children, and the children seem to be more mature than you are. They seem to know exactly what they want out of life. They have taken you by surprise. You seem to know very little about them and very little about yourself; you'd better sit down and do some thinking.

The house was quiet now, with Elizabeth living in town, Avery back at the University, Henry at the news office all day,

Jonathan and Jane at school until the early afternoon, and Henrietta, although often audible, usually occupied with Susie and the puppy in the yard or the kitchen, or with Amos and the pony in the stable. Sitting in the rocking chair at the sunny window of her big bedroom, mending, darning, making small garments for the little girls, Janie had uninterrupted hours for thought.

It was then that she asked herself the question: Was the life she had visualized for Avery the best of all possible lives, and if it was, if it at least set up the framework for a good life, could he not attain it within the ministry? Could he not follow his own high calling and at the same time achieve the human satisfactions and joys to which her heart clung? Why did she always think of the ministry as a muted, gray world, solemn and cold, set apart by righteousness from ordinary humanity? She remembered the old, old Bishop of her childhood, a noble and beloved old man, his shaking hand upon her bowed young head when she was confirmed, his old voice murmuring the wonderful words, "Defend, O Lord, this Thy child with Thy heavenly grace. . . ." She thought of the present Bishop, old himself now, son of one of the state's outstanding families, on his way to becoming a legend because of his charm, gentle humor and godliness. The other clergymen she had known came to her mind, beginning with Henry Harrison, who had come through the Yankee lines to bury Grandpa and had refused to pray for the President of the United States the Sunday after the surrender. The Reverend Mr. Arthur Hammond had been kind and cordial to her during the few years when she had gone to the Presbyterian Church with Avery, and a tower of strength at the time of Avery's death. The present rector of St. John's, Dr. Owlsley Davis, was a man of fire and eloquence. He had a charming wife and two pretty daughters, and they had made the rectory a center of pleasant activity for the young people of the congregation. There was nothing gray and dour about these men, nothing detached and cut off. They were good men full of good works, leading normal and one might suppose happy lives. Why, then, did she have this feeling about the ministry? It was the Calhouns, of course. The shadow of the Calhouns. Avery and the Reverend Mr. Strachan Calhoun seen, known, lived with—grandfather and great grandfather for generations back, unseen but felt, going before the family like the Biblical pillar of cloud. These were good men too; as Mrs. Calhoun had said, good and godly men, but they did live in a cold gray world, they did worship a harsh and vengeful God. And Avery was a Calhoun. The Calhoun blood was strong in his veins, as witness his startling likeness to his father. But Avery was not like that, he was different.

The fear of the Calhouns and the reality of Avery began a struggle in Janie's mind. I have always been so glad that he was different, that he was warm and friendly and happy. Until he said he wanted to go into the ministry I never thought of his being like the Calhouns, except to be pleased that he had inherited his father's good looks. And now here we are, right where his father was before him, wanting to get into the ministry. But this Avery is really different. I couldn't have been mistaken all his life. He is a different kind of person, he has a different kind of religion. Certainly nothing, not the theological seminary nor holy orders nor the work of the ministry could change his basic character and temperament. Perhaps all the stern righteousness of a long line of Calhouns had been leading up to this, this gentle flowering of the spirit, this glad outpouring of warmth and light. "I can think of no happier calling," Avery had said.

Janie seized upon the statement. Happy. He could serve God happily, lovingly, gaily, not conscience-driven but willing, without sternness or self-righteousness. In this, and perhaps in this only, lay his happiness. Perhaps even for his father, if he had followed his conscience into the ministry, he would have found there a happiness he never knew.

Having laid the ghost of the Calhouns, Janie turned to another question. God obviously meant something to Avery that He did not mean to most people, certainly not to his mother. What did He mean to Avery that made him long passionately to live his life to the glory of God, that made him glow with an inner light at the prospect of taking the word of God to his fellow men?

It was to Janie a staggering experience to glimpse the inner world in which Avery must have dwelt as he progressed, under her ardent eyes, from childhood to young manhood. To realize what spiritual hunger he must have felt to lead him to say of the Bishop, "I can't tell you how splendid it was to talk to someone like that." The old feeling of guilt, the sense of having failed the first Avery by lack of understanding and sympathy was now renewed. Had she failed the second Avery in the same way, by lack of understanding of his deep spiritual needs? What kind of spiritual life did she herself have, that she should have found it so difficult with the father, and now with the son, to enter into the inner realm of being which to them was so important? What did God mean to her?

To answer that question Janie entered upon a mental pilgrimage which absorbed her thoughts for weeks during that sunny spring. She went on with her normal life, getting the children off to school in the morning, having breakfast with Henry, ordering the meals, supervising the servants, marketing, mending and sewing, working in the garden, going in town to parties, or to pay calls. It was a gay season, a beautiful spring, and there was a burst of entertaining after Lent and the Easter holidays.

Through all these activities and gaieties Janie, who usually floated along with the interests and pleasures of the moment, or coped with problems as they arose, found herself wandering in unaccustomed ways of thought. She returned constantly to the question: What did God mean to Avery that He did not mean to her and what did God mean to her?

24

Palm leaf fans rustled like leaves in a summer breeze. It was hot, even in the lofty dimness of St. John's Church. June sunshine flooded through the rich colors of the Transfiguration of Christ over the altar; His white robe was luminous. The candles on the altar burned without a flicker, there was not a breath of air stirring. People entered the church in a steady stream, moving sedately down the aisles, taking their places in the pews, bending their heads in silent prayer, straightening up, looking around the church, picking up the palm leaf fans.

Janie, too scared to feel the heat, sat stiffly at her end of the pew. Jonathan, home for the summer from the Episcopal High School, sat next to her and then Jane, in her ruffled white dotted swiss dress and white "lingerie" hat with pink ribbons. Henrietta sat next to her father at the other end. The children were excited. Avery, graduated from the Seminary and newly ordained, was going to preach his first sermon; at least his first here in his own town, in his own church, among his own people. The Reverend Murrell Anderson, rector of St. John's, had invited him, proud of this new recruit from his parish. Janie wished he had not done so. She wished that he had at least waited until Avery was used to preaching sermons. To be sure the Bishop had told her at graduation that her son had a splendid "pulpit personality," and certainly she, who knew him so well, should have confidence in his abilities.

All the same, he was too young and inexperienced to be preaching sermons and anyhow he was Avery and she was scared.

She felt a wave of impatience at her men. Why must they push themselves into positions of public prominence, where she must suffer agonies of nervousness for them, instead of going on with their private lives like most men? Henry had decided to go into politics. He was running for the State legislature against the incumbent delegate, a man named Marsh who lived somewhere out in the county. The primary would take place in July; Henry had been campaigning through the county for several weeks. Last week there had been a rally here in town, at Calisthenics Hall, and Janie had gone. Ladies didn't do much in politics, of course, but the wife of a candidate in his own town was expected to put in an appearance. Henry would have been hurt if she had not. She had suffered this same nervousness then, but she needn't have. Henry was good. He used his worst grammar and the crowd loved it. He walked up and down the platform and waved his arms and joked and cajoled and argued. People said he was going to get the nomination. This was different. A political speech was a rough and ready thing, but a sermon . . . And anyhow, this was Avery. A baby, really, in spite of the height and breadth of him.

The organ prelude died out and the congregation bowed its collective head at the sound of Dr. Anderson's voice from the back of the church: "May we worship the Father in spirit and in truth, for the Father seeketh such to worship Him."

The organ and the voices of the choir soared in the processional hymn, the congregation stood up, the choir passed down the center aisle, and Janie longed to turn around and watch Avery as he walked by Mul Anderson's side. As it was, she saw only his back until he reached the chancel and turned. In his black clerical robe, the white surplice, the green stole accenting the blackness of his hair, he was as striking a figure as she had ever seen. He was beautiful; she had always thought he was beautiful, but up there in the chancel, against the background of vested choir, altar, stained glass, organ music and the solemn, sonorous words of the service, there was a quality about him which transcended mere physical handsomeness, a richness and radiance that slowly penetrated the nervous tension, the self-consciousness gripping her. It reached her heart and brought tears to her eyes. I am blessed, she thought. God has been good to me in giving me such a son; what have I done to deserve it?

Now the sermon hymn was finished and Avery was in the pulpit. He raised both arms to give the invocation; the wide sleeves of his surplice spread out like white wings along his upstretched arms. His voice was resonant, carrying clearly but not loud: "Let the words of our mouths and the meditations of our hearts be always acceptable in Thy sight, O Lord, our strength and our redeemer."

Avery had chosen for his text the fourth verse of the Ninety-first Psalm: "He shall cover thee with his feathers, and under his wings shalt thou trust; his truth shall be thy shield and buckler."

As he talked Janie had the curious sensation that this was a stranger standing in the pulpit, this tall young man in the white robe and the green stole, his dark head outlined against the light from the stained glass window almost as if an aura surrounded it. This could not be her son, the baby she had carried in her arms, the boy she had loved and guided and taught as he grew to manhood. He did not read his sermon, he preached it, simply, earnestly, eloquently, sometimes leaning forward in the pulpit as if to draw closer to the congregation, sometimes spreading his arms in an all-embracing gesture, his face glowing with the meaning of what he was saying, his voice vibrant. It was a young sermon, it made no pronouncements, it laid down no laws. It was quite simply a plea for faith, for trust in God. The simile of the hen gathering her chicks under her feathers, guarding them with her wings, the assurance of security to be found under the protection of God; the strength and reality of God's truth, that the soul of man was a spark from the Soul of God, born for eternal life; the mercy of God as the loving Father of all mankind, these were the points he made. A simple sermon, moving her to the depths of her consciousness. Although Avery did not look at her once, Janie felt that every word was aimed directly at her. Each word sank into her consciousness as a pebble sinks into a still pool, sending ripples through her whole being. Almost subconsciously she realized that the church was very quiet, most of the palm leaf fans were still

253

now. Avery finished his sermon, paused, said: "God be merciful unto us, and bless us; God make his face to shine upon us, in our goings out and comings in. Amen."

Janie went through the rest of the service in a state of happy exaltation. She felt at peace, reconciled to God and man, happy with a joy that transcended ordinary happiness. The offertory anthem, the final prayers and benediction, the recessional hymn, all flowed past her without penetrating her conscious mind. When the choir had passed out and Mr. Anderson's voice came from the rear of the church: "In leaving Thy house, O Lord, may we not leave Thy presence," Janie moved with the rest of the congregation. The children filed out of the pew sedately. Henry stood aside in the aisle to let her go first; he smiled and squeezed her hand, and she knew he was congratulating her because Avery had done so well. All along their slow progress down the aisle people were doing that. They leaned around each other to congratulate her. "He was wonderful, honey." "You should be proud, Miss Janie." "He has a gift, my dear Janie, he certainly has a gift." Janie smiled at them and thanked them. She appreciated their praise, she was glad to hear it, but her own heart was telling her more about Avery than they could say.

Avery and the rector, still in their vestments, were standing in the vestibule shaking hands with the congregation as they filed out. Progress was slow, everybody wanted to speak to Avery. Janie slipped out of the line as they approached and stood in a corner of the vestibule. Sara Anne came over to her and hugged her.

"Darling," she said, "I can hardly keep from crying, he is so wonderful."

Sara Anne looked very pretty in a blue silk dress that Janie had given her. Carey was with her and little Sara Anne, their one child, finally and triumphantly produced after repeated miscarriages and stillbirths. She was a pretty child, a year younger than Jonathan, blond like her father, lacking her mother's vivacity. Janie returned Sara Anne's hug. They clung to each other for a moment and Janie rejoiced as always, in this dearest of all friends.

When the last of the congregation had filed out and the vestibule was almost empty, Janie went over to where Avery was standing and took his arm. She did not speak, words always deserted her in the presence of strong emotion. She squeezed his arm and he smiled down at her, and she knew that words were not necessary.

2

Avery had come home only that morning. He was to have two weeks of vacation and then begin his first assignment. Janie had had no time to talk to him. She waited until the big Sunday dinner was finished, and the children had gone out in the yard to play. Henry settled himself in the library, surrounded by Sunday papers. He had gone by the Arlington Hotel to pick them up after church, as he always did. The *Herald* was not published on Monday mornings, so he had no reason to go to the office, and he spent Sunday afternoons reading newspapers as avidly as if he had not seen one for a week. He scattered them all around the library until, as Janie complained, you had to wade through newspapers to get into the room.

"On Sundays you make the library look just like your office," she had said to him once. Henry had grinned wickedly at her and replied: "That's what I want to do. You won't let me go to the office on Sunday so I just bring the office here."

Janie and Avery went into the back parlor. The room was cool and dim. The windows had been closed and the shades pulled down against the morning sun. Now the sun had passed over to the other side of the house. Janie raised the shades and opened the door onto the side porch, a miniature replica of the front porch with its fluted white columns and Palladian gables. When the house had first been built, many years ago, by great-great Grandfather Marshall Meade, newly come to the wilds of this Piedmont country from the old settlements of the Tidewater, there had been a corresponding porch on the western side, leading off the dining room and giving access to the kitchen path. That had been taken off by Grandpa, before Janie was born, when he added the back hall to the house and built the long corridor connecting the kitchen with the house.

Janie stood for a moment at the open door, looking down the path to the rose garden. The air was sweet with warm summer smells. The spicy fragrance of pinks in the perennial borders stood out clearly against the composite sweetness of roses, sun-warmed box hedges, magnolia blossoms and the

Concord grapes hanging in heavy purple clusters from the arbor. The two things that had always brought beauty close to Janie were the church services and the garden. Today, with Avery here and with the exaltation of his sermon still with her, they seemed fused into one.

Avery came over to the door and put his arm around her; they stood together looking down the garden path. Janie struggled with words to express her feelings.

"Avery, you—I thought your sermon this morning was wonderful. I was very proud of you."

"Thank you, Mother." He had recently taken to calling her mother, and she liked it.

They stood in silence for a few moments, then Janie turned away from the door. "Tell me, honey, about your plans. All I know is that you are going to be in New York."

"Yes, I have been invited to St. Mark's, in New York."

"That's nice," Janie said placidly. "It would be nicer if you were going somewhere in the South, but New York is not so terribly far from home, and it will be nice to have Emily there, she has always been fond of you, and Jerome and that snippy little Mathilda, though I don't expect she will contribute much to your pleasure."

Avery laughed and ran his hand through his thick, dark hair. "Darling," he said, "I don't expect I will be seeing much of Aunt Emily and the cousins, I won't be moving in their circles. My parish is in lower Manhattan, on the East Side in the slums, where the immigrants live."

"Oh, Avery," Janie cried, horrified. She remembered that on one of her rare trips to New York—she had been there only three times in her life—she had been taken through one of the slum districts as a sight she should see. "Those awful people. The dirt and the smells. Darling, why? Why did they do that to you? Couldn't the Bishop have prevented it?"

"I asked the Bishop for it, Mother."

"You asked for it?" Janie was incredulous. "Why in the world—Avery, I just don't understand you."

He had been moving restlessly around the room, now he came and stood in front of her chair.

"Listen, Mother. You belong to a missionary circle at the church, don't you?"

"Yes."

"You ladies sew for the heathen, and have bazaars and raise money for the missions, don't you?"

"Yes, of course."

"Why do you do it?"

"Why?" Janie searched her mind. "Well, it's a worthy cause."

"Yes, but what is the cause?"

"Why, to carry the blessings of the Christian religion to the benighted people who worship heathen gods. To maintain the missions and improve the conditions of the people."

"Exactly, to take the word of God, as brought to mankind by Jesus Christ, to the people of the world and to try to help them to improve the conditions under which they live. Has it ever occurred to any of you to look around you and see how many people in your own country, right here in your own town, need help and encouragement and the word of God brought to them?"

"Of course it has, Avery," Janie said indignantly. "We take baskets to the poor every Thanksgiving and Christmas, and the children's mite boxes at Easter go to buy clothes for poor children, and when anybody is sick we try to help."

Avery made a curious little gesture, as if brushing aside these things. "Yes, I know, dear. It is a little hard for a family to live on help at Thanksgiving and Christmas and Easter, but of course it helps. I am talking about something a little more—fundamental." He seemed to be struggling for words. "This country has some of the richest people in the world—millionaires, huge fortunes, growing up overnight all through the North and Middle West—and it has some of the poorest, great areas of desperate poverty, the Negroes of the South, the immigrants of the North. When you were in New York the Tysons took you on a trip through the slums as a sight to see, something to look at, like Grant's Tomb or the Statue of Liberty. It would never occur to the Tysons that they had any responsibility for the people in those slums."

Janie felt puzzled and, to her surprise, antagonistic. "Well, have they, Avery?"

Again Avery ran his hand through his hair. It was a gesture with which she was becoming familiar; he used it whenever he was talking earnestly, trying to explain or communicate an idea. "Perhaps not," he said. "Who am I to judge? There are

257

some sayings of Jesus that seem to me to apply, but then, who among us lives up to the sayings of Jesus? It's a case of 'Am I my brother's keeper?' Perhaps not. Perhaps the Tysons have no responsibility toward the poor and the suffering, but there is one thing I do know, Mother, and that is that I, as a minister of the Church, do have a responsibility toward those people."

Shrill squeals came from the back yard. Through the window Janie could see Jonathan on his horse, with Henrietta perched in front of him. He was holding her carefully. Jane followed behind on the pony. They were probably going to ride up the hill to the spring.

Avery paid no attention to them. "I could have looked for a nice parish church in a nice Southern town," he went on. "Or I could have asked for an assignment in the foreign missionary field. I chose to ask for a mission here in our own country, among the poor, the downtrodden, the sore of heart —you remember what the State of Liberty says,—who come flocking to our shores from all the countries of Europe, hoping to find the Promised Land. Some of them find it, there are infinite opportunities in this country; others will in future generations, but for most of them it is a cruel disillusionment. You saw what it was like. They need help, dear. I won't stay there always, you know, but that is where I want to begin, among the poor and the suffering. It was to them that Jesus spoke first of all, you know."

There was silence in the room for a few moments. Janie found it hard to speak. "Oh, darling," she said finally, "of course you are right. It is just that I can't live up to you, Avery, you are too good for me."

He laughed at her, and leaned over to stroke her cheek with a gentle finger. Then he became serious. "You mustn't say things like that, honey. You have always had an exaggerated opinion of my qualities. It makes me feel foolish."

"But you are good, Avery, you were born good. God gave you a quality of goodness that most people don't have. I have always known it."

"God gave me a desire to be good," he replied, "but goodness has to be cultivated. I hope I can learn true goodness."

"You see things I don't see," Janie said. "When they took me down into those crowded, dirty streets, with their noises and smells and awful-looking people, I just curled up inside and wanted to get away as fast as I could. It never occurred to me to want to help them. I—Once—" She hesitated. She had never spoken of this to anyone. "Your father once told me that I was a light-minded woman. I reckon he was right."

"No, my father was wrong," Avery said gravely. "He should have said a happy-hearted woman, and a happy heart is a gift of God. I hope you never lose it. Keep a happy and an understanding heart, and seeing eyes."

"You will have to help me to understand and to see, my dear. You will have to open my eyes to the things I have never even thought about."

Two weeks later Avery boarded the train for New York. Janie did not cry when she went to the depot to see him off. The facile tears that always came when she said goodbye to Avery had no place in the emotions she felt now. She knew that this tall young son of hers, fully grown to manhood, was leaving her as he had never left her before, taking on a man's work, going into places she could not follow, living through experiences she could not imagine, and yet she felt an even stronger bond between them than she had known in the happy years of his boyhood.

25

"It ain't decent," Henry said. "It just ain't decent."

"Was it any decenter when the Readjusters voted the illiterate Negroes by the thousands in every district in the state, to carry every election the way they wanted it to go? Government by illiteracy! Do you think that's decent?" John Waverley asked.

"No, that wasn't decent either."

The men around the long conference table stirred impatiently. The clock on the wall said ten minutes of five. They had been sitting there all afternoon, as they had sat many afternoons and mornings during the last months, saying the same things over and over again. Every man in the room knew where every other man stood on this issue; every man had expressed his views repeatedly. Opinions had become hardened and set by the long discussions and arguments. The committee had recessed for long periods to give the members time to think it over, only to meet again and say the same things. Most of them were unhappy about the whole situation, but none of them was willing to give up his own opinions, nor could any of them think of an acceptable way out of the dilemma. The old Senator, chairman of the committee, sat in silence at the end of the table, his handsome chin sunk into his collar. They were all deeply disappointed in him; they had expected leadership from him, and none was forthcoming. Leadership was what they needed.

"Now listen, Henry," said Stuart Gaines with a sort of

weary patience, "you've got to be sensible about this thing. Moral scruples are all very well, but we are dealing with a reality. For mo'an thirty years—thirty-five years—we have sat here in this state and watched the Republicans and the Readjusters controlling the illiterate Negro vote. You know that."

"Of course I know it."

"And you know that the only way we have been able to get around that and get control of our government again has been by using illegal methods of disfranchising the illiterate Negroes."

"So what you want to do now is to legalize the illegal disfranchising of illiterate Negroes," Henry said.

"Exactly!" exclaimed sandy-haired, scrappy little Thomas Burns, slapping the table with the palm of his hand. "That's exactly what I want to do."

"We have had the damnedest corruptest government in this state ever since the war," Gaines went on, "and we have been a party to it. We can't deny that. Oh yes, you can say the Democrats were fighting fire with fire, and we have been, but the result has been that we have substituted our form of corruption for theirs. Now we have been sent here by the people of Virginia to write a new constitution and take the corruption out of our government and make it possible for gentlemen to be gentlemen in their politics once more."

"And Henry Forbes Darby sits there and keeps saying that it ain't decent," said Thomas Burns.

"I keep saying that it ain't decent to disfranchise the illiterate Negroes and let the illiterate whites go on voting," Henry said. "I keep saying—disfranchise illiteracy, and then for God's sake educate the illiterate."

"Well, ain't we educating 'em?" asked Burns.

"No, we ain't," said Henry.

"We got schools for 'em."

"Yes, we got some schools for 'em, but we don't make 'em go to the schools. There are Negro boys and girls growing up all over this state who can't read or write, and in the western part of the state, in the mountains and the other side of the mountains, there are white boys and girls growing up who can't read and write, and everybody knows it and nobody does anything about it."

"And those white boys and girls in the west come from some of the best old Anglo-Saxon stock in the state, whose ancestors had the guts to come over here in the early days

261

and go out and open up the wilderness, and you want to put them on the same level as Negroes whose fathers were slaves and whose grandfathers, or at least great-grandfathers, were naked savages in Africa."

"Well, if they are such damn good old Anglo-Saxon stock," said Henry, his voice rough with irritation, "why in hell don't they get themselves educated?"

"Gentlemen," said the chairman.

"I'm sorry," said Henry.

"There is not one word in this suffrage article," said Colonel Martin Willoughby, "which provides for the disfranchisement of illiterate Negroes while at the same time allowing illiterate whites to vote. And Mr. Darby knows that."

Colonel Willoughby was an old man with white hair and mustache and an aquiline nose. He always wore wide-brimmed hats and black broadcloth frock coats in the winter, white linen suits in the summer. He looked like a storybook version of a Confederate colonel, and liked it. He spoke carefully, with perfect diction; his speeches were always models of stilted, complicated but correct English. Henry considered him pompous and conceited, but because of his years and his prominence in the state he commanded respect.

"There is not a word written into the article, sir," he replied, "because we have all got sense enough to know that under the Fourteenth Amendment to the United States Constitution no overt provision for discrimination would stand up, but nobody can deny that the 'understanding clause' is a device to make it possible for the election judges to allow illiterate white men to vote while refusing to allow illiterate Negroes to vote."

"Nobody is denying it," said Thomas Burns.

"Well, there it is," Henry said. "I will say, as I have said a dozen times, that if you will take out the understanding clause, and if you will provide that every voter must be able to write his own name and prepare his own ballot without help from anybody, I am with you. I will accept the poll tax and I will accept the requirement for the payment of a dollar a year in property taxes, but I am going right on saying that the understanding clause and the provision for election watchers to help illiterates prepare their ballots are hypocritical and an invitation to corruption, and it ain't decent."

Voices were raised all around the table. Some were there who agreed with Henry, in varying degrees. The majority did not. The old Senator at the end of the table looked up at the clock, then sat up straight and gaveled for silence.

"It is growing late," he said. "Do I hear a motion for adjournment?"

Henry and Stuart Gaines came out of the building together. "Another wasted day," Stuart said. "When is this thing going to end? Where are we going to find a solution?"

"I don't know," Henry said. "What we need is a leader. It is easy enough to write the rest of the constitution, but this suffrage question is a problem. We need a man with vision to select a course and eloquence to persuade us, another Jefferson or a Madison or Patrick Henry."

"The age of giants is past," Stuart said. "We have to get along with common clay. Goodnight."

He went on his way down the sloping park outside the capitol building. Henry stood still for a few minutes in the early twilight. The air was cold and fresh, it was good to breathe after the smoke-and-emotion-filled air of the conference room. He loved this view of Richmond at this hour of the evening, looking down on the lights of the city from the hill. He turned to look back at the stately columns of Thomas Jefferson's Capitol, a beautiful building dedicated to a beautiful concept of human freedom, degenerated now past recognition. What would the generation of giants have done with this problem? Jefferson, George Mason, Madison, Monroe; John Marshall, who believed in power; Patrick Henry, who hated power; John Randolph, who believed in justice but not equality, what would they have done about this question of Negro suffrage? Even Thomas Jefferson, the greatest of them all, who fought for manhood suffrage, fought and lost, even he thought of it in terms of white men only. For all his noble ideals and splendid affirmations he was dealing, they were all dealing with a cozy little agricultural world, Anglo-Saxon, isolated, protected on one side by vast stretches of ocean and on the other by vast stretches of untouched wilderness. What would they do with this new-century world, this great sprawling country, the industrialization, the swarming masses of foreigners coming in from God knew where, the almost indecent power of the vast aggregations of wealth in the North, the poverty of this defeated state and the still-green prejudices and passions of civil war? What would Thomas Jefferson do about Negro suffrage, the great liberal who owned slaves all the days of his life and, apparently, felt no sense of illogic when he wrote, and meant with his whole heart, "All men are created equal"?

Giants these men undoubtedly were, the brief and brilliant flowering of a transplated English civilization, come together at a momentous epoch and stamping their imprint not only upon their own time and their own people but influencing the thinking of men throughout the world for centuries. This was all true, but standing where he was, on the hill in front of the Capitol in Richmond, in the cold November twilight of the first year of the twentieth century, Henry Darby thought that they would have had a harder time dealing with the problems of their people now than they had then; harder to agree upon and proclaim the great ideals which united them in the last quarter of the eighteenth century. Perhaps not; perhaps he was only trying to justify the confusion of his own generation. Perhaps they would have had the wisdom to know how to deal with the Negro problem, what to do with the dead weight of Negro illiteracy that hung like a pall over the politics of the state.

Presently he went down the hill, crossed the street and started his walk to the hotel. This always seemed to him a cheerful hour, the evening homegoing, lights coming on all over the city, shining through the windows of the stores and houses he passed, people hurrying along the streets intent on reaching home after a day's work, carriages bringing ladies home from afternoon calls or tea parties. Tonight he felt no cheer. He was tired. This constitutional convention had dragged on for months now and showed no signs of ending. He had said that the rest of the constitution was easy to write, but as a matter of fact almost every article was befogged by bickering and dissension. The delegates to the convention found it hard to agree on anything, and most of them had a great deal to say. It was wearing on the body and the nerves, the unending flow of argument and discussion, the migrant living, back and forth between Richmond and home, between the paper and the convention. A feeling of depression at the stupidity of men and his own ineffectiveness had been growing on him recently.

Tonight he tried to throw it off. Janie and little Jane were waiting for him at the hotel and he didn't want to appear gloomy to them. He walked slowly along the streets, breathing in the cold air, looking into the shop windows, watching the people he passed. He felt better by the time he reached the hotel.

Jane threw herself into his arms when he went up to the suite he had taken for their visit. When he was there alone he kept a room at Mrs. Carson's boardinghouse on Grace Street.

"Oh, Papa," Jane cried. "I am so glad to see you. Can't we go down and have supper now right away? I want to start getting dressed for the ball."

"But honey—we aren't even invited until ten o'clock."

"Oh, I know. But I just can't wait. I thought if I started getting ready the time might go faster."

This was Jane's first ball, and she was filled with ecstatic excitement. She had been going to the dances of her own young crowd at home for a year now, but this was to be a big, formal ball, given under the auspices of the Society for the Preservation of Virginia Antiquities and attended by the rank and importance of Richmond. When Janie's cousins, the Christopher Peytons, had invited them to sit in their box on this occasion, and had said that young Jim Peyton would like to escort Jane, she had exploded into a storm of pleadings. Henry thought she was too young to go, and so did her mother, really, but neither of them was proof against little Jane's blandishments. Each thought the other spoiled her terribly. She was, Henry knew, the daughter of Janie's dreams, the daughter that Elizabeth had never been and Henrietta showed no promise of becoming. To him, she was a continuing miracle. He could understand Jonathan and Henrietta, but how a homely old codger like himself had managed to father a creature so enchanting as Jane was a source of grateful wonderment to him. Small, pretty, gay, brown-eyed and golden-haired, filled with beguiling ways and vast enthusiasms, she seemed to him irresistible.

"She's too young," he said when the invitation arrived.

"I know she is," Janie had agreed, "but oh, Henry, there is no time in her whole life when a girl enjoys things like she does when she is sixteen and just beginning to grow up."

"She ain't sixteen."

"Well, almost. And it comes on a Friday night so it won't interfere with school."

Of course in the end they had said she could, and she had been bubbling with happy anticipation ever since.

"You look tired, honey," Janie said to him now. "Has it been a bad day? Having supper early won't make the time pass a bit faster, Jane, so calm down. Your father ought to rest for a while."

"I ain't tired physically," Henry said, "I'm just tired of arguing. There ain't any sense in having supper this early, though. I'm going to sit down and read the paper."

"You and your paper," said Janie.

Jane went into her room to look, for the hundredth time, at her new ball gown. It was made of white China silk, as befitted so young a girl, trimmed with pink rosebuds. There was a ruffled taffeta petticoat to go under it, and a wreath of matching rosebuds to go into her hair. Janie's was the most elegant dress she had ever had, but Henry was not sure he liked it. He admitted that it was striking, but he preferred pretty dresses. This was black velvet. It was cut low in the back and the fullness of the skirt extended into a short train. A broad panel of white satin trimmed with passementerie extended from the square neckline in front all the way down to the hem of the dress.

"You ought to have a diamond necklace to wear with that," he said when he first saw it, and Janie had laughed.

"All right, give me one," she said.

"When we sell the rest of the Fairview land, perhaps I can," he said, and then was sorry he had said it, because the thought always saddened Janie.

Instead of a diamond necklace she wore a moonstone and diamond brooch on a silver chain, and in her hair the little diamond clasp that he had given her the Christmas the paper first began showing a healthy profit. She looked lovely, and he reversed his opinion about the dress. He was filled with pride in his womenfolk in comparison with the other ladies at the ball. In his opinion nobody could touch them.

The special feature of the ball was a pageant depicting the presentation of Pocahontas, the Princess Matoaca, at the court of James I in the year 1616. Prominent young people of Richmond society took the parts of the characters involved, the King and Queen, the little Indian Princess and her husband John Rolfe, and the courtiers. The ballroom was decorated with a happy mixture of American patriotism and British royal elegance. The boxes were draped in red, white and blue bunting; gilt ballroom chairs interspersed with potted palms lined the walls beneath. The dais was covered with a red carpet and draped with the red velvet curtain used for amateur theatricals. Two tall gilded chairs stood in its center for the King and Queen, and a red satin cushion for the Princess to kneel upon. The courtiers were elegantly dressed; the Princess Matoaca was costumed in careful conformity to the famous portrait of Pocahontas but the radiant young lady who wore the costume could have borne little resemblance to the Indian girl.

Following the presentation the courtiers danced a "Saraband" for the entertainment of the King and Queen, a dance described in the society columns of Henry's paper on Sunday as "a festive revel with the dignity of a minuet and the coquettishness of a Virginia Reel."

Henry danced the opening figure with Janie and then he was through. The livelier dances were too much for him.

"My dancing days are over," he said.

"Nonsense, Henry, you're not that old," Janie said.

"When a man gets well along in his fifties he ought not to be expected to cavort around the floor like that," he replied, motioning to the swirling couples on the dance floor.

Leaving Janie surrounded by friends in the Peyton box, he wandered out to the lobby of the ballroom and met Justin Vaughn.

"Come and have a drink with me," Justin said.

"I need one," Henry replied, "but where?"

"They have set up a bar over here for the gentlemen."

With his glass of whiskey and water and a cigar, Henry began to enjoy himself. He liked Justin Vaughn, who represented one of the northern Virginia counties at the Constitutional Convention. They were not on the same committees so their liking had not worn thin from too much friction.

At first they talked casually about the world in general. It was a difficult time, they agreed. Everywhere you looked there was trouble; the Boer War in Africa, the smoldering aftermath of the Boxer Rebellion in China, the Philippine Insurrection, the still-fresh tragedy of President McKinley's assassination, and the large question mark posed to the country by the Rough Rider in the White House. Barring the fact that he was a Republican, Henry was pleased by what he saw there. Justin was not.

"He's got the Wall Street boys sitting on hot cakes," Henry said gleefully. "They don't know where he stands."

"He's too young and untried," Justin said, "and too brash and full of himself. There's no telling what he might do."

Inevitably, they came back to the subject of the new constitution. Henry did not want to talk about the suffrage article so he spoke of education.

"It is what we need most," he said. "We've got to get the compulsory school attendance provision, I've promised myself that I won't go home until we do. It is the only way we can destroy illiteracy in this state."

Justin nodded. "It's having rough sledding. Leaving out any question of the racial issue, some of the rural delegates look on education with suspicion, and some of our friends consider education the prerogative of gentlemen."

"They're fools," said Henry.

"No, they're not fools. Most of them have plenty of sense. It is just that they are rooted in the old ideas, the old concepts of society."

"Well, it's about time they got uprooted. This is a new century and a different kind of world. We got a democracy on our hands. Education is basic, and they ought to be able to see that."

"We are not an intellectual people, Henry. You have to admit that. We draw our strength from the spirit and the heart more than the mind. Virginians have always admired valor more than brains, and the solid virtues more than wit and genius."

"I ain't asking for genius and only the good Lord can give us brains," Henry said. "I'm just asking for some good sound education right down to the bottom. Right now it don't look to me like we got either brains or education or leadership."

"We've produced some pretty good brains in our time," said Justin, "and some pretty good leadership. We have made for ourselves a pretty good life in a grand old state with an illustrious history and a fine tradition back of it."

"There you go! That's what's the matter with us. We are too blamed self-satisfied. We don't want to improve anything because we are perfect already."

"Not perfect," Justin said consideringly, as if giving thought to the idea. "Not really perfect, but good. Pretty damn good!" He drained his glass and stubbed out his cigar with quick jabs in the ashtray. Then he threw back his head and laughed at Henry's face. "Never mind, Henry, never mind. I am going to vote for your compulsory attendance law. I know education is necessary. I just get tired now and then hearing you new fellows crying down the old ways."

"But damn it, man, we've got a world in which the old ways don't fit. You can't get anywhere holding on to 'em. You have to cope with a new world in its own terms, not in eighteenth century terms."

"All right," said Justin Vaughn. "All right, I'll cope, but sometimes under protest."

When they went back to the ballroom Janie was sitting in the Peyton box talking to Colonel Willoughby. Henry joined them.

"Oh, Henry, you've just missed such a lovely figure," Janie told him.

"To my great advantage," the Colonel said, bowing gallantly. "Mrs. Darby consented to dance it with me."

"This was my favor," Janie said, showing him a brightly colored little Japanese fan. "Isn't it pretty?"

Henry sat down, and the Colonel, to his relief, wandered off.

"The others are all dancing," Janie said. "The Colonel was good for the figure but not the waltz."

"I should think not. He must be eighty."

The orchestra was playing "And the Band Played On." The floor was a swirling mass of waltzing couples. Henry watched them until he located Jane. He had caught glimpses of her during the evening, radiant and gay, always with a different young man.

"Ain't that the Tyler boy Jane is dancing with?" he asked.

"Yes," Janie said. "Tommy Tyler. He has been giving her quite a rush."

There was something in her voice that made Henry turn and look at her sharply. She was watching Jane and Tommy Tyler. He sat in silence for a few minutes while Janie followed the pair with her eyes as they glided around the floor.

Presently Henry spoke. "She ain't quite sixteen," he said.

Janie started and turned to him. She blushed and stammered a little.

"Why of course, Henry. I wasn't thinking—I didn't have any idea—"

"Yes, you did. You were sitting there with visions of Meriden floating around in your head."

"Well, it would be nice," Janie said, abandoning pretense.

"It ain't likely to happen in the first place, and if it did it wouldn't be nice."

"Of course I have never liked the Boyds," Janie went on, "but Tommy is not like them. He's a Tyler. He is like Raiford Tommy and Kate are the only ones of the children who are."

"Listen, sugar," Henry said. "He is the youngest of five children. How much chance do you think he has to inherit Meriden?"

"Oh, but the others don't want it," Janie explained earnestly. "Raiford Junior has gone into business in New York and he has married a Yankee girl, from Boston, I think. Angela is engaged to a New York man, I have always heard she hated living out there in the country. And Ranny is going to be a lawyer; you can't practice law and live at Meriden. That leaves only Tommy and Kate. I shouldn't be a bit surprised to see Tommy get Meriden in the end."

"I'll tell you something else," Henry went on. "Tommy Tyler has a bad reputation. He's dissipated. He drinks too much, and he goes with a pretty wild crowd at the University."

"Oh, no, Henry." Janie's face was stricken. "How terrible. He looks like such a nice boy. Are you sure?"

"I have heard it from a lot of people. And if all that wasn't enough to discourage any hopes of a romance, just remember that Jane would have Martha Boyd for a mother-in-law."

He laughed a little at that, but Janie sighed. "Oh, well, yes, I reckon you're right. But it seems a pity. It would have been so nice."

It was very late when they got back to the hotel that night and Henry was really tired. Janie and Jane seemed as fresh as when they started, and bubbling with excitement. Women liked this kind of thing, he supposed. He didn't see how they did it. Some men did too, look at all the society hounds. The papers were full these days of the goings-on of New York society. He got into bed and stretched out gratefully. Drowsily, he wished somebody would tell him what ought to be done about the suffrage article. He wished that most of Janie's early romantic dreamings had not centered around Meriden. It was like a fairy-tale castle in her eyes, and even with the injection of the Boyds she couldn't be realistic about it. Meriden's days were numbered, in his opinion. Soon he was asleep.

26

Jane Darby came down the stairway at Fairview, feeling as if she were floating on air. The pink chiffon of her full gored skirt flowed around her as she stepped. She tried to come down slowly, sedately, but to save her life she could not help taking the last steps at a run. When she reached the hall she pirouetted gaily and even the taffeta foundation of her dress stood out in a flaring circle around her, revealing the lace-trimmed petticoats underneath. She was going to the dance with Tommy, he would be here any minute now; she would dance with him over and over again, and he would press her hand and whisper in her ear, and she would smile at him, and their secret would be a shining treasure between them. They were going to announce their engagement after the Christmas holidays and be married in April. Because it was a secret Jane had to keep on going around with her other beaux. She had been to dances this Christmas with Melvin Pratt and Harry Russell and Jim Sprague, and even her cousin Dwight Wilcox, who after all was only her second cousin and very devoted to her. But tonight was Tommy's; tonight and the New Year's Eve cotillion. And soon every dance, every day, every moment, would be Tommy's.

When they heard her in the hall Mama and Papa came out of the library to look at her. Papa just stood and beamed, but Mama looked her over carefully.

"It's lovely, honey," she said. Jane's dress was new. There

had been much discussion about it. Mama thought it might be too old for her, not the material but the way it was made. "I don't think it is too low in the back, and the gored skirt makes your figure look very nice."

Susie came to the dining room door and watched her admiringly. "You ready for the flowers, Miss Jane?" she asked.

"Yes, Susie, I'm ready."

Susie came back with a square florist's box, and Jane lifted the lid and looked lovingly inside, sniffing the fresh fragrance of violets. Violets! Five hundred of them! Five bunches, each with a deep crimson rose at its center. When they had come from the florist that afternoon Jane had worried for fear that the crimson roses would clash with the pink dress, but they didn't, they looked lovely. Each bunch was wrapped in florist's dark green tinfoil, but just to be sure about the new dress a clean handkerchief was placed first and the bunches of violets were pinned through it and the dress and the corset cover to the corset underneath. They were clustered close together and made a great splash of vivid color against the pale pink chiffon, extending from her belt to the young curve of her breast. Everybody exclaimed over them, and Jane did a little posturing before the mirror over the pier table in the hall, turning this way and that to get the effect.

There was still a crowning glory to be added to the costume, her new evening wrap. Papa had given it to her for Christmas. It lay across the arm of the carved oak cathedral chair now, waiting to be put on, a deep sapphire-blue cut-velvet cloak, with white fur collar and cuffs and a white satin lining. It was the most elegant thing Jane had ever had; it made her feel like a princess to slip her arms into its satin lustrousness as a young man held it for her, and snuggle down into its soft warmth.

Tommy was late. Jonny had gone in town a long time ago to get Sara Anne Morgan, whom he was carrying to the dance tonight. Henrietta, home from school for the holidays, was sitting glumly on the steps, her knees drawn up almost to her chin, watching. She had not said a word, about the dress or the flowers or anything. She was in one of her moods, probably jealous because she was not invited to this dance She had been to a dance of her own younger set last night, she was too young to go with the older crowd, but you never knew how Henrietta would feel about things.

She wished Tommy would come on, she would hate to miss the opening figure. The dance was being given by Mr. and Mrs. Henry Daniels for their daughter Arlene, and there had been all kinds of rumors about how elegant it was going to be. The Darbys didn't know the Daniels as well as they knew most of the people in town. Mrs. Daniels was not a Virginian; she came from Philadelphia, and she had money of her own, which Papa said was a good thing because Hank Daniels couldn't make a living if his life depended on it. Jane had known Arlene when they were children, but she had been off at boarding school for the last four years and hadn't taken much part in things when she was at home, so Jane did not know her well. There were rumors that Arlene's dress had been made in Philadelphia and Mrs. Daniels had sent to New York for the favors, and the refreshments were coming down from Demonet's in Washington. Everybody was excited about it.

She heard the sound of horses coming up the driveway and rejoiced. Tommy always brought a carriage when he came to take her somewhere at night. With the other young men she usually went on the streetcar, but when Tommy was going to a dance or any evening entertainment he came into town from Meriden and spent the night with one of his friends or one of his Boyd cousins, and rented a carriage to take his girls to parties. Recently there had not been any girls but Jane.

Papa opened the door for him as he came across the porch, and Jane's heart melted as he entered the hall, all the six feet two of him, the broad shoulders, the brown hair, the brown eyes, the darling crooked smile. Nobody in the world would have called Tommy Tyler handsome, but he didn't need to be. He had something else. Everywhere he went the girls were crazy about him. She had tried so hard not to fall in love with him, she had pretended to herself and to him for a long time, but she had always known, deep down inside herself ever since the ball in Richmond three years ago. And he had fallen in love with her, out of all the girls he had known, here in town and at the University and in Richmond, where the Tylers often went, and even in New York, where Angela Tyler lived since her marriage, and out of them all he had chosen her. She knew that he loved her; he had been courting her devotedly now for nearly two years, and he had

273

promised to give up drinking, and they were going to be married. Happiness was like a song in her heart.

Tommy smiled at her first, and then spoke to Mama and Papa and Henrietta and Susie. He had beautiful manners. Papa picked up her evening wrap but Tommy took it away from him and held it for her. She touched her violets.

"They are so lovely, Tommy," she said.

Tommy's face was red. She thought it must be very cold outside, so she pulled the cloak around herself warmly, being careful not to crush the violets. They went out into the darkness, calling goodnights, and Tommy helped her into the carriage. He got in after her and closed the door. The coachman clucked at the horses and the carriage started off, its lights making flickering shadows on each side of the driveway. The horses went faster when they reached the main road. Tommy put his arm around her and she rested her head against his shoulder. He bent his head and kissed her, a long, hard kiss, and she relaxed in his arms. He rubbed his face up and down against hers; his clean-shaven beard scratched her cheek and she loved it. Her cloak had fallen open, he stroked her throat with his hand; the hand moved down and curved around her breast. Jane was filled with exultant emotion.

"Darling," she said. "Darling Tommy."

He kissed her again, and this time the pressure of his mouth hurt her lips. The pain cut through the haze of happiness in which she had been lost, and suddenly a hateful thought came to her. Tommy had been drinking. She was not sure, but the idea was there. There was a faint odor. This would account for the red face and the roving hands, for the roughness of his kisses. This was not the gentle Tommy she had always known. She pushed away from him and sat up straight.

"No," she said. "No, Tommy."

He took his arm from around her. "All right, ma'am. Just as you say."

It was not just as she said, however. Two or three times during the drive he tried to renew his lovemaking. He would sit quietly for a while, and then his arm would reach out to her. Each time she pushed him aside. She was becoming more and more convinced that her suspicions were correct, and she was sick with disappointment. He had promised. He had promised on his word of honor and by his love for her.

She had believed him. She sat in silence and Tommy also seemed to have nothing to say.

They came to the long, steep hill leading down into town. The horses went slowly, placing their feet carefully on the rough cobblestones, holding back the carriage. Down Twelfth and along Market Street to Calisthenics Hall. Lights flooded from the building and Jane was glad to see that couples were still going in. They were not late. She went into the ladies' room to leave her cloak. Emmy Duval was there. Emmy also had a new dress and they admired each other. Connie James came to the door and called to them.

"You all come on out," she said. "You've never seen anything like this. You wouldn't recognize the old Hall."

They went out into the ballroom and gasped. Calisthenics Hall was used for everything, from church services to political rallies to dances and receptions. Jane had seen it decorated in many ways, but never anything like this. Mrs. Daniels had converted the stage of the Hall into a drawing room. There were sofas and chairs and tables, and red-shaded lamps, and great bowls of red roses and carnations. There were even red velvet hangings at the windows across the back of the stage and all down the sides of the hall, and tables holding clusters of holly or bowls of red flowers were interspersed with little gilt chairs all along the walls. The orchestra, which usually sat on the stage, was hidden behind a bank of evergreens and holly in one corner, and in the opposite corner towered an enormous Christmas tree, gaily hung with small, brightly wrapped packages.

"They are the favors," whispered Connie. "Mrs. Daniels brought the velvet hangings from her own house."

All the lights along the walls of the room and in the big central chandelier were covered with small red shades, giving a warm glow to the whole hall, and from the four corners of the room to the chandelier were strung festoons of red and green Christmas decorations. It was breathtaking, it made Jane feel gay and excited just to look at it.

The orchestra was making little tuning-up sounds behind its green barricade, so Jane and Tommy hurried up to the make-believe drawing room on the stage where the receiving line stood, Mr. and Mrs. Daniels and Arlene and all the chaperons. When they came down off the stage Tommy got a dance card for Jane and began scrawling his name all over it, for dance after dance. Obscurely, to her own surprise, Jane protested.

"No. No," she whispered. "Remember, Tommy, not too many."

Tommy handed her the card and she scratched his name off several of the dances. Other young men crowded around, asking for dances and soon the card was filled. The orchestra struck up a waltz, to give the late stragglers a chance to get there before the opening figure, and she and Tommy danced. With the music and the warm lights and gay decorations, with Tommy's arms around her, she forgot her fears and the strange revulsion she had felt a few minutes ago and she happily gave herself up to the dance. They swooped and circled and glided, and Jane again felt as if she were treading on air.

Arlene led the opening figure with Walker James. It was a pretty, intricate figure; they marched and paraded and wove in and out and separated and came together and stooped under an archway of uplifted arms. As the men passed by the Christmas tree Arlene's younger sister, Marcia, and a cousin of the same age, Harriet Eubank, lifted two of the little packages from the Christmas tree and gave them to each gentleman, one for his lady and one for himself. You could tell the difference by the shape, the girls' favors were square, the men's long and narrow. When the figure was over and they opened the packages it was found that the girls had small gilt-trimmed bottles of perfume—"imported French perfume," they said, with awe in their voices, and the men had slender silver pencils. They were accustomed to pretty baubles as favors, beribboned canes or boutonnieres for the men, fans or paper parasols for the girls, or humorous toys that exploded and made the girls squeal. These were real presents and they were all impressed. By the time the second figure came, however, and it turned out that the favors for the girls were pins shaped like silver bows, and the men had silver stickpins, Jane lost her enthusiasm. It was sort of ostentatious, she thought. This was the kind of thing the rich people in New York did; it was not appropriate here, where so few people could have afforded to give favors like these. She and Emmy decided that Mrs. Daniels was just showing off.

By that time Jane was again miserable. There was now no doubt that Tommy was drinking. Whenever he was not dancing with her he disappeared, and each time he came back the

276

signs were more apparent. His face was brick-red now, his voice was thick, he was not altogether steady on his feet. Jane did not know what to do. She was frightened and embarrassed. She did not want to make a scene and she was afraid that if she refused to dance with him he would make one. This clumsy, suddenly coarse-featured man with the thick voice was not Tommy, her Tommy, her darling Tommy. She wanted to get away from him. She thought of going into the ladies' room and pretending to be ill, but she knew that the maid would call Mrs. Daniels or one of the chaperons and there would be complications. She was so poor at pretending. She might appeal to Jonny or Dwight, or any of her beaux, but the thought of appealing for help against Tommy was unthinkable.

The music started and she saw Tommy coming toward her across the floor. She would dance this one dance with him and then she must think of something to do. She watched him approach.

"You've been drinking," she said accusingly.

"Jush a lil-l-l," he replied, and put his arms around her. They started to dance. It was one of the new two-steps. Tommy, who was usually such a good dancer, was clumsy and uncertain, he wavered and turned in the wrong directions. He kept stepping on her pretty new pink satin slippers, dyed to match her dress. They bumped into other couples, and he kept drawing her closer and closer in spite of her efforts to keep the proper distance between them. He was crushing her violets. All the generations that lay behind her were speaking in Jane's blood now, voicing the inviolable rule "no lady ever lets herself be made conspicuous." She knew she was conspicuous, she felt that everybody was watching them, everybody must see what a state Tommy was in.

"I think we had better not try this, Tommy," she said quietly. "We had better stop."

"Awright, lesh stop." He stood still but he did not release her. Instead he pulled her closer and crushed her to him, then bent his head and kissed her. Incredibly, there on the dance floor, surrounded by her friends, by her mother's friends, he kissed her. It was not just the hard pressure of his mouth on hers which she had felt in the carriage on the way there; this was different. It was a moist, lingering, drunken kiss. His mouth was half open; there was motion in his lips as they pressed against hers. It was horrible, he was horrid. She struggled against him, and managed to give him a quick push. It was not a hard push, because she was held so closely against him that her arms had little leeway, but it was too much for Tommy. He lost his equilibrium and fell backward, throwing out his arms as he fell. He crashed into Eunice Maybank and John Foster, and then lay sprawled on his back on the floor. Eunice, startled, screamed and everybody turned in that direction. Most of them stopped dancing and stared; every eye in the hall was turned upon them. Jane stood in frozen horror.

Mrs. Daniels came over to them. Her eyes and her voice were icy. "I am afraid that Mr. Tyler is in no condition to remain in the presence of young ladies," she said. "Will you see that he is taken out?"

She looked vaguely around. John Foster and Walker James sprang forward and pulled Tommy up from the floor. He looked dazed. They each took an arm and half lifted, half pulled him out of the hall. Jane turned and ran. The maid in the dressing room looked startled as she rushed in. She ran through the cloakroom into the washroom, and did not stop there, but shut herself up in one of the two booths. She leaned up against the wall, panting, trembling all over, trying to control herself. I must not cry, she kept telling herself. I must not cry, I must not give way. I have got to go back out there and face them all, I must not cry. As she pressed against the wall she could feel the small bulk of her engagement ring between her breasts, Tommy's beautiful diamond solitaire. She wore it in a chamois-skin bag pinned with a safety pin on the inside of her corset. She knew it was safe there, because even if the pin came undone the tiny bag would be held between her chemise and the tightly laced corset. The pressure of it made her want to cry more than ever; she moved so she would not feel it.

She heard someone come into the washroom and she struggled hard for composure. Presently a soft voice spoke. It was Emmy.

"Jane, honey, come on out. Come on, sweetie."

Jane took a deep breath and unlocked the door.

"I am so sorry," Emmy said, "but I am not going to talk about it now. I just want to say that this is Tommy Tyler's funeral, not yours. You are just the innocent victim, you had nothing to do with it. Come on back and show them that. Hold your head up and show them that you don't care."

"But I do care, Emmy."

"I know you do, darling, but just for a little while pretend you don't. Pretend that this thing has nothing to do with you. Jonny told me to tell you that," Emmy added, "and in a little while he will take you home."

Jane glanced at herself in the mirror. It did not seem possible, but she looked just the same. There were no marks of tragedy on her face, her hair was still in place, a shining mass on top of her head. Some of the violets were crushed, and she carefully pulled them out of the bunches.

In the cloakroom they met Mrs. Daniels coming in. "I am so sorry, my dear Jane, that this should have happened to you at our party. Mr. Daniels and I feel very badly about it, and Arlene too. I will write to your mother tomorrow. I would not have invited the young man if I had known his reputation. I thought he was an accepted member of your crowd."

Even in her extremity loyalty to Tommy rose up in her. "He is, Mrs. Daniels," she said. "I have been to lots of parties with him and this is the first time I have ever seen him when he was—was not himself."

Janie thought Mrs. Daniels looked skeptical and she realized that people had been telling her that Tommy Tyler drank.

"It is very unfortunate," her hostess said vaguely, and they all went back into the Hall.

Jim Sprague was waiting outside for Emmy. Jane had lost her dance card, she had no idea with whom she was supposed to dance this dance, but when she appeared several of the stags standing on the sidelines moved toward her. Dwight Wilcox got there first and she was glad. He was in the family and there would be less strain in keeping up appearances with him.

"I'm sorry, little girl," he said as they moved onto the dance floor. "It shouldn't have happened to you."

Jane smiled up at him but said nothing. She could hold her head up and smile and dance, but conversation was beyond her. Somebody found her dance card and brought it to her. She had the next dance with Harry Russell. Harry always talked a blue streak himself, and he took up most of the dance telling her about a scrape he got into at the University. At the next dance Jonny came over to her.

"Ready to go home, honey?" he asked.

A wave of relief came over Jane. "Oh, yes, Jonny. Please, will you take me home. Sara Anne won't mind, will she?"

"No, Herb Spencer will take care of her. Get your coat. I will pay our respects to Mrs. Daniels."

They went out into the quiet street. Jonny pulled out his watch and looked at it under the light on the corner.

"We'll just make it," he said.

The last streetcar went out to Greenway at midnight. In the old days when everybody lived close together in town they all walked to the dances and parties; those who lived too far away to do that came in town and spent the night with friends. Since the town had spread out so, however, the people who gave parties lasting after midnight had to lease a special car from the company to take their guests home. They all went at once. When the orchestra had played "Turkey in the Straw" and "Home, Sweet Home," as many times as it could be persuaded to do so, they would all troop down to the brightly lighted waiting streetcar. After the big dances the girls would have to sit on each other's laps and the boys would stand up hanging on the straps, and the car would go swaying gaily down the streets all over town, wherever the streetcar lines went, letting couples off at anyplace they wanted to get off. Sometimes just for fun the motorman would clang his bell as he zoomed along, though he didn't need to because the streets were empty at that time of night. They all thought that was very funny, but the next day the streetcar company was apt to get complaints from people who didn't like being waked up in the middle of the night, so now it was against the rules for a motorman to sound his bell unless he needed to. Sometimes the car would wait until a boy escorted his girl to her front door, or sometimes he would catch it on its return trip from the end of the line in any one direction. Whenever Jane came home like that from a late party the motorman would obligingly wait until her beau took her up to the house and dashed back down the driveway, because otherwise he would have had no way to get back into town. It was all lots of fun and usually Jane looked forward to those gay, noisy nocturnal rides, but tonight it would have killed her.

She and Jonny walked down to Main Street and stood waiting on the corner. Jonny was sweet; he knew she didn't want to talk so he said nothing. In just a minute or two the streetcar came in sight around the curve from the Union Station. They boarded it and sat in silence all the way to Fairview. What Jane wanted more than anything was to get to her own room and let the tears come. She couldn't hold them back much longer.

There was a light in the front hall when they reached Fairview and in the hall upstairs. Jonny put out the lower light as they went up the steps. When they reached the upper hall Mama opened her door and came out in her dressing gown. She looked surprised; when she saw Jane's face she looked concerned.

"Darling. Baby, what in the world is the matter?"

That was the end of the line for Jane. She went to her mother, put her arms around her neck and broke into sobs. Papa came out into the hall, his hair standing up all over his head.

"Great guns, Jonny," he said, "what happened? What's wrong with her?"

Jonny's voice was tight with anger. "That heel of a Tommy Tyler got dead drunk," he said. "He made a spectacle of himself, and ended by standing still in the middle of the floor and kissing Jane, right there before everybody. Then he fell down flat on the floor, so drunk he couldn't get up. He had to be carried out."

Jane cried harder when she heard it told in plain words. Mama held her close. "My poor little girl," she said. "Darling, I am so sorry."

Henrietta came to her door, sleepy-eyed but inquiring. Papa and Jonny were talking in low tones. Mama took charge.

"You all go back to bed," she said. "Everybody go to bed. We'll talk about this in the morning. Come on, Jane, sweet, I'll get you into bed."

Jane let herself be led into her own room. She found a handkerchief and tried to stop crying. Mama was turning down her bed.

"I'll unhook your dress, darling," she said, "and then run downstairs and warm some milk for you while you are undressing. That will make you sleep."

With the dress unhooked Jane found herself still tightly held in it by the violets pinned at her belt. She pulled the pins out one by one, and as each bunch was freed she threw it violently on the floor. She was aiming at the trash basket, but her eyes were so full of tears that few of them reached it. The little purple bunches lay all around the floor. When she unlaced her corset and unpinned the little chamois bag she did not throw that to the floor. She held it to her cheek for a moment and then locked it carefully away in a small leather box in her top bureau drawer.

2

When she came down to breakfast the next morning, Mama was sitting at the table drinking coffee. Papa and Henrietta had finished and Jonny had not come down.

"Good morning, precious," Mama said. "I hope you slept well."

"Yes, ma'am," Jane said. She had not slept well, and she knew her eyes were red-rimmed from crying.

"Susie, tell Baizy to make Miss Jane some hot cakes," Mama said. "Here is your coffee, or would you rather have tea?"

Jane did not want coffee or tea, or hot cakes or the roe herring that Mama urged upon her. Her throat felt as if it were solid, and it was hard to swallow. She toyed with the food. Papa was wandering around. He came to the door and spoke to her and then went away. Later he came back.

"Finished your breakfast, honey?" he asked. He sat down at the table. "I want to talk to you, little girl."

Jane felt as if she could not stand it. Why couldn't he wait, didn't he realize how hard it was for her to keep any control of herself?

"I don't want to make you any unhappier than I know you are anyhow," he said, as if answering her question, "but we got to face some facts, honeybunch, and I think we better do it right now. We've been worried about this thing right from the beginning. We tried not to say anything at first because we hoped it would blow over, and then when we saw your

282

heart was set on marryin' him we hoped he would change and settle down, but that's all over now. Everybody knows that Tommy Tyler drinks like a fish. You knew that, Jane. He ain't gonna change."

"I knew that he sometimes drank too much," Jane said, speaking carefully. "I did not know that he drank like a fish, as you put it. I had never seen him before when he was— under the influence." She could not bring herself to speak the word drunk. "We talked about it and he promised to stop. He promised not to take another drop. I thought he meant it."

"I reckon he meant it, honey," Papa said. "I reckon he meant to stop. But promises like that don't mean a thing, not a thing. When that habit gets hold of a man it ain't a question of promises. Now what I want to say is that you can't marry Tommy Tyler. We can't let you marry him. Your mother and I can't sit back and see you marry a man who will make your life a misery, who will subject you constantly to public and private humiliation."

For the first time in her recollection Jane was angry with her father. Didn't he know that she knew she couldn't marry Tommy as he now was? Didn't he realize that that was why her world was shattered and life seemed a dreary, barren stretch, impossible for her to face? She wanted to scream, to get up from the table and run. Precariously she held on to her self-control.

"I have no intention, Papa," she said, "of marrying Tommy until I am sure that he has given up drinking for good."

Papa started to say something, but Jane saw Mama make a warning gesture that stopped him. "All right," he said, "that's a promise?"

"That's a promise."

"And in the meantime you won't see him, you won't go anywhere with him?"

"No," Jane said. "No, Papa, I won't promise that. I won't marry him, but I am going to see him. I am going to see him no matter what, as long as he wants to see me."

Papa got up and went to the window, where he stood staring out into the yard. Presently he turned and came back to the table.

"Very well. I think it would be much better if you didn't, but I reckon we can accept that for the time being."

"Can't you eat your breakfast, honey?" Mama asked.

283

"No, I can't," Jane said.

She jumped up from the table and ran. As she went up the steps in the front hall she heard Mama say: "You see, Henry. I asked you to wait." She sounded cross.

Jane did not stop to hear what Papa replied. She ran into her room, closed the door and buried her face in the tumbled pillows on her bed.

That afternoon Tommy came. Jane was alone at home. Jonny and Henrietta were off on their own separate activities, and Mama had driven in to call on Aunt Kate. Jane suspected that the family was gathering to discuss the situation. She heard the horse come up the driveway; she heard the doorbell ring. When Ella came to tell her that Mr. Tommy was there she still sat quietly in her chair, gathering her forces. She knew what she must do; spirit and body were torn with the knowledge. Presently she stood up and went to the bureau. Even her feet felt heavy. She unlocked the little leather box and took out the chamois-skin bag. The small white satin box in which the ring had come lay at one side. She transferred the lovely, gleaming thing from the bag to the box, closed it, and with it in her hand went slowly downstairs.

Tommy was standing in front of the mantelpiece. Jane stopped in the doorway and they looked at each other across the room. He looked awful; his face was gray and there were dark circles under his eyes. There was no sign of the dear, crooked smile that always made him look like a mischievous little boy. Jane knew that she looked awful too, with red-rimmed eyes and unpowdered face. It did not matter.

It was Tommy who broke the silence. "There is not much to be said, is there, dear?"

"Yes, Tommy, I think there is a lot to be said."

"I meant that there is not much I can say, except that I would not have had it happen for all the treasures of Araby. I am so desperately sorry, darling. And I promise—oh, Jane, I promise that it won't happen again."

"We might as well sit down," Jane said. She moved to one of the tufted blue satin sofas and took her seat. Slowly Tommy came and sat beside her.

"I am afraid promises won't do much good, Tommy. You promised before, you know."

He threw back his head and shook it, a characteristic gesture, as if he were trying to shake off his troubles.

"I know," he said. "I know."

"I have some things to say, Tommy. First, we can't announce our engagement next month, as we planned, and we can't be married in April. I think you had better take this back." She held the small box out to him.

Tommy stared at it as if it were some loathsome object. "Oh, for God's sake," he cried. Jumping up, he went over to the window, his hands jammed into his trousers pockets. Presently he spoke. "I don't want the ring, Jane. It's yours, I gave it to you, for better or worse." There was a tinge of bitterness in his voice. "I don't want it back. I have no use for a diamond solitaire."

"I have no use for it either, Tommy, now."

"Then throw it away." His voice was rough.

Jane sat looking at the box for a long time. Tommy stared out of the window. "No, I won't throw it away," she said finally. "If you don't want it, I will keep it, in the hope that some day I may wear it, proudly."

He came quickly back to the sofa. "You mean—"

"Oh, darling, don't you understand? I will marry you any time—any time at all, that I am convinced that you have stopped drinking. And I will wait as long as I have any hope that time will come."

He reached out for her hand and held it tightly. "Bless you, my dear. But oh, Jane, it would be so much easier for me to stop if you would marry me now."

"No. No, I don't think that is true, Tommy. If you can't stop in order to make our marriage possible, I don't think you could stop if we were married. And—I must say this, Tommy —the man you were last night is not the man I love."

Again Tommy shook his head. "I don't remember a thing about it, honey," he said. "I never do when I get drunk. At first I didn't believe the things they said I did, but I have learned that I have to believe them. But I assure you that all the lurid details of last night have been given to me by various people, including your brother Jonathan, who came to see me this morning, breathing fire and smoke."

"Oh, Tommy, I'm sorry. Jonathan shouldn't have done that."

"He gave me to understand with considerable force that he would knock my block off if he ever saw me with you again. I don't believe he could, you know," for just a moment the smile came to Tommy's face, "but I would hate to have him try. I told him it was none of his damn business, that whether I saw you or not depended entirely on you. Right?"

"Right. You should know, though, that Papa said the same thing this morning. I don't mean that he made threats, but he asked me not to see you any more. I told him that I wouldn't marry you until I was sure, but I intended to go right on seeing you."

"Bless you again, darling." Presently he stood up. "I reckon I had better go. Right now I don't feel up to any run-ins with indignant fathers or brothers. Or even reproachful mothers."

He pulled Jane up from the sofa and, holding her hands, stood looking down at her.

"All right, darling, I expect you are right. We'll have to wait. I couldn't be sorrier." He hesitated. "May I kiss you?"

The humbleness in his voice hurt her. She went into his arms.

"Oh, Tommy, darling, please try. Please, please."

He pressed his face against her hair. "I will. God knows I'll try."

27

When Miss Bessie Mason died in 1908 at the age of eighty-seven there was a funeral such as the town had never seen before. People came from all over the state. The Governor was there, and both Senators, and several members of the Virginia delegation in the House, including Henry, of course, who acted as one of the honorary pallbearers. Miss Bessie's pupils over the years, many of them quite old now, with their husbands and children and sometimes their grandchildren, came pouring into the town. All the undertaker's carriages and all the livery stable carriages were used, and everybody in town who owned a carriage came in it and brought others. Some of the people came to town in automobiles, but were not allowed to bring them near the church or take them in the funeral procession because they frightened the horses so badly.

Janie and Jane went to the funeral in the victoria. It seemed more suitable for a funeral than the surrey. Henrietta did not want to go, she had hardly known Miss Bessie and Janie saw no reason why she should go. Jonathan and little Sara Anne went with Sara Anne and Carey in a livery stable carriage. St. John's Church would not hold all the people who came, they were standing up at the back and in the wide vestibule and even out on the steps. Janie had never seen such flowers. They were banked in masses all over the chancel and the cross aisle in front of the chancel, and the funeral procession was delayed in starting for the cemetery because it took so long to load them into the funeral carriages. The procession stretched out for blocks, and the streetcars could not run for a while as it moved out Twelfth Street.

Miss Bessie was an institution in the town, and everybody felt that something was lost when she died. Eighty-seven was a good old age and she had grown very feeble, so you could not be really sorry for her sake, but it saddened Janie to see all the old people go. The world was changing so fast that you just could not keep up with it. All the aunts and uncles were gone now except Aunt Josie Ashby, who lived with Mary and her family. Mary's husband had done real well and they had a nice house with plenty of room for Aunt Josie. It was funny that she, who had had the hardest life, should live the longest.

When the services in the cemetery were over, Henry went back into town to see what was going on at the newspaper office, and Jane went home with Emmy Duval Foster. Janie lingered a long time because she saw so many old friends, "girls" whom she had not met up with since their school days. It was good to see them again and she enjoyed the little reunions, but it made her feel old because the passage of time was so plainly marked on most of them, and of course she knew it must be on her too. Everybody was probably thinking how old everybody else looked. When you saw yourself in the mirror every day, and you saw your close friends every few days, you didn't realize what age was doing to you, but when you saw somebody you had not seen since she was eighteen years old—well, there it was.

When she got back into the victoria and told Amos to go home she was in a mood of sentimental nostalgia. Life was going by, she was growing old, the world was changing, the sands were shifting under her feet. Look at this street they were driving along, which had once been the old country road into town. It was now Fairview Avenue. She had given up some more land to the city so it could be widened again, and sidewalks had been put in on both sides. Wherever possible the city had left a line of trees between the sidewalks and the street and had planted others, so now it stretched out, a wide tree-shaded avenue all the way to Greenway, with new houses set back in big yards almost as far out as Fairview. They had sold off all the Fairview land now except a strip big enough for their own use. A year ago electricity and city water had reached them. They had running water in the kitchen and had turned the little hall room over the kitchen corridor into a bathroom. Most wonderful of all, a telephone had been installed. That was the most revolutionary thing that had happened. To be able to stand in the back hall at Fairview and order your groceries and invite people to dinner and make engagements and call the children up to see how they were, this was nothing short of miraculous. It was all fine, and she enjoyed the comforts and conveniences as much as anybody, but somehow today, with Miss Bessie Mason dead and all the old girls looking so old, and the constant worry about Jane and Henrietta heavy on her heart, it made her feel forlorn and insecure.

They drove past the house that Jonathan and little Sara Anne had recently built, and that made her feel better. She didn't have to worry about Jonathan; he was certainly a bright spot for her to look at. It was wonderful that he had fallen in love with little Sara Anne Morgan. They were very happy. Just two months ago they had had their second little boy, named David because they liked the name. "Just think, Janie," Sara Anne had said when Carey Morgan Darby, the first son, was born, "we are co-grandmothers." It was another bond between herself and Sara Anne.

The house was smaller than most of the houses on Fairview Avenue. Jonathan and Sara Anne were very young to build their own home, but Henry was so glad to have Jonathan come on the paper with him, instead of studying law as he had meant to do until he fell in love and wanted to get married right away, and the paper and the investments were doing so well. The little house the young people had rented when they were first married was tiny and very hot in summer, so when the second baby was coming Henry had half given and half loaned Jonathan the money to build. Janie was glad they had had sense enough to build a Georgian house instead of a modern one with turrets and cupolas and what not. It was simple and small but well-proportioned. Later, when Jonathan was established, they could add wings to it and it would be really very pretty.

Ordinarily Janie would have stopped to see the babies. She knew that Amos was waiting for her to tell him to stop, but today she did not feel like it. She said nothing and they drove on past. Soon she heard an automobile coming behind them. Janie hated automobiles. The carriage horses were always frightened and sometimes they acted up badly. Amos would have to get down off the box and hold their bridles until the contrivance got past. This one did not pass them, however. It drove up behind the victoria and stopped, and Janie heard a man's voice calling her. Turning, she saw Raiford Tyler.

She had seen him at the funeral but they had merely bowed to each other with the formal detachment that people use at funerals. Now he got out of his absurd-looking contraption and came up to the carriage.

"Hello, Raiford," Janie said. "I'm mighty glad to see you. It has been a long time."

"Saw you at the funeral," he said, "but didn't have a chance to speak. How are you, Janie? You look mighty well, and pretty."

"Heavens, Raiford, you are still a flatterer. I have just been thinking how old all my contemporaries look."

"Not you. You and Sara Anne still look mighty pretty to me."

Poor Raiford. He looked terrible himself. At one time he had been fat and pouchy, now he was thin and haggard. It was too bad. Janie had heard that he was having an affair with an actress in New York. It was shocking, of course, but she almost hoped it was true, and if it was true, she hoped the actress was pretty and soft and loving. Raiford deserved something more in life than Martha Boyd.

"I hope Martha is well," she said politely, wondering why she had not come to Miss Bessie Mason's funeral. She realized suddenly that it had been a long time since she had seen Martha anywhere.

"She's all right," Raiford said shortly, and that was that.

Emptiness seemed to surround the subject of Martha, and Janie knew, what she had often heard rumored, that that marriage had gone to pieces. Well, what could you expect? She tried to fill the awkward gap.

"You have been in New York, haven't you?"

"Yes, I get up there from time to time. Have some investments to look after, and I like to see the grandchildren. Rai has three now, and Angela two. Nice little tykes."

"And Ranny is practicing law in Boston. Why Boston, Raiford?"

"God knows. His grandparents would turn over in their graves. And Kate has gone and got herself married to a man in California. Never heard of him before. She went out there on a visit and just got married. Life is a funny thing, Janie. The Tylers have lived in Virginia for more than two hundred and fifty years, and now here they are scattering all over the United States. Tommy is the only one left at home."

They looked at each other and Janie knew that they had got around to what Raiford wanted to talk about.

"What are we going to do about them, Janie?"

"What can we do about them, Raiford?"

"Why don't you take her away somewhere?"

"We have taken her away, over and over again. You know that, Raiford. Before this thing developed, when we saw it coming, we sent her off to school in Washington, during Henry's first year in Congress. And after the engagement was broken we went to Washington, we spent more money than we could afford and gave her a wonderful winter there. She had a lovely time, parties and beaux, several eligible young men were interested. We have sent her for visits with Emily in New York and with Avery and Susan in New Jersey. We have done everything but move away, and we can't do that. This is our home. Besides, it wouldn't do any good, she won't look at anybody else."

"If she would just go on and marry somebody, that would settle it."

"If she just would. He might marry somebody else and that would settle it too. At least it would end the suspense for Jane. I think she keeps right on hoping."

Raiford shook his head. "I am afraid there isn't much hope. He can't help it, Janie, he just can't help it. It's born in him. He tries, he certainly tries, but the thing is too big for him." He stood in silence for a few moments. The horses shook their heads and pawed restlessly, but neither Jane nor Raiford noticed them. "He used to be sort of wild, you know. He had a lot of girls, and he gambled a lot and ran around a lot. He has his own money, their grandfather left money to each of the children. I used to get pretty mad with Tommy. I don't know, Janie, I reckon I haven't been the best father in the world. Anyhow that's all passed now, all except the drinking. That's what he can't manage. There aren't but two things in

291

the world that Tommy wants now. One is Jane Darby and the other is Meriden, and he can't have either."

A carriage drove past and a lady bowed. Janie returned the bow, but she did not even notice who the lady was. Raiford made a vague motion with the hat he held in his hand.

"I can't let him have Meriden, Janie," he went on, "and he is the only one who wants it. He is good at it, too, he is a good farmer. That's the Tyler coming out in him. He could make the place pay if he could just stay sober. It doesn't seem fair somehow."

It was not only not fair, it was tragic, and Janie could think of nothing to say in the face of the tragedy.

"I worry about that pretty little girl of yours," Raiford said. "She ought not to be trapped like this."

Trapped! That was exactly what Jane was, trapped and caught and held by her foolish, unreasoning, invincible love for Tommy Tyler. Tears came into Janie's eyes. She reached out and put her hand over his as it rested on the frame of the carriage.

"It is good of you to worry about her when you have so much to worry about yourself, Raiford. It is all a tragedy, and it is hard for me to see any sense in it, but Avery has tried to teach me to believe that God always has a reason and He will show us a way out."

"Avery is a dreamer," said Raiford, with a touch of the scorn that worldly men feel for the unworldly, "and too good for us ordinary mortals. I don't think God has a thing to do with this situation, it's the work of the devil. But God or devil, we have got to make the best of it, I reckon. It's been good to talk to you, Janie, it has sort of eased my mind."

"Come to see us sometimes, Raiford," Janie said. "We would like so much to see you."

"Yes, I will. Get Amos to hold your horses' bridles until I get by you."

He went back to his automobile and with much sputtering cranked it and drove off, waving to Janie as he passed.

As the carriage drove up to the front porch of Fairview Janie saw a buggy there, the horse tethered to the hitching post. Sounds of music were coming from the house. As usual, Henrietta and her beaux. Janie stood on the porch and listened. Henrietta was playing her guitar and singing a French song. She had studied French for four years at school in

Washington and she spoke it very well. Not only spoke it but sang it. Miss Bessie Mason's French of thirty-odd years ago was not equal to Henrietta's songs, and Janie had no idea what they were saying. They might be perfectly innocent, she hardly thought the school would have taught her the kind of naughty songs that Janie associated with Paris, but the way Henrietta sang them certainly made them seem very wicked, and Janie shuddered at the thought of what they might be saying. Her only consolation was that she did not believe the young men who listened to the songs with such pleasure knew any more than she did what they meant. Henrietta could make the guitar sound as if it were a part of the song, and she would sing in her husky contralto, slowly and meaningfully, looking at the boys out of the corners of her eyes, or fast and gaily, the unknown French words falling off her tongue in a charming cascade. When she finished a song she would put back her head and laugh, just as she used to do, only now the sound that came out was a throaty, gurgling laugh instead of the shrill shriek of the past. The finishing process had done the most amazing things to Henrietta.

Janie went into the front hall and moved toward the stairway. She saw that two boys were in the back parlor with Henrietta. They all stood up as she appeared. "Good evening, Mama," Henrietta said politely. "You are so late, the funeral must have taken a long time."

"Howdy, Mrs. Darby," the boys said. One of them was Macon Lacey. She did not know who the other was, though he seemed to know her.

"Yes," she said. "It was so big, there were hundreds of people. And I saw a lot of old friends to speak to. Don't let me disturb you, go on with your music. I am going up and rest a while, Henrietta."

In her room she took off her hat, fluffed up the elaborate puffs which covered her head, and looked at herself critically in the mirror over her bureau. She was fifty-three years old. Her hair had not begun to turn gray but it had faded. The shining luster of it was gone. The natural color in her cheeks was gone too; Dorine's Liquid Rouge was put to daily use now. Her face was fuller than it had been, there were lines across her forehead and around her mouth. Still and all, she didn't do so badly. She didn't honestly think she looked as old as so many of the people she had seen at the funeral today.

She did not lie down, but sat in the rocking chair by the front window. From force of habit she picked up a piece of embroidery and worked on it as she thought about Henrietta. This youngest of her children was now eighteen years old, grown, graduated, finished. She was as smart as a whip, she knew many things that her mother did not know, she read books that her mother had never heard of, by authors she had never heard of. She had done remarkably well at school. The headmistress had recommended that she go to college, and Janie knew she had surprised everybody by approving of the idea. Girls were going to college more and more now, and with all the suffrage agitation she was developing a decided leaning toward women's rights. Henry thought it was terribly funny. Little old stick-in-the-mud going in for things as new and progressive as women voting and girls going to college.

Henrietta had not wanted to go to college, however. The music teacher at her school had told Janie that her daughter had a fine contralto voice and recommended that she go to New York and study and make something of it. Henrietta had not wanted to go on with her music.

"What do you want to do, honey?" Janie had asked.

"I don't want to do anything, Mama. I'm lazy. I just want to stay at home and enjoy myself."

Well, that was all right. That was what she herself had done, what she had always expected young ladies to do until they got married. But Henrietta was such a strange young lady. It was disturbing to see what the growing up and the schooling had done to her. It was not just that the squeals and the shrieks and the shrill voice and the violent activity had been calmed down into a contralto voice and a gurgling laugh and a sort of lazy vitality. It was as if the whole nature of Henrietta had changed. From being excessively outgoing, affectionate, excitable, she had become quiet, withdrawn, almost as detached as Elizabeth. Not that there was anything cool about Henrietta. She smoldered. You felt that the detachment was simply a lid she had placed on her emotions. You felt that she might burst into flame at any moment. It was disquieting and Janie didn't know how to deal with it. She had an unhappy idea that it was Henrietta's reaction to the realization that she was homely. And she was homely, there was no denying that, though Janie always denied it to Henrietta herself.

When Henrietta was just beginning to grow up, and would look at herself in the mirror and cry despairingly: "I'll never be pretty, Mama, you know I won't," Janie would say: "There are different kinds of prettiness, Henrietta. A girl can be charming without being pink-and-white pretty. You have a good complexion and you must take care of it. You are going to have a nice figure, and you must learn to hold yourself properly and walk and dance gracefully and be well groomed and stylish, and above all to control your voice."

Well, Henrietta had done all these things. Her skin was fresh and clear, she had a nice trim figure and a definite sense of style. Though she startled Janie by the kind of clothes she wanted to wear. She moved with slow grace and danced beautifully, and heaven knew her voice was controlled. Still, there it was—her features were irregular, her mouth was too big, her eyes a nondescript brownish gray, her lashes and brows colorless, and her hair mouse-colored, fine and straight as a poker. Taken all together, Henrietta's appearance was distinctly unattractive—until she moved or spoke or laughed or sang. Then something happened. The homely features were lost in something that was neither homely nor unattractive. Certainly not to young men. That was the most amazing thing about Henrietta, she was terribly popular with young men. They flocked around her, she had more beaux than Jane had ever had. When this phenomenon first began to manifest itself Janie had been astounded and puzzled. Later she became worried. There certainly was something suggestive and —well, come-on-ish, in Henrietta's manner with boys, and a horrid thought persisted in her mind. Finally she spoke to Henry; men knew about these things.

"Henry, you don't suppose—do you think—that Henrietta is—*fast?*"

Henry was indignant. "For God's sake, Janie," he said, "of course she ain't. What put that idea in your head?"

"Then why in the world do the boys flock around her the way they do?"

Henry laughed at her. "Because she's got something. I always told you she had. Men don't just fall in love with pretty women, Janie. Look back over the history of the world. Henrietta has got personality; she's got—allure."

Janie considered that doubtfully. "It doesn't sound very nice."

"Why not? Men and women are attracted to each other, Janie, because that's the way the good Lord made the world. Sometimes it's just because they are men or women, sometimes it is a pretty face or a pretty figure or a pretty voice or because they are good and kind or what not, but sometimes it's something, some quality that reaches out from inside and attracts them, draws them like bees to honey. Look at Tommy Tyler. He certainly ain't good looking or anything special at all, even when he's sober, and yet the girls are crazy about him; older women too, not just our little Jane. It's a gift, and Henrietta has got it. It don't make people happy, I don't think, but there it is."

So there it was. Young men swarmed around homely little Henrietta, and she flirted with them or treated them with a high hand, smoldered at them or looked at them with lazy indifference, sang to them, danced with them and, down underneath, it seemed to her mother, watching, was not very deeply interested in them. Janie had seen her refuse to go to a dance for no reason except that she did not feel like it, or turn down an invitation from a young man because he had bored her the last time she went out with him. Perhaps that was part of her system, of her "allure." Janie didn't know, it was all strange to her.

She heard somebody coming up the back stairs, and Henry came into the room. "Hello, honey," he said.

"I came in the back way, because I didn't want to get involved with that crowd downstairs."

"There aren't but two of them."

"Well, they are making enough noise for six."

They certainly were. One of the boys was banging on the piano now, and they were singing.

"I told Ella to bring me my toddy up here."

"That's nice. It was quite a funeral, wasn't it? Everybody I ever knew was there, and lots of people I never saw before. Where do you suppose they came from?"

"All over the state, I reckon. Everybody knew Miss Bessie."

"On the way home I saw Raiford, in that automobile of his. We had quite a talk. I'm afraid, Henry, that that isn't a very happy family. Raiford looks awful."

Henry grunted, but said nothing. Ella came in with a pitcher of hot water and Henry's toddy on a tray. Henry went to the washstand and washed his face and hands with much

296

splashing and sputtering. Although they had the bathroom now, they still did not have hot water. They were going to put in central heating and hot water as soon as they could afford it. Janie went on with her embroidering.

"Jane went home with Emmy Duval Foster," she said. "She is going to spend the night with them and go somewhere, to the Russells', I believe, to play five hundred."

"Good," Henry said. "I like to see her go out with her friends. She works too hard at that painting of hers. She's getting too quiet. She ain't but twenty-two years old, Janie."

"I know. It's too bad, but oh, Henry, I am so glad for her to have the interest the painting gives her. And she's good at it, you remember her teachers at the Corcoran Gallery that winter she was in Washington said she was really gifted."

Henry sat down with his toddy and the *Richmond Times.* The singing was still going on downstairs.

"You know what I got on my mind, sugar?" Henry asked. "Before long I am going to start an afternoon paper."

"For heaven's sake, Henry, isn't one paper enough for you?"

"There ought to be an afternoon paper in this town, and if I don't start it somebody else will."

Henry was in a constant state of irritation over the presidential election. He grumbled about it every time he read a paper. Big, fat old William Howard Taft lumbering around the country making dull speeches, and William Jennings Byran. He had been mad about it ever since the Democratic Convention had nominated Bryan last June.

"You might think the Party was bankrupt," he stormed. "Why in the devil can't we think of somebody to nominate? Ain't there any other Democrats?"

"What's the matter with Mr. Bryan?" Janie had asked.

"The chief thing the matter with him is he can't get elected. He's a forward-looking man and an eloquent orator and all that, but he's tried twice before this. He has said everything he's got to say. If he couldn't get the people with him before what makes 'em think he can now?"

Janie had begun to take some interest in politics since Henry went to Congress and she spent so much time in Washington. He was running again this year and was campaigning through the district, but not very hard because he was unopposed. The Republicans knew there wasn't any use putting up a man against him. Janie had stopped being frightened when he made speeches, he was a veteran now. She was not even scared when he made speeches in the House of Representatives. She could smile at herself when she remembered the time he made his maiden speech in Congress. He had not opened his mouth all during the first session he was there, a freshman representative was supposed to keep quiet, and when he began to make plans to speak in his second session she was not only scared but worried.

"Now listen, Henry," she said. "You have got to remember that you are representing Virginia, the Old Dominion. You are speaking for Virginians. Please don't get up there and talk the way you do when you are campaigning around here at home."

"Don't you worry about that, sugar," he said. "Don't you worry a bit. I ain't going to let those Yankees catch me saying ain't."

And he hadn't. Sitting up in the members' gallery, tense with nervousness, Janie had seen Henry stand up on the floor of the House, looking distinguished in his cutaway coat and gray striped trousers, with his high flaring collar and black bow tie, and heard him deliver an address on the iniquities of the Republican tariff in English as polished and perfect as anyone could desire. Not only were there no ain'ts or double negatives or "he don'ts," but he used scholarly allusions and Latin phrases and words that Janie had to go home and look up in the dictionary. It was a very creditable performance and she decided to stop worrying about Henry.

The music-making had ceased now, and the house was quiet. Presently the gong sounded for supper and she and Henry went down. Henrietta was waiting for them. With the going down of the sun the October evening was chilly, and Amos had built a fire in the dining room. It flickered in the polished floor and the gleaming silver. The new electric chandelier, hanging over the dining room table in a great green glass cone, edged with a fringe of beads, was lighted and everything looked very pleasant and cheerful. Janie had recovered from the depression of the afternoon.

28

The house was so quiet that it seemed to Janie you could almost hear the silence. Certainly you could feel it, it hung heavily in the atmosphere, and it began to get on her nerves. There wasn't a soul in the house except herself and the servants, and no sounds were coming from the kitchen. She wondered where Ella and Sally were. Now that the new kitchen and pantry had been installed close up to the dining room, where the kitchen corridor and storerooms had been, the sound of the kitchen noises could frequently be heard in the house. Sally was a talker and she and Ella seemed to enjoy each other. It was such a contrast to Baizy, who had always been quiet and during the latter years of her life had hardly talked at all. She missed Baizy and Susie and old Zeb, they had been a part of her life ever since she could remember, and the new ones were not as good.

It was hot and sunny and peaceful. There wasn't a breath stirring. Maybe that meant it would rain and they wouldn't have to water this afternoon. She got up and went to the window, but the sky denied her hopes. She sat down and picked up her darning again. She was darning Henry's socks, and if there was anything duller in the world than darning a man's socks she didn't know what it was. But she had been so busy all during Avery's visit, she had not darned a sock or sewed on a button for Henry the whole month that he and Susan and young Bland had been there. They had left two days ago and it was not until this afternoon that she had worked herself up to settling down to the job. That was why the house seemed so silent, there had been so much activity going on in it. It seemed to her that young Bland made more noise than either of her boys had ever made. Susan tried to quiet him, but Janie liked to hear him. It had been wonderful having them for such a nice long visit. She had grown really fond of Susan. She was a nice girl. Not exactly what she would have wanted for Avery, of course; she was neither beautiful nor brilliant nor exceptional in any way, and Janie knew in her foolish heart that she had hoped for all these things for him, but she was a sweet-faced, capable girl, utterly devoted to Avery, as well she might be, and well qualified to be a minister's wife. Her father was an Episcopal minister, and though Susan had been born in Ohio and had lived in Missouri before they went to New York, both the Reverend Mr. Bascom Bland and his wife were Virginians of good families; she was a Gordon of Dinwiddie County. There was nothing against Susan, and the more she saw of her the better she liked her. It was nice that they were going to Atlanta, Avery was finally getting the kind of parish he ought to have, though of course his New Jersey church had not been bad.

The sound of a lawn mower cut through the silence, and Janie was glad to hear signs of life about the place. That would be George, the boy she was trying to teach to be a gardener. She went to the side window and called to him.

"George, I'm afraid we will have to water again this afternoon. It doesn't look like it's ever going to rain."

"Yassum," came back to her over the noise of the lawn mower. He was a good worker, he just didn't know anything.

She looked at the clock on the mantel. It was nearly five o'clock. Heavens, she would have to hurry. Henry would be coming soon. She finished the sock she was darning and piled them all back into her workbasket. She would have to sort and roll them tomorrow and then get after Henry's shirts.

She changed into blue crepe de Chine dress, thinking how the world had changed. Here she was a woman past sixty and still wearing bright colors. Mama never wore anything but black and gray after she passed forty. She smoothed up her black hair, powdered her nose, and went downstairs. It was cool in the wide front hall and there was a breeze on the porch. They liked to sit on the porch in the early evening. The trees shielded them from the street and yet they could see the streetcars and carriages and automobiles going by, and the strollers. She was sitting there rocking peacefully when Henry drove up the driveway in the automobile. Janie still thought he looked funny in it and was inclined to laugh at him. He always seemed too big for it, somehow. Henry certainly had put on weight. She ought to make him diet, but she hadn't the heart to insist on it.

She had stood out against the automobile as long as she could, until finally Henry had said: "Now listen, honey, you can keep the horses and carriages until the cows come home if you want to, but I'm going to get me an automobile."

He had, and he had learned to drive it and Janie went with him in it when they went to parties or the theater at night, but she still kept the horses and the victoria and the surrey, and Amos always drove them to church on Sunday. It was a losing fight, though. Everybody had automobiles, and now here was the problem of the carriage horses. When Betsy died last week she knew it was the end, but she wasn't going to admit it right away. Both the horses were so old, it had been obvious for quite a while that she was going to have to face up to the question pretty soon. It did not make sense to buy new carriage horses now; she would just have to tell Henry so. She waved to him as he drove around the circle past the porch and on to the old kitchen, which they had turned into a garage. He put up the car and went upstairs by the back way to wash up.

When he came down to the porch his toddy was waiting for him on the little bamboo table by the rocking chair that he liked. He kissed Janie and sat down with the paper. He had his afternoon paper now, the *Evening Sun*. He had put Jonathan in charge of it and it was doing very well. He took a sip of the whiskey and opened the paper. It had big headlines across the top. He shook his head.

"Things look mighty bad," he said.

When Henry spoke of "things," unspecified, looking bad, he usually meant that the stock market was going down, and this surprised Janie because everything had been doing so well. "You mean the stock market?" she asked.

"No, I mean the situation in Europe. Germany has declared war against Russia."

"Germany and Russia? For heaven's sake, Henry, why?"

"Franz Ferdinand. The murder of the archduke."

"But he wasn't either German or Russian."

"No, but he was Austrian. And Austria and Germany are allies. Russia and Serbia are allies, and Austria has declared war on Serbia and Russia has got to defend her. They are all tied together over there, Janie, by treaties and spheres of influence and balance of power and all kinds of things that thank God we don't have in this country. France is going to be drawn into it, as sure as you're born, and it will just be a Lord's blessing if Great Britain can keep out of it."

"How perfectly awful."

"It is awful, and all for one miserable little Austrian archduke. Europe is a powder keg, Janie, and that fool at Sarajevo lighted the match."

Sitting there in the peaceful late afternoon, with the sinking sun casting long black shadows of the cedar trees across the driveway and the cheerful sounds of the street coming to them, it was hard to imagine a whole continent rising up in arms. War! How well she knew what war could do. It had been—heavens above, it had been half a century since the tides of war had swirled up around this peaceful place and receding, had left ruin behind them. It had taken all those years to get back to where they were, and of course the world had never been the same and never would be. Did those men in Europe realize what they were doing when they declared war against each other? Well, thank goodness it was way off there in Europe, across three thousand miles of ocean. It was no concern of this country, though of course everybody would be sorry to see European fighting and killing, specially if England got involved. She ought to have gone abroad before this. Why in the world hadn't she?

Henry went on reading his paper, and presently Janie came back to their own affairs.

"I had such a nice letter from Jane today," she said. "I left it on the hall table for you to read."

Henry looked up and said "Good," but then he went on reading, and Janie knew that he was too absorbed in the paper to take in what she had said, because any mention of Jane always commanded his immediate attention. She waited until they went in to supper. The extra leaves had been taken out of the dining room table, but with just the two of them there they still seemed a long way apart. It made Janie's heart ache to think that it might easily get to be that way permanently. If Jane and Henrietta should get married—not that Jane was likely to marry now, but surely Henrietta would, and Jane was so occupied with her painting that you never could tell when she would be at home. She had gone to New York to study two years ago, and she was spending the summer now at the artists' colony at Woodstock, New York. Jane, it seemed, had turned out to be more than just "gifted." She was a real artist. Her work had been shown in several exhibits, and now she was going to have a one-woman show at the Corcoran Gallery in Washington. Janie thanked God that she had this interest, because certainly there was now no slightest lingering hope that Tommy Tyler might change. The Keeley cure had been the last resort, and when that failed there was nothing else to do. Jane knew it, of course, but when Tommy was sober and she was at home they still saw each other constantly, they still went out together, and the violets still came. Almost every week the big box of dewy-fresh, fragrant violets. Violets were going out of fashion now, orchids and gardenias were the things, but it was violets that Jane loved and that was what Tommy sent her.

"Jane seems to be having a very nice time," she told Henry. "You must read her letter. She is working very hard, her show has definitely been set for the first week in November."

"Sold any more pictures?" That was what got Henry, people bought Jane's paintings. They paid money for them, and it filled him with pride. "Hot dawg," he would say, "she's the smartest little gal in seven counties."

"She didn't say anything about it, and I don't imagine so. I think she is holding everything for her show."

"I wish they'd wait until Congress is in session in December, then I'd be there anyhow."

"Well, we'll have to go up for it whether Congress is in session or not."

"Nothing from Henrietta, I reckon."

"Heavens, no. You know how she is about writing. I am sure she is all right with the Dwight Wilcoxes, and the Old Sweet is always gay at this time of year. She is probably having a lovely time, she always does at the Springs."

She waited a few moments, and then spoke again. "Henry, I have decided—I reckon I'll have to give up the horses and carriages."

He smiled at her. "I'm glad to hear it, honeybunch. It's the only sensible thing to do."

"Sensible," said Janie, annoyed at the calm way he accepted this momentous decision. "I don't care about being sensible. And what in the world am I going to say to Amos?"

He grinned. "That's what is the matter with you, I reckon. You're scared of Amos."

She was, for a fact. The next morning she went out to the stable to talk to him, and she didn't know when she had done anything she hated more. Amos was in the carriage room. He had a soft chamois cloth in his hand and he was polishing the shining dark blue frame of the victoria.

"Good mawnin', Miss Janie," he said.

"Good morning, Amos." She sat down in a split-bottomed chair. "I want to talk to you. I'm afraid, Amos, that with Betsy gone we will have to give up the horses and carriages." Amos went on polishing, he did not speak. "Bounce is old too, we would have to get two new carriage horses and now that Mr. Henry has the automobile, it just doesn't seem sensible." She used Henry's word without thinking.

Amos put down his cloth and turned to face her. "Now lissen to me, Miss Janie," he said. "Now you jus' lissen to me. I ain't gonna drive one of them things. I ain't gonna drive 'em. I don't know nothin' about 'em and I ain't gonna learn."

"Of course not, Amos," Janie said soothingly. "Nobody expects you to drive the automobile."

"Then what is I go'n do, Miss Janie? 'Thout my horses and carriages, what is I go'n do?"

That, of course, was the question. "There will still be the riding horses," she said.

Amos brushed that aside angrily. "Don't nobody use 'em hardly ever. With Miss Jane and Miss Henr'etta away so much and Mist' Henry gittin' too old to ride. They been out to pasture all summer."

Janie knew that was true. The girls still rode, but not enough to justify keeping two riding horses. It would not be long before they too would go. What could she say to this man whose usefulness was being destroyed? It wasn't fair, it simply wasn't fair what this changing world was doing to older people, caught in the destruction of all their ways when it was too late for them to learn the new ways. Back in the old days people could expect to live out their lives in the same pattern, but not now. In his early boyhood, right after the war when they were so desperately poor, Amos had worked in the fields and the orchard and the vegetable gar-

304

den or anywhere he was needed, but for many years his life had been centered in the stable. What would he do without his horses and carriages? Suddenly a thought came to her.

"Amos," she said, "how would you like to come in the house and be our—our butler?" Dear Lord, there had not been a butler at Fairview since the war, not since the day in 1865 when Jackson had walked away.

Amos considered this in silence, and gradually a pleased grin spread over his face. "Yassum," he said. "Yassum, I reckon I'd like that right good. I could wear my outfit."

His outfit was his blue coachman's livery. He could of course wear that on special occasions, but she would have to find some way to persuade him to a less grandiose apparel for everyday wear.

Henry laughed and laughed when she told him. "We need a butler about as much as we need a seagoing motorboat," he said.

"I know, Henry, but we've got to do something with Amos, and this pleases him. He can be real useful around the house, and he certainly can't drive the automobile. And that reminds me, who is going to drive me around when you are at the office or in Washington?"

"George."

"George? The yard boy?"

Henry grinned at her. "He's a fine mechanic. He's crazy about machines and drives real well. That's why I hired him. I knew that sooner or later we would need him."

"Oh, Henry!" Janie exclaimed. "You provoke me so. You are always *right*."

When Henrietta came home from the Springs she was much amused by the household changes.

"My, my, aren't we grand?" she said. "A butler and a chauffeur. Dad must have discovered a gold mine." Henrietta had taken to calling her father Dad.

"It don't cost any more for Amos to buttle for us than it did for him to take care of the horses, and it don't cost any more for George to drive the car than to cut the grass and pull up weeds," Henry said.

"And who is going to cut the grass and pull up the weeds?" Janie asked.

Again Henry grinned at her. "George can, when he ain't driving you around."

The next day, as Henry had predicted, Germany declared war against France. That evening she issued an ultimatum to Belgium, demanding free passage to French territory. Four days later she invaded Belgium and England was in the war. It was like the firecrackers of her childhood, that you spread out on the ground and lighted at one end, and they went off in separate explosions as the flames crept along. All during the hot August days and on into the autumn, when the trees were laden with apples and the crows were cawing over sunny fields, the papers carried great headlines telling of the new developments, new tragedies of the great war. Proud little Belgium crushed beneath the iron heel of Germany, France invaded, Namur and Liege taken, the battle of the Marne fought and won. French names became a part of the everyday vocabulary, the Aisne, the Meuse, Verdun, Mauberge, Ypres. New ones every day. Every day Janie read the papers, filled with horror and wonderment that such things could happen; filled too with a growing cold hatred of the Germans and a warm admiration for the Western Allies. The British Expeditionary Force was so wonderful, she had always been sentimental about the British, of course, and the French and Belgians were splendid.

One crisp October day, when the mountains were incredibly blue and the leaves on the trees shimmered in the sunshine, Janie drove back to Fairview from a meeting of the Women's Auxiliary of St. John's in the parish hall.

As George drove her up to the house she saw another car parked there, and recognized Tommy Tyler's. He would probably stay for lunch, and she wondered vaguely whether Ella would have enough food. Tommy came out of the front door as she went up the steps, however, and she was startled. He looked like a ghost and he acted like one. He passed her by without looking at her or seeming to see her, and went and got in his automobile. It was some kind of foreign car, you did not have to crank it. He just started it up, backed around and zoomed down the driveway at terrific speed.

Janie stood looking after him. For heaven's sake, what was the matter with him? He did not seem to be drunk. He had held himself straight and walked steadily, but something was certainly wrong. She went into the hall and turned to the front parlor, looking for Jane. At first she thought the room was empty, and then she saw. Jane was standing against the front wall of the parlor near the corner, her back pressed against the wall, her head thrown back against it, her eyes closed, her hands straight down at her sides, the palms flat against the wall. Her whole body seemed tense with the pressure it was exerting against the wall. She looked as if she were trying to sink into it, to lose herself completely in the surface of that pale yellow wall.

Janie was frightened. She moved forward and Jane opened her eyes without moving. Again Janie stopped. She had never seen such desolation as looked out at her from Jane's eyes.

"Oh, Jane darling. Darling," she cried. "What is it? What has happened?"

Jane moved away from the wall, but her body did not relax. She stood tense and straight, her arms at her sides.

"He is going to Canada tonight," she said, "to enlist in the Canadian Army. He is going to fight in France."

Janie stared at her uncomprehendingly and she repeated it slowly, carefully, as if she were speaking to a child. "Tommy is going to join the Canadian Army, to fight in France."

"But Jane, honey, why on earth—we are not involved in this war, why—"

Jane threw back her head and gave a bitter little laugh, a terrible laugh.

"Yes," she said, "why in the world would Tommy Tyler go off to fight in a war that doesn't concern him, that is none of his business? Can you think of any reason, Mama?" There was irony in her voice.

She went out of the parlor and slowly climbed the stairs. Janie heard the door of her room close. She made no effort to follow. She knew that Jane must be left alone. This was evidently the supreme tragedy of her life. Dear Lord in heaven, what can I do to help this child? What can anybody do? Only Thou, oh Lord, can reach her. Perhaps Avery might, Avery with his unshakable faith in the love of God. She didn't believe the love of God could penetrate the desolation she had seen in Jane's eyes, could reach across that abyss of misery. It could for Avery, of course, but not for Jane, nor for herself, she was afraid, when she was faced with tragedy. Why, why, why must Jane be so inextricably tied to Tommy Tyler, why must he always bring her unhappiness? And to himself, too, of course. What depths of misery he must have been sunk in to justify going off like this to fight in an alien war. Perhaps it was just as well.

Jane did not come down for lunch. Janie sent a tray up to

her but it came back untouched. Neither Henry nor Henrietta was at home for lunch that day—they had lunch and late dinner now—so Janie ate alone in the big dining room. A dozen times during the afternoon Janie started to knock on Jane's door, but always held herself back.

When Henry came home that afternoon and she told him about it he was worried.

"Damn him," he said, "there just ain't any end to the trouble that man causes her."

He insisted on going in to speak to Jane. Janie didn't want him to, but he would do it. Sometimes Henry was awfully pigheaded. He knocked on her door and when he got no answer he opened the door and went in. Janie stood in the doorway behind him. Jane was lying face down on the bed, her head buried in the pillows. Henry went to the bed and when she did not move he said: "Little sugar."

Jane rolled over and sat up on the side of the bed, all in one motion. There was a certain fierceness in the motion. Her eyes were red, her face looked swollen and blotched from crying. She did not look like Jane. She looked like a different person.

"Go away," she said. Even her voice sounded strange. "Both of you go away. I don't want to see you, I don't want to talk to you. You made me promise not to marry him. You had no right to do that. This is my life, and his. I ought to have married him, no matter what. I told him so this morning. I told him I would marry him. But it is too late—too late—"

It ended in a long wail, and again Jane rolled over on her face, sobbing. Henry and Janie stood, uncertain, appalled. Jane raised her head and said: "Go away. Go away." So they went.

Henry closed her door quietly and they went into their room. His face was pale and he wore the puzzled expression of a hurt child.

"She didn't have any call to say that," he said. "She knew she couldn't marry him. She always said she couldn't."

Janie was so crushed by Jane's misery and her resentment that she took it out on Henry.

"I told you not to go in there," she said, "but you would do it. You just would do it. I told you."

Henry turned and went downstairs. She heard him close

the library door. She sat down in the chair by the window and rocked silently, torn between her own resentment at Jane's unfairness and her pity for the poor brokenhearted child.

The next morning Jane came down to breakfast as usual. Her face still showed the ravages of tears and tragedy, but she was quiet and composed. She made no mention of yesterday's scene, and for some reason neither Janie nor Henry felt at liberty to mention it. Afterwards Janie wondered if it would not have been better to have spoken of it. Words at first might have softened the edges of the hurt, before they could harden into a small core of mutual resentment, not allowed, as time went on, to interfere with deep affection, but never quite forgotten.

After breakfast Jane went up to the back guest room which she used for her studio because it faced north, and painted. A few days later she had a letter from Tommy, he was in Toronto. So life went on, but there was a quietness about Jane now that almost broke your heart. Janie kept thinking about the words of Sir Edward Grey at the beginning of the European war: "The lamps are going out in Europe one by one. They will not be lit again in our lifetime." Janie's light had gone. It had been flickering for a long time. Janie wondered if it could ever be lit again.

The brilliant autumn days went by. Henrietta had taken up golf, and she poured into it all the latent energy you always felt she had but she never seemed to use. Richard Ames, Elizabeth's eldest child and only son, was on the high school football team, and his father glowed with pride. Hugh insisted on taking Janie to some of the home games to see the splendid performance of her grandson. Richard was a fine boy, she was devoted to him, and Elizabeth's two little girls, Betsy and Jane, were sweet. Grandchildren were so satisfactory. Jonathan's four were adorable. The two little boys were in school now, but the little girls were hardly more than babies.

Jane's show in November went off very well. She got good criticisms and sold several paintings. She was going in more and more for portraiture and from this show she got several commissions for portraits. As always Janie thanked God that she had this gift and this interest to help fill the emptiness of her life. The Lord giveth and the Lord taketh away.

It was a pleasant winter. The war in Europe was distressing, of course. You grieved over the destruction of the Louvain Library, the desolation of the bombarded French towns, the terrible loss of life, but people could not help feeling thankful for the good old United States of America, for the detachment and security it offered, and for the prosperity the whole country seemed to be feeling. Prices were going up, of course, and labor was demanding higher wages, but business activity was keeping pace, and Henry said it was a fine thing, if it didn't get to the point of inflation. Janie was learning what inflation meant and trying to take an intelligent interest in public issues, partly because she thought the wife of a Congressman ought to, and partly because if you were going to advocate women's voting it was important for women to know what they were doing.

There was a lot of entertaining at Christmas time; Janie gave an evening reception and later on in the winter an afternoon card party, with refreshments sent down from Demonet's. There were some splendid plays at the Academy of Music, with dinner parties beforehand, and Amos got to wear his outfit a good many times. Henrietta had to stop playing golf when the weather got cold, but she was deep in amateur dramatics, at which she was very good. Jane went to Washington several times and stayed at the hotel with her father for sittings with the people whose portraits she was painting. Letters came from Tommy, first from Canada and then, after an interval of silence, from France. And violets came, regularly every week now, because Tommy had left the order with the florist. Jane never wore them; she took them up to her room and put them in water in a Lalique bowl on her table.

After the first of March the letters stopped coming. Tommy was killed in the second battle of Ypres. Janie heard about it through the newspaper office, when the word came over the Associated Press wires. Henry was in Washington; he was coming home that night. It was Jonathan who called her up to tell her.

"Would you like for me to come out there, Mama?" he asked.

"No," she said. "No, I can break it to her."

When she hung up the telephone she sat for a few minutes on the hall sofa to gather her forces. Then she went upstairs and knocked on the studio door.

"Come in," called Jane.

The room was a mess, of course. The big four-poster bed had been pushed into one corner, the room was filled with canvases, tubes of paint, palettes, brushes in cans. Jane really should have a better studio. She was sitting now at her easel in front of the big north window.

"Hello, Mama," she said.

"Darling, I have bad news for you." No use trying to beat around the bush.

Jane put down her brush. "Tommy?"

"Yes. There has been another battle at Ypres. The Canadians went in and Tommy was— "

"Killed." Jane finished the sentence for her. Her face grew a little paler, that was all. She sat looking out of the window, looking a long way off.

Janie went to her, held the pretty golden head against her breast and cuddled it.

"Oh, my honey, my darling, I am so sorry. If there was just something I could do to help."

"Thank you, Mama, you're always so sweet. There isn't anything anybody can do."

There wasn't, of course. Tommy was dead in a foreign country, thousands of miles away, in a foreign army, fighting for a foreign cause. It was not even as if there were any funeral preparations to make. He would be buried over there.

"There never has been," Jane said, and Janie felt that was a fitting epitaph for this whole tragic, long-drawn-out situation. There never had been anything that anybody could do about it, including Jane and Tommy themselves.

Jane came down to lunch that day, pale and quiet but composed. There was no shutting herself off in her room this time, and Janie had the feeling that she had already faced the ultimate tragedy before this happened. When Henry came home that night she said to him: "You know, Henry, I believe Jane has always known that Tommy was not coming back. I believe she knew he didn't *intend* to come back."

"I never thought of that," he said, "but it's possible. It seems sort of likely, when you come right down to it."

The next day Janie decided to drive out to Meriden to call on the Tylers. It seemed the least one could do, and the only way she could think of to express sympathy. She did not mention it to Jane, who was working in her studio. Janie felt that it was more than she should be called upon to do. Instead she telephoned to Sara Anne and sent the car in town for her. Together they drove out to Meriden. The country was still wintry but here and there the new pale green of weeping willows stood out against the browns and russets, and the mountains were very blue.

It was always such a pleasure to be with Sara Anne. She was still just as pretty as she could be, in a nice settled way. If you looked carefully you could see flecks of gray in her hair, but its general effect was still brown, and her eyes were as warm and merry as ever. She had on a brown suit which Janie had given her. That had become an established thing now; every spring and fall Janie passed to Sara Anne any of her clothes that she did not intend to wear any more. That happened frequently among their friends and relatives in the town, the prosperous ones turned over to the unprosperous the nice clothes they had finished with. Sometimes Janie bought things with Sara Anne in mind, and this had been true with the brown suit. There was a standing joke among their friends about the time Janie had come from Washington with a new green afternoon dress, and Sara Anne had looked at her reproachfully and said: "Now Janie, you know that green is not becoming to me."

Everybody had given up hope long since that Carey would ever make any money. His two attempts to set up his own agency had failed, and he had settled down as an agent with the John Price Insurance Company. They had gone back to live in the old Lewis house on Sycamore Street when Sara Anne's father had died, and they scraped along, but the house was getting mighty dilapidated and the neighborhood had gone down terribly.

They turned into the long driveway at Meriden and went toward the big pillared house. "It was sure a long time ago," Sara Anne said. "Think what has happened since then."

"Heavens yes. It has been—" Janie started to figure.

"Don't let's count it up," Sara Anne said. "Let's just say it was twenty years ago." They both laughed, because they knew it had been nearly forty years ago.

Meriden had a butler. He took their calling cards, ushered them into the parlor and disappeared. It had been years since Janie had been inside this house. In spite of all the Boyd money the Tylers had done little entertaining after the first few years of their marriage, and none at all since the children grew up and married and went away. It was a great shock to see it now, so different from her early recollections. She remembered that some time in the 1880's, not many years after Martha and Raiford were married, the whole house had been done over, and here it was, in limp and faded Victorian elegance. We thought it was beautiful then, but isn't it awful, she thought. The two lovely long parlors had been separated by folding doors, closed now and painted a dark mahogany, as was all the woodwork in the room. The walls were dark green and almost every inch of them was covered with paintings and photographs and wall brackets and knickknacks. Dejected looking red velvet curtains hung at the windows, a red velvet cover with gold fringe was draped over the closed piano, and a round table with an embroidered red and green cloth stood in the center of the floor. The room was so cluttered with red and dark green velvet sofas and chairs that you almost lost sight of its size and splendid proportions.

Janie and Sara Anne sat in silence in straight carved chairs with velvet seats. The house was absolutely quiet. Noiselessly, a starched, becapped nurse came into the room.

"Mrs. Darby? Mrs. Morgan?" She looked inquiringly from one to the other.

"I am Mrs. Darby, and that is Mrs. Morgan," Janie said.

"Mrs. Tyler is not well," the nurse said, in a voice that obviously did not come from this locality. "She has asked me to tell you that she is so sorry not to see you. She appreciates your coming very much, but she is not up to seeing visitors."

"Why, of course not," Sara Anne said. "We hardly expected to see her. We just wanted to extend our sympathy."

"Mrs. Tyler appreciates it."

"Is Mr. Tyler here?" Janie asked.

The nurse shook her head. "He was in New York, you know, when—the word came. He has not been able to get down yet."

"And the other children."

Again the nurse shook her head. "Mrs. Burton of course could not get here." That would be Kate in California. "And two of Mrs. Hilary's children have measles." That was Angela in New York. She did not mention Raiford Junior or Ranny. "There not being a funeral, you know—" She left the sentence hanging in the air.

313

"Yes, of course," Janie said, rising.

A curious shuffling sound came from the hall. The nurse appeared to be much upset. She moved quickly toward the hall but before she reached it Martha Tyler appeared.

"Mrs. Tyler," the nurse remonstrated. "You must not. No, no, you really must not."

Janie stood frozen in shocked horror. Martha Boyd was almost exactly the same age that she was, but the woman standing in the wide archway could have been a hundred. Her hair was gray and hung in wisps, her face was colorless and lined and as expressionless as if it had been a mask. She had on a shabby red velvet dressing gown which seemed to match the curtains at the windows.

"Janie," she said. "Janie Meade. And Sara Anne." She looked at them in a dazed sort of way, out of sunken eyes.

"Yes, honey," Sara Anne said, recovering more quickly than Janie, and moving toward her.

Tears welled up in the sunken eyes and ran down Martha's cheeks. Suddenly she raised her hands and covered her face. "Go away," she said. "Oh, go away."

She turned toward the hall and in turning swayed and almost fell. The nurse caught her and put an arm around her waist. "Harold," she called, and the Negro butler appeared and took Martha's other arm. Between them they lifted her up the wide and lovely stairway that was one of the beauties of Meriden.

Janie and Sara Anne let themselves out the front door. Janie took long breaths of the clean, fresh air. They got in the car and George started for home. They sat in shocked silence for a few minutes. Presently Sara Anne spoke.

"Janie, wasn't that awful? Just perfectly awful. Not a soul in the house with her but that nurse and the servants. Not even a friend, much less a relative. And what in the world do you suppose was the matter with her? Was she drunk or do you suppose they had given her some dopey medicine to quiet her?"

"I don't know," Janie said. "I just don't know, Sara Anne, but I never saw anything so sort of terrible."

"And Meriden! It used to be so lovely, would you believe it could ever be like that? Oh, Janie, will you ever forget that night? I thought I might fall in love with Raiford then, and you did fall in love with Avery."

They drove on in silence, sunk in their memories.

Janie did not know what was the matter with Martha Tyler but she had a strong suspicion, and that night after dinner, when Henrietta had gone off somewhere with a beau, and Jane had gone up to her room, she spoke to Henry about it.

"Sara Anne and I drove out to call at Meriden this afternoon."

"I am glad you did."

"Nobody was there but Martha. Neither Raiford nor any of the children, nor any relatives or friends. It was pathetic."

Henry looked at her over his glasses but said nothing.

"And Henry, I don't like to say this, maybe I shouldn't, but I have heard that Martha drank, and honestly, she was either drunk this afternoon or—or something else."

Henry put down his paper. "I am surprised you saw her," he said. "Martha Tyler has been a drunkard and a dope fiend for years, Janie. She sits out there at Meriden and drinks and drinks and when she can't get anything to drink she takes dope. She has lost everybody who should be close to her. Tommy was the only one who could stand it, and you know why that was."

Janie closed her eyes. How horrible, how unspeakably horrible. Poor Raiford. Poor, dear, gay young Raiford Tyler. She opened her eyes.

"You've always known?"

"I have known for a long time."

"And you never mentioned it."

"What was the use?" Henry asked wearily. "The whole thing was bad enough as it was. They tried to keep it a secret, they've always imported their servants and nurses from New York. I hoped Jane might be spared that knowledge at least."

Had she been? Had Jane known? Had Tommy ever told her, by way of explanation, of at least partial justification for himself? Poor, poor Tommy. She would have had so much more sympathy for him if she understood. She remembered Raiford's words the day of Miss Bessie Mason's funeral: "He can't help it, you know, Janie. It's born in him."

Janie found it hard to sleep that night. The terrible picture of Martha Tyler kept rising up before her. She lay in the darkness beside the gently snoring Henry and thought about the purposes of God. Whenever she came face to face with

315

the stark tragedies of the world she remembered her fight against the first Avery's concept of the avenging God, the Jehovah of the Old Testament, who issued orders to His people through the mouths of the prophets and punished those who disobeyed. She had not accepted that concept then and she did not now. On the other hand was the second Avery's belief in the God of the New Testament, the loving Father, helping, guarding, guiding, manifested on earth in Jesus Christ and speaking through His mouth. How could one accept that belief in the face of this useless, hopeless, sordid tragedy of the Tylers? And all the other terrible tragedies that were going on throughout the world, of course, but at least in the war it was possible to conceive of God having a purpose, the forces of good against the forces of evil, met at Armageddon. But what about the Tylers?

Through Avery she had come to believe that God had a purpose and a plan, and that for each individual the most important purpose of life was the developing of the divine soul that God had put in him. Sorrow was part of the process, of course. Sorrow was a teacher, as were happiness and joy and love. You could believe that as a generalization, but how could you believe that Martha Tyler was learning anything for the good of her immortal soul in the long twilight of drunkenness in which she lived? Or Tommy by following in her footsteps? Or had he learned? Perhaps that was exactly what he had done. Perhaps he had learned a certain peace at the end and strength, and the courage to go out and die, an honorable death, fighting in a good cause, rather than continue the life of degradation that Meriden offered him. And her darling little Jane, caught in the web of the Tyler tragedy? Oh, yes, it was easy to believe that she was growing and developing. You could believe in the purposes of God when you looked at Jane, but when you thought of Martha Tyler you could only wonder.

29

Henrietta was behaving very strangely. Janie had noticed it for several days. Her usual mercurial temperament seemed to be much exaggerated. She was all ups and downs, vague moonings around the house, doing nothing, and violent activity. Now Henry was looking at her in puzzlement. They had left the dinner table and come out to sit on the front porch in the early evening.

"You ain't going down to the Armory tonight, honey?" Henry asked.

"No, Dad."

"Every girl in town is going to be there. I bet every beau you got is in the Home Guard, and they're leaving at midnight. This is the first time, I reckon, since the Civil War that the Home Guard has been called out for anything but local duty, and they're going all the way to Mexico. You ought to go down and tell 'em goodbye."

"They really are going to give them a big send-off tonight, Henrietta," Janie said. "There were all kinds of preparations going on when I was downtown this afternoon. I thought we might all drive in later on."

"I'm not interested," Henrietta said, looking dreamily off into space.

Jane smiled at her sister. "I think," she said, "I really do believe that Henrietta is in love."

"I am," Henrietta said, flatly.

Janie wouldn't have been any more surprised if the sinking sun had begun to rise in the western sky. "Why, honey! Why —are you fooling?"

Henrietta turned and faced her. "I am not fooling, Mama. I am in love. I am so much in love that I don't care one least little scrap about the President calling out the Home Guard to go to Mexico. I hope they catch Pancho Villa, I hope they don't get killed, and I hope they come home soon, but personally—" she snapped her fingers, "it doesn't mean that to me."

"He ain't going to Mexico?"

"He's not going to Mexico."

"Well, for heaven's sake, Henrietta," Janie said, "who is he? Don't just sit there and talk about being in love and not tell us who you are in love with."

"I am in love with Giles Hammond." Henrietta managed to put an extraordinary amount of feeling into her expressive voice as she spoke the name.

Well! Giles Hammond was the son of Mr. Lawrence Hammond, president of the Citizens National Bank, a widower of long standing. Being an only child and motherless, Giles had spent most of his boyhood off at school. He had graduated from West Point and was in the regular Army, and was to be seen only occasionally in the town. He had been at home on leave recently, she had seen him several times with Henrietta.

"But, honey, this must be very sudden and very recent," she said.

"It is very sudden and very recent. That's the pity of it, it is just a crime that we didn't meet sooner."

"Why, you have known him for years."

"I mean really meet—to see each other. I didn't think about him one way or the other, and he didn't think about me except as that homely little Darby girl. Oh, yes, he did, Mama," she said as Janie started to remonstrate. "He told me so. It doesn't make the least bit of difference, he doesn't think I am homely now. That's why he told me, he can't imagine why he ever did. He thinks I am almost—not quite but almost—beautiful. Isn't it wonderful?"

She jumped up and ran over to her mother and hugged and kissed her. Henrietta was so seldom demonstrative that Janie was moved. Then she went back and sat down.

"I didn't mean to tell you tonight," she said. "Giles had to

318

go to Richmond. He'll be back tomorrow and we meant to tell you then. We want to get married right away."

"What do you mean, right away?" Henry asked.

"I mean right now, tomorrow or the next day."

"Oh, darling, you can't *do* that," Janie cried.

"Yes we can, Mama. Now listen." She drew her chair up close to Janie and spoke earnestly. "I am twenty-six years old and he is twenty-seven. We could have been married five years ago, when he graduated from the Point, if we had had sense enough to know it. We have wasted all that time. He has only two weeks of his leave left and he says he doesn't know when he will get another one. With all this Mexican trouble and the submarine situation with Germany getting so bad, there isn't any telling what will happen. Giles thinks that no matter what President Wilson can do we are bound to get into this war, and he is in the regular Army. We just simply can't waste any more time. Even as it is we will have only about ten days for a honeymoon, because he has to be back at Fort Benning two weeks from today."

"Of course, honey," Jane said. "You must get married right away."

"But what about a wedding?" Janie asked.

Henrietta laughed. "We'll get married, Mama. It will be quite legal, I promise you. We just can't have a regular big wedding. Anyhow, imagine me in white satin and a lace veil."

"I don't see why not," Janie said indignantly.

Henry did not say anything. He just pulled Henrietta down on his lap and kissed her.

So it was that two days later Henrietta and Giles Hammond were married in the front parlor at Fairview. It had been two of the most hectic days of Janie's life. "What are we going to do about a trousseau?" she had wailed, and Henrietta had laughed and said: "Give me a check and I'll buy a trousseau after we are married." All the same, Janie had insisted on taking her downtown and buying her a few proper things for a girl to have on her honeymoon. They had to be ready-made, of course, but it was surprising what you could get already made in the stores nowadays.

Henrietta was pleased with everything her mother bought her, and she agreed with all the plans that were made for the hurried little wedding, but she seemed totally incapable of taking any action herself. This was a different Henrietta, soft, complaisant, smiling. The child was a chameleon, Janie thought. You could not keep up with her changes. Giles came back the next day when the family were all sitting around the luncheon table. Henrietta went into his arms and it almost made Janie cry to see them. So Henrietta was not going to explode after all, she melted instead.

Jane took over the task of calling people up and inviting them to the ceremony. Janie had no idea who was coming and she didn't care, and certainly Henrietta didn't. "Just keep it small," she kept telling her sister, and it was relatively small, but when you added Elizabeth's family and Jonathan's family and Aunt Josie and all the cousins and all the close friends, it was not really so small after all. The fact that most of the young men in town were on their way to Mexico did cut down the numbers.

Henrietta was married in a long tan linen suit "with brown accessories," so the paper said. She wore an enormous brown straw hat weighted down over one eye by a clump of tan and green roses. Very dashing, but as far as possible from what Janie considered a proper wedding costume. She had to admit, however, that Henrietta looked stylish. She carried green orchids that Giles had had sent up from Richmond, which nobody in town had ever seen before. Mr. Hammond, looking a little dazed by these fast-moving events, acted as his son's best man, and Henry gave Henrietta away. That was all. Janie remembered Elizabeth's wedding and Henry's dismay at the prospect of taking part in two more big church marriages. He needn't have worried.

After the ceremony they had a wedding cake and champagne in the dining room. The bride and groom cut the cake with his sword, which was a nice touch, but then Amos had to scurry around in the kitchen getting the sword cleaned and polished up again. The young couple went away in Mr. Hammond's new Stutz automobile for a honeymoon which would include a stay at Hot Springs and a trip up the Shenandoah Valley.

Everybody stood on the porch and waved goodbye as they drove off. Janie felt sad and a little frightened by the thought of the vulnerability of youth. How many more sea changes would Henrietta undergo, she wondered. She edged up to

Henry and put her hand into his. He squeezed it hard, and Janie wished all the people would go away so he could take her in his arms and kiss her and comfort her.

It was lonely at Fairview after Henrietta left. The household consisted only of herself and Henry and Jane, and as each of them went away from time to time she was, for the first time in her life, occasionally left alone at Fairview. Not alone really, because Ella and Amos lived in the house now, in the room over the new kitchen, but alone as far as the family was concerned. Henry and Jane tried not to go away at the same time, but sometimes they could not help it. Henry was doing a lot of politicking, and Jane had to go to Washington for sittings with the people whose portraits she was painting. She kept a tiny studio there now, in a little building behind a big house in Georgetown which had been somebody's stable.

Mr. Wilson was running for re-election, and though it seemed incredible to Janie that there should be any question about it, it seemed that there was. Henry was worried. The Republicans were united now, there was no third party to divide them and give the Democrats a better chance, and of course they had the money. Henry was working hard with the Democratic National Committee and making speeches wherever they wanted him to; not around here, because of course Virginia would go for Mr. Wilson, but in Maryland and Kentucky and even up into Indiana and Ohio. All during the early fall he was coming and going constantly.

One afternoon in September when he was at home and was having his toddy and reading the afternoon paper in the library, Janie came into the dining room from the pantry with a bowl of flowers for the table. Suddenly she heard explosive sounds and saw Henry go stomping angrily along the hall to the telephone in the back hall. She went to the door to see what the trouble was and heard him give the operator Jonathan's number.

"Is Jonathan there?" he demanded after a moment. "Well, tell him to come out here fast. You hear, Sara Anne. Tell him I say to get here damn quick. I want to see him."

He slammed down the receiver and stomped back to the library. Janie followed him.

"For heaven's sake, Henry, what's the matter?"

"The damn young whippersnapper!" He was walking up and down the floor, thumping the newspaper. "Who does he think he is? I'll wring his neck."

Henry was seldom profane, and as a matter of fact, seldom angry. She could see how mad he was now, so she decided it would be better not to say anything to him. She went out and sat on the porch, leaving Henry to his angry mutterings, until Jonathan drove up to the house in his car. It was only a short distance from his house to Fairview when you came by automobile. He parked at one side of the circle and walked across and up the steps, and Janie watched him affectionately. He was a tall, blond young man, more like the Meades than any of her children. It was too bad that he and Henry did not get along better. It wasn't that they didn't get along exactly, they were devoted to each other, but they just didn't think alike. There was a preciseness, a sort of rigidity about Jonathan that seemed strange in Henry's son. Perhaps that was a Meade characteristic, going back to Grandpa. Anyhow, Henry didn't know how to cope with it. They looked at things from different points of view, especially in political matters, Jonathan being very conservative and Henry being given to all kinds of forward-looking ideas.

Jonathan took off his hat with a little bow when he saw his mother on the porch, and came over and kissed her. He had beautiful manners.

"Good evening, Mother," he said.

Janie followed him into the library.

"I understand that you want to see me, Father," Jonathan said.

"You're dead right," Henry replied. "You're just dead right. I want to see you and I want to know what you mean writing an editorial like this." He thumped the newspaper.

"I don't approve of the Adamson Act," Jonathan said.

"Well now, ain't that something." Henry's voice dripped sarcasm. "Ain't that just something. Young Mr. Jonathan Darby don't approve of the Adamson Act. Ain't that too bad. You against labor unions? You in favor of strikes? You like ten- and twelve-hour working days for the laboring man? Would you rather have all the railroads on strike than give them an eight-hour day? Is that what you want?"

"I want the President not to yield to every demand made by labor," Jonathan said stiffly. "I have been opposed to his policies in regard to labor right along. I was opposed to the Clayton Anti-Trust Act, at least to the labor provisions of it."

"And so right in the middle of a hard campaign, running neck and neck, you come out and stick a knife in President Wilson's back."

"I didn't stick a knife in his back, Father," Jonathan said. "I just expressed an opinion. Certainly as editor of the *Evening Sun* I have the right to express an opinion."

"You expressed your own personal and private opinion as if it were the official position of the Darby newspapers, and you know damn well it ain't the position of the Darby papers. You know it ain't my position in Congress. You know I voted for the Clayton Act and the Adamson Act. You know I am supporting the President up to the hilt and campaigning for him all around the place. The Republicans could pick up this editorial in my paper and make something out of it. It could hurt both the President and me."

"I'm sorry, sir. I don't want to hurt you or the President, but I do think I am entitled to have some discretion about the editorials I write."

"You said it!" Henry exclaimed. "Discretion is right. That's what you need. Now listen, young man. You don't have to write editorials in favor of things you don't believe in, you can write about the weather if you want to, but don't you come out with mean polemics against the things the Democratic Party believes in and the things Woodrow Wilson believes in and the things I have stood for all the years I have published these papers and served in Congress. And if that don't suit you, any time you want to resign as editor of the *Evening Sun*, you just resign. I don't want you to go, you understand, you're my only son and I want you on the papers and I want you to have the papers when I'm gone, but if the urge to express a contrary opinion on fundamental political policies gets too strong for you, you'll just have to express them somewhere else. I ain't goin' to have the two Darby papers pullin' each other's hair out in public."

Janie felt sorry for Jonathan and kissed him as he left, his face rigid with anger. "Give my love to Sara Anne and the children," she called. All the same, she agreed with Henry. Jonathan was a little too full of his own opinions.

Henry came home for the election, of course, from a last-minute whirlwind campaign trip. Jane was in Washington.

Janie and Henry went down to the *Herald* office after dinner that night to get the returns. The place was swarming with people and crowds were banked in the streets outside watching for the bulletins that the *Herald* flashed on a lighted screen. All evening they stood there, yelling and cheering, or groaning when the returns were bad, or just standing in silence, and as the evening wore on they were more and more silent, because it looked as if Mr. Wilson was going to be defeated. Charles Evans Hughes was carrying the big states of the North and East, and that was where the votes were. Before midnight it was all over. The *Herald* turned off the lighted screen, the crowd dispersed, dejection settled on everybody. Henry was crushed.

"It just ain't reasonable," he said. "Here we go and get ourselves a great man, a real leader, and what do we do? We throw him to the German submarines and elect Old Hairy-face." Sometimes Henry called Mr. Hughes Old Bluebeard, disrespectfully and most inappropriately. "What do they want to do, get in a war with Germany?"

Henry and Janie drove back to Fairview and went to bed. Early the next morning before it was daylight Janie was awakened by a soft knocking on the door. She sat up in bed and turned on a light.

"Come in," she called, and Ella's head appeared cautiously through a slowly widening crack.

"Miss Janie, ma'am," Ella whispered, "that phone been ringing and ringing. The office want to speak to Mister Henry. They say wake him up. What we goin' to do 'bout that?"

"We are going to wake him up," Janie said. Ella disappeared and Janie shook Henry into consciousness. He was always hard to wake up. He put on a robe and slippers and stumbled sleepily downstairs. After a moment or two Janie could hear him yelling all the way up from the back hall. At first she was frightened, but in a moment she realized that the yells were joyous. He came back upstairs, moving faster than she had seen him move for a long time.

"California went for Wilson," he called. "Hot dawg, Old Hairy-face ain't elected after all. Wilson has just got it, thank the Lord. We got more sense than I thought we had. But man, man, it's close."

He was putting on his clothes, getting into his trousers, tying his shoes, rummaging for a clean shirt.

"Henry, you haven't washed."

"Haven't got time, got to get to the office. I can go dirty for one day for Woodrow Wilson."

"You can't go without some breakfast."

"Haven't got time, honeybunch. Whole paper has got to be changed. First edition is already printed, we got to hold it back and print another. We'll get something sent in from the hotel."

He started out of the door. "Henry, you haven't combed your hair." Henry's hair always stood up in tufts over his head when he had been asleep, and now that it was thin and gray it was very funny-looking. Janie wanted to laugh.

"Oh, hell," he said, and going over to the bureau, gave it a few licks with comb and brush. Then he left, and that morning, hardly any later than usual, the *Herald* appeared with triumphant roosters crowing on the masthead and four-inch headlines saying: *Wilson Re-elected*.

30

Dr. Payne came out of the bedroom and closed the door behind him. Janie and Jane, sitting in tense silence on the hall sofa, leaned forward.

"Don't look so tragic, Miss Janie," the doctor said, smiling at her. "He's going to be all right."

Janie stood up, shakily. "Oh, Doctor, thank you," she said. "Thank you."

He laughed. "Don't thank me. Thank the good Lord and Mr. Darby's strong constitution."

"It's—it's his heart?"

"Oh, yes, it is his heart. He has had a heart attack, a thrombosis, but if he does what he is told and takes care of himself, he will be all right. Not quite as good as new, perhaps, he'll have to be careful, but good for a long time yet."

Janie drew a deep breath. "What should he do?" she asked.

"Well, right now he has got to stay in bed and keep perfectly quiet. He will have to be in bed for at least two months, maybe longer. We'll see. And he has got to be quiet. It doesn't matter what happens in Congress or at the newspaper office. He'll have to forget all that. You are going to have to see to it that he stays quiet, Miss Janie."

"All right, John, I will."

"Not an easy job, I imagine. Miss Myers will stay with you as long as you need her. She has her instructions and she knows what to do. I will come back tomorrow. If you need me before that, call me."

After he had gone Janie and Jane still sat on the hall sofa. "Now what am I going to do about Henrietta?" Janie asked.

"You can't possibly leave Papa, so I'll go in your place, Mama."

"Oh, Jane, I hate for you to do that. I know you have engagements in Washington."

"They are not important. I can easily postpone them."

"I do feel that Henrietta ought to have somebody from her own family with her, going to that big old strange hospital."

Jane laughed. "Everybody has babies in hospitals now, Mama. Nobody has them at home if they can help it. Sara Anne went to the hospital when the two little girls were born, you remember."

"I know, but she had all her family right here with her, and Henrietta is in a strange place, among strange people, and Giles is just as likely as not to be out on some training detail, walking twenty miles or target practicing or something, when the time comes for her to go to the hospital."

"You mustn't worry about her, honey," Jane said. "People have been very kind to her, she has made friends out there, and you know she keeps telling you that the Army takes care of its own. Of course a sister isn't as good as a mother, but she is better than nothing, and I will just take your ticket and reservation and go on out there tomorrow in your place."

"Thank you, darling."

Janie went into the quiet darkened bedroom. Miss Myers, the trained nurse, was sitting in the rocking chair by the front window. Henry lay in the big bed. His eyes were closed, but he opened them when he heard Janie come in and reached up and took her hand as she stood by his side.

"You ain't going to let this keep you from going out to Henrietta, are you, sugar?" he asked.

Janie drew a chair up to the bedside and sat down. "Jane is going," she said. "The girls are devoted to each other, she'll be every bit as much of a comfort to Henrietta as I would be. I am going to stay here with you."

"Ain't this the devil?" Henry said, and closed his eyes again.

He looked white and weak. He had had a bad attack and

327

Janie had been terribly frightened. He had been pushing himself too hard. All that campaigning and speech-making a year ago and then the strenuous session of Congress, with everything getting worse all the time and the United States being drawn into the war. Henry had taken that hard. Woodrow Wilson had been re-elected on the slogan "He kept us out of war," and then five months after the election he had to go before Congress and ask it to declare a state of war with Germany. But by that time there just simply wasn't anything else to do; the whole country was back of him by then, with Germany declaring unrestricted submarine warfare and killing American citizens all over the high seas, with no concern for human life or property or international law or decency or anything.

After all, Henry was seventy-three years old. A man that age couldn't do the things a younger man could do without thinking about it. There had been all the long extra session of Congress called by the President to pass the legislation necessary to fight the war, and the problems at the newspaper office caused by all the young men going away. Every man in town of the right age had volunteered, except those with such heavy family responsibilities that they couldn't. There had not been a man drafted from the town, because the number of volunteers had exceeded the draft quota right along. That filled Henry with pride. "I always said this was a good town," he would say. "A fine town, fine people. It makes you proud."

In her own selfish heart she rejoiced because her sons were too old to go to war and her grandsons too young. All except Richard Ames. He had not actually reached draft age, he would not have had to go, but he volunteered just the same. He was down at Camp Lee now training with the other boys from the town in the Eightieth Division. It was too bad, he had been in his second year at Washington and Lee. Hugh had been much upset and she supposed Elizabeth was too, but you never could tell about her. And of course there was nothing anybody could say. When the country was at war the young men must fight. It was funny about Giles Hammond. You would have thought that he would be among the first to be sent to France, and she had agonized over that probability for Henrietta's sake, but instead he had been assigned to training duty and transferred from Fort Benning to Camp Zachary Taylor, outside of Louisville.

Henry opened his eyes. "All the Darbys die of heart trouble," he said. "It is a good way to go, only I ain't ready to go quite yet."

The thought of Henry's dying terrified Janie. She had a sudden appalling vista of what life would be like without Henry. She squeezed his hand. "Darling," she said, "you are nowhere near going. John Payne says you will be perfectly all right if you will just behave yourself and do what you are told."

"I reckon I'll have to."

The next day Jane took the train for Louisville, and a week later a telegram came from Giles: "Baby girl born this morning. She and Henrietta are doing fine. Letter follows."

The letter that followed was from Jane. Everything was all right, she wrote. Giles had not been off on a training detail when the time came, and both of them had been with Henrietta right up to the time she went into the delivery room. It had been an easy birth considering the fact that it was a first child.

Both Giles and Henrietta were simply enchanted with the baby. Henrietta said tell Mama that she was unbelievably beautiful. She was a sweet little thing, though of course you couldn't tell a thing about her at the age of two days. She weighed seven pounds and had blue eyes, of course, at birth. Although she was practically bald there was a fine golden fuzz over her head. She would probably be a blonde. Louisville was a charming city, rather stately in its residential sections, and the Seelbach Hotel was very comfortable, but Camp Zachary Taylor was the most godforsaken place she had ever seen, interminable rows of unpainted wooden buildings separated by unpaved dirt streets, dusty in dry weather and mudholes when it rained. Of course that was true also of Camp Lee and all the new hastily built training camps. Giles had confided that though he had wanted to stay there until after the baby came, now he hoped to be sent overseas. In that case Henrietta and the baby of course would come back to Fairview. She, Jane, would stay with Henrietta until she left the hospital and was settled back in her apartment. Henrietta said please thank Papa, only she said Dad, again for the money to get a nurse. Giles had engaged one who would be waiting for her.

It was all very satisfactory and Janie was delighted. She

could not imagine Henrietta with a baby, but she had learned long ago that even the flightiest girls, when they had babies, settled down and learned how to take care of them. She was glad the child was a girl. She had a feeling that if anything happened to Giles a girl would be more comfort to Henrietta, though she had no idea why she thought that. Certainly she had worried more about her daughters than she had about her sons.

Jane came home, with glowing messages from Giles and Henrietta, and Janie invited Mr. Hammond to dinner one night to hear her firsthand reports. He was a nice man, but he had lived so long alone that he always gave you the impression of not knowing exactly how to deal with people. He was stiff and shy, but his face lighted up at mention of Giles, and he seemed to be delighted by the thought of the new little granddaughter. Everybody hoped they would see her soon, and Janie forbore to mention that this was likely to happen only if Giles went overseas soon.

The bright October days went by. Jane went to Washington to fill all her postponed engagements. Henry stayed in bed and behaved himself as told to do. He did not, in fact, seem to feel like doing anything else. Janie was with him a great deal. Miss Myers was very competent, she felt quite safe in leaving him in her care, but Henry wanted her there and she stayed with him as much as she could. She read the papers to him endlessly. She shuddered over the execution of Mata Hari, justified, perhaps but terrible all the same. She thrilled over the first entry of American troops into the war during the last days of October and grieved over the first American casualties in the early days of November. She was interested in the downfall of the short-lived Russian Republic and the seizure of power by the Bolsheviks, but somehow Russia and the Eastern Front seemed so remote that the war in the East had almost no reality for her. Sitting there in the big, quiet bedroom, hardly reached by outside noises now that the windows were closed against the sharp autumn air, with Miss Myers crocheting silently over by the window and Henry lying quietly in bed, it was indeed hard to project yourself with any sense of reality into the great events that were taking place throughout the world.

Winter and spring came and went. Henry was allowed to get up out of bed at Christmastime, then to move around the house, and finally to resume a normal existence. He resigned his seat in Congress, however. John Payne had been very firm about that. "You can do one thing or the other, Mr. Darby," he said. "Either Congress or the newspapers, but not both. If you take care of it, your heart will be good for a long time, but you must be careful. You must not push yourself."

During those months the faraway war took possession of your life. You read the papers each day, avidly; you read the casualty lists with your heart in your mouth and you saw many familiar names there. You worked at the canteen set up by the ladies of the town in the Union Station, where the long troop trains passed by constantly on their way to Norfolk and the transports. You worked with the Red Cross, endlessly rolling bandages. You knitted socks and sweaters for the troops, and helped to package and ship them. You tried to conserve flour and sugar over Ella's protests. You bought Liberty Bonds and strangely, almost unbelievably, you sold them, from booths set up on street corners and platforms raised for public rallies. And you waited, everybody waited, for the next great battle, for the next casualty list, for the next great event, for the next pronouncement by the President, for the next sign of Germany's weakening. You waited for the end of the war.

One afternoon in May, when Henry had come home from the office early, as he usually did now, and was resting on the sofa in the library, she heard someone coming up the porch steps and a familiar voice calling to her.

"Grandma."

She went quickly to the door. Richard Ames stood there. He put his arms around her and squeezed her.

"Oh, my dear boy," Janie said. "I am so glad to see you. How are you? You look simply wonderful in your uniform."

He laughed. He was a nice-looking boy, not handsome but well-set-up, with a pleasant open face and nice smile.

"How is Grandpa?" he asked. Henry of course was not his grandfather by blood relationship but he was by affection.

"Come on in here, boy," Henry called now. They went into the library. "I'm mighty glad to see you. What you doing here?"

"Oh, I got a short leave and ran home to see the family," Richard said. If he had added: "The Division is going overseas pretty soon now," his meaning could not have been clearer. In recent weeks boys had been coming home on these brief, sudden leaves. It was understood by everybody that they were granted for the purpose of saying goodbye to their families, but it was mentioned by no one. The departure of troop transports was always the deepest of secrets.

Richard sat down and told them about life at Camp Lee. It was all right, he said. The training was pretty strenuous but he reckoned it was good for you. He had put on fifteen pounds since he had been there. The food was awful but you were so hungry you went on and ate it anyhow. It was certainly better than you would get when you got out in the trenches. The people of Petersburg had been wonderful to them, and the people at City Point too, where the huge Du-Pont plant was manufacturing ammunition. Things were always gay when you could get away from training long enough to go anywhere. There were some mighty pretty girls in Petersburg. No, no particular one, he liked lots of them, and of course they were not any prettier than the girls here at home.

It was a pleasant visit. Henry and Richard did most of the talking. Janie sat watching this boy, the oldest of her grandchildren, marveling at the casualness with which he talked of everyday things while poised on the brink of a great and terrible adventure. How did he really feel, she wondered. Dimly, from far away, she remembered other men going off to war. Papa, riding Black Prince to join his company in town, looking gay and dashing in his new gray uniform, expecting to be home soon. Later Jon, quietly and without gaiety, knowing by that time what the war involved. Grandpa, in his white linen suit and wide-brimmed straw hat and his old musket, going out to stop Hunter's men. Those men had been fighting on their own ground, for their own land, a land which had been invaded by an enemy. They knew what they were fighting for; they were like the French in this war. There was a closeness and a reality to those goings-off-to-battle that this war lacked, with its silence and its secrecy, its great transport ships slipping down the waters of Hampton Roads in the dark of night to the vast, submarine-infested ocean, to pick up their convoys and start the long slow journey to a foreign land and the strange, dug-in warfare being conducted there. Was it all unreal to this boy, sitting there telling Henry about his training program and the new weapons and equipment they had been taught to use? Did he know what war was, or was he filled with the high excitement of youth?

Presently Richard stood up. "I must get on back home now," he said. He shook hands with Henry. "It is good to see you looking so well, sir. I am not going to worry about you any more."

"That's right, boy. No use worrying about me. Take care of yourself."

Janie went out onto the porch with Richard. He put his arms around her and hugged and kissed her. "Goodbye, Grandma," he said.

"Goodbye, darling. God bless you and watch over you." She watched him with pride as he started down the steps. "You do look splendid, honey. You know, Richard, I have come a long way from Appomattox, a long way, but I certainly am glad you are not wearing a blue uniform."

He laughed at her and came back and hugged her again. "There aren't any blue uniforms in the Army any more, Grandma," he said. "Or gray ones either. There is nothing but good old American khaki."

She stood on the porch and watched him walk briskly down the driveway to the streetcar stop outside, then she went back to the library with Henry. There was silence from Camp Lee for a time until, weeks later, they learned that the Eightieth Division had landed in France. Four months after that young Richard Ames lay dead in the Argonne Forest, with blood all over his good old American khaki.

At the end of September, when word came of Richard's death, it was eighteen-year-old Betsy Ames who called to tell her. Her voice was choked with tears. A few minutes later, while she was waiting for George to bring the car around, Henry called. The family had been notified first, of course, but the casualty list had reached the paper shortly thereafter.

With tears streaming down her face Janie drove the short distance to Elizabeth and Hugh's new house, built on one of the side streets cut through former Fairview land from Fairview Avenue. Betsy met her in the front hall. Her eyes were red and she burst into tears again when she saw her grandmother. They stood with their arms around each other for a few moments.

"Mama is up in her room," Betsy said, wiping her eyes.

333

"Go on up, Grandma. I am going to bring up some hot tea."

Janie went up the stairway and knocked on a door at the front of the house.

"Come in," Elizabeth called.

She was sitting in a wing chair by the front window. She rose as her mother entered. Janie went toward her, wanting to take her in her arms and pour out words of comfort. Elizabeth, however, turned her cheek to be kissed as usual.

"Oh, darling," Janie began. Elizabeth's calmness deprived her of words. "My honey, I am so distressed, so desperately sorry."

"Thank you, Mama," Elizabeth said. She sat down again.

Janie sat down also. She sat and looked at Elizabeth. Dear Lord in heaven, would nothing move this woman? "Thank you, Mama," was what she had said when Janie wished her happiness in her coming marriage. It was what she had said when Janie congratulated her on the birth of her son, it was what she said now when she tried to give her sympathy on the death of that son. The still, cool pool of Elizabeth's consciousness seemed to run shallow and unruffled.

"Where is Hugh?" Janie asked, for something to say.

"I think he is downstairs in his den." Janie understood how Hugh would be grieving over Richard, his son and his firstborn. "Jane hasn't come home from school. She doesn't know yet," Elizabeth added.

Betsy came into the room with a tea tray and set it on a small table in front of her mother. "Drink that, honey," she said. "It's good and hot. And try to eat something." There were sandwiches on the tray, and a plate of tea cakes. "We haven't had any lunch," she explained to Janie. Then she left the room quickly.

"Will you have some tea, Mama," Elizabeth asked, and "Yes, I think I will," Janie replied. "Just the tea, strong, with nothing in it."

Elizabeth poured the tea and handed it to her mother. She started to pour herself a cup, and then Janie saw a strange thing happen. Elizabeth's hands began to tremble. They shook so that the cup rattled in the saucer and the stream of tea from the teapot spilled onto the tray. She put the teapot down and dropped the cup and saucer. They fell on the tray, the saucer broke and the cup overturned. The hot tea seeped

334

all over the pretty lace mat. Elizabeth made a little groping gesture with her hands and cried: "Oh, Mama, Mama."

Janie went to her, knelt by the side of her chair and took her in her arms. Elizabeth put her head on her mother's shoulder and sobbed. She cried for a long time. Having started she seemed not to be able to stop. Janie held her close. For the first time in her life, for the first time since Elizabeth was a tiny baby to be carried in one's arms, she felt the closeness, the oneness, the communion, she had always longed for with this child of hers. Dear Lord, how much emotion had been hidden all these years under the calm, smooth surface, the cool, clipped voice. She found herself crooning over Elizabeth as if she had been a baby.

31

Jane Darby gave a sigh and put down her palette and brush. Absent-mindedly she wiped her hands on her blue smock. This was it. She really did believe she had got it at last. She had been working all day on this portrait. Working hard. It came over her suddenly that she had had nothing to eat since breakfast. She had not thought of it before, now she was hungry. She went behind the screen which cut off one corner of the room, where she had rigged up a makeshift kitchenette, just a shelf with an electric grill, a coffee percolator and a chafing dish. It was inconvenient, you had to go into the bathroom to get any water, but it was all she needed, really. She stayed at the hotel and had her meals there or with friends, but so often when she was working in the studio she did not want to go out for lunch, and that was when this little corner was useful.

She put fresh coffee and water in the percolator and plugged it in. To the sound of its cheerful gurgling she opened a little cupboard to see what was there. Looking doubtfully at various cans, she glanced at her watch. Heavens! It was nearly five o'clock. It was too near dinner-time for real food, she would just have cheese and crackers with her coffee. Taking a plate with her she went back into the studio and stood off, eating crackers and looking at the portrait while she waited for the coffee to perk.

It was good. It really was good. There had been something

in that boy's face she had not been able to get for a long time. Something in the last photograph, that was. The room was littered with pictures of him, from the time he was a small boy on. As soon as she had her coffee she would have to begin to pick them up. His name was Warren Upsalom. He had been killed in France last fall, one of the early American casualties. He was an only child, his parents were crushed, they wanted a portrait of him. They had brought her innumerable pictures, clippings about his athletic activities, his school yearbook, various small possessions, his letters from France. She could have gone ahead with the portrait long ago if it had not been for that last photograph, taken in his uniform in Paris, during a brief leave when his regiment had been brought back after weeks in the trenches for a rest period before returning to the front, and death for him. It was his face then, the expression in his eyes, that she had not been able to get. Over and over again she had painted in the features and lost the expression. Angrily she would clean the canvas and begin again. That morning she had concentrated as she sometimes could when painting. She had lost herself, given herself up completely to that boy's face, his eyes, the qualities she saw there and divined from his letters, a fine courage, a calm acceptance of self-sacrifice for a cause, an almost spiritual surrender to something bigger than himself. The words of Alan Seeger's poem came into her mind: "I have a rendezvous with death." That was it. These were the eyes of a boy looking death in the face, sorrowfully, wistfully, but unafraid. There was nothing in his other pictures to suggest this self-surrender; he looked and acted like an active, alert, normally self-centered and thoughtless American boy. This was something that had to come to him, she thought, in darkness and cold and mud and terror and death, something not in the normal experience of youth, something born of sorrow.

There came to her the look on Tommy's face that last dreadful day when he had come to say goodbye to her, a final goodbye. He too had been looking death in the face, intentionally, deliberately; looking at death as a friend and a welcome deliverer. Looking through her and past her to a longed-for haven. She would never forget it.

She rose and went to a pile of canvases leaning against the wall at the back of the room, under the big north window.

She pulled one out and put it on a bookshelf and sat down and looked at it. It was a portrait she had painted of Tommy from memory, after his death. No one else had seen it, she kept it for herself. She had not painted him as he had been the last day. She had painted the young Tommy, the one she had first known, gay and charming with his crooked smile and his tousled brown hair. Death was a stranger to him then, life the ultimate desire. Looking at Tommy she turned the surge of emotion that came to her upon Warren Upsalom. Thinking of Alan Seeger's rendezvous with death, she painted with passion and sorrow and longing. When she finished she had what she had been seeking.

The coffee was perked now and she poured herself a cup, hot and black, and picked up another handful of crackers. She would straighten up the studio a little and get the paint off her fingers and go back to the hotel for an early dinner.

The portrait of Tommy still stood on the bookshelf. Jane pulled a chair up to a small table, put her coffee cup on it and sat looking at the portrait. The young, young face, the gay mouth and eyes, the devil-may-care cock of the head on the shoulders. As she looked it came to her that if this beloved Tommy was here with her now, in person, he would seem to her very immature. She had learned so much of weariness and sorrow since Tommy looked like that. Even if she supplanted the young face with the older, worn face of the later Tommy an unbridgeable chasm would stretch between them, because she had gone on living and he had not. Life was a hard taskmaster, it made demands that must be met. Those who lived could mourn but they could not share life with those who died. Tears came to her eyes. Dear Lord, must even this be taken from her? Death was ruthless and life without mercy. When death took the loved one, life, by the mere fact of living, took the love itself, leaving only a sad memory and an ache of the heart. The emotion of the morning, which she had poured into the portrait of Warren Upsalom, was in reality only the memory of emotion.

There came a rat-tat-tat on the door, followed by a loud banging. She knew who it was. She sat quietly for a few moments, collecting herself. The banging continued. She went to the door, and there he was. Bradford Long.

"Greetings, my love," he said. "Let me in. I'm on the point of committing suicide or murder. I need to be rescued."

338

He came in and dropped into an armchair, hat, overcoat and all.

"Where I come from," Jane said, "men take off their hats when they come in the house."

"Where you come from, love, men are gentlemen, so you tell me. I'm not."

"You might try it. It would be an experience for you."

He took off his hat and sailed it across the room. It hit against the screen and fell to the floor.

"You couldn't be persuaded to give me a drink, could you?" he asked tentatively.

"I haven't got a drink," Jane said.

"I was afraid of that. All right, I'll settle for coffee."

"There is some fresh coffee, just made, in the percolator."

He sat and looked at her. "Do you mean I've got to get it myself?"

"You certainly have."

"Where I come from, women wait on their men."

"You are not my man," Jane said. "Thank heaven."

Bradford slowly got up, dropped his overcoat and went to the shelf behind the screen. Jane watched him without moving. She liked Bradford, in spite of, or perhaps because of, his exuberance. He always cheered her up and she was glad to see him now. It was lonely at the hotel without Papa, and she felt like celebrating, now that she had got what she wanted and the portrait was finished. She knew he would take her out to dinner. All the same, he had to be held down, hard and constantly.

Coming back from the percolator with his hot coffee, Bradford noticed the portrait of Tommy that Jane had put on the bookshelf. He stared at it.

"Well, well," he said, putting down the cup and picking up the canvas, "what have we here? Is this our young hero, our dear departed?" His voice was flippant.

Jane crossed the room swiftly and took the portrait away from him.

"Bradford Long," she said, "don't ever try to be facetious about Tommy Tyler."

His face softened. "I know. I'm sorry, little girl," he said. "I apologize. It's just that I am a little jealous, you know, and then I have had a hellish day."

Jane put the portrait back behind the others against the wall. Bradford sat down and drank his coffee.

"I am a newspaperman, you know," he said. "I'm used to my freedom. This thing of being tied to a desk with a bunch of nitwit superiors over me is getting me down. I don't know why in hell the newspaper picked me to loan to the Treasury."

"I do," Jane said. "You are one of the best publicity men in the business. It takes somebody like you to be good at publicity, and the Treasury needs publicity for the Liberty Bond drive. You are just doing your bit."

"I get no sympathy from you, my love?"

"None, and Brad, will you please stop calling me your love. It makes me feel like a fool."

"But you are, you know."

"Hah!" Jane said derisively.

"You don't believe it, do you?"

"No, I don't."

He shook his head sorrowfully. "I can't make you believe that I entertain a high degree of affection for you, and all because I offended your girlish sensibilities by proposing an extramarital relationship between us."

"All because I don't believe you've got it in you to really love a woman, Brad."

He sat looking at her consideringly. "If I asked you to marry me, Jane, would you do it?"

"I would not."

"Why not?"

"For many reasons, Brad, my dear," Jane said, "all of which add up to the fact that I don't want to."

"A good forthright statement," he replied. "I must admit that any girl who married me would lead a hellish life. Temperamentally and professionally I am not a marrying man. I'm a wanderer, here and there, come and go, off again on again. I am one of the few real adventurers left in this grim modern world. And yet sometimes when I look at you I am tempted. I really am tempted to give marriage a try."

"Well," Jane said. "And I should feel honored?"

"You should indeed. It is the first time in my life that I have been so tempted."

"Be reassured, Brad, you are perfectly safe. I haven't the

340

faintest intention of marrying you, or of getting involved in what you so delicately call an extramarital relationship."

"Nevertheless, I am going to hang around for a while, just in case," he said. "Time heals all wounds, Jane."

"But the wounds leave scars," Jane said.

Bradford had finished his coffee. "Take off that smock and wipe the green paint from your cheek, and I'll buy you a dinner," he said. He went behind the screen to put down the cup and came back in front of the easel, where it stood facing the big north skylight, with its back to the rest of the room. "What have you been occupying yourself with today?" he asked, and stopped to look at the portrait on the easel. He stood in silence. Jane was picking up the scattered photographs of Warren Upsalom. Finally Bradford let out a long, low whistle.

"Wow," he said. "Man alive, you've got something here, Jane. This is good, my girl."

Jane went on sorting the pictures and putting them in the top drawer of a secretary. Bradford spoke again, and there was suppressed excitement in his voice.

"Listen, Jane, this is it. This is exactly what we need. You've got to let me use this portrait. We have to have a poster for the new Liberty Loan drive. I have spent the afternoon fighting the dumb cluck who happens to be my chief. He wants to use a horrible mawkish thing that shows a little girl, or maybe it's a boy, I don't know, anyhow a child with its arms stretched out and the picture of a soldier behind it and a caption saying 'Buy Bonds to Help My Daddy.' Can you believe it? But this— Who is he?"

"His name is Warren Upsalom. He was killed in France last winter."

"This says it all, without a word. We wouldn't need a caption. That face says it all. It would jerk tears—and money, out of Old Stonyman. You'll let me have it, won't you, Jane?"

"I can't," Jane said. "It is not mine. It belongs to the boy's parents. They have paid me for it, you will have to ask them."

"Who are they?"

"They are Mr. and Mrs. Howard Upsalom. They live in Baltimore. I can give you their address."

"Hah! Tomorrow we go to Baltimore. I would go to San

341

Francisco for that portrait. We will go to Baltimore and take it with us, and we will turn our combined blandishments upon Mr. and Mrs. Howard Upsalom. They can't resist us. Hurry up, girl, I want to celebrate." As Jane took off her smock and started toward the little bathroom across the vestibule to get the green paint off her cheek, he called to her. "In case I haven't mentioned it before, you are a damn fine artist. And I am the best damn publicity man in the United States."

"And one of the world's great egotists," Jane said.

So it was that soon the portrait of Warren Upsalom, by Jane Darby, began appearing on bulletin boards and road signs, posters and pamphlets, at meetings and rallies from one end of the United States to the other. His haunting eyes and sad young face became familiar to millions of people, and the name of Jane Darby known to thousands.

32

October was a beautiful month that year, if you could enjoy it, if your heart had not been heavy with a weight of sorrow. The mountains were soft in their autumn haze and the days were crisp and sunny. Great things were happening in Europe. The Quadruple Alliance was breaking to pieces. Bulgaria and Turkey had signed armistices with the Allies, the Austro-Hungarian Empire was splitting, Germany was exchanging peace notes with President Wilson. It looked like the beginning of the end. And yet the troop trains kept passing through Union Station, men kept pouring into France, the great Meuse-Argonne battle went on endlessly, the casualty lists made your heart ache. Here at home a new worry appeared in the spreading epidemic of Spanish influenza. You began to read about it in the papers, a strange new disease in its virulence and deadliness. People died of it almost overnight. It was worse in the big cities, of course, though a few cases developed right here in town, and in the Army camps.

Henrietta and Giles were still in Louisville. "Giles is almost crazy with impatience," Henrietta wrote, "and I really do feel sorry for him, because it is awfully important to him. He simply can't bear sitting out the war here in this place, and he absolutely hounds the C.O. I wouldn't tell him so, but oh, Mama, just between you and me, I do rejoice over each day he stays here in safety." Finally she wrote: "Giles has at last got his overseas orders. When the present contingent of trainees goes over, which will be in November, he will go with them, and Lynne and I will come to Fairview." Now she wrote that the influenza was bad at Camp Zachary Taylor. She was afraid to let the baby go outdoors, and if it got any worse she thought she would come home even before Giles sailed.

Henrietta had named the baby Carolyn and called her Lynne. "I wouldn't think of naming her Henrietta," she had written, "and there are already too many Janes and Elizabeths in the family. Do you mind, Mama?"

Janie did not mind. She was always amused and touched by Henrietta's exaggerated enthusiasm over the baby. Her letters were full of the child and of her beauty. "You wouldn't believe it, Mama. She is just simply perfectly beautiful. Aren't the genes or the hormones or whatever it is that makes babies what they are supposed to skip over a generation each time? Well, they have certainly done it with Lynne. It is incredible that I could have produced anything as lovely as Lynne, even with Giles' help."

Jane, coming back from a trip to Washington, reported that conditions were terrible. The city was unbelievably crowded; the new army of government war workers were piled on top of each other, living three or four in a room, in halls and attics and anywhere that provided a roof and a bed. They worked in temporary wooden buildings hastily put up on the Mall and in the parks; they ate from cardboard boxes sold in the buildings and the streets near the buildings. No wonder the epidemic spread like wildfire. All day long, Jane said, you could hear the wails of the ambulance sirens going by, taking people to the hospitals. She would not go to Washington again until this was over, and she had told the real estate agent to rent her studio. She didn't have the heart to keep it for occasional use when space was so badly needed. The woes of the world seemed endless that fall of 1918. The only thing you could do was to keep busy and not think about them.

One day in early November, when the papers were full of the abdication of the Kaiser and his flight to Holland, when it really did look as if the war must end any moment now, Janie was resting in her room after a strenuous morning in the Red Cross workroom. She heard an automobile drive up to the porch and the doorbell ring, and soon Sally came up to tell her that Mr. Hammond was calling. Strange, she thought, he was so formal he didn't usually drop in like this. Hurriedly dropping her kimono and putting on a dress, she went downstairs. Mr. Hammond was standing in the front parlor. His face was gray. He looked very old.

"Mrs. Darby," he said, without waiting for a greeting, "I— I am sorry to disturb you but I—have had word from the War Department that—Giles has died of Spanish influenza."

Janie was so shocked that she was speechless. Giles, in perfect safety at Camp Zachary Taylor. The futility of words came over her. What was there to say?

Mr. Hammond went on. "I am much grieved to tell you this, but Henrietta is ill also."

Janie cried out and caught his arm. "She is not—dead?"

"No. Oh, no, but she is ill. They have taken her to the hospital. The telegram from the War Department told me only about Giles. It was followed immediately by a telegram from his commanding officer, extending sympathy and telling me about Henrietta. He knew my address through Giles, of course, he was very fond of the boy. The baby—is all right, but they thought it best to take her to the hospital also." All Mr. Hammond's words seemed to come out with difficulty.

"I am going out there to bring him home, and to see about Henrietta and the baby. I came to you instead of Henry because I thought you would want to go too."

"Oh, yes. Yes. Yes, of course. When can we go, Mr. Hammond? How soon can we go?"

"There is a C & O train leaving at five o'clock," he said. "I have taken the liberty of making a reservation for you on it."

The next few hours were so hectic that Janie had little time to think. Henry was called from the office. Both he and Jane wanted to go with her, and she was quite short with them about it.

"There is no possible sense in all of us going, and I can't be worrying about you, Henry, on top of everything else. Now you stay here and take care of yourself, and Jane, you stay here and take care of him. Mr. Hammond has made all the arrangements and he knows exactly what to do. I'll send you word as soon as we get there."

Jonathan came out and drove them all to the station. Mr. Hammond was already there. It was a quiet group that stood waiting for the train. When it rolled into the station Henry put his arms around her. She clung to him for a moment, she was sorry she had been cross with him.

"Goodbye, sugar," he said. "I wish I was going with you."

"No, darling, it wouldn't do any good. I can take care of Henrietta and the baby better than you could, and certainly both of us shouldn't go, with Mr. Hammond doing everything that needs to be done."

"She's going to be all right, don't you think, Janie?" he asked, seeking comfort.

"Of course, honey," she replied, trying to give it. "Take care of yourself, Henry."

"You take care of yourself," he said. "Keep away from people as much as you can and put Glycothymaline up your nose and gargle with it every few hours."

Janie patted his shoulder. "Imagine your telling me that." She had been telling him that ever since the epidemic started.

Mr. Hammond had reserved a drawing room for Janie and she was thankful for the privacy. They had dinner together in the dining car. It was a pretense for both of them, they did not want food. She must eat something, Janie told herself, she would be faint if she did not. Mr. Hammond merely picked at his food. They ate almost in silence. He was not an easy man to talk to in the best of circumstances. In the face of this sorrow it was impossible to maintain a conversation. She went to bed as soon as the porter had made up her berth, but it was a long time before she could go to sleep.

When they reached Louisville the next day Mr. Hammond bought a copy of the *Courier-Journal* in the station and opened it when they were settled in the taxicab. Large headlines stated that an armistice was to be signed that morning. Smaller headlines underneath said that representatives of the Allies and the German Army would meet in Marshal Foch's railway coach near Compiegne for that purpose. He held out the paper for her to see, and the irony of it moved her so that she reached out and pressed his hand. He caught it and clung to it, and she left it there all the way to the hospital. If there had been any mirth in her she would have laughed at the picture they presented to the outward eye, two elderly people on the most formal terms, clinging to each other's hands in a taxicab.

When they reached the hospital they entered a busy, swarming lobby, and waited in front of a curved counter-desk behind which two starched nurses were busy with people, coming, going, inquiring. When their turn came and Mr. Hammond gave their names one of the nurses ushered them into a small room at one side. A tall gray-haired woman with a calm face, wearing a white uniform, rose to greet them.

"Mrs. Darby," Mr. Hammond said, "and I am Lawrence Hammond."

The woman spoke to him first. "May I express my sympathy, Mr. Hammond," she said, in a voice that matched her face. "I am so sorry that you had to come on this sad journey." Then she looked at Janie.

"How—how is she?" Janie faltered.

"It grieves me to tell you this, Mrs. Darby, but Mrs. Hammond died last night, shortly after midnight."

Janie swayed, and Mr. Hammond caught her and led her to a chair. She sat with a hand over her eyes, fighting to hold on to herself.

"May I get you some water, Mrs. Darby?" asked the woman, head nurse, superintendent, whatever she was.

Janie shook her head. She was not going to faint, but all the forces of her spirit were concentrated on not giving way, not screaming and crying here, in this place, where death was a routine occurrence and human tragedy had little significance. Mr. Hammond stood with a hand on her shoulder, trying to give comfort by touch as she had done in the taxicab. He was talking to the women. She heard their voices, she knew what they were saying. The nurse was giving him the name and address of the funeral parlor where Giles and Henrietta lay together. They were discussing arrangements. Giles' commanding officer had made reservations for them at the hotel, he would like to call on them this afternoon. There were other friends who would like to call. The woman rang a bell, and when the door opened she said: "Bring the Hammond baby here, please, Cecile."

Janie lowered her hand and looked up. The tall woman held the baby in her arms. A pair of wide blue, wondering eyes looked at her out of an exquisite little face. Even through the shock and sorrow that racked her she was conscious of surprise. The child was beautiful. What she had thought was fond and foolish mother-talk from Henrietta was true. Golden ringlets covered her head, her eyes were gentian-blue, her features almost cameo-like in their clear perfection. The genes had certainly skipped a generation, many generations, in fashioning this child.

She stood up and held out her arms. The baby came to her willingly. Janie held her close and pressed her cheek against the soft curls. Another little life, another little girl. Would she go on to tragedy, as her own little girls had done, her tragic little girls? Jane eating her heart out in silence, and her little Henrietta, her funny, strange, darling little Henrietta, dying alone in this great, bare, impersonal hospital. Suddenly a picture came into her mind through all the years that lay between. She saw hot sunshine on a dusty, country road, and a tired, shabby, gray-clad figure sitting on a tired horse, and heard a tired young voice saying, "Don't weep for him, ma'am. Tears are for the living." She buried her face in the baby's clean white dress to hide the tears that were rolling down her cheeks, but she could not hide the sobs that shook her body.

Part IV

33

The blue and gold enamel clock on the mantelpiece, under its domed glass cover, registered a quarter to ten o'clock. Its golden balls turned evenly, smoothly, backwards and forward, as they had been turning for heaven knew how many years, certainly since long before Janie was born. Janie kept glancing at it, filled with impatience and irritation. I am getting to be downright crotchety, she thought. Old people do, and I must not let myself get that way. All the same, why in the world would Arthur take so long to carry the eggs to Maria Jennings and the custard to old Mrs. Hamlin?

She sat down and picked up a piece of knitting. Ever since the World War, when she had made so many socks and sweaters, she had found that knitting soothed the nerves. She had expected Arthur back with the car long before this, and there was so much to be done this morning that it was annoying to have to sit there and wait when she was all ready to go downtown. She must do some marketing, and she was taking some old clothes to the Salvation Army, and Sara Anne was not well, she did want to stop by and see her. She wanted to get to the hospital to see how Toni Russell was doing, she had had an operation for gallstones and at her age that was pretty serious. Toni was older than she was, though not much, of course. She had to go by Garrett and Wright's to get some white wool to edge the little pink sweater she was knitting for Helen, Jonathan's older daughter who was expecting a baby. Another great grandchild, heaven help me, this will be ten. It was hard to realize. And then she simply must get to the bank to talk to Harry Updyke about the financial situation. There was so much poverty and want everywhere these days, and her income had been so much cut down by the depression that she could not do half of what she wanted to do. Harry insisted that the securities were perfectly good, they were all blue chips, all she had to do was to ride out the storm, but all the same it was a problem to meet her commitments and keep up her charities and run the house. Of course Jane helped with the house, bless her, but Jane's income was as badly cut as hers. At 12:50 she must be at the Southern station to meet Jane, who was coming from Washington.

Upstairs Lynne's radio was blaring forth sounds that passed as music in her ears, and Janie was as always filled with astonishment at modern youth's imperviousness to noise. Not only were they impervious to it, they demanded it. Lynne would turn hers on when she went upstairs to study in the evening, and when Janie protested she would say, "But Gram, I can study so much better with the radio on."

Janie was glad Jane was not working in her studio in the stable. She had made a charming place out of the old stable and spent much of her time there, but Lynne's room was at the back of the house on that side, and when she turned the radio up to a high notch and the windows were open the sounds could easily be heard in Jane's studio. Sometimes Jane did not mind, but if she was really working and wanted Lynne to stop the noise, she told her to stop and Lynne would do it. Jane adored the girl, but when it came to discipline she was even firmer than her mother.

Well, thank goodness they did not have to worry about Lynne's college expenses. Mr. Hammond was going to take care of them. Mr. Hammond would do anything in the world for Lynne, and though he was hit by the depression like everybody else, he lived so quietly and had so few expenses, that he still could and did do lovely things for her. He had taken her to Europe last summer, a year ago, when she was sixteen; or rather, to be more accurate, Lynne had taken him. He confessed to Janie when they came back that he had simply trailed along and paid the bills. He was pretty well worn out by the time he got home.

The radio was turned off. Janie looked at the clock again. Eight minutes to ten. Really, she would speak to Arthur about this delay. She wondered, as she had many times, whether they could get on without Arthur. The only way she knew to economize on the house was to cut down on the number of servants. Both Jane and Lynne could drive a car, but Lynne was going off to college in the fall and Jane was too busy with her own work to be readily available. Since Amos died Arthur was the only man around the place, and he was needed for so many things. Besides, if she let Arthur go it would simply add to the terrible unemployment. There would just be one more person for the charitable agencies to take care of. Jonathan was facing that problem on the newspapers. He was trying so hard not to discharge his employees, but it was hard sledding. They had all agreed to a cut in their wages and salaries rather than in personnel, and that helped.

She heard footsteps coming down the stairs and in a few moments Lynne stood in the doorway. Janie had tried to learn to school her face to immobility in dealing with Lynne, because she knew there was nothing the child liked as much as startling her elders, and she hoped she did not show now how startled she was. She sat looking at her granddaughter.

I lived through Henrietta's French songs and her come-hither ways, she thought. I lived through the lost generation of the twenties with Betsy and Jane Ames and Jonathan's children—the knee-length skirts, the Charleston and the Black Bottom and the bootleg liquor. I have accepted short hair and women smoking in public. I have tried to go along with the times, but nothing has ever prepared me for Lynne.

To begin with, she was five feet ten inches tall, a young goddess. A golden goddess. She was gold all over. Her golden hair waved prettily around her head, her brows and lashes were golden; not colorless as her mother's had been, but a gold that glinted in the sunlight. Her skin was golden, tanned by the sun now to warm brown-gold, fading in the winter to ivory-gold. Against this golden background the blue of her eyes and the vivid red of her lips stood out in startling contrast. That was another thing Janie had had to get used to. Delicately tinted cheeks out of a top bureau drawer she had known all her life, but violently red lips out of a small tube carried in purse or pocket and applied anywhere at any time, that was something else. Lynne had on a bright yellow, open-throated shirt and a pair of brief blue pants which, Janie knew, went by the name of shorts among the young. She could think of no more appropriate word for them. She had occasionally seen girls wearing them at the Country Club and had looked upon them with cold distaste. She had never seen Lynne so clad before. The incredible length of slender golden legs ended in yellow socks and white tennis shoes. She carried a tennis racquet in her hand.

"I'm going out to the Country Club to play tennis, Gram." Lynne's voice was like Henrietta's after it had been cultivated, but with Lynne it was natural.

"I gathered that impression," Janie said. "And after you have played tennis, what are you going to do?"

"I expect I'll stay for luncheon. They are trying it out, you know, serving lunch every day, and if people don't do it they will probably stop."

"Is it your idea that you are going in what you have on?"

Lynne looked down at herself with innocent eyes. "Why yes, of course."

"Then I think you had better change your plans. You can't possibly go into the clubhouse in that outfit."

Lynne came into the room and sat on the arm of a chair. "Listen, Gram, darling, you simply must get over the idea that there is something immoral about a girl's legs."

"I am not talking about morals," Janie said. "Morals are something different. I am talking about suitability, about conduct appropriate for a young lady."

"Gram, I've got news for you. There aren't any ladies any more."

"And I have important news for you, Lynne," Janie said, tartly. "There are still ladies. There will always be ladies in any society that has passed the primitive stage. They may not be called ladies, and the social customs surrounding them may vary widely, but the qualities that make a lady are inherent in civilized society, and there must always be women who guard and preserve them. Among those qualities are good taste and personal dignity. I know that the costume you have on is now considered proper for the tennis courts, and if you want to change into it after you get to the Club and wear those outrageous shorts while you are actually playing tennis

353

I will make no objection, though I would much prefer that you didn't, but you simply must not sit around the clubhouse and have luncheon or play bridge dressed like that."

The old blue eyes and the young blue eyes looked at each other, levelly, gravely, for a few moments and then Lynne's red lips parted and she laughed gaily. Going out into the hall she came back in a minute tying around her waist a full, wrap-around blue skirt that matched the shorts beneath it.

"See?" she said, as she adjusted the ties into a bow in front. Janie saw. "So I have been taken for a ride," she said.

"Just a little one, Gram. I wanted to see what you would do. You were positively noble, darling."

"Thank you. I hope you will remember my words."

"Heavens yes! You were downright impressive."

She looked charming in the blue skirt and yellow shirt. She handled her splendid young body with grace. There had been a time when she first began to shoot up like a beanstalk that she was self-conscious about her height and had tried to lessen it by slouching and bending forward, but that had passed. She held herself now as straight as an arrow, and she moved with full-bodied vigor.

"Is someone coming for you?" Janie asked.

"Oh yes, that Curtis Russell creature."

"I can't imagine why you don't like him. He seems such a nice boy, and he is so tall and long-legged and well-set-up that I should think he would suit you."

Lynne towered over many of the boys she knew, and in such cases she looked calmly over their heads and ignored them. She was interested only in those who, at least, matched her own height.

"The Lord loveth not the legs of a man or the strength of a horse," Lynne said. "It's in the Bible," she added in response to Janie's inquiring look.

A loud honking came from outside. Nowadays, it seemed, young gentlemen honked for their young ladies instead of coming up on the porch and ringing the doorbell.

"There he is now," Lynne said. She picked up her tennis racquet and started out, then came back and bending over, kissed Janie on the tip of her nose. "You are so cute, Gram," she said. With a wave of the racquet she went out.

Janie was intensely amused. Mrs. Henry Forbes Darby,

seventy-nine years old and a pillar of the community, cute. Arthur drove up in the car a minute or two later.

"For heaven's sake, Arthur," Janie said, "what took you so long?"

"Miss Janie, ma'am, that old Miz Hamlin, she wanted me to do things for her. She wanted me to bring in wood for her kitchen stove and take out the ashes. She's such a poor, helpless old lady, ma'am, I didn't like not to."

"Old" Mrs. Hamlin, Janie knew, was some years younger than herself, but she was poor and helpless. Old women living alone always touched her heart.

"Of course, Arthur," she said. "That was right."

Toni Russell was not so well when Janie went to the hospital to see her. She did not get by to see Sara Anne because before she knew it it was time to meet Jane.

At the station Janie waited in the car while Arthur went to the incoming train to find Jane and carry her bag. Janie watched her daughter coming through the crowd across the station platform. She was a distinguished woman now and she looked it. Jane had made her life into a career and herself into a personality and a personage. She carried herself well and she wore her clothes well. She had cut her hair short and as it was not naturally curly she had permanent waves from time to time. "A most inappropriate name," Jane had commented. "It seems to me you are having so-called permanents all the time."

"Only once every six months, lamb," Jane replied, "and six months is relatively permanent in this day and age."

Now she had on a brown surah silk dress and a small beige and brown hat. She too wore lipstick and her mouth was vivid.

"Hello, darling," she said as she climbed into the car beside her mother.

Janie kissed her. "I am so glad to see you, honey. I was just thinking as you came across the platform how distinguished you look."

Jane smiled at her. "You are sweet to say that, Mother."

"Did you have a good trip?"

"Splendid. The little Phillips boy was wonderful, I was glad to have a chance to paint him. I got just exactly what I wanted."

355

Jane had gone in more and more for children's portraiture. She still painted adults, and for her own deep satisfaction landscapes, but children had become her specialty. She was pretty highhanded about it; she painted only those she wanted to paint, and she charged what seemed to her mother, having no knowledge of the value of a painting, exorbitant prices. Sometimes, when a family could not afford the price and the child appealed to Jane, she asked permission to do the portrait as a gift; but she would make no concession in her scale of prices. During the boom years of the twenties people had clamored to have Jane Darby paint their children. It was not that she flattered them. Her children were not necessarily pretty or charming, but she got something in a child's face, the essence of childhood, that made her portraits distinctive. Now in the depression years not many people had the money to indulge in expensive portraits of themselves or their children. Jane, quite contentedly apparently, spent most of her time painting her beloved blue mountains, the hazy hills and red earth.

Luncheon was ready when they reached Fairview and they went into the dining room as soon as Jane had taken off her hat and washed her hands.

"Where is Lynne?" she asked.

"Having luncheon out at the Country Club," Janie said. "They have started serving plate luncheons every day in the effort to make some money and hold on to their employees."

Janie rejoiced at the affection that existed between Lynne and Jane. It was a happy thing for Jane, with no children of her own, to have this child upon whom to lavish her love—and for Lynne to have someone of her mother's generation, who might be expected to understand the ways of modern youth better than grandparents. Though, even before Henry's death, Janie exerted the final authority in Lynne's upbringing, Jane took charge of many aspects of the girl's life, especially her clothes. She and Lynne were now deep in preparations for Lynne's going away to college. Mr. Hammond had sent Janie a check and told her to buy whatever the child needed. What she needed appeared to consist largely of sweaters and skirts, shirts and terrible garments known as pedal pushers, which, bad as they were, were at least better than shorts. They were, of course, some dresses to be included in Lynne's outfit. Janie was afraid she was going to freeze to death, and was much concerned for the warmth of her clothes.

"It must be terribly cold way up there in Massachusetts," she said.

"Not much colder than it gets here, Mother," Jane said, "though of course they do have more snow. I am sure we are getting Lynne plenty of warm things."

Lynne was going to Wellesley. When she had first expressed a preference for that college Janie had been annoyed.

"We have good colleges right here in Virginia, Lynne," she had said. "Why need you go to Massachusetts?"

"I don't need to, Gram," Lynne said. "I just want to."

"But why do you want to?"

"Oh, lots of reasons. To see the world, to meet different people and see how they live. To keep up with the Joneses, maybe."

"The Buford Joneses, I suppose," said Janie sarcastically, but Lynne looked at her calmly and said: "Well yes, now that you mention it. Allen Jones is going to Harvard this year, and Marcia Armstrong to Radcliffe."

Lynne knew about old Jiminy Jones, but he was too far back in time to mean anything to her. The present generation of Joneses and Armstrongs, Marcia Jones having married Kern Armstrong, were very nice young people. Who cared if their great-great-grandfather had been a dirty old man who kept a stall in the marketplace? Young people cared nothing about family now.

Jane thought it was fine for Lynne to go to Wellesley. "It is more exciting to go a distance away from home, Mother," she explained, "and I think it is good for her to get completely away from us in a different background. Not that Wellesley is different, really, but Lynne won't know anybody there and will have to stand on her own feet."

Jane herself was very cosmopolitan. She had been to Europe a number of times and had spent that fatal winter in Paris. She liked to go to Woodstock in the summer and had driven all over New England and she went to New York often, being very fond of the theater. In Washington, she had friends from all over the world. Occasionally she brought some of them to Fairview for a weekend. Of course Janie enjoyed having guests in the house, but she did find it difficult to cope with bearded French artists who kissed your hand and whom you could not understand, and Russian expatriates who clicked their heels at you and bowed from the waist. The British of course were charming.

Bradford Long was not among those whom Jane brought home for visits. No word had ever been spoken about it, but both knew clearly that there was no welcome for him in that house. It was at the time of Henry's death that Janie learned about Bradford Long.

Jane was in Washington. It was in the winter of 1929. She kept an apartment there now, and in that prosperous time she was very busy with her painting. Henry had a heart attack that afternoon; it was his third coronary. When Dr. Payne came by late that night he told her he did not think Henry could live until morning. After he had gone Janie sat in the semi-darkness of the big room and faced it. He was eighty-four years old, it had been twelve years since he had had his first attack. She had been blessed in being able to keep him so long. Now he was going. Henry, who had brought the fullness of life to her, who had been the center of her life for nearly fifty years. She was going to have to learn to live without him. She felt old and cold and lifeless herself. The nurse that John Payne had sent sat quietly in a corner. There was nothing that she could do. Henry was unconscious. There was nothing that Janie could do either, except sit there and wait. Yes, she could call Jonathan, he would want to be there.

She stood up and wearily went across the hall to Jane's room, to use her phone. Jonathan, awakened, said that he would come immediately. Janie sat there by Jane's bedside table for a while, thinking. She had talked to Elizabeth that afternoon, there was no use calling her in the middle of the night. There was nothing she could do. Lynne was asleep. Janie wished she had sent her to stay with one of the relatives that afternoon; a death in the house was hard on a child. She would get Jonathan to telegraph Avery. What should she do about Jane? If Henry went before morning Jane could not get there. She ought to know, however. It would be better to tell her now, rather than after it happened. She supposed she had better call her, though it was an awful time. It was nearly one o'clock. She sat thinking about it. Action was difficult for her, but finally she made her decision, dialed Long Distance and gave Jane's Washington number. She heard the local operator talking to the Washington operator, heard the ring of a telephone, and then a sleepy man's voice said "Hello."

Janie's mind snapped out of its daze. How terrible, to wake people up at this time of night with a wrong number. "Oh, I beg your pardon," she said. "I am so sorry." She put down the phone as quickly as she could. Dialing the operator she repeated Jane's number. She heard more conversation between the operators but paid no attention. This time Jane's voice came to her.

It was hard for Janie to speak. "You're father is ill," she said. "Dr. Payne says he can't live through the night."

"Oh, darling," Jane said. "Oh, Mama." Then there was silence. "I will come immediately. There is an early morning train, I'll be on it."

Janie went back and sat by Henry's bed. Jonathan came and they sat together. When the sun rose Henry was still breathing, still unconscious. Elizabeth came and went, Jonathan telegraphed Avery. Jane arrived. The morning went on, the long vigil continued. The doctor came.

"It's just a question of hours," he said. "Minutes, perhaps."

Janie did not want to leave Henry's bedside. She refused to go downstairs for lunch, so Ella set a table in the wide upstairs hall by the front window and served Janie and Jane there.

There was something in Jane's manner that puzzled her mother. She kept looking at her inquiringly, expectantly. When Ella had cleared the table and gone downstairs, and they were still sitting in the hall, Jane said: "I am sorry about last night, Mother. You must have wondered."

Janie looked at her. "What do you mean?"

"When Brad answered the phone."

Suddenly Janie's mind was alert. She remembered the man's voice. "I thought it was a wrong number."

"Oh!"

The two women sat looking at each other. Neither spoke. Then Jane straightened up in her chair and said: "It was not a wrong number, dear. It was Bradford Long, the newspaper columnist. He was there with me. He was asleep, he answered the phone without thinking."

Again there was silence. "What are you trying to tell me, Jane?"

"I am trying to tell you that Bradford Long and I have been—lovers, I expect that is the best way to express it, for years."

Janie sat perfectly still. She could not have moved.

"Oh, darling, don't look like that," Jane cried. "It's not that tragic, is it?"

Janie did not answer. All the forces of her spirit were concentrated on meeting this new blow that had fallen upon her.

"I have known him for years, you know," Jane went on. "Ever since the World War. This began the winter I spent in Paris. He was there then. I know this is a terrible time to tell you, honey. I wouldn't have, of course, except that I thought —that you would be wondering. I thought it would be better to be frank about it."

"Why don't you marry him?" Janie's voice was hard.

Jane gave an impatient little gesture. "Brad and I don't want to marry each other, Mother," she said. "He is not a marrying man and I—I am not a marrying woman. We both want our independence."

"Independence," Janie said scornfully. "Independence only means loneliness."

"Oh yes, loneliness," Jane said, as if loneliness was a normal human condition, to be accepted and discounted. She tried to explain. "He is a newspaperman, a columnist, a correspondent. He goes into all the far places of the world, Tibet, the Gobi Desert, Mongolia, the South Sea Islands. You know, you read his pieces in the paper. He has to be free, it's the breath of life to him. He goes at a moment's notice and he stays months at a time, sometimes years. If you took that away from him he would wither, he would die on the branch. And I—I have my painting. It is terribly important to me, now. It is the thing on which I have built my life. I'm sorry, dear, but you will just have to forgive us. It is not your way, it is probably not the right way, but it is the way we want it. It is the way we can have each other and still have our own individual lives."

"Thank God your father did not know," Janie said.

"Yes, it would have distressed him. I am glad, though, for you to know. I would not have chosen this time to tell you, but I have hated the deceit."

She did not speak of my distress, Janie thought, but even while thinking it, she understood. Women were tougher about women than men were. As great a shock as it was to her, it was not as great as it would have been to a man who had idealized and romanticized women all his life.

Janie stood up and moving slowly she went back into the darkened room and sat by Henry's bedside. He was going. He was leaving her. She would have to face this strange new world alone. A world of shifting sands, changing standards, insecurity. How could she ever feel the same toward Jane? She thought of Jane as she had been, and the tears rolled down her cheeks. That Jane was gone. There was nothing to be done about it. We interfered in her life once, she thought. I'll never do it again. Not that there was anything she could do. Jane was grown, adult, independent, famous in the art world. She was forty-three years old. Even during that winter in Paris she had been thirty-five. She knew what she was doing.

Henry died that night. For a while nothing mattered to Janie, including Jane's immorality. Everybody was very good to her. Life went on. Lynne was a joy and a delight. Jane was —Jane. She looked just the same, talked and acted just the same. Bradford Long was in the Congo. His name was never mentioned.

34

Janie Darby sat in the soft candlelight, at the head of the flower-decked, silver-laden table, and looked down its length at her family. It was her eightieth birthday and they were all making a great to-do about it. It was the occasion for a big family reunion, and this dinner party was its climax. Every leaf had been put into the dining room table. It stretched all the way across the big room, and it took two lace tablecloths to cover it. The biggest silver candelabra filled with yellow candles stood in the center, and at each end alabaster bowls of yellow and white chrysanthemums. The great green glass cone which had hung over the table when electricity was first brought to Fairview had long since been removed and a crystal chandelier hung in its place. Tonight, however, the room was lighted only by candles, on the table and the sideboard and the serving table and mantelpiece. Their warm glow softened the faces and lowered the voices, though there was plenty of lively conversation.

Avery, as the eldest son, sat at the foot of the table. Down the sides were ranged the children and grandchildren, the husbands and wives, Sara Anne Morgan who rated as one of the family, of course, and who had lived with Jonathan and little Sara Anne since Carey's death; and Jerome Tyson, who to Janie's great pleasure had come down from New York for her birthday celebration. Since Emily's death it had been hard to keep in touch with the Tysons. Mathilda had never been much interested in her Virginia relatives. Jerome was always friendly and affectionate, and they always saw him when they went to New York, but it had been years since he had been to Fairview. Only two of the grandchildren were absent, Bland Calhoun who unbelievably was in Sao Paulo, Brazil, building a bridge, having gone into engineering instead of the ministry to his father's disappointment; and Lynne who, having just gone to Wellesley three weeks ago, could not turn around and come back so soon. Sally Darby, Jonathan's youngest, was also in college but she was a junior at Sweet Briar so it was easy for her to come home for the celebration.

Janie took little part in the talk but her mind was busy. Here she was, eighty years old, the acknowledged head of this big family, the matriarch. The beginning of it all, the center from which the strands spread out. She, little Jane Peyton Meade, not very well educated, certainly not very wise, not seeing her way clearly, stumbling and fumbling, but always loving, always trying according to her limited insights to accomplish the best results. Here tonight, at this table, she could see the results of her life. Now look out, Miss Janie, she told herself. Don't get the bighead, don't give yourself airs. God is the source and God the guide. You have only been His instrument. The purposes of God! How well have you fulfilled the purposes of God? That is what you must judge your life by.

Avery. Sitting way off at the other end of the table, so splendid, so heartwarming. The white flame that had lighted Avery's eyes in the past had mellowed to a penetrating glow. His whole being radiated warmth. You absorbed warmth from him, you felt it when he entered a room. Avery was a bishop now, the Bishop of Oklahoma. It still seemed strange to Janie. "But Avery," she had said when he first told her about it, "you have never had the slightest connection with Oklahoma." He had laughed and said: "Bishops don't have to be native sons, dear." All the same, she could not remember a Bishop of Virginia who was not a Virginian.

She had gone out there for his consecration. It was shortly after Henry's death and everybody thought it would be good for her to get away. It was the first time she had ever been west of the Shenandoah Valley. All the family came down to the depot to see her off, and they behaved as if she were a baby they were sending off all by itself.

"Now Mother," Jonathan said, "I have spoken to the porter and given him a tip, and he will look out for you and help you when you change trains in St. Louis. Stay in your own drawing room—you can have your meals sent there if you want to—and remember to tip the porters and the waiters and I am sure you will be all right."

"Jonathan," Janie said, "it seems to me that I have showed normal intelligence throughout my life. I don't know why you should all think I am a complete fool." She looked around at the circle of worried faces.

Betsy Barnett laughed and hugged her. "It's because you look so pretty and so helpless, darling," she said, "and you are so trusting. We are afraid a big bad wolf might eat you up before you get there."

"Big bad wolves are usually looking for tenderer morsels than seventy-four-year-old ladies, Betsy," Janie said, "and anyhow I am neither helpless nor trusting."

"Just stay in your own compartment, Mother," Jonathan repeated when he had got her settled and kissed her goodbye.

"I have no intention of staying in my own compartment, Jonathan," Janie said.

And she didn't. She went into the dining car and she sat in the lounge car and she talked to strange people. She got into an argument with a Republican from Michigan, and other people in the lounge car gathered around and cheered them on and Janie flattered herself that she had not let him get away with a thing. Later she found to her surprise that she really liked him, so long as they kept away from politics. She compared notes on progeny with a grandmother from Arizona and listened with amusement to the jokes of a Catholic priest on his way to New Mexico, and she decided there were a great many nice people in the world no matter where they came from.

The trip itself was exciting and revealing. Going through the vast stretches of country hour after hour, the farms and forests, the villages and towns, the long waits in the great bustling, echoing stations of the cities, crossing the Mississippi and the Missouri, the flat tablelands stretching away in the distance. She had never seen land like that, flat as the palm of your hand, flat as a carpet laid on a floor, unrolling continuously as the train moved forward. She especially liked to go to the back of the observation car at the end of the train and stand watching the carpet unroll—the long, straight lines of the railroad tracks narrowing until, to the watching eye, they seemed to meet in the distance. She had always known that this land was there, of course, just as she knew that the Sahara Desert existed in Africa and the Himalaya Mountains in India, but it had little reality to 'her. The United States to her mind, except for the eastern seaboard, was a map marked off in different colors to show the states, with names printed in varying sizes of type. She knew the shape of the country, the shape of many of the states; she was familiar with the blue waters of the Great Lakes at the north and the Gulf of Mexico at the south, the Atlantic and Pacific oceans, but she knew these things as they were printed on the map. Now here she was seeing them in reality, real land, filled with real people. America. The United States of America.

The consecration was the most magnificent and moving spectacle she had ever witnessed. It had a deeply spiritual impact upon her, and she thought that any man who had himself gone through that ceremony and experienced its heights of splendor and depths of humility must thereafter live on a higher level of spirit than is given to most men. She was sure that this was true of Avery. As a matter of fact it always had been true of Avery. He lived in a rarefied world, for which she could not give herself credit. All she could say of herself in regard to Avery was that at least she had not obstructed the purposes of God.

Elizabeth? No slightest trace of beauty remained with Elizabeth now. She had put on weight with the years, her dark hair was gray. The skin which had always had a tendency to sallowness was now definitely sallow. Her manner was as cool, her voice as clipped as ever, but the shallow dark pools of her eyes had taken on depth. They too had acquired warmth, and never since the day of young Richard's death had Janie doubted that deeps of emotion lay beneath them. Elizabeth's husband was a successful and apparently a happy man; the dull position in Mr. Fosdick's shoe factory had turned out very well indeed, Hugh Ames was now vice-president of a thriving business. Elizabeth's two daughters,

Betsy and Jane, who had seemed so wild to their grand-mother ten years ago, were now married and settled, the doting mothers of small children and prominent in many community activities. Except for the one great tragedy of Richard's loss, Elizabeth's life had been a good life.

And Jane. What report could be rendered to God about Jane who, according to all the standards she herself recognized, should have ruined her life and yet so obviously had not? Ruined something in herself, perhaps, something soft and yielding and generous, but not her life. Jane looked very pretty tonight, in a moss-green lace and chiffon dinner dress. Her short hair was still golden, her features cameo-clear. The warmth had gone from her eyes and the sweetness had left her face, but strength had taken its place. She looked distinguished, important. To her mother's eyes she did not look happy, and Janie asked herself as she had a hundred times, what she could have done to help this child to a better fulfillment of the purposes of God. For the first time it occurred to her that perhaps Jane was fulfilling the purposes of God. She had long known that the soul could draw sustenance from tragedy; perhaps it could learn also from what the world called immorality.

Janie turned her eyes from Jane to Jonathan, sitting half-way down the length of the table between Susan Calhoun and Betsy Barnett. The infinite variety of the human pattern was borne in upon her. Could any people be more different than her children, sitting here at the table? Jonathan, the conservative, the rigid, the eminently proper. A handsome man, courtly of manner, shrewd of mind, limited—it simply must be admitted—limited in outlook. Sometimes you could hardly help smiling at Jonathan. He could be downright pompous. It was almost amusing to think what he would say if he knew about Bradford Long.

At the moment he was being shaken to his roots by Franklin D. Roosevelt. That any President should do the terrible things that man in the White House was doing shook his faith in human nature and representative government, but that a Democrat should do them, a man he had voted for, a party he had supported all his life, and his father and his father's father! The fact that his father would have loved Franklin Roosevelt and rejoiced in what he was doing had no effect upon Jonathan. It was incredible, the man simply wasn't a Democrat.

"What is a Democrat, Jonathan," Janie had asked.

"A person who follows the doctrines of Thomas Jefferson," Jonathan said.

"Which doctrines? The one that says all men are created equal? The one that says government must be by the consent of the governed? The one that says any people have a right to change their form of government, even to the point of revolution, whenever they want to?"

"The doctrine that that government is best which governs least," Jonathan said. "The doctrine that advocates local self-government and the rights of the states to control their own affairs."

"It seems to me we fought a war about that," Janie said. "Anyhow, certainly one of these doctrines is as Jeffersonian as the other."

Nevertheless Jonathan was a successful man, a kind man, a good husband and father, a man who did his part in the community. She thought she could render a good report on these children of hers, in so far as they reflected the results of her life. What about herself, she wondered. What could she say that she had done with the inner spirit in her eighty years of life? What had she made of mind and heart and soul according to the purposes of God? Answer that if you can, Janie Darby, she told herself.

After dinner they all went into the parlors. The Ashby and the Peyton and the Wilcox and the Richardson cousins were coming out for the cutting of her birthday cake, a grand affair that did actually have eighty tiny candles on it. They all came trooping in, the cars were parked all around the circle and down the driveway, and they brought greetings and kisses and little presents for Janie. All day people had been giving her presents, some useful, some pretty fripperies destined to clutter up bureau drawers and closet shelves. Jane had reserved her present. It was brought in after the cake had been cut and eaten and toasts had been drunk to Janie in champagne. Arthur came in with an easel and set it up by the piano in the back parlor. Jane and David Darby lifted in a framed painting and set it on the easel. A hush fell over the crowded rooms as everybody paused to look at it. It was a portrait of Janie. She had not known that Jane was painting a portrait of her, and as she looked at it now she was startled. Do I really look like that, she asked herself. The woman who looked at her from the canvas bore her features, but to her she seemed a stranger. Jane, who had an uncanny ability to see through the outer shell and get down to the very essence of personality, saw her like that. What did she see? How could one read that face? It was strange. You saw yourself all your life in the mirror. You stood before the mirror and fixed your hair and powdered your nose and put on Dorine's Liquid Rouge. You put on dresses and hats and stood off to get the effect. You knew every line of your face and figure. But always you saw yourself through your own eyes, and those eyes were conditioned to a certain idea of yourself which you carried through life. You knew perfectly well that your hair was white and that there were lines in your face and that you had begun to show the withered throat of old age, but while you saw those things clearly you still saw them in the light of the golden-haired, delicate-featured, sweet-faced person you had been in the beginning. You never got away from yourself. This woman did not fit that concept. A life was written in that face, but what kind of life? What did it say, with what qualities did it speak? Here was the same question she had asked herself earlier in the evening.

After the silence there was a rush of exclamations, ohs and ahs and "how splendid," and "congratulations, Jane." Jonathan did not like it.

"Mother is prettier than that, Jane," he said, with a suggestion of reproach.

"There is more in that face than prettiness," Avery said. "It's—wonderful, Jane."

Jane said nothing. She was like that about her painting. She did it. There it was. It was herself. She never explained or defended or commented. You either saw or you did not see, you felt or it left you cold, you liked or you disliked.

Janie thanked her for the portrait. She was touched, she was pleased. She was deeply appreciative. "I know it is a wonderul portrait," she said. "I will have to let you know later, after I have looked at it some more, whether I like being that woman or not."

Jane kissed her. "You should," she said.

The next morning, when the leaves had been taken out of

the dining room table and the candelabra put away, and the wrapping from the birthday presents picked up, and some order brought to the house, and when Jerome Tyson and Avery and Susan had gone for a drive through the country-side to see the early fall foliage, and Jane had gone out to her studio, Janie went into the back parlor to study the portrait. The thing that surprised her most about the woman on the canvas was not the indisputable lines of age so clearly drawn there, but the strength that showed in the face. There was strength even in the carriage of the head and shoulders. But I am not strong, she told herself. I have never been a strong character, I have never been sure of myself. Where did Jane find that strength? She went to the mantelpiece and looked at her familiar image in the mirror, the piled-up white hair, the wrinkles around the blue eyes, the lines from nose to mouth, the soft, faintly pink cheeks from which the roundness had departed, the withered throat. She saw no signs of strength in her own face in the mirror, no signs of wisdom or confident personality. Jane had just put them there, she decided. Jane had put them there because she thought they ought to be there.

Later in the day she found Avery looking at the portrait. He reached out his hand and drew her to him and they stood together studying the canvas.

"Jane is not only a very fine artist," he said, "but she is also a genius at reading character. I suppose the two things go together as far as portraiture is concerned. This is a wonderful piece of work."

"She looks like an old curmudgeon to me," Janie said.

"She looks like a wise and benevolent lady to me, one who has never been defeated and never will be, one who has inner resources of strength and spirit."

"But Avery, you know I am not like that at all. Heaven knows I am not wise. Years ago you started me out looking for the purposes of God, and I have never yet been able to figure out the purposes of God. And I certainly am not benevolent. I am irritable and impatient and prejudiced, and narrow-minded, I reckon. The world is full of people I don't like."

Avery's face lighted up with a smile. "Very reprehensible," he said. "You are supposed to love your enemies and do good to them that despoil you. But I could mention some counterbalancing characteristics of this person we are talking about. She is kind and considerate and completely without malice. She has never turned away a beggar or abandoned a friend. She is generous to a fault, and she hides her light under a bushel. For years she has been carrying on charities about which no one knows except the agencies through which she works. Since the depression started she has been taking care of several Negro families without even going through the agencies."

"How do you know that?" Janie demanded.

"I have ways of knowing."

"Harry Updyke told you. He had no right to do that. The bank has no right to tell anybody how I spend my money. Does Jonathan know?"

Avery put back his head and laughed. "Don't tell me you are afraid of Jonathan," he said. "The woman in the portrait wouldn't be afraid of anybody."

"Of course I am not afraid of Jonathan," Janie said impatiently, "but he would disapprove. He would think that I ought to hold on to my money in the present uncertain state of the world. I would have to explain, and he would argue. I don't want to argue."

What she meant was that she did not want to be questioned or interfered with. She wanted to do things the way she wanted to do them. Realizing this, she felt for the first time a kinship with the woman in the portrait. A gleam of amusement spread over her face, and she smiled at the painted features.

35

During the Christmas holidays of Lynne's senior year at Wellesley Janie began to detect a difference in this surprising young granddaughter of hers. The Christmas and spring holidays were always whirlwind affairs, filled with ringing telephones, blaring radios, parties and dances, comings and goings, the house full of young people, most of whom were strangers to Janie. She had known the boys and girls her children went with, she had known most of their parents, but now the town had grown so, there were so many people she had never seen or heard of, the young faces around Lynne seemed to change so constantly, that she gave up trying to know who they were during these short, hectic homecomings. Summers were the times Janie loved, when Lynne came home and settled down to a normal routine. A lively routine, to be sure, full of activity, interspersed with visits to college friends or trips to the springs, but still leisurely by comparison, long enough to get reacquainted with Lynne and to recognize her friends. Some there were, of course, whom Janie knew and could place, the Lacy girls and Ginny Foster, and the Armstrongs and the Boyds and the Russells, and of course all the innumerable cousins. Among the young men there was always Curtis Russell, and there was also another young man, named Grant Emory, always to be found following Lynne. It was a source of great satisfaction to Janie, however, that Lynne seemed to have no favorites. She gave no indication of emotional attachment for any of the young men she went around with. Janie knew better than to call them beaux. When they first began coming to see Lynne and she had spoken of them as beaux, Lynne had closed her eyes and shuddered.

"Gram, please," she implored. "Please. I cringe. They are not beaux, they are dates."

"Nonsense," Janie said. "Dates are things you have with beaux, they are not the beaux themselves."

"They are in my book," Lynne said.

After that Janie refrained from calling them beaux, but she positively refused to call them dates, so there seemed to be nothing for it but to speak of them as young men, or as "your friends."

This Christmas vacation seemed outwardly like all the others, the activity, the noise, the partying, the honking of horns at the front door, the general confusion. It was Lynne herself who seemed different. Splendid-looking she was, blue and gold, more like a young goddess than ever, but a little quieter, a little less flamboyant. More mature, Janie decided, and of course that was natural. She had grown up in the nearly four years of her college experience. She seemed no longer to get pleasure out of shocking her elders, and her natural sweetness was more evident. It showed particularly in her dealing with her grandfather. Mr. Hammond was not well, and even in the hurry and bustle of the holidays Lynne went to see him almost every day. He was not well enough to come to Fairview for Christmas dinner, so Lynne suggested that they all have dinner with him, in the big, silent house where he had lived alone so much of his life. It was not what Janie wanted. She liked her own Christmas dinner in her own dining room, but the old man was failing fast and it was certainly a kind thing to do, so she agreed. Mr. Hammond's worship of Lynne was touching to see.

Janie began to notice that whereas in previous hectic Christmas holidays, when there was some kind of a party every night, Lynne had slept well into the morning each day, she now came down for breakfast, clad in a yellow quilted satin robe that made her look like a slim aspen tree, and showed great interest in the morning mail. There was always a great deal of it, letters and Christmas cards from all the unknown—to her grandmother, friends and acquaintances of these years away from home, but there was always one letter, one special letter. Janie thought nothing of it until she began to recognize the handwriting, bold, decisive, written in black ink. It came every morning, and Lynne never opened it at the breakfast table. She saved it until she went back upstairs to her room.

Janie spoke to Jane about it. "Has Lynne said anything to you about a special young man?" she asked.

"No, she hasn't," Jane said, "but I think there undoubtedly is one. She acts like it, in the first place, and it would certainly be surprising if there wasn't."

"Oh dear," Janie said, "I wonder who he is."

Of course she wanted Lynne to marry, and of course she was old enough, having had her twenty-first birthday in October, but please not quite yet. Please let me have her for a little while longer. Just a little while. It was not really a prayer, just a spoken wish. And please, when it does happen, let him be the right man for her, something special, something splendid. Please, Lord, give her happiness in her marriage. That was a prayer.

In the brief intervals between her comings and goings Lynne sent out a good many letters and cards herself, and Janie suspected that among them were frequent replies to the bold handwriting. One morning when she was preparing to leave the house to go marketing Lynne called to her from upstairs.

"Gram, wait a minute, please ma'am." She came running down the stairs and handed Janie a letter. "Mail this for me, will you, sweetie."

She handed Janie an envelope. She handed it to her directly, face up, address visible, and there was something challenging in her manner. Janie, glancing at it, saw the address and, being taken by surprise, exclaimed without thinking: "Heavens, what a name!" It was addressed to Mr. Anton Cziermanksi. "Cher—Ser— How do you pronounce it? Where did it come from?"

"It is pronounced Chermanski," Lynne said. "As if it was *Ch*, and it comes from Poland. You had better learn to pronounce it, darling, because I am going to marry him."

Janie stared at her. She was speechless.

"Perhaps I shouldn't spring it on you like this, Gram dear," Lynne said. "I have been trying to decide how to break it to

373

you, and it just suddenly came over me to come right out and tell you."

"From Poland," Janie repeated wonderingly. "Lynne, who is he?"

"Let's sit down," Lynne said, and led the way to the hall sofa, the polished applewood sofa upholstered now in faded green brocade which had stood in the front hall at Fairview for two hundred years. "He is a very poor and very brilliant young man who is doing graduate work at the Massachusetts Institute of Technology and is working in a filling station to pay for it. That is the way I met him, at the filling station when I went there for gas."

Janie sat quite still. She felt incapable of motion or of speech. Lynne went on.

"He hasn't got a drop of Virginia blood in his veins and he never heard of an FFV. It may console you a little that he is not a Yankee either. He was born in Poland, though his parents brought him over here when he was just a baby."

"Who are his parents?" Janie asked through stiff lips.

"They are small farmers, his father is named Milan Cziermanski, they own a farm in the central part of Massachusetts, nearer Springfield than Boston."

"What were they in Poland?"

"Peasants," Lynne said flatly. "They were peasants, Gram. They came to this country twenty-five years ago to better their condition. And they have, they have done pretty well; but there are five other children, Anton is the oldest, and they are all going to college. They are all smart, all good students. One brother has graduated and two sisters are in college now. The youngest brother will go next year. His father helped Anton through college, but when it came to his graduate work he has to do that on his own. That is why it has taken him longer than it would otherwise. He has to have a job to keep himself going."

"Does he speak English?" Janie asked. What she meant was, does he speak English like an American or like a Pole come to America. She meant to be disagreeable, and she saw that Lynne understood her intention. The girl gave a short little laugh.

"He speaks English well," she said. "He also speaks Polish and French and German. He is studying to be a scientist, he is taking his Ph.D. in physics. Anton knows more than all the generations of Meades and Peytons and Darbys and Hammonds put together."

Janie did not bother to answer that, to her, completely irrelevant statement.

"You are not planning to marry this—person any time soon, I hope," she said, and again she sensed a hardening in Lynne.

"I would like to marry him in June, when I graduate, but he won't agree to that. It will be another year before he can get his degree and then he will be in a position to get a good job. There are opportunities for young scientists these days. So we are going to wait until the following June, 1940."

Bessie came to the dining room door, "Miss Janie, ma'am, you forgot your list."

"Thank you, Bessie," Janie said, taking the paper. She stood up, and the letter to Mr. Anton Cziermanski fell to the floor. She left it there and went toward the front door. Lynne picked it up and stood looking at her grandmother. For once in her life she seemed to be nonplused.

"I'm sorry, Gram," she said.

"I am very sorry," Janie replied.

"I expect I shouldn't have told you so suddenly."

"I hardly think a gradual approach would have helped."

She went out onto the porch, closing the front door behind her. Arthur held the car door open and she got in, hardly knowing what she was doing. He headed toward downtown but presently he turned and asked: "Where we going, Miss Janie?"

She had intended going to the market to see if she could find any special delicacies for Lynne's last two days at home, but now she changed her mind. What difference did it make what they had to eat if Lynne was going to marry a foreign peasant who worked in a filling station in Massachusetts? That was what came of letting her go to Wellesley to college, and what came of letting her have her own car during her senior year. She had been opposed to both things, but Jane and Lynne had talked her into it. Arthur was waiting for an answer, and she made a sudden decision.

"I'm sorry, Arthur," she said. "I wasn't thinking. I don't want to go downtown, I want to go for a drive out in the country. Turn around at the next corner, please, and take me out the Old Turnpike."

The early January day was clear and cold. The trees were bare, the sky pale blue, and the mountains seemed so close you could almost see the trees on them. Wrapped in her warm lap robe Janie settled back for a long drive. Eighteen months. She had eighteen months of grace before Lynne planned to marry this stranger. Anything could happen in eighteen months. This might be just a passing infatuation. Lynne was young, she might easily meet someone more appropriate in the interval. Perhaps she could take her to Richmond next winter, or to Washington. These were the thoughts that went through her mind, but they carried no conviction. I am just whistling in the wind, she admitted to herself. That is not the way we do in this family. We always seem to fall in love so definitely, so immutably. Mama and Papa. Herself and Avery. The God-sent rightness of her marriage to Avery had been as clear as crystal to the nineteen-year-old Janie. Elizabeth and Hugh, Jane and Tommy, Henrietta and Giles Hammond. All unshakable, immovable. And it was not always right. It had not been right for her with Avery; it certainly had not been right for Jane with Tommy. But what could you do, what could you say; how, as a matter of fact, could you know?

If only she could go to Sara Anne for advice and comfort. But Sara Anne was gone. She had died nearly a year ago. Janie had felt a desolation she had never known before. She knew it could not be true, knew that the death of parents, husbands, children must go deeper than the death of even the most beloved friend, but at the time of her death, when she faced for the first time a world that did not contain Sara Anne, she thought she had never felt such sorrow. All her life, from her earliest childhood memories until that moment, Sara Anne had been with her. She was, as a matter of fact, the only one of them all who had gone with her the whole way, who had covered with her her entire life-span. The lovely face, the merry eyes, the charming voice, the laughter and sympathy and companionship, had always been with her, always to be counted on, gone now with the flickering-out of Sara Anne's life. A small life, limited, never far from poverty, without important achievements, as the world counted importance, but lived with such high style, with such courage and humor and gaiety. There should have been a sounding of trumpets when Sara Anne crossed over. Perhaps there had been, Janie often thought. Perhaps trumpets had blown when Sara Anne entered the immortal gates, trumpets and banners flying in crisp sunshine against a deep blue sky.

Now there was no one to whom Janie could go for comfort. Almost no one of her generation was left. Toni and Johnny Russell, Maria and Corbin Pratt, Tom Gordon, Jennie Lee Davis, the lifelong friends, the cousins, gone now. Raiford Tyler, dead these ten years. It was the thought of Raiford that made her decide to drive out to Meriden. She had had it on her mind for some time.

They drove at a decorous forty miles an hour, but even so it was amazing how soon they came to the crossroads where you turned to go to Meriden. Janie remembered the long, long drive it had been in her childhood.

"Turn right here, Arthur," she said.

This had been a narrow, back-country road when she first knew it. Now it was hard surfaced, but still narrow and winding. Meriden was three miles off the turnpike. When they reached the whitewashed fence which had been put around the entire estate during the prosperous Boyd-Tyler years she instructed Arthur: "Drive slowly along here, Arthur, until I tell you to stop."

The car crawled past the imposing entrance gates, put up by Raiford when the white fences were built, and went on until Janie found a place where the house was clearly visible from the road, through the trees.

"Stop here," she said.

Janie sat and looked at Meriden. Lovely, gracious Meriden, home of romance and of gaiety. Its bare windows looked back at her with an empty stare. One of the upstairs shutters had come loose and hung at a crazy angle. The white columns were scaled and chipped. A wilderness of weeds and vines had grown up around the house. It looked unutterably forlorn. Empty, forsaken, abandoned. She had known it would be like that. She had not been to Meriden since Raiford's funeral, ten years ago, but she knew very well what had happened to it. She knew that the stock-market crash and the depression had practically ruined the Tylers. The ironworks and foundry and machine shops and plow factory which old Ranny Boyd had founded and from which he had made his fortune were still running and the Boyds in town were still well-to-do, but the Tylers had sold out in the

377

twenties. They had been beguiled by the easy enticements of the stock market. Raiford did not live to see the catastrophe, he died in the fall of 1929. The children could not have kept Meriden if they had wanted to. In 1930 it was sold to a man who wanted to make an inn of it, a resort. He spent money doing over the house, building a swimming pool, tennis courts. He should have known better. Meriden was too remote, too far from the tourist lanes, too inaccessible. Even the Old Turnpike was not a through highway now. As the depression grew worse and the patrons did not come, the project had to be abandoned. The house stood empty for several years. The property was finally sold for taxes, at auction, sold for a song, to the owner of the adjoining farm. He wanted the land, he did not want the house. It was thrown in with the purchase, because there was nothing else to do with it. Nobody wanted Meriden now. Some of the woodwork was sold to a museum, some of the mantelpieces were sold to a builder, some of the chandeliers were sold to Colonial Williamsburg. The empty shell stood there now, looking at her through its dirty windows, slowly decaying. Perhaps some day somone would have mercy on it and tear it down. Perhaps its mellow old bricks would be bought by someone who knew their beauty and would go into the making of another house. She hoped so, devoutly. Old things, old people, old houses, when their usefulness had passed, should be allowed to go in dignity. Today she felt old, almost for the first time. She recognized her age, she accepted its limitations, but she had not felt old in spirit. Today she did, old and unwanted.

"All right, Arthur," she said presently. "Let's go home."

Lynne was not there for luncheon that day. Janie and Jane were alone. Depression covered Janie like a fog; she found it hard to carry on a casual conversation, and Jane also was unusually quiet. Silence could be such a comfortable thing between two people accustomed to each other's presence, at ease. It frequently was so with Jane and herself, but today there was a sense of strain. Presently Jane spoke.

"Lynne is worried about you, Mother," she said. "I am afraid she did not pick the best way to tell you her news."

"As I told her, I hardly think the approach would have made any difference. It is the fact that distresses me. Have you known about this young man?"

"Only for the last few days. She gradually worked up to
378

telling me. She didn't know how to tell you." Janie said nothing and Jane went on: "I don't know him, of course, but from what Lynne has told me he seems to be a very intelligent—brilliant, she says—very hardworking, quite admirable person, and those are characteristics which I know you value. Of course he is not what we would have wished for Lynne, I doubt if you and I would think that anybody was good enough for her—but certainly he could be much worse. The important thing is that he is what she wants and please, Mother, please don't make it hard for her."

Jane looked her directly in the eyes, and Janie knew exactly what she meant. The gloom of the day increased. So the old resentment was still there. So unfair, Janie had always felt, so really perverse of Jane, because certainly she knew that she herself had made the ultimate decision, she herself had known with utter clarity that she could not live with the kind of man Tommy Tyler was when he was drunk. Still, a promise had been exacted, and the promise had been kept.

Well, so there it was. Jane had deprived her of any possible weapon in fighting this marriage of Lynne's. However unfair it might be, she would not be able to make any effort to break it up without thinking of Jane's broken love and Jane's twisted life. There was nothing she could do. Nothing but sit quietly and let Lynne become Mrs. Anton Cziermanski.

She went up to her room immediately after lunch and lay down. She tried to read the paper and found herself bored with the world. Finally she went to sleep, but when she woke up from her nap depression was still with her. What I would like to do, she thought, is go to bed with the sulks and have my dinner sent up here. She refused to allow herself that piece of childishness, however. Instead, she did her hair over and put on a blue lace dinner dress, and made an entrance into the living room and demanded a glass of sherry before dinner.

36

If it had not been for Anton Cziermanski the year following Lynne's graduation would have been a very happy one for Janie. It was a joy to have her there for that precious fall and winter and spring, filling Fairview with young life, bringing interest and pleasure to the two quiet women who lived there. With Lynne at home Jane felt freer to be away and she made frequent trips to New York and to Washington. Janie did not know where Bradford Long was, his columns were not appearing in the paper, which might mean that he was in some distant and inaccessible part of the world, or it might mean that he was at home with nothing to write about. Janie herself still maintained a reasonably active routine. She marketed and shopped and went to church on Sundays and attended the meetings of the Women's Auxiliary. She still occasionally went to parties, she drove out in the afternoons and sometimes she went to the Country Club, and she saw to it that the house was at all times prepared for any sudden influx of Lynne's friends. She realized that the tempo of her life was slowing up, however, and when she thought of next June and the impending marriage she sometimes felt old and useless, as she had the day she learned of Lynne's engagement to Anton.

At first Lynne seldom spoke of him. The bold, black-addressed envelopes came almost every morning; answers went out in Lynne's equally firm, smaller and blue-inked handwriting, but for a while she maintained a definite reserve about him. As the weeks went by, however, this gradually faded, and she began to speak of him naturally. Anton was going to have his oral examinations. Anton had had his orals and passed them. Now he could concentrate on the final stages of his dissertation. He was beginning to put out feelers about jobs. He had written to know what Lynne would think of the Government. The Bureau of Standards in Washington. He could probably make more money with one of the big corporations, but those jobs were in great demand now, and he thought he would like the work with the Bureau of Standards, and Lynne would like being in Washington. What did they think, Lynne wanted to know. Janie didn't think anything at all, Jane thought it would probably be a good idea at least as a beginning.

When Christmastime approached Lynne announced that she was going to spend part of the holidays with Anton.

"I mean I am going to Boston," she explained. "I'll stay with Cindy Simms, I won't go until the day after Christmas, darling, so don't look so horrified. It isn't as if the holidays were the only times I had to be at home this year. Anton thinks he will almost have finished his dissertation by that time and will be able to turn it in soon, so he will have some free time. I will only be gone a week."

Janie knew there was nothing she could do about it even if she had not established an armed truce with Lynne in the matter of Anton. Her granddaughter was of age, twenty-two years old now, and financially and temperamentally independent. Mr. Hammond had left her everything he had when he died last summer, and though what he had was not what he had had before the depression, it was quite enough to make Lynne comfortable and secure. Janie therefore said nothing in response to Lynne's announcement. Silence had been her tactic throughout this whole situation, and she retreated into it now. Jane, however, put it into words when Lynne had left the room.

"You are going to be defeated, dear," she said. "You might as well make up your mind to it. Lynne is going to marry Anton, and you had better accept it and be gracious about it."

Janie thought about that all the time Lynne was away. She concluded that Jane was right. In the first place, she realized quite clearly that she would not take the responsibility of stopping this marriage even if she could. Who was she to know where Lynne's happiness lay? Why therefore be surly

381

and sulky just because it was not what she would have chosen for Lynne? And in the second place, she couldn't stop it if she wanted to. She decided to make a graceful retreat. She began being gracious about it as soon as Lynne returned from Boston. She inquired politely about Anton and was told that he was very well and very busy and they had had a wonderful time together. Then she said: "Tell me about him, Lynne, what kind of person he is."

Lynne' face was radiant. She was enchanted at being asked to talk about Anton. She came and sat close to her grandmother.

"He is wonderful, Gram. I am not just saying that, he really is. He is something special. He is good and kind and thoughtful, you should see him with his parents and his younger brothers and sisters. And he *is* a Brain, everybody who has come in contact with his work says so. He has the most beautiful manners—" Her voice fell dreamily and she seemed to wander off after the absent Anton.

"Is he tall enough for you?" Janie asked.

Lynne's enthusiasm overflowed. She jumped up and pulled herself to her full, astonishing height. "Gram, he is. Isn't it wonderful, isn't it fabulous? Even with heels he is taller than I am, I mean when I have on heels. At the wedding," she went on confidentially, "I am going to wear low heels, they won't show under a long wedding dress and I want to emphasize his height, but I am not going to have to go through life wearing flat heels. I can wear 'em as high as I want to. Isn't it perfect?"

At Easter time Mrs. Henry Forbes Darby announced the engagement of her granddaughter, Miss Carolyn Darby Hammond to Mr. Anton Jan Cziermanski, of Boston. It sounded quite impressive in the newspaper. Jonathan, although outraged by this foreign invasion, published a large and handsome photograph of Lynne with the announcement. Everybody was properly excited, although most of Lynne's friends already knew about Anton.

So for the first time since Elizabeth's marriage forty-four years ago, Fairview was to have a wedding with all the "works," as Lynne expressed it. Henrietta's hasty little wedding did not come into that category.

When it came to planning the event there were problems to be faced. First, Anton was a Catholic and Lynne was not. Anton did not intend to give up his religion and neither did

Lynne. A non-Catholic could not be married in a Catholic church and a Catholic could not agree to be married in any other church. Obviously therefore it must be a home wedding. That would limit the number of people who could be invited to the ceremony. If you could count on the weather it could be a garden wedding, very charming, in the late afternoon, but suppose it rained? In the end they decided to invite a limited number of people to the ceremony in case it should have to be held indoors, and then invite everybody in town to the reception. If the weather was good there would be plenty of room in the garden and if it rained and they all stepped on each other's toes in the house it really wouldn't matter.

The thing that worried Janie most was what to do about the elder Cziermanskis. Obviously they must be invited, but what in the world could she do with them? Lynne had not talked much about them. Janie knew that Anton had taken her to see them once, but Lynne had maintained a curious reticence about her prospective parents-in-law. She had mentioned, however, that Anton's parents spoke English with difficulty, and Janie felt sure that whatever gloss the son had managed to acquire was not shared by the foreign-born older generation. She could not imagine them as part of the kind of wedding gaieties that would surround Lynne's marriage. She spoke of it to Lynne one morning at breakfast.

"What should we do about Anton's parents, Lynne? Of course they must be invited, and I suppose we ought to ask them to stay here at Fairview. There isn't going to be enough room here for all the bridesmaids and relatives and everybody. I suppose we can parcel them out with Elizabeth and Jonathan and the other members of the family."

Lynne took a bite of toast before she answered. "Gram, there is a shock coming to you," she said then. "Whatever objection you may feel to my marrying Anton is as nothing to the way the Cziermanskis feel about Anton's marrying me."

Janie stared at her. "You mean they don't want him to?"

Lynne put back her head and laughed her red-lipped, full-throated laugh. "They certainly don't, lambie. They don't indeed."

Janie could hardly believe it. "But why, honey? Why in the world—"

"Lots of reasons," Lynne said. "First there is the matter of religion. I am not a Catholic, and they take that hard. Second, I am not a Pole. Third, I am not a farm girl. I don't know how to cook, I don't know how to milk a cow, I don't know how to work a field of beets. I don't know how to do anything useful, according to the Cziermanskis' definition of usefulness. And it is quite true, I don't."

Janie considered this in silence for a few minutes, and gradually it seemed very humorous to her. She began to laugh. She and Lynne sat and laughed together. It made the whole thing seem better. Obscurely, the fact that the Cziermanskis did not want Anton to marry Lynne improved the situation immensely.

"You see, Gram," Lynne went on, "when Anton was in school he made friends. He was always brilliant and terribly attractive. The sisters in the parochial school and the Catholic priests pushed him. He won a scholarship to Harvard and made friends there and went around with people who were—different from his own family. Cindy Simms knew him before I did. I met him at the filling station when he was working for his Ph.D., but she met him in his undergraduate days, with boys from some very proper Boston families. So he sort of grew away from his own people—not in affection, he is devoted to them and sweet and lovely to them, but in ways of living and thinking. They don't like it, and when I came along I sort of—epitomized, dramatized, whatever you choose to say, Anton's withdrawal from the ways of the old country. So they have washed their hands of this whole outlandish marriage of his." Again they both laughed. "Invite them by all means, Gram, but I can assure you that they won't come."

Well, that was a relief. Janie wrote what she hoped was a cordial note to Mrs. Cziermanski inviting her and Mr. Cziermanski to be guests at Fairview for the coming wedding. Sure enough, a stilted little reply came back, written in a fine, stiff handwriting, regretting that Mr. and Mrs. Milan Cziermanski would not be able to accept Mrs. Darby's kind invitation. So that worry was laid to rest.

2

Anton was to arrive several days ahead of the wedding accompanied by his next younger brother, who was to be his best man and the only member of his family present. The two young men were to stay at Jonathan and Sara Anne's. Fairview was going to be filled with bridesmaids. Cindy Simms was to be Lynne's maid of honor, and she was having six bridesmaids, three of whom were college friends from various parts of the country, who were to stay at Fairview. The other three were home-town girls, Jennie Duval, Hester Lacy, and Miriam Wilcox, one of the cousins. With four visiting girls in the house, and Avery coming for the ceremony, all the Fairview guest rooms would be occupied.

The Cziermanski brothers were the first to arrive, and the night of their arrival had been kept for a strictly family dinner. They were to go straight to Jonathan's house from the station, and would come out to Fairview with Jonathan and Sara Anne for dinner. There were to be no other guests. Elizabeth and Hugh had been invited, of course, but Elizabeth was having so much trouble with her arthritis she thought she had better not try it. The wedding would be about all she could manage.

Janie had given the meeting with Anton considerable thought. She wanted to impress him, but she was not sure exactly what impression she wanted to give. If she liked him she wanted to be gracious, if she did not like him she wanted to be haughty. She thought it probable that she had assumed the guise of an ogre-ish *grande dame* in his mind, knowing as he must that she had not wanted Lynne to marry him. She wanted either to live up to that impression or to dispel it, depending upon her feeling when she saw Anton. She wished it was not June so she could wear her black velvet. That was her most impressive getup; however, she had a new black chiffon and lace dinner dress which she had bought for whatever evening entertainments the wedding would involve her in. It was almost as good as black velvet. She piled the white hair on top of her head, applied the merest touch of liquid rouge to her cheeks, donned the black chiffon, and put on the pearl necklace, almost her only handsome piece of jewelry, that Henry had given her on their fortieth wedding anniversary. Then she went down to what she still called the front parlor and took her seat in a yellow brocaded wing chair to await Anton's arrival.

Lynne had met the boys at the station when they came in on the late afternoon train, and had dashed home to change while they changed at Jonathan's. She was rushing around upstairs. Jane came down, and Janie thought she looked tired. Perhaps she had put too much of the wedding preparations off on her. They smiled at each other affectionately.

"Darling, you're wonderful," Jane said. "You look exactly as you should look. The matriarch, the chatelaine of Fairview. I am sure you would impress any young man from Poland by way of the filling stations of Massachusetts."

Jane always saw through her. Janie glanced at her portrait, hanging now in the back parlor. In the five years it had been there she had come to feel very much at home with that old lady. She recognized herself in ways she had not thought of until Jane had presented her with the clear image.

Jane was only in her early fifties—Janie had to count back now to remember the children's ages—fifty-four it would be, but her hair had begun to turn gray several years before. It was not becoming to her.

"Touch it up, darling," Janie had advised. "I don't mean for you to be a peroxide blonde, but I am told that there are rinses nowadays that keep the glint in your hair."

Jane had laughed and laughed at her. "Who says you don't move with the times?" she asked.

"I have always believed in a woman's making the best of herself," Janie said.

Jane had taken her advice. Her pretty golden hair was still golden. She too had on a new dress, a gold and green print that fitted her nicely. Jane had always had a pretty figure.

They heard a car drive up, and voices on the porch. Sara Anne opened the front door and the three men followed her in. Lynne rushed down the stairs and across the hall, a whirlwind in blue chiffon. She took one of the young men by the hand and led him into the living room, to where her grandmother sat.

"Here he is, Gram," she said triumphantly. "This is Anton."

Janie's first impression of Anton was of his height, the second was of his eyes. Such eyes! She searched for an adjective for them and found one. Limpid. Trite, perhaps, but that was what they were. Limpid, brown and soft and clear, with a surprising depth to them. Limpid brown eyes in a thin, distinguished face. He was looking at her seriously, almost inquiringly, with no hint of a smile. She put out her hand.

"I am very glad to meet you, Anton," she said. "For a long time I have had to carry around a blank picture of my prospective grandson. I am glad to be able to fill in the details."

She surprised herself very much by saying that. Now his face broke into a smile.

"I too have looked forward to this meeting," he said, "with anticipation and perhaps a little trepidation."

"Did Lynne paint me as an ogre?" she asked.

"Not at all. But I think she did not do justice to your graciousness."

"She has got on her company manners," Lynne said. "Don't be taken in by her, you should see her when she gets on a rampage."

They all laughed at the idea of Gram going on a rampage. The brother was presented to Janie. He was called Raddy. She had no idea whether that was his name or a nickname or what it signified. It did not matter. He seemed to be a pleasant, ordinary young man. She paid little attention to him; she was watching Anton.

Arthur came in with cocktails and a glass of sherry for Janie. She sipped her sherry, saying little, watching everything, thinking her own thoughts. Granting Harvard and friends among proper Boston families, it was still remarkable that this one-generation immigrant boy, coming from what Lynne said firmly was a peasant background, had acquired such a polish. Good manners, of course, were inherent, they came from innate kindness, considerateness, good taste, but the complete rightness of everything Anton did must have been acquired. Perhaps he had been boning up on Emily Post; if so he was certainly an apt pupil. The exact degree of deference shown to her, of friendliness for Jane, of adoring admiration for Lynne, all were perfect. There was no over-eagerness, his movements were unhurried. He did not jump up to take her sherry glass, but in a casual sort of way he was there when she was ready to put it down. He supplied the light when Jane wanted to smoke. He listened with amused interest to Sara Anne's latest anecdote about her grandchildren. He talked knowingly with Jonathan of the news from Europe. It was he who pulled out Janie's chair when they went in to dinner. His table conversation was lively and amusing, but never self-assertive. It was all perfect. Was it almost too perfect, she wondered. Was he acting a part? Lynne was enchanted, you could see.

When Elizabeth married Hugh Ames, Janie had thought him a very dull young man. Jane's unshakable devotion to Tommy Tyler had always been a source of puzzlement to her. Giles Hammond had left almost no impression upon her. But

Anton Jan Cziermanski came of a different breed. It was easy to see why Lynne had fallen in love with him. No doubt he had the quality now known as sex appeal, the thing Henrietta had which Henry had called allure in a more reticent age, but there was more to it than that. He was Romance with a capital R. He was Lochinvar, he was Romeo, he was Leander. He was Avery riding Midnight to the sound of trumpets. He held in his hands the gossamer strands of romantic legend, and however unfashionable pure romance might be in the eyes of this sophisticated generation, Janie did not believe for a moment that it had lost its appeal to the heart of youth.

All during dinner and when they were back in the living room, Janie watched Lynne and Anton. They made a splendid couple, certainly. So tall, so dark and so fair, so filled with bright vitality. They had an elan, a flair; their happiness flashed between them like shafts of summer lightning. If this marriage was not right it should be, they seemed made for each other. If it was not to be a good marriage it could not be foretold. Only the reality could prove it. God grant that the reality would prove the rightness.

When Sara Anne and Jonathan and the two brothers were leaving, Anton came back into the living room to speak to Janie.

"I hope you do not hate me for taking Lynne away," he said. "Someone would, of course, it was bound to happen, but I am sure you know that no one could take her away from you in affection."

"She is very dear to me," Janie said. "She has been the joy of my old age. All my hope now is that she will be happy."

Something happened to Anton's face, and Janie was sure that this at least was not an act.

"She is very dear to me, too," Anton said. "My constant prayer is that I can make her happy."

"I think you can," she said, and meant it.

3

The weather was perfect for the wedding. An altar was set up at the end of the perennial-bordered garden path, in the opening of the boxwood hedge leading to the rose garden. Rows of small folding chairs were ranged on each side of the path. It always amused Janie that the chairs everybody rented for festive occasions came from the undertakers. The sun shone but, though there was almost no breeze, not enough to ruffle the candles on the altar, it was not too hot for comfort. The air was sweet with sun-warmed boxwood and magnolia and mimosa blossoms. As far as Janie knew this was the first time a wedding had ever taken place in the garden of Fairview, and yet she could think of no more perfect setting. The bridal procession came out of the side door from the back parlor, down the steps and along the path. The bridesmaids were charming in crisp green or yellow organdie dresses and big, flower-wreathed garden hats. Lynne looked lovely and radiant in her cream-colored wedding gown. Avery performed the ceremony, and he looked beautiful and distinguished in his bishop's robes.

It was not exactly a secret but few people knew that for Anton's sake and the comfort of his family he and Lynne had gone in town that morning and had a private ceremony performed by the Catholic priest at Betsy Barnett's house. There wasn't going to be any question about their being married from whichever side of the religious fence you looked at it. Jonathan gave Lynne away and then came and sat beside his mother on the front row of chairs. Janie sat on her uncomfortable little chair and wanted to cry. She always wanted to cry at weddings, but this was more than mere emotionalism. She felt sad and lonely. Here was the whole family around her and yet today she felt as if the family was slipping away from her. It is only Lynne who is going, she kept telling herself, and of course she is not really going. It didn't do much good.

The last few days had been very trying. The bridesmaids had arrived, the house was filled with strange people, everybody was always rushing out to go to a party or rushing back to change for the next party. The phone rang, the doorbell rang, presents arrived and had to be unwrapped or unpacked and great mounds of wrappings removed from the library, where the presents were being displayed. The only way Janie lived through it all was to retreat into her own inner consciousness and ignore it. Yesterday she had come back again to the world of reality. She and Jane gave a buffet supper for the wedding party last evening. Avery arrived in the afternoon, and after the supper and after the wedding rehearsal, the young people had gone off to a party at Jennie Duval's home and she had a chance to talk to Avery.

He looked tired. Susan was not well. She was in the hospital, he was going to have to fly back immediately after the wedding. The news about her was not good. He had written this to Bland, asking him to come home as soon as he could.

"He is still in Copenhagen?"

"Yes, but I think his project there is just about finished. Susan wants to meet her new daughter-in-law. So do I, of course."

Bland had recently married a Russian girl. One could only be thankful that she was a White Russian, exiled since childhood, and not a Communist.

"The family is getting quite an international tinge, isn't it? What do you think of Anton?"

"Very intelligent, very personable. You can't know, of course, what lies underneath but," he smiled, "I would call him a good risk."

Watching him now, standing in front of the altar with Lynne, making his vows in a strong, vibrant voice, Janie agreed that he did indeed seem like a good risk.

After the ceremony when the reception began, Janie sat in the carved cathedral chair from the front hall, which had been brought out to the yard for her and placed in the shade of the copper beech, and shook hands with successive waves of strange people who descended upon Fairview. Sometimes there were familiar faces, often there were familiar names. Jane, who stood by her side and introduced them, seemed to know them all, and of course Lynne knew them. Everybody said the same things. Janie got tired of it. What a lovely day, what a lovely setting for a wedding, what a lovely bride, what a handsome groom. A group of young girls giggled and said they had better go to Boston to college, there was nothing like that around here. This annoyed Janie and she spoke with some asperity.

"I don't expect you would find many like that in Boston either," she said. "They come only occasionally."

It was not that she was defending Anton. She spoke from the memory of Avery, softened now by time, and for the honor and prestige of Virginia. Boston indeed! She realized that the girls did not understand, but it didn't matter.

Late afternoon shadows cut across the sunny stretches of the lawn. Some of the guests began to go. Those that remained went into the house with Lynne when she went to

change, and watched her throw her bouquet to the bridesmaids from the landing of the stairway. Cindy Simms caught
it which, everybody agreed, was right and proper for a maid
of honor. Janie sat down in the parlor, it was cooler there
than outdoors. Jane came and sat beside her, stretched out
her feet and fanned herself.

"Somebody get me a plate of food and some champagne
and a cigarette," she said. "I haven't had time for food or
drink and I am starved."

Raddy Cziermanski and one of the bridesmaids scurried
out to the kitchen, and Miss Lucy Magee, who had done the
catering for the wedding, now that Demonet's in Washington
was no longer in existence, hurried in with more food than
Jane could possibly eat.

"You poor darling," she said. "Imagine, nothing to eat."

Lynne came downstairs, radiant in a sweater and skirt
combination. They were going to take an automobile trip and
they would not tell anybody where they were going.

When Anton came to say goodbye to Janie she kissed him.
"It is a good thing, young man, that I am eighty-five years
old," she told him, "or I would marry you myself."

He smiled, with the merest suggestion of a bow, charming
and slightly foreign. "Miniver Cheevy, born too late," he
quoted, and she liked him better than ever. She was very
fond of that poem.

Lynne put her strong young arms around Janie and hugged
her hard. "Now you be good, Gram," she said. "Don't you do
anything I wouldn't approve of. And as soon as we get settled
you are to come up to Washington to see us. We'll paint the
town."

They all went out to the front porch to wave them goodbye. Janie was glad there was no foolishness, no bells tied to
the car, no white streamers or "Just Married" placards. Only
calls and handwaving and smiles and goodbyes. As the car
disappeared down the driveway she knew that this was the
end. Not the end of life, nor the end of the love that existed
between Lynne and herself, but the end of her contact with
life. From now on she would be merely an observer. Her work
was finished. That was why she felt sad and lonely. She
would watch the world go by through the windows of Fairview.

37

The world that was to be seen through the windows of Fairview was changing rapidly. The dusty old country road which had become the wide, tree-lined avenue filled with carriages and strolling couples and families sitting on front porches in the summer dusk, had entered upon a new phase. It was definitely "going down." It was becoming an attenuated extension of the downtown section. "Business" was coming out that way, but it was little business, small shops, little eating places, drugstores, a neighborhood moving picture theater. The streetcars clattered past out to the city limits at Greenway; beyond Greenway Fairview Avenue became a highway, streams of through east-west traffic passed the entrance. A through bus line came down the Avenue, great trucks lumbered past. So many of the people who had built the big houses, set back in their big yards, at the turn of the century and in the early 1900's had moved back from the Avenue, toward the river on one side, up the hills on the other side. The houses were becoming rooming houses or overnight tourist stops, or were being cut up into small apartments. The Buford Jones house, first to be built on Fairview land, had been sold to the Catholic Church, it was now a girls' school. The Henry Daniels house had been torn down to make a parking space for the moving picture theater. The oncoming tide had not quite reached Fairview, or rather, it had jumped over the neighborhood of Fairview and begun again near the amusement park at Greenway. Ranny Boyd still lived in the gingerbread-Victorian house he had built in the 1890's, but Ranny's wife had died, the children were scattered; Ranny was older than Janie. Undoubtedly the house would soon go the way of its neighbors. The Duval house on one side of Fairview and the Marshall house on the other side were still occupied by their families. They, with a few others, formed a small green oasis in the arid stretch of Fairview Avenue. They would not last long.

Janie found this transformation very sad. She grieved over it in her heart. It was, she supposed, her fault. If she had not sold Fairview's three thousand acres the town would have had to go in some other direction. She told herself that sometimes when she saw new evidences of the Avenue's decline, but she knew that it was not true. As Henry had told her, she could not have played King Canute. She could not have stopped the oncoming waves then any more than she could stop them now. She could not have sat there stubbornly holding on to the land telling the twentieth century to go somewhere else. The twentieth century would have its way in the end. It in turn would be destroyed by the twenty-first. If you lived long enough the transience of human life became apparent to you. When you stood on a slightly higher hillock of time you began to get a clearer perspective. You might not be able to see the purposes of God, but you could see that movement and change were necessary to carry out those purposes. Not good in themselves necessarily, but opening the way for good. You must not let yourself grieve for a street or a house or a way of life. That is, you must try not to grieve. It was hard to do.

The changes worried Jonathan. "This is getting to be a poor neighborhood, Mother," he said. "Really I think you should sell Fairview before the property values go down any more. You and Jane are here alone, and it is getting harder and harder to get servants to stay with you. You could buy a smaller house on Prospect Avenue, somewhere near me, or perhaps take an apartment . . ."

"Jonathan," Janie said, "now listen to me, my dear. If Fairview should burn to the ground, and I did not burn with it, I expect I would have to find some other place to live. But while Fairview stands, and I live, I am going to stay right here."

Jane agreed with her. "It is too bad about the street, Jonny," she said, "but I don't see that that is any reason for us to move. This is where we belong. I don't think either of us could be happy anywhere else, I know Mother couldn't. And where would I find anything like my studio?"

Jane's stable studio was a charming place, and a great joy to her. Janie had not the slightest intention of following Jonathan's advice and selling Fairview, but she was glad that Jane's studio provided a good practical reason for not doing so that Jonathan could accept. He ceased his urging for a while but when a year later the city bought the big side yard of the Ely house exactly opposite the entrance of Fairview, and set about building Engine House No. 4, he began again. Janie had to be very firm with him.

"Let me alone, Jonathan," she said. "Just let me alone. I don't want to talk about it any more."

The engine house, however, was a blow. They cut down the trees in front of it, breaking the green stretch of the Avenue at that point. The alarms went off any time day or night, the engines dashed out, sirens screaming, fading gradually in the distance, to be followed by the clanging bells as the engines returned. All the family worried about it, except Betsy Barnett, who took a humorous view of it. Janie was sure she did it to tease Jonathan. Betsy, not pretty, but trim-figured and vivid, considered Uncle Jonathan rather a stuffed shirt, and enjoyed sticking pins in him. So when he said: "All right, Mother, I won't talk about it any more, but I don't see how you can possibly live right opposite that infernal noise," Betsy laughed gaily and said:

"Why, I think it is wonderful. Gram will take up with all the firemen, and pretty soon you will see her dashing around town on the fire engine, going to all the fires."

Janie did not take up with the firemen and she did mind the sirens, but there was nothing to be done about it, so she accepted it. Thank heaven both she and Jane were good sleepers.

Avery came to spend Christmas at Fairview that year. He was lonely since Susan's death. Lynne and Anton came also. Anton had expected to take a real vacation and they were going to stay for two weeks, but after Pearl Harbor occurred and the United States was plunged into the war he had to give up that plan and come only for a few days at Christmas. Lynne, however, came on as they had planned. She was expecting a baby in March. The fact was very evident and

Janie had assumed that would mean a quiet holiday season. She looked forward to family gatherings and long, quiet evenings at home. She could not have been more mistaken. Lynne made no concessions to the approaching arrival of the baby. The old holiday routine began as soon as she stepped into the house, the ringings of the phone, the comings and goings, the partying and general confusion. Lynne had some pretty maternity clothes, including two evening dresses, the skirt and separate smock that the girls all wore nowadays, and she dressed herself up and dashed around with as much verve as she had during her college holidays. Janie had never quite stopped being surprised at the casual public acceptance of pregnancy shown by the present generation. It was all right, it was fine. She liked the lack of self-consciousness, she approved of the girls' refusal to allow months to be taken out of their lives with each baby, but it was still a little startling to an old lady who in her time had tried to hide her pregnancy as long as possible and then had more or less stayed at home when it could no longer be hidden.

It was a pleasant Christmas, with Avery and Jane and Lynne and Anton all there at Fairview. The war, of course, filled everybody's mind. Janie found it hard to accept. Twice in a lifetime was too much, she said, people ought not to be called on to go through it all again.

"You talk about the purposes of God," she said to Avery, accusingly. "How can you find God in the terrible things that are happening in the world today?"

"The war is not the purpose of God, of course," Avery answered patiently. "The war is anti-Christ. God's purpose lies in man's inner triumph over war. Some day the spirit will triumph over evil and there will be no more war."

"Well, considering the amount of evil there seems to be in the world, I am afraid it will be a long time before that happens."

With the entry of the United States into the war Janie had assumed that Anton would immediately go into the service. He was of military age and he must have deep feelings about the fate of his native Poland. She was surprised, therefore when it appeared that he had no such intention. There was a reticence in his manner which kept them all from asking questions. Lynne, however, tried to explain it.

"He is doing some scientific research work, Gram," she

said. "He wanted to go into the Army, he would have liked to be sent to Europe, but the Government thinks he can be more useful where he is."

Although Janie's three grandsons were all beyond the regular military age, they had all been drawn into the services by 1943. Almost immediately after Pearl Harbor Bland Calhoun came back from Europe, joined the Army Engineer Corps, and returned to Europe in uniform. Carey Darby, Jonathan's oldest, now managing editor of the *Evening Sun*, went to Washington to serve in the Army Bureau of Public Relations. David, two years younger, went into the Naval Reserve and commanded a PT boat in the Pacific. His family went to California in the hope of seeing him occasionally. Of the great-grandsons only Richard Barnett, Betsy Ames' son, was old enough to serve. He volunteered in the Army Air Corps. God grant that history would not repeat itself, Janie prayed.

Anton remained in Washington throughout 1942. In 1943 he was transferred to the Clinton Engineering Project in Tennessee. Lynne and the baby went out there to be near him. Lynne's baby was a little girl. She insisted on naming her for Gram.

"I don't care how many Janes there are in the family," she said. "My daughter is going to be named for you."

Janie was gratified, but she could not help being amused at the curious admixture, Jane Meade Cziermanski. Janie had no idea what Anton was doing. She felt sure that she would not understand it if anybody told her, but the subject was never mentioned. Lynne and Anton seemed to be very happy, he was apparently serving his country in some necessary way, and Janie would have been, for Lynne's sake, deeply thankful for its remoteness from the fighting front, if she had not constantly remembered the "perfect safety" of Camp Zachary Taylor in World War I. She wondered if Lynne ever thought of that.

2

Janie sat alone in the library at Fairview, in front of the blazing fire. It was very cold, unusually so for early December. Eudora had said that the thermometer on the back porch stood at 30 degrees that afternoon, it must have gone down a good deal now. A thin drizzle had been falling ever since lunch-time, with the coming of darkness it began to freeze. Looked at through the windows of the library the world seemed covered in ice to Janie. The bare branches of the trees glittered with white fire, the cedar trees of the driveway looked like filigreed glass where they caught the reflection of the street lights at the far end and the lights of Fairview outside the windows. Very lovely to look at, but terribly dangerous. She was getting more and more worried. It was nine o'clock and Jane had not come yet. She should have been there hours ago. She was coming from Washington by bus, and Janie did not know what bus she had planned to take. She was always very vague about her times of arrival, she had said only that she would be there for dinner.

Janie had called the bus station. Road conditions were bad, the man said, all the buses were late. Yes, ma'am, there was a bus due from Washington at 6:50, but it was late, he didn't know how late it would be exactly. Had a little trouble near Culpeper, nothing serious, it would be along pretty soon now, he thought. She had waited dinner until seven-thirty and then had told Eudora to go on and serve her. Eudora was not going anywhere but she liked to get through her work and make herself comfortable in her own room. Quite naturally, of course. It was well that they had because they could not have waited this long.

Jane was very busy with her painting. Everybody seemed to have plenty of money these days and so many people wanted Jane Darby to paint their portraits, or their children's portraits, or their dead sons' portraits. Sometimes they came here and stayed at one of the hotels in town and had their sittings in Jane's studio at Fairview, but sometimes she had to go to Washington for the sittings. Since Lynne's marriage she had tried not to be away more than one night at a time. In the old days she had driven herself up and back, but with gasoline rationing she could no longer do that. She had to use buses or trains, less flexible and much less convenient, but in a way it was a comfort to Janie. She had never liked the casual way Jane ran around in her car, frequently at night. She wished Jane would not accept so many commissions and push herself so hard. Why should she, she wondered. The inner compulsion of the artist she supposed, the joy of achievement. All the same, she thought Jane looked tired, and she worried because she knew that it was only because of her that she ran back and forth so much. Bradford Long was not in Washington now. He was serving as a war correspondent with General Clark's Fifth Army in Italy, living with the troops, going where they went, writing very moving dispatches from the fighting front. She read them every morning in the paper. Of course Jane did too. Letters came from him, not constantly but often enough for Janie to know that the bond between them was still strong. She always felt happier about Jane when Bradford Long was in some other part of the world.

At nine-fifteen she heard a car come up the driveway. Thank God, she really was beginning to be frightened. She rose and was in the front hall when Jane opened the door and came in. Cold air blew in with her.

"Devilish weather," she said. "Hello, darling. Sorry to be so late." She kissed her mother, her face felt icy. It looked white and pinched. "I am frozen, simply frozen stiff."

She went into the library and stood against the fire screen, holding out her hands to the blaze. "Lord, this feels good."

"What happened, honey?" Janie asked, sitting down again in her chair by the fire.

"The roads are icy," Jane said. "Just solid sheets of ice. The road crews are out now with sand and ashes, but at first we didn't know what was happening. It just looked like the road was wet. Somewhere on the other side of Culpeper the bus skidded. It ran over a low stone coping and crashed into a tree. It didn't turn over and nobody was hurt, just shaken up a bit, but it did a lot of damage underneath the bus. The driver turned off the engine, fast, he must have been very skillful, and the gas leaked out, and of course the heat went off. That was the trouble. We all nearly froze. We had to sit and wait while they sent into town for somebody to come out and patch things up, and then we had to wait in town for some more patching. We went into a drugstore and had some hot coffee, but it didn't do much good. And then we simply crawled the rest of the way, with no heat on in the bus."

She had taken off her coat and hat and gloves, and pulled up a footstool as close to the fire as she could get, but she was still shivering. "They wired for another bus to meet them at the station here. This is a through trip, it goes all down into the South. The poor people who are going through are going to have to wait until it gets here. I was thankful that this was

398

the end of the line for me. Is there anything to eat? I'm starved."

"Eudora left your plate in the warming oven," Janie said. "I hope it is still hot. There is coffee already made in the percolator, plug it in and it will be hot in a minute."

"I want a drink," Jane said.

It was so seldom that Jane wanted a drink that Janie realized she must be chilled.

"There is sherry in the decanter on the sideboard," she said, "but I expect you want whiskey. You know where it is."

Jane came back presently with her plate and hot coffee and a tall drink on a tray. She sat on the floor with her back to the fire screen and put the tray on the footstool, and ate and drank with relish. By the time she had finished she seemed to feel better. She inched a little farther away from the fire and lighted a cigarette. Her face still looked pinched.

"You had better go to bed, darling," Janie said. "You must be worn out. Take a hot bath and put an electric pad at your feet."

Jane stood up. "All right, I think I will." She bent over to kiss her mother. "I hope you didn't worry about me, honey," she said.

"Of course I worried about you," Janie said. "I worry about you frequently."

Jane stroked her cheek. "Poor Mama," she said, reverting to her childhood name.

Jane occupied the other front room upstairs, over the library, opposite Janie's room. Early the next morning Janie was awakened by a sound. She thought it came from Jane's room, she had a feeling that Jane had called her. It was still dark. She sat up in bed, and the sound came again. It was Jane calling her, in a strangled voice. She got out of bed; she moved slowly nowadays, she could not run as she wanted to do. It was very cold. She caught up a robe but did not stop to put down the window, and went across the hall to Jane's room. Her light was on, she was lying in bed, her face dead white. She was clutching her left breast and seemed to be in great pain.

"Call Dr. Payne, please, quickly." She struggled with the words.

"Oh, my darling," Janie cried. "My dear, what on earth—"

"Doctor, Doctor," Jane said, through stiff lips.

399

Janie turned and went as quickly as she could into her own room, switching on the light as she went. Dr. Payne's number was written on a pad attached to her telephone. It stayed there always. She dialed it, fumbling a little in her fright.

"I am so sorry to disturb you," she said when she heard his voice, "but Jane is ill. She seems to be in great pain, in her chest. Will you come, please, right away."

"Miss Janie, listen to me," Dr. Payne said calmly. "Listen carefully. She has some pills, they should be right there with her, on her bedside table or on her bureau or in her bathroom. They are marked 'As needed for pain.' Find them and get her to put several under her tongue, as many as she needs. I will get there as soon as I can."

"Thank you."

Janie put down the receiver and went through the hall into the back corridor to call Eudora. She was in too much of a hurry to go all the way so she banged on the wall and called: "Eudora, Eudora, wake up. Wake up. Miss Jane is ill. Come to her room."

She heard muffled sounds and turned and went back to Jane's room, to see if the pills were on her table. Jane was quiet now, the paroxysm seemed to have passed. She was lying motionless on the bed. As Janie approached the bed and stood looking at her panic seized her. She reached out and shook Jane's shoulder.

"Jane, Jane," she called. Slowly she took her hand from the slim, lace-clad shoulder, knowing that Jane had gone. In those few minutes, while she was calling the doctor, while she was calling Eudora, Jane had gone.

For the first time in her life Janie Darby fainted. The world became a spinning black void. The floor rose up around her. She felt herself going and tried to catch herself against the bed, but all she did was to pull Jane's blue eiderdown quilt into a soft mound on the floor. She fell on the bedside rug. When Eudora, sleepy-eyed, in felt bedroom slippers, shuffled in in answer to her call, she found Miss Jane motionless on the bed and Mrs. Darby motionless on the floor. She thought they were both dead and ran screaming from the room. She was still screaming when Dr. Payne came. He had to deal with her hysterics downstairs before going up. He shook her and slapped her, and when that did no good he went out to the pantry, got a glass of water and

400

threw it full into her face. The screams became sobs and snuffles.

"Pull yourself together, girl," Dr. Payne said sternly. "Wipe your face and come on upstairs. I'll probably need you."

He went straight to Jane's room. By that time Janie had regained consciousness and had managed to prop herself up into a sitting position on the floor against a wing chair near the bed. That was as far as she could get. The doctor took one look at Jane and concentrated on the old lady. He bent down and picked her up and carried her to her own room and put her in bed. She seemed to be dazed. Her eyes were open but she stared unseeingly in front of her. Shock, of course. Her pulse was good, she had an amazing heart. It was lucky that she had not broken any bones in falling, a woman of her age. Eighty-eight, wasn't she? He had the records at his office. A wonderful old lady.

The maid, dry but sullen and still frightened, stood in the doorway.

"What is your name?" he asked.

"Eudora," she said.

"Eudora, this house is very cold. Put down any windows that were opened for the night and turn up the heat. And please find a hot-water bag or an electric pad for Mrs. Darby's feet."

There was a water bottle and glass on the bedside table. He searched in his bag for what he wanted, then put his arm under Miss Janie's head and propped her up.

"Swallow this, Miss Janie, dear," he said. She swallowed like an obedient child, and he put her back down and covered her up, and went on into Jane's room. There was nothing he could do here. Poor little lady, poor dear lady. He had always been fond of Jane Darby. Such a pretty, gay young thing she had been, when he too was young. And a very fine artist, so they said, the people who knew about art.

Perhaps he should feel guilty about this, but how could he have known? She had come to him a month or two ago, two months he thought it was, about a pain she sometimes felt in her heart. She didn't want her mother to know about it. He had examined her and done a cardiogram and there was no sign of anything wrong. But you couldn't tell about angina, and he had given her the pills just in case, and told her to keep them always with her. He looked now, and there they were, on the bedside table. Either she had not had time to take them or they had done no good. He picked up the blue eiderdown quilt and covered her with it, then went to the telephone. When he had made the necessary calls he dialed Jonathan Darby's number. It was still only seven o'clock, he knew he would awaken the household. The lifelong habit of the morning-newspaper man of going to bed late and sleeping late in the morning. Jonathan answered the phone. He was so shocked when the doctor told him that John Payne thought he might have to go there to revive him.

"I'm sorry, Jon," he said. "It is a terrible thing, but there was nothing to do but tell you. You had better come on over here, and bring Sara Anne with you. I am trying to get a nurse to stay with your mother but the chances are slim. Nurses are scarcer than hens' teeth these days. I will stay here until you come."

He went to find Eudora and found her in the kitchen. She was dressed now.

"Eudora," he said, "Miss Jane has died very suddenly, apparently from a heart attack. I have given Mrs. Darby a mild sedative, she will sleep for several hours. Mr. Jonathan and Miss Sara Anne will be here soon, and I expect you had better do something about some breakfast. They won't have had any. Neither have I, for that matter."

When Janie woke up from her sleep her mind was completely clear. She remembered everything and she knew that there was something she must do. It was as if her mind had gone on working while she slept and she had arrived at a decision. Betsy Barnett was sitting by her bed. She sat up.

"Hello, darling," Betsy said. "I am glad you have waked up, Gram." It was Lynne who had started calling her Gram, but now all the grandchildren had adopted the name.

"Where is Jonathan?" Janie asked.

"He was here until just a little while ago. Aunt Sara Anne went home and he went to the office, to attend to the notices and—the telegrams—" Her voice choked.

Janie had no time for tears. "I must speak to him. I wish I had been awake when he was here. Call him on the phone, will you, Betsy, please."

"Jonathan," she said when she heard his voice.

"How are you, dear?" he broke in. "Such a terrible shock for you, Mother, I am—"

"Listen, Jonathan, there is something I want you to do, as quickly as you can. Find out how to reach Bradford Long, and send him a cable."

"Bradford Long," said Jonathan incredulously.

"Yes, Bradford Long. He is one of Jane's oldest and dearest friends. You will probably send telegrams to some of her friends, certainly Mary Cullen and the other young woman she has spent so many summers with, and others will see the notices in the papers. But Bradford Long is with the troops in Italy, he won't see any notices, and I know, Jonathan—please don't argue with me, I am not up to arguing—but I know she would want him to be told."

"All right, dear," Jonathan said.

"With your newspaper connections you can find out how to reach him. Send him a cable for me. Say *Jane died sudden Heart attack Funeral here*—when, Jonathan, when have you set the funeral?"

"We were waiting to consult with you, Mother. This is Friday, I should say Monday morning."

Janie did some rapid calculating. If he got the cable today he could fly. Of course he might not get the cable, he might be where he could not be reached. Of course he might not be able to come, he might not want to come. None of that was her business. The important thing was for her to let him know.

"Say Monday afternoon," she told Jonathan, "and sign the cable with my name, Jonathan, Mrs. Henry Forbes Darby."

He got the cable. Late on Saturday afternoon a reply came: *Will get there Thank you.* It was signed Bradford Long.

So it was that at the funeral of Jane Darby there was a tall, lanky man, with gray eyes and balding hair whom nobody in town knew personally but whom everybody recognized from the little square picture of him which headed his column each morning in the *Herald*. Bradford Long.

His presence there was not conspicuous. A good many of Jane's friends came for the funeral, Mary Cullen and Anita Drew, and others from New York and Washington. Some of their faces were familiar to Janie, some she did not know. They went from the church to the cemetery and at the conclusion of the services there they came up to speak to her, quietly and sorrowfully. She acknowledged their greetings, but they were like shadows thrown against a wall, two-dimensional. They meant nothing to her. Jonathan and Sara Anne and the young ones, the grandchildren, would take care of these out-of-town visitors. She went slowly back to her car, holding Avery's arm. He had flown in from Oklahoma yesterday. Before she reached the car Bradford Long overtook her.

He put out his hand and said: "This was very kind of you, Mrs. Darby. I appreciate it." He had a deep voice.

They looked at each other, across an immeasurable gap. So many questions she would like to ask, so many things she would like to know about Jane that she would never know now. It was too late to bridge the gap. She took his hand and pressed it firmly. Who was she to judge him?

"She would have wanted you to know," she said.

A small spasm passed over his face like a sudden gust of wind, and was gone.

"Yes," he said, "I think she would have."

He shook hands with Avery and turned back to the others. Janie and Avery and Lynne got into the car and drove back to Fairview. She would never see him again, she knew.

Lynne had flown in that morning and would have to fly back to Oak Ridge that evening. The baby had a slight cold, she was afraid to bring her, and though Anton was there and a kind neighbor friend was keeping her during the day, Lynne thought she must get back that night. She would come later with the baby and stay with Gram for a while.

Avery stayed with her for a week. He was of course a great comfort. At first she found it hard to speak of Jane. The shock of her sudden death had set up a barrier to speech; it seemed somehow irreverent to talk about her. Avery helped to break that down. He spoke of Jane naturally, affectionately. He reminisced about her, he rejoiced at the place she had won for herself in the world of art. Condolences poured in, from all over the country; newspapers wrote editorials about her and later some of the specialized magazines. Jonathan collected them for her and brought them to her. Gradually Janie found herself able to think of Jane as she was during all the years and not as she had been in that horror-filled moment in the cold December dawn.

Immediately after the funeral Janie said to Avery: "Jonathan and Elizabeth are going to try to make me give up Fairview, and I am not going to do it, Avery. I know I am being a stubborn old woman, but I am going to end my days in this house. Please try to head them off, I am so tired arguing about it."

Evidently Avery did head them off. The subject was not mentioned; instead the family concentrated on making adequate arrangements for Gram's care. When Avery left a couple had been engaged who would live at Fairview, a man named Harvey and his wife Lucinda. Between them they would do all that was necessary. They seemed reliable and everybody was pleased.

A great problem was what to do with Jane's things. All the paintings in the studio, all her personal belongings. Both Elizabeth and Sara Anne offered to help her with them though it was getting harder and harder for Elizabeth to get around, but Janie could not face it. It was not until the end of January, when Lynne came to pay a visit with little Jane, that she worked herself up to going over Jane's possessions. Jane had left a will, with bequests to nieces and nephews and friends, to art foundations and museums, but what to do with the pretty clothes, the lacy underwear, the coats and sweaters and shoes and gloves and bags? Jane had always dressed nicely. And the jewelry. She did not have much, but she had a few really good pieces. Janie sat in front of the bureau in Jane's room, with her jewel case in her lap, going over the small collection. When she lifted the velvet tray she found in the bottom compartment a little turquoise ring that Jane had had as a child, the seed pearl necklace which had belonged to her great-grandmother and which Janie had given her on her seventeenth birthday, as her mother had given it to her, and a small white satin box, yellowed and slightly discolored by time. Opening it, she saw the diamond solitaire that Tommy Tyler had given Jane that happy Christmas so long ago. The beautiful stone flashed up at her, blue-white and brilliant, in its old-fashioned setting, a slender gold ring with tiny platinum prongs holding the diamond. So long hidden, never worn. It was then that Janie put her arms on the bureau and cried. It was the first time she had been able to shed tears since Jane died.

38

Janie awakened to a cold and silent house. She came out of her sleep slowly, drowsily, as she always did, and felt at first that it must be very early. Then she was puzzled because she could see gray November light coming around the edges of the drawn shades at the windows. She sat up in bed and shivered. Turning on her bedside lamp she saw that it was five minutes past eight o'clock. Gracie was late. She should have turned up the thermostat and come to awaken her at eight o'clock. A little later she would bring Miss Janie's breakfast on a tray.

It had been almost a year since Jane's death and in that time Janie had allowed herself to contract a habit she had always scorned, having her breakfast in bed. It seemed so pointless to get up and dress and go downstairs to sit alone at the big empty dining room table and eat her small breakfast. Now she reached for her robe and slipped stiffly out of the big four-poster. Going to the front windows she raised the shades and saw that it was indeed a gray and cheerless day. The room seemed very cold and she closed the small crack in the window, which was all she opened at night nowadays, remembering all the years she and Henry had opened wide the four windows of the room and sometimes had been almost swept out of bed by the winter winds that blew through. She wondered why they had done that; it was considered healthful. She moved slowly out to the hall to turn up the thermostat. Awareness increased, and the silence of the house invaded her consciousness. A horrid suspicion came to her; leaning over the well of the staircase she listened. Not a sound came from the lower floor. Turning she went down the back hall to the door leading to the servants' rooms and back stairs to the kitchen regions.

"Gracie. Henry," she called.

When no answer came she knocked on their door, opened it, closed it and came away. They had gone. Harvey and Lucinda, the couple who had come just after Jane's death, had stayed six months and left. Henry and Gracie had been with her five months. That was the way it was these days; only those whose servants had been with them a long time could keep them. There were so many war jobs available, so many new opportunities where those who had gone into domestic service could earn more money with shorter hours and greater independence, it was very natural. Natural, but hard on an old lady. She went back to her room and began to dress. The old should die, they had no place in the world, and if the good Lord wouldn't let them die then they ought to go on and live in docile dependence with their children, if they had any children.

Don't let yourself be bitter, Janie, she told herself. You have been infinitely blessed. This is just a minor inconvenience.

The house had begun to warm up when she went downstairs. In the pantry she fixed coffee in the percolator and plugged it in, she got out bread for toast. She thought she had better boil herself an egg, food was apt to be sketchy that day. She set herself a place at the pantry table and sat down to eat the egg and toast and drink the coffee and consider the situation.

Of all the changes that had taken place in her lifetime this was to Jane the most pervasive, calling for the greatest adjustment. This revolution in service! This do-it-yourself-world! It was all right for the young ones, who had known no other. The middle-aged ones, some of them at least, could adjust, but for the old it was hard.

Janie checked over in her mind the changes she had witnessed since the isolated country living of her childhood, the successive revolutions in ways of living which she had accepted and assimilated. Streetcars, electric lights, telephones, automobiles. Furnace heat, city water, moving pictures, radios, television. Airplanes, shrinking the world so unbelievably. Bradford Long flying from Italy for Jane's funeral. Bland Calhoun flying from Germany to Oklahoma when his mother died. Supermarkets, frozen foods, labor-saving devices. Electric stoves, coffee makers, toasters, dishwashers, clothes washers and driers, freezers, blenders, what not. All supposedly taking the place of the hewers of wood and the drawers of water who had, since the beginning of time, been a part of human existence. All assuming to do for everybody what, since the dawn of history, some had done for others. All good, all fine, all contributing to a better life for more people. All dedicated to the great god democracy.

Now that the house was warm and she had had food and was drinking her second cup of good hot coffee, Janie's sense of humor returned to her, and she was amused at herself as she always was when she came face to face with democracy. She believed in democracy, deeply, but she much preferred not to live with it. Henry had believed in democracy, Avery did. It was remarkable how often Henry and Avery had arrived at the same conclusions, approaching them from such different directions. Henry's beliefs were strictly secular, based on human dignity and the rights of man, on the writings of Thomas Paine and Thomas Jefferson; Avery's were religious, based on the sayings of Jesus Christ two thousand years ago. They usually came out at the same place. Janie, in between them, had accepted democracy in theory from both points of view. It was right, but it was terribly uncomfortable. Theory could be so far removed from everyday living. Say what you chose, no electrical invention dreamed up by the mind of man could take the place of human hands, human strength and skill. All these gadgets and savers helped, but they still required the human element. It took men and women to operate them and to do the work they were designed to help. It was unquestionably easier to make a cake by using an electric mixer than your own right arm, but the fact remained that somebody had to mix the cake and pour it and bake it. It was much pleasanter to buy a dressed turkey at the grocery store than to go out in the barnyard and kill and pluck and dress the turkey, but all the same somebody had to prepare the dressed turkey and stuff and bake it. It was a fine thing to be able to put dirty dishes in a dishwasher, but what about cutting the grease out of the pots and pans and scouring them? What about washing windows and scrubbing and waxing floors and polishing furniture and silver? What about ironing after the clothes had been washed in an electric washer? These were things that very old ladies could not do, especially those who had never done them or expected to have to do them. And if you didn't do them yourself who did, in this fine new democratic world?

Janie remembered the saying of Will Rogers back in the Republican twenties, that it was a pity the Democratic Party had adopted the slogan: "Equal opportunity for all, special privilege for none." It should advocate, he said, "Special privilege for all, equal opportunity for none," and then it would get elected. Of course what the Republicans really believed in was: "Special privilige for some, equal opportunity for none." That was what was the matter with Jonathan. He was at heart a Republican, but he hadn't realized it yet. He kept talking about Jeffersonian Democracy, when what he meant was the special privilege of those who had inherited or knew how to amass property and wealth. Personally, she admitted, she liked a little special privilege. She had had it all of her life; it was hard to get caught with equality in your old age. At least, however, she recognized special privilege when she saw it, she smiled at the conflict between her principles and her desires, and she tried to be philosophic about the situation. She had a strong conviction that democracy was not only right, it was inevitable. The twentieth century was actually the century of the common man, dedicated to the leveling processes of democracy, like it or not.

When she had finished her breakfast she telephoned the employment agency. Mrs. Marbury was terribly sorry Henry and Gracie had left; they had seemed so reliable. Yes, she would try to find Mrs. Darby someone else, but she knew what the situation was. Janie knew. She tried to call Mary Davis' house. Mary was Baizy's Lucy's granddaughter, Lucy herself had died five or six years ago. No one answered. They were probably all working, she would have to wait until tonight when they would be at home.

Elizabeth telephoned, as she did almost every morning, and was horrified to learn what had happened.

"You must come over here and stay with us until you get someone, Mama," she said. "You can't stay there by yourself."

409

"I may get someone in a few days, honey," Janie said. "Let's wait and see."

"Well, Hugh will come for you and bring you here for dinner," Elizabeth said, "and we will get one of the children to stay with you tonight."

"If you get hold of Betsy or one of the children, you might ask them to run over to Emmy Brown's house. She might know of someone."

Janie had been contributing to Emmy Brown's support for years. She knew the old woman would help if she could.

In the months that followed this situation developed repeatedly. Janie gave up trying to keep a couple and concentrated on having a cook and an occasional yard man. They came and they went. Sometimes they told her they were leaving, sometimes they simply disappeared. When this happened she would call the employment agency or one of the Negro families she knew and try to get someone else. In the meantime she would boil herself an egg and make some toast for breakfast, the house had to do with a lick and a promise, the grass did not get cut or the hedges trimmed or the leaves raked, depending upon the time of year it was. Sara Anne and Jonathan, or Hugh Ames, or one of the grandchildren would bring her food or take her home to have dinner with them, and one of the great-grandchildren would sleep at Fairview so she would not be alone in the house at night.

"I know I am a nuisance," Janie said to Jonathan. "Just a stubborn old nuisance."

"You are not a nuisance, Mother," Jonathan said gently. "You must never say that. We do worry about you, but if this is the way you want it, this is the way we want it to be."

Jonathan was really very sweet.

2

Mrs. Thompson was a large woman. In an age when the female figure was for the most part lightly restrained by elastic girdles, she always looked corseted and boned to the teeth, giving a nostalgic reflection of the hourglass figure fashionable at the turn of the century. Janie watched her come plodding heavily up the driveway. On the porch she made a great to-do of stomping the snow off of her galoshes and shaking it from her coat, then she rang the bell. Bertha came to let her in, smiling broadly. Bertha liked Mrs. Thompson. So did Janie, really, though she wished she would not call her dearie. She called her that now.

"Well, well, how are you this morning, dearie?" she asked cheerfully. "And how do you like this weather?"

"It is beautiful to look at," Janie said, "but I am glad I am not going anywhere in it."

"It ain't bad," Mrs. Thompson said. "It's real nice, sort of soft and feathery so it ain't slippery. I just stopped by to see how you're getting on with the Bishop away." Avery had gone to an ecclesiastical conference in Philadelphia. "I'm going to the grocery store, you and Bertha need anything?"

"Yessum," Bertha said. "Want I should get up a list, Miss Janie?"

"Why, yes, if Mrs. Thompson doesn't mind. I expect, though, that we could get Smith and Allen's to send us what we need." Janie clung to the old grocery store. It was the only one in town that still delivered, and she knew it was having a hard fight against the supermarkets.

"Better let me get 'em for you," Mrs. Thompson said. "With this snow and all, no telling when deliveries would get here."

"But you couldn't carry the bundles in this weather."

"Bless you, no." Mrs. Thompson beamed at her. "I'll just get 'em put up and Jim will stop and pick 'em up on his way home to lunch."

Jim, her husband, drove a taxicab. He was a great convenience to the neighborhood. The oasis around Fairview had gone now. All the old families had died off or moved. The big houses had been turned into small apartments or used as offices; the spaces in between were filled with little shops. Through Avery, Janie had come to know many of her new neighbors and had established firm friendships among them. Avery had retired and come back to Fairview to live. In no time at all he seemed to know everybody in the neighborhood, and he drew Janie into a circle of warm friendliness. Avery made friends with everyone, simply by being Avery. He exuded friendship, and Janie lived in the reflection of his warmth. Mrs. Thompson, who had an apartment in the old Marshall house next door, and little Mrs. Ellis, who ran the bakery shop a few doors down the street, and old Mr. Wyeth Cram, whose father had bought Ally Martin's livery stable way back in the 1880's and who had lost his money in the depression; Mr. John Taylor, owner of Taylor's Laundry and Dry Cleaning Co., Inc., across the street, and Mrs. Taylor, who lived above the laundry, Miss Jennie Saunders, who ran a little shop which defied classification, selling anything that happened to occur to Miss Jennie as being a good idea to sell, and Mrs. Martin Jones, whose son Marty was a policeman; these were the people Janie saw now, who were always running in to inquire how she was and do small kindnesses for her. These and the firemen. Avery drew much pleasure from the firemen, and it amused Janie to see the tall, white-haired, distinguished-looking retired Episcopal Bishop, in his clerical garb, sitting in a chair on the sidewalk in front of the engine house talking and laughing with a group of firemen.

With Susan gone and Bland and his family always off somewhere, Avery had felt drawn back to Fairview. His coming was the greatest happiness that Janie had known in recent years. She could have asked for no greater joy in her last years than to have him here in the empty house with her, to have his daily companionship and the light of his spirit.

By that time Bertha had appeared. Bertha was the answer to prayer, the solution to all domestic problems. She was a big, amiable woman, not young, the widow of a railway porter. She had her pension from the Railroad Retirement Board. She had a married daughter who lived in town. Bertha did not want to live with the daughter, and Janie knew so well how she felt that an immediate bond was established between them. Bertha liked living at Fairview and taking care of Miss Janie, and when Avery came she was delighted. With Bertha and a yard man who came twice a week Fairview settled back into an orderly existence.

Mrs. Thompson departed with Bertha's list of groceries, and later red-faced, red-haired Jim Thompson, as thin as his wife was portly, drove up in his taxi and delivered the bags. Mrs. Ellis ran in with a pan of hot rolls from her bakery. Elizabeth telephoned and Jonathan stopped by to see her on his way home that afternoon. Everybody was so good to her. She was greatly blessed, she knew. Sometimes she reproached herself for not appreciating her blessings more acutely.

Janie was going up in her nineties now. Emotions were muted. Time drifted by for her; it had no particular purpose, no direction, it merely drifted. Day followed day, pleasantly for the most part. The emptiness and loneliness that Jane's death had caused had been filled in by Avery; the heartache had been mitigated by him. She could not be actively unhappy when Avery was with her. They lived quietly and comfortably. Bertha was not the best cook in the world but that made little difference to either of them. She had lost her interest in food and Avery was on a diet. He was frequently called upon for church activities, to take the services at St. John's or to go to conferences or preside at community meetings, but for the most part he lived a quiet and peaceful life, and spent much time in the library at Fairview. He read a great deal and Janie tried to. Her eyes were not very good, but with her glasses she got on well enough. The trouble was her attention wandered. They listened to the radio, they drove out in the afternoons and went to church on Sundays. The relatives came to call; they had big family reunions at Christmas and sometimes in the summer when the out-of-town grandchildren came home for visits. Sometimes Janie enjoyed such gatherings, but sometimes they were too much for her and she withdrew into her inner self and let the activity around her flow past her. Elizabeth hardly went anywhere now, she was almost a cripple from arthritis, but her daughters, Betsy Barnett and Jane Eubank, and their children seemed to take part in everything that went on in town. So also did Jonathan and Sara Anne and their two who lived in town, Carey and Helen. David came over from Roanoke frequently and every summer Sally, who lived in Birmingham, came home for a visit. Janie was devoted to Sally, she was a charming girl. She seemed to have a great many children.

"Only six," Sally said. "I think maybe I will stop with that."

Janie was having a little trouble with the great-grandchildren. They were beginning to grow up now, and sometimes she could not remember whose children they were or what their names were. She forgot other things too, and it worried her. Whenever she was depressed over not remembering things she fell back on the kings of England. There had been a time when she had questioned the usefulness to her of the kings of England, but now she found them a great comfort because, when she turned to them, there they all were, each taking his proper place in the long procession from William the Conqueror to—Queen Victoria it had been when she first learned them, now on to George VI. She might not be able to remember the name of a great-granddaughter or whom Laura Ashby's son had married, but she could always go through the list of splendid blond Plantagenets, the Tudors and the Stuarts and the Hanoverian line. It was very comforting to her.

Janie enjoyed the afternoon drives with Avery more than anything. Sometimes they drove around the town, to see the changes and the new developments. Sometimes they went out into the country and tried to find the old country roads they used to know. One afternoon they drove up the steep slope of Prospect Avenue, past Jonathan's house, where they frequently went, and on up to the rock-tipped top of the hill, where in the old days they used to walk and look out over the wide untouched stretch of fields and forests and hills and mountains. As near to the top as possible, before Prospect Avenue began to go down on the other side of the hill, an overlook had been built. Avery parked the car there, and they sat in silence, flooded, submerged by memories.

Janie could see herself there as a child, puffing tiredly behind Peyton; as a young girl, slowly climbing the hill through the woods, past the spring and the place where the trailing arbutus grew, to sit at the top and dream of the life ahead of her. She could see herself with Avery, the first Avery, in the summer days of their courtship, and later in her tragic widowhood, alone or with this Avery, this white-haired man beside her as a little boy. She and Henry used to come here, and here she had walked with the children many times. From this point she had watched the whole world change. All changed now except the mountains. They still stood in blue majesty across the western sky. Perhaps some day man, with his new machines, would level them off too, would lay them flat, but not yet. Man had not yet been able to destroy the mountains of the world.

She said this to Avery and he told her it was pure pessimism. "Why do you have such a low opinion of the human race?" he asked.

"After Hiroshima, how can you tell what we might do?"

He nodded. "Yes, after Hiroshima."

After Hiroshima they knew what Anton Cziermanski had been doing at Oak Ridge, Tennessee. Not long after that, after the end of the war, he was transferred to Los Alamos in

New Mexico, where he was continuing his experimental research. Man now knew, it seemed, how to destroy himself; he was seeking to learn how to turn the forces of destruction to his own salvation. Anton and Avery sometimes discussed these things when the Cziermanskis came to Fairview for a visit. They had three children now, two boys having followed little Jane. Avery and Anton liked each other and found much to discuss. Just as Henry's secular political philosophy had so often agreed with Avery's religious convictions, so did Anton's scientific approach.

"We know too much, sir," Anton said to Avery, "and we know too little. We don't know how to handle our knowledge. Man can so easily destroy himself."

"You are reckoning without God when you say that," Avery replied. "Do you imagine for one moment that God is going to let man destroy himself? God created the human race for a purpose, and the purposes of God still stand."

Anton smiled at him. "I don't question the purposes of God. Perhaps I should say man can so easily destroy his present civilization and a good part of the present generation of the human race."

"Man is certainly capable of infinite stupidity," Avery said, "but somehow I trust the guiding hand of God to keep him from the ultimate folly. Only God can save us, but I don't doubt that He will."

Avery never doubted, and he had little patience with those who did. Possessed of a vast tolerance for human foibles, he accepted people as they were and shed a sort of benign goodwill upon them. Only toward the cynical and the unbelieving did he show irritation.

"Sinners I can forgive," he would say. "I can understand them, we are all sinners in some degree. God can help the sinners, it is the doubters and the unbelievers who are beyond help. The little people who try to limit God to the confines of their own small finite minds. The ones who say 'God can't exist because I can't understand him. I can't see or touch him so he can't be there.' The ones who say, 'God couldn't have done that because it is contrary to natural law, and God is bound by my understanding of natural law.'" Avery, usually so calm and benign, would become almost agitated when he discussed such people. He would pace the floor much as Henry used to do when arguing against unseen political opponents. "How much do they know about natural law?" Avery would demand. "Science is opening up new laws all the time that nobody knew about a generation ago. How much do you think the ordinary person knows about splitting the atom, or what an atom is, for that matter? But because men found a way to split the atom and cause unbelievable physical destruction everybody accepts it. If God, who created the atom, had done that these little people would have said it was a miracle and therefore could not have happened. They must always have a man-made explanation. God can't, but man can, that's what they believe."

God was so integral a part of Avery's life that, living with him in the quiet companionship of those years, He entered into Janie's life in a way she had never been able to bring about by herself. Just as Avery drew her into a warm circle of human relationships so he drew her into the secure world of God's love. Her life, past and present, seemed good to her.

It was Avery, however, who brought the peace and the deep content, not she herself. She found that out after Avery's death. Again she was left alone, so deeply alone that for a while nothing could reach her. She lived in an empty world, a cold void. God was not there, and no human relationship meant anything to her. The children—only Elizabeth and Jonathan were left now—the grandchildren, the great-grandchildren, the neighbors, were all kind and attentive. They did what they could. Out of the first emptiness came bitterness, and out of the bitterness a pervading, all-absorbing question: Why must I go on living? Why am I kept here, far beyond my own generation, almost beyond my children's generation? Why?

She knew what Avery would say; to complete some plan of God's as yet incomplete; to learn something as yet unlearned, to kindle a spark as yet dormant. But why her, when others went so easily, surely knowing no more of God's purposes than she knew? And what? And why? Mind and heart and spirit were concentrated on those questions.

39

It had been so long since Janie had had a new hat that, though she could not honestly say that she was excited, she was interested as she dressed for church that Sunday morning. When she had prepared for church the week before she had been vaguely dissatisfied with herself. She had hardly thought of her appearance since Avery died, and she had to admit that she had let herself go. It had come over her that Mrs. Henry Forbes Darby, even at ninety-six, owed it to herself to look like a lady and not a frump. She decided that the place to begin was a new hat.

She had come slowly back from the arid place of her desolation. It was strange, she thought, how insistent life was. As long as that mysterious current ran through your body, as long as this physical shell breathed and moved and thought, life made its demands and you had to meet them. So here she was once more thinking about her appearance.

Shopping was difficult for her, but she made an effort and went downtown. Betsy Barnett took her. They went to Garrett and Wright's. Janie had been shopping there since it was Wright's Emporium way back there when she was a little girl. If she could find a pretty new hat which would go over her hair, still worn piled up on top of her head, she was sure it would be at Garrett and Wright's.

Main Street amazed Janie. There were so many people and not a soul that she knew. Some of them spoke to Betsy and some of them included her in the greetings, but to Janie they all looked like strangers. Inside the store, however, it was different. The older employees were all familiar to her. Some of them called greetings and some came out from behind their counters to speak to her, and Mr. Garrett hurried up and almost embraced her, he seemed so pleased to see her. He personally escorted her up to the millinery department on the second floor. The elevator girl was named Daisy; she and Janie were very glad to see each other. Mr. Garrett told Mrs. Warburg, head of millinery, that if she didn't have what Mrs. Darby wanted to send to New York and get it. That was not necessary, however; Janie found a very nice hat. Looking at herself now in the mirror she nodded approval. It fitted nicely over her hair and around her face, and it had an iridescent coq's feather across one side to give it some life. The next time she went downtown she thought she would buy a new dress. Her black faille was all right, but it was pretty old. The mink coat was old too, but a mink coat was a mink coat. It was a handsome one, and she would pay no attention to styles as far as it was concerned.

Jonathan and Sara Anne were coming by to take her to church. Avery's car still stood in the garage but there was no one to drive it now. Janie was dependent on the members of the family, or Jim Thompson's taxi when she wanted to go somewhere on her own, which was seldom. It was Bertha's Sunday off. Every other week she spent the day with her daughter and Janie had Sunday dinner with Jonathan or Elizabeth or one of the grandchildren.

Putting on her coat, Janie picked up her white gloves and her purse, and stopped for a moment to look at herself in the cheval glass. Yes, she did very well, the hat was a great help. She had fixed her hair with care and she had put on a touch of lipstick. Even she had come to it. She did as well as could be expected, she thought, except her shoes. She looked down with distaste to her feet. She had always worn pretty shoes until recently; now she had on what she called "old-lady clodhoppers." They were ugly and clumsy, made out of black kid with untapered heels and ties that wouldn't stay tied. Dr. Herndon made her wear them. Dear John Payne had died and she missed him. Dr. Herndon was nice, a good doctor, very modern and up to date, but she would have liked to finish her days with Dr. Payne. The shoes were too big for

418

her. Even with the shoestrings pulled tightly together they were too big. She had told the shoe man that, but he only smiled at her and said he thought she would find them comfortable. People treated you like a child when you got old.

As she came down the first flight of stairs to the landing she heard Jonathan's car coming up the driveway. She started down the second flight, holding carefully to the railing as she always did, but hurrying a little because Jonathan always tried to help her and though stairs were hard for her, especially in the big old clodhoppers, she did not want to be helped. Hurrying, her foot turned in the shoe, giving her a jerk that caused her purse to slip from her hand. She reached to catch it, taking her hand from the railing for a moment, and then she felt herself falling. With great clarity she was conscious of the sensation of falling, of reaching again for the railing and missing it, of hitting the steps and landing on the floor at the bottom. She heard a cry from Jonathan, felt excruciating pain, and lost consciousness.

When she came to herself she was still lying on the floor, but there was quiet movement all around her. People were coming and going, people were standing in the hall, Jonathan was kneeling by her side, the front door opened, she heard low voices. Somebody knelt on her other side and she realized it was Dr. Herndon. He pushed up the full sleeve of her coat and stuck a hypodermic needle into her arm. Then he stood up. She knew he was talking to Jonathan but the voices were far away. She drifted off into unconsciousness.

This time when she awoke, she was in the hospital. It was the first time in her life that Janie had been a patient in a hospital. She stayed there two months and hated every moment of it. She hated the bare, clean hospital room, the hard hospital bed; hated the ministrations of doctors and nurses, their professional cheerfulness, their secretiveness, their questioning. She hated the food; hated the impersonality, the publicity—being pushed on stretchers through long public corridors with unknown people staring at the old woman passing by, being handled by strange masked figures under great glaring lights. She tried to be quiet and decent about it, she tried to behave like a lady, but her whole being was tied into tense knots of passionate revolt. People were kind to her, they came to see her and brought her delicacies and sent her flowers. She thanked them but she was not mollified.

When she finally left the hospital and went home she knew she would never walk again. She had broken both her hips. The doctors had done their best, they had put pins in the hips and done all the modern things, but the old bones would not knit, the legs would not bear the weight of her body. At first she was too glad to be at home again, to be in her own room in her own bed with her own things around her, to mind very much. A practical nurse was engaged to take care of her, but after a few weeks they let her go. Bertha could take care of Miss Janie. Jonathan bought her a wheelchair, and each morning Bertha would lift her in her strong arms and put her in the chair, and she could wheel herself around and look out of the windows and watch the busy life of Fairview Avenue in front, or at the back the yards of the houses on the side streets going off from the Avenue.

One morning when Bertha had settled her comfortably in the wheelchair Janie said to her: "Bertha, do you think you could get me downstairs in this chair?"

Bertha looked doubtful. "Yessum, I think I could get you down all right," she said. "We could put the brake on the wheels and go down one step at a time, and you could hold on to the railing, but Miss Janie, I don't believe I could get you back upstairs again."

Janie thought about that for a while. A few days later she said: "Bertha, when you get time will you step across the street to the engine house and ask Captain Higgins if he would come over and see me some time at his convenience. I want to speak to him for just a few minutes."

Captain Higgins came that afternoon. He was a grave, gray man, gray of hair, of eyes and of face, as if the ashes of many fires had settled on him. He was dignified of bearing and courtly of manner. He and Avery had liked each other very much. Janie had rolled herself out into the wide upper hall and was sitting at the front window, looking out over the portico.

"Well, well, ma'am," the Captain said. "It certainly is good to see you. We certainly have missed you, Miss Janie."

"Thank you, Captain," Janie said.

"You're looking mighty well, ma'am."

"I am well. The trouble is, I can't walk."

"Yes, we heard about that. We are all mighty sorry, Miss

Janie, mighty sorry. But as the Bishop would of told you, ma'am, God's will be done."

"I know, Captain, and I am not protesting. It doesn't make so much difference to an old woman like me. There is just one thing, I would like to be able to get downstairs, and for that I need some strong young arms."

Captain Higgins was looking at her doubtfully. Janie knew he had no idea what she was leading up to.

"I have been wondering—I don't know whether you can do this, Captain, and if you can't I am sure you will say so—but I have been wondering if you could lend me two of your firemen for about five minutes each evening to lift this wheelchair up the front steps. Bertha can get me down in the morning, but I think it will take two men to get me back up."

The Captain's face did not change, but Janie knew that this was a request new in his experience. Never before had he been asked to lift old ladies' wheelchairs up the steps every night.

Presently he nodded. "Why yes, Miss Janie, I don't see why not. We've got a Rescue Squad, we are all the time being called to get cats out of trees and babies out of drainpipes, I don't see why we couldn't lift your chair upstairs at night."

"It would be deeply appreciated, Captain," Janie said.

After that every evening at eight o'clock sharp, two firemen came out of the engine house, crossed the street, and were admitted to Fairview by Bertha. Janie would be waiting for them; they would get on each side of the wheelchair and lift it up the stairs by the arms as easily as if she had been a baby. Sometimes they stood and talked to her for a while, always they greeted her smilingly, cheerfully. They joked with her and told her about the weather and gave her bits of neighborhood news. She came to know all of them and from time to time she tried to do little things for them. She sent them magazines and boxes of candy, and a turkey at Thanksgiving and a ham at Christmas, and fruitcake and hot biscuits, which were the only two things Bertha was really good at making. They all grew to be great friends, and Janie looked forward to their coming each evening.

So now she spent her days in the front parlor, the living room of Jane's and Lynne's designation, or across the hall in the library. She found it hard to read nowadays, her attention wandered and her eyes hurt. Elizabeth gave her a television, which she was sure Mama would enjoy as she herself found it such a comfort. Janie did get some pleasure out of it. She was fascinated by the gadget that allowed her to sit across the room and turn it off and on or change the channel at will without moving. Bradford Long was doing a series of news commentaries on the television now, and she listened to him every week. His face and his voice became as familiar to her as Jonathan's.

For the most part Janie just sat and looked out of the window, or closed her eyes and thought about the past. She lived in the past. Partly this was because the past was all there was; there was no future for her and the present had no meaning; but it was also because she was searching for what her life should have taught her. Her mind ranged over all the years and all the people she had known. She remembered little things: Miss Bessie Mason's big yellow cat, Josephus, who sat in a rocking chair on one side of the potbellied stove in Miss Bessie's big classroom, in which the girls would no more have thought of sitting than in Miss Bessie's corresponding chair on the other side of the stove; the way Henry's coattails flew out behind him as he walked up and down the floor when he got mad; Sara Anne twinkling her eyes at the boys when they were very young; Uncle Tim Ashby sitting with his big feet on the porch railing of Aunt Josie's boardinghouse on Market Street, as lazy as all get-out. Backward and forward the long procession went, she lived with them vividly. The only one who did not come alive, who refused to move through her recollections with the grace of reality, was Avery, the first Avery. He seemed to her like the splendid romantic figure of a storybook tragedy. The old mind and heart could not recapture the ecstasy and the misery he had brought her.

Sometimes Janie was interested in what went on in the world around her. She entered into the presidential campaign of 1952 with vigor. Adlai Stevenson seemed to her another in the great tradition—Thomas Jefferson, Andrew Jackson, Woodrow Wilson, Franklin Roosevelt. She put her television to good use during those months, listening to the news avidly, hearing every speech that was made. She read the papers too, but the papers made her so mad that she resolved over and over again to have nothing more to do with them. The *Her-*

ald and the *Evening Sun* both remained technically Democratic, but their support of Mr. Stevenson was so lukewarm as to be practically nonexistent. She scolded Jonathan and Carey. They were polite but reticent, and Janie had a hateful suspicion that they were personally supporting General Eisenhower. She never pushed it far enough to find out, however, because if it was true she did not want to know it. She tried the Richmond papers and they were worse. She sent Bertha to the drugstore down the street to get Washington papers and the *New York Times*, but nowhere could she find any papers who were supporting Mr. Stevenson. The press was a great black Republican forest.

Janie was appalled also to learn how many of the neighbors were supporting Mr. Eisenhower. She could not understand it.

"He's a hero, ma'am," said Miss Jennie Saunders, "a real hero."

"But he is a Republican, Miss Jennie, and you know you are a Democrat."

"He ain't a real Republican," Miss Jennie said comfortably. "He never had anything to do with politics. He's just running on the Republican ticket to beat Harry Truman."

"But Harry Truman is not running for the Presidency," Janie said patiently. "Adlai Stevenson is."

"Well, it's all the same thing," Miss Jennie said.

Some of the firemen were for Eisenhower, even Alec Brown, one of Janie's favorites.

"Stevenson talks over everybody's head, Miss Janie," he said.

"Now that's just nonsense, Alec," Janie said crossly. "You know it is not true, you just heard somebody say that. You can't make me believe that you don't understand perfectly well what Mr. Stevenson says."

He grinned at her. "Well, he uses such grand words, and his voice don't sound like other people's. Eisenhower is right down to earth. And he is such a fine man, Miss Janie."

"And what if he is? Lots of people are fine men. You can't elect a President of the United States on that basis."

It was no use, however. They were impervious to logic. The Thompsons were for Stevenson, she was glad to say, and so was Bertha. And so was Captain Higgins. A few days before the election he came to see Janie.

"I just want to say, ma'am, that I'd be glad to send the Rescue Squad ambulance to take you to vote next Tuesday, if you would like."

Janie was very grateful. She had been wondering how she was going to get to the polls. Nobody in the family had said a word about it, they seemed to take it for granted that she would not vote. It annoyed her.

"Thank you, Captain," she said. "I would like it very much." An idea came to her. She remembered Betsy Barnett's teasing of Jonathan when the engine house was first put up. "But you know, I think it would be very nice to go to the polls on the fire engine, or perhaps the hook and ladder. We might as well show ourselves. There don't seem to be many of us."

Captain Higgins nearly choked with laughter. It was the first time Janie had ever seen him laugh. He roared.

"Well, you've got an idea, Miss Janie, you certainly have got an idea. We might not be able to do just that, but you wait, let me see what I can work out."

They did not go on the fire engine, but on the morning of election day Captain Higgins and Young Tom Purvis and three or four other firemen drove up to the porch of Fairview in a bright red Fire Department pickup truck, and lifted Miss Janie, wheelchair and all, onto it. Bertha got in next and then the firemen, and they drove through the streets, not fast as if they were going to a fire, but clanging the bell as if they were coming back from one, to attract attention. People turned around to stare at them. Janie sat up straight in the wheelchair with a kind of grim satisfaction. She wore the new black hat she was going to wear to church the morning she fell down the stairs. It had been in its box on the closet shelf ever since. She had on her mink coat, though it really wasn't cold enough for a fur coat, and both she and Bertha wore the biggest Stevenson buttons that Bertha had been able to find at the Democratic Headquarters downtown and Bertha held up a Stevenson poster so everybody could see.

When they reached the American Legion Hall, which was the voting place for their precinct, and the firemen started to lift Janie out of the truck, all the people standing around the entrance began to laugh and clap. They rolled Janie into the voting booth first and then she sat at one side and waited while Bertha and the firemen all voted. People came up and spoke to her and congratulated her on getting there. Randall Hoffman, who was something in the Democratic organization, Janie couldn't remember what, hurried up and shook hands with her.

"Mrs. Darby, it certainly is good to see you here, ma'am. Thank you for coming. You certainly made an entrance."

"We might have brought a brass band, if I had thought of it," Janie said, and everybody laughed.

Photographers began taking her picture. Young Tom Purvis rolled the wheelchair onto the sidewalk and the photographers followed. They got them all to pose, with Bertha standing behind the chair and the firemen on each side, and they kept on taking pictures as they got back into the truck again. Janie waved at them and everybody clapped again. Then they clanged their way slowly back to Fairview.

Janie was sure that Jonathan would not publish any of the pictures in the *Herald* or the *Evening Sun* because he would be horrified not only that his own mother would do a thing like that, but that any lady of a good Virginia family would make such a spectacle of herself, no matter what her age. She had enjoyed it very much; she spent the rest of the day watching the television.

Jonathan did not use the pictures, but one of the Richmond papers did, and one of the Washington papers, with little articles about who she was and how old she was. For days people were sending her clippings. Several days later a letter appeared in the *Herald* protesting the use of a Fire Department truck for political purposes. Jonathan published that; Janie supposed he thought he had to, but nobody paid any attention to it.

The trip to the polls, however, was the only satisfaction Janie got out of the election. When the returns came in that night and even before she went to sleep she knew, from the radio in her bedroom, that not only had Eisenhower been overwhelmingly elected, but that Virginia and several other Southern states had gone Republican, all her pleasure and excitement drained away, like air from a pricked balloon. She had not thought that she could still feel emotion so keenly.

The day after the election Jonathan did not come to see her and Elizabeth did not telephone. Of course in the ordinary course of events there were some days when Elizabeth did not call her and a good many days when Jonathan did not stop by, but Janie felt that their silence on that particular day was intended to emphasize their disapproval of her conduct. Or else it came from a guilty conscience for having voted Republican, as she was almost sure they all had done. Anyhow, she was glad not to talk to them. She was in a very bad humor. She knew better than to allow herself to be in a bad humor. She knew that if Avery had been there she would have struggled to overcome her resentment, but there she sat alone, with the television going into ecstasies over General Eisenhower's election, and she allowed the smoldering fumes of bad temper to have their way. In spite of all she had learned in life the Old Adam was still strong.

The day was not empty, however; she had other visitors. The first was David Darby. He had driven over from Roanoke that morning on business, and he was always sweet about coming to see her when he was in town. He came in without ringing the doorbell, shed his overcoat in the hall and stood in the archway looking at her.

"Well, well, Mrs. Darby," he said, "I hear you made quite a scene yesterday. You cut yourself a figure."

"Yes, I did," Janie said with satisfaction. "I wanted to ride the fire engine, but we compromised on the truck. I hope the family are all shocked."

"In varying degrees." He came over and kissed her and drew up a chair.

"What does your father say about it?"

"I'd hate to tell you." He grinned at her cheerfully. "He is nothing less than horrified. He can't imagine what has come over you. He thinks the Fire Department has had a very deleterious effect on your character."

"Good," Janie said. "I owe him that for all the double-faced, damning-with-faint-praise editorials I have had to read all during this campaign. And Carey too."

"Carey thinks it would have been all right if the Fire Department had taken you to vote in an ambulance," David said.

"Not a single member of the family suggested taking me to vote, in an ambulance or anything else."

"And Helen thinks," David went on, "that it would have been all right if you hadn't clanged the bell. Personally, I like it just the way it was. I'm all for it and I wish I had seen it. I

426

am only sorry that you took all that trouble to vote for the wrong man."

Janie looked at him. "Does that mean that you didn't vote for Stevenson?" she asked.

"I certainly did not. I know how to pick a winner when I see one."

So there it was. He was the first one who had admitted it to her. "Your ancestors would turn over in their graves," she said.

"What do you want to bet?" David always had an impudent twinkle in his eyes. "The world has changed, Gram darling."

"David Darby," Janie said, "don't you sit there and tell me that the world has changed. I have been watching it change for ninety-seven years. There isn't anybody living who knows any more about the world changing than I do. But there are some things that don't change. Republicans don't change."

"Well, Democrats do," David said. "I'll bet my ancestors wouldn't recognize this Democratic Party we have got now."

Janie wasn't going to get into that because she thought it was true. "David," she said, "I appreciate your coming to see me. I am very fond of you, and I don't doubt that I will get over this, but right now I don't want to look at a grandson of mine who voted the Republican ticket. Now you go on away and give me time to get over it."

He laughed and stood up, patting her on the head, affectionate and slightly patronizing, as the young are to the old. Not that he was so young himself, David must be going up in his forties.

"I hope it won't take you long, Gram," he said. "We are coming over to spend Thanksgiving with Mother and Father, and I would hate not to see you."

Janie said nothing. David put on his coat and delivered one parting shot as he left.

"I'm afraid you will be mighty lonely, honey, if you won't have anything to do with Eisenhower supporters."

This merely confirmed what Janie already knew. She sat quietly for a while and thought about it. All these Virginians turned Republicans, whom she was accusing of betraying the faith of their fathers, were really clinging to tradition as much as she was. She was clinging to a name, to an old loyalty, and

427

to a prejudice. They were clinging to a way of life, to an old order which she believed to be dying and which they could not save, any more than she could have saved the Fairview plantation. Every age had a purpose to accomplish, as every individual had. You had to believe that to make any sense out of life. You had to believe it when you looked back over the history of dynasties and empires and eras. The twentieth century had swept over Fairview as irresistibly, as implacably as a lava flow forced up into eruption by hidden forces at the earth's core, destroying it. Something else had been created in its place. The twentieth century was sweeping over the old orders of the world, destroying here, building there. Learn to control and direct the hidden forces, that was all you could do, you couldn't stop them. These children and grandchildren of hers, these friends and neighbors, clinging to the substance of the past, were blaming one political party for the slow submergence of the old order and taking refuge with the other, which might delay but could not prevent the steady progression of the age of democracy. This was her conviction, but she knew very well that conviction or not, she would still have clung to the old loyalty and the old prejudice.

Later that afternoon one of her great-granddaughters came to see her, bringing a young man. Janie was pleased because she knew where to place her in the family. She was Marjorie Eubank, Jane's daughter, Elizabeth's granddaughter, a pretty dark girl who showed the Calhoun strain. She introduced the young man as Kern Armstrong. They came to tell her that they were going to be married.

"Mother is giving a party the Saturday after Thanksgiving, and she and Dad will announce it then," Marjorie said. "We wanted you to know, Gram."

"Thank you, that's very kind of you, Marjorie. When will you be married?"

"Not until summer," the girl said sadly. "Kern is studying law at the University, he's just in his first year. Right after New Year's I am going to business school to learn stenography so I can get a job and help out until he graduates and gets established. We'll be married as soon as I finish."

That seemed to be the way of the world nowadays. Perhaps it was a good way, better than waiting for years. Perhaps not.

Kern Armstrong was a nice-looking boy with a resonant

voice and intelligent gray eyes. He was also a great-great-grandson of old Jiminy Jones, his mother being Marcia Jones, daughter of Buford Jones, Jr. Well, what did it matter? Let Jiminy's dirty hands and tobacco-stained beard be finally buried. All citadels fell with time. A Republican South and intermarriage with the descendants of old Jiminy Jones! A gleam of humor came to her and she smiled at the illogic of putting the two things together. It was like Miss Jennie Saunders saying that Adlai Stevenson and Harry Truman were all the same thing.

The young couple thought she was smiling at them, as indeed she was. She wished them happiness and thanked them for coming to tell her. They left holding each other's hands and smiling, glad that that duty was done.

Janie was tired when the firemen came to take her upstairs that night.

40

One of the firemen at Engine House No. 4 was called Young Tom Purvis. He was a tall boy with blue eyes. There was something about his eyes, something about him, in fact, that attracted your attention. He looked at you with a wide blue stare that was almost disconcerting. Stare was not the right word, Janie knew, but there was a directness, a sort of intensity about the way he looked at you, as if he were trying to get right down inside you. It was a questioning intensity, and Janie came to the conclusion that he was questioning a world he did not understand, searching and probing for the answer to a puzzle that eluded him.

He came to her attention the first spring of her invalidism, before she had grown to know all the firemen at the engine house. He and Alec Brown came one evening to lift her chair upstairs, and she encountered for the first time that wide, blue, questioning gaze. One morning a few days later the doorbell rang, and when Bertha answered it there was Young Tom Purvis, asking to see Miss Janie. She was sitting in the front parlor.

"Good morning," she said. She could not remember his name, she was not sure she knew it.

"Mawnin', ma'am," he said. "I am Tom Purvis."

"How are you, Tom? Come on in and sit down."

He stood looking at her. He was not shy, just a little hesitant, as if feeling his way. In his hand he held a small parcel, wrapped in foil. He came into the parlor and offered it to her.

"I thought you might like this, Miss Janie."

She opened the neatly folded covering of foil and there, on a bed of wet oak leaves, lay a clump of trailing arbutus. The small, delicate blossoms looked up at her wide-eyed.

"Oh, Tom," she said. She lifted the little parcel and buried her face in it, inhaling the sweet fragrance, and for an instant, one magic instant, the years fell away and she was a little girl again, kneeling on the hillside where the trailing arbutus grew.

"I'm glad you like it, Miss Janie," Tom said. He drew up a chair and sat down. "I thought you would. I said to myself, there's a lady who would like arbutus!"

"Where did you find it?"

"Back here behind Fairview. You know, Orchard Road on one side of your yard only goes back a block, and Sunset Road on the other side runs into Prospect Avenue and that goes all the way up the hill to the top and down the other side. Most of the houses on Prospect Avenue are built on the upper side of the road and even those on the lower side have yards that go back just a way, and in between there are woods. Real nice woods, like it was in the country. I walk up there right often. Up there in the woods there is a spring that comes right out of the rock, and runs down and makes a little pool, and on one side of the pool the arbutus grows."

Janie could hardly believe it. "I didn't know it was still there," she said. "It has been so many years since I went up there."

"Did you know about it, Miss Janie?"

"Tom, I have known about that spring ever since I was born. All that used to belong to Fairview, you know. What has happened to the stream?"

"There ain't any stream, just the pool in a little hollow and some marshy ground on the down side. I tried to find out what happened to the water that runs off. I reckon it has gone underground." He laughed. "Made me think of the people in Europe during the war, and now too, I reckon, when things get too bad they go underground."

Later she asked Alec Brown about Tom.

"His father was a fireman too," Alec said. "Old Tom, a mighty good friend of mine. That's why we call this one Young Tom. This boy did his stint in the Army when he finished high school and was in the fighting over in Korea. While he was gone his dad died and his sister got married, their mother died a long time ago, and he was sort of at loose ends when he came home, so he joined the Fire Department. I think he thought it woulda pleased his dad. But he don't belong there, Miss Janie. I don't mean that he ain't a good fireman. He is, but his heart ain't in it and he don't sort of fit in with the other men. He is different, Miss Janie."

"He is different," Janie agreed, "but I don't quite know why."

"There ain't anything wrong with him, you understand. He did real well at school, and in the Army too. At least, I don't know how well he got on with the men but his Army record was good. He got an Award of Merit in Korea. He just ain't like anybody else, and people don't like other people who are different."

"How does he get on with the men at the engine house?" Janie asked.

"They laugh at him some, but they are right good to him, because he is Tom Purvis' son and because he is younger than any of them, but as time goes on it ain't going to be so good."

"Has he always been different, Alec?"

"Yessum. His dad used to worry about him like all get-out. He never liked to play games like the other boys, used to like to go wandering off by himself in the woods. He liked to go fishing, but whenever he caught a fish he would throw it right back in the water. Things like that; they just don't make sense to most people, Miss Janie. He's crazy about animals, has a way with them. His mother used to have an awful time with the stray animals he brought home. He's got two-three of them over at the engine house now. I sort of worry about him, Miss Janie."

Janie began to worry about him too. He came to see her frequently, not only to lift her upstairs at night, but during the day on his off time. Often he brought her little gifts, a bunch of daffodils from his sister's yard, or lady slippers or wild bleeding hearts from the woods. He never stayed long, showing an innate consideration for an old lady who tired quickly, but he liked to stop by and talk to her for a few minutes. Sometimes he asked questions that Janie found it hard to answer. One day he said: "You must know an awful lot, Miss Janie. You must be mighty wise."

"Oh, Tom, I certainly am not. I ought to be wise, with all the years I have lived, but I find that wisdom is hard to come by."

"No'm, I'll bet you are. I'll bet you know a lot about life. I wish I did. I keep wondering about things, Miss Janie, why things happen to some people and not to others. When I was over there in Korea, for instance, in the fighting and people getting killed all around me, or being wounded and suffering so bad, and people's homes getting blown up and little lost children wandering around crying and starving sometimes, and nothing ever happened to me, Miss Jane, I just went right along through it all and never got hurt. Now why was that, Miss Janie?"

"God has other plans for you, Tom."

"Yessum, but why me? Why not some of those other fellows?"

The question found an echo in Janie's mind. How often had she asked, "But why me, Lord, why me? Why am I kept on so long beyond my time?"

"Take that old colored man who froze to death last winter, you mighta seen about him in the paper," Tom went on. "He lived in one of the old shacks down by the railroad tracks, you know, between the tracks and the river, and he froze to death in his shack. I mean, just froze solid because he didn't have any heat. Plenty of coal and wood and oil all around and everybody warm except that old man, and he sat there and froze to death. And take this, Miss Janie, you live to be a real old lady, but the Jenkins little boy—they run the shop, sort of a five and ten, in the next block, and their little boy, just four years old, died yesterday with some funny blood disease that the doctors don't even know what it is. Now, Miss Janie, does all that make sense to you?"

"No, Tom, it doesn't make sense to our human minds, but we must believe that God has some overall purpose, some plan for each one of us, which would make sense if we could understand it. I wish you had known my son Avery, he could have helped you to believe that."

"Yes ma'am, I've heard about the Bishop. And that's what I do believe, Miss Janie. You know what I think? I think those Oriental fellows, Hindus, ain't they, who believe that we come back over and over again to lead different lives at different times and places, I think they are right, and that what happens to us each time is because of what we have

433

done or haven't done in previous lives and what we need to learn. That's why some people have it good and some bad, and next time it may be just the other way around. What do you think about that, Miss Janie?"

"I think it sounds very logical, Tom. It certainly accounts for the apparent injustices."

"I have been going down to the Public Library and reading some books about it. They're mighty interesting, Miss Janie."

It was apparent to Janie that Tom Purvis did not belong in the communal life, the rough-and-ready comradeship of a fire engine house. She wondered whether he tried to talk about reincarnation and the purposes of God to the other firemen.

That was the day she asked him what, if he had his choice, he would like to be. There was no hesitation in his answer.

"I want to be a veterinarian, ma'am. I like animals, I get on real good with animals. I am saving my money now, Miss Janie, so some day I can go off and learn to be a vet and set myself up in business, have an office and a little animal hospital."

After that, Janie had a project in her mind about Tom Purvis, but she did not quite know how to work it out. It took some thought. When Lynne and Anton came to spend Christmas at Fairview that year, the project crystallized. The Cziermanskis had four children now: Jane, and Anton Jr., and Henry Darby Cziermanski and Lawrence Hammond Cziermanski. Janie never ceased being amused by this mixture of names.

"You should have another little girl, Lynne," she said, "so that you can give her your own pretty name."

"Well, I certainly have tried," Lynne said cheerfully, "but these miserable little boys keep coming." She smiled lovingly at the latest of the miserable little boys, a plump, brown-haired baby now propelling himself across the polished floor on the seat of his absurd little pants.

Lynne had put on weight. The willowy figure of girlhood was gone, she was a big, handsome woman. Well, thirteen years and four children would naturally make a difference. She was obviously happy, but Janie found herself obscurely disquieted by the quality of her happiness. It seemed docile, passive. She had said that she wanted the world and would get it when she married Anton, and apparently that was true. Anton and the children were her world. And why not, Janie

434

argued with herself. Surely a happy marriage was a gift of God. She too had been placidly happy during the early years of her marriage with Henry, when the children were young. She had already known tragedy, however; by then she had known the difference between happiness, and unhappiness. She had drawn happiness up out of the ashes of conflict and misery. Lynne had never known anything but happiness, granted by God or fortunate circumstance, accepted but not earned. What did such happiness prepare you for? You are being captious, Janie she told herself when these thoughts came to her. This is old age speaking. Old age and a long view.

Thirteen years had made a difference in Anton too. He still wore an aura of romance, he would still draw the eyes of any woman in sight, but now he wore it with an air of authority. He was no longer the young Lochinvar. He was a man obviously in control of his world. She had long ago decided that he was not acting a part in any respect. The almost studied perfection of his outward attitudes was a reaching out for a state of perfection craved by the inner self.

One morning when Lynne had taken the children to spend the day with Jennie Duval Foster's children while she and Jennie went Christmas shopping, and Janie and Anton were in the front parlor, Tom Purvis came to see her. He brought her a big clump of mistletoe which he had gone into the woods to get for her. She introduced him to Anton and watched them with interest. When he had gone Anton said: "An unusual young man, Gram. Tell me about him."

Janie told him what she knew. "He is, as you see, different. He doesn't belong in the Fire Department. I have something in my mind for him, and I think, Anton, I am going to ask you to do me a great favor."

"I'd be happy to do you a favor, Gram," Anton said.

It was hard for Janie to explain it. "I am the victim of a conspiracy," she began, and then she laughed at his expression. "Don't look at me as if I were suffering from delusions, Anton. There is a conspiracy, a beneficent one, engaged in by Jonathan and John Updyke at the bank and to some extent by Henry Taylor, our lawyer. They are all protecting me, from myself and from those who prey upon the guileless. They have never approved of my—my private charities. They think I am too much governed by emotion and that I am an easy sucker. They watch me like hawks. I want to give some money to Tom Purvis. He wants to be a veterinarian and that's what he ought to be. He gets on with God and with animals, but people don't know what to make of him. If I give a check for a considerable sum of money to a strange young man there will be a terrific hullabaloo." Her eyes twinkled. "Especially a young man belonging to Engine House No. 4. Jonathan has never trusted the Fire Department since the election last year."

Anton laughed.

"They couldn't stop me from doing it, you understand," Janie went on firmly, "I am in full control of my affairs, but they could make a row and take away a lot of the pleasure of doing it, and probably make Tom think he ought not to take it. I don't want anybody to know anything about it."

"So you want me to engage in a conspiracy against the conspirators, is that it?" he asked, smiling.

"Exactly. It isn't that Jonathan would grudge the money," she hastened to add. "He is a kindhearted man and a generous one. He gives to a lot of good causes and works for them and cooperates in the papers, but he has a nice, orderly mind, he likes to give to causes and organizations and agencies, and sometimes I like to give to people. Of course it is natural to think that a very old woman, who doesn't always pay attention to what's going on around her, is likely to do something silly. I don't exactly blame them, but sometimes it makes me mad. Anyhow, I want to give some money to Tom without anybody knowing it."

"All right, Gram. How do we do it?"

"I have a lockbox upstairs, and in it there are some Government bonds. I bought them during the war. I don't remember now why I had them here or why I kept them here, everything else is in the bank, but I think I came to feel that it would be a good idea to have something that I could get at easily. And I want to know, if I sign them and if I give you a power of attorney, couldn't you go into any bank and cash them, preferably a bank in some other town, Richmond, for instance?"

Anton leaned back in his chair and laughed. "You're wonderful, Gram," he said. "It will give me great pleasure to liquidate your bonds for you. I don't expect to go to Richmond, but Lynne and I are going to run up to Washington before we go home, and I can take the bonds to the Treasury and cash them at the source. Nobody will know anything about it."

Janie sighed. "Oh, Anton, you are such a comfort."

He was. That was a strange thing. She felt a closeness to Anton that she could not explain. Here she was, confiding to him what she wanted to keep secret from Jonathan, her own son, and from John Updyke and Henry Taylor, who had helped her with her affairs ever since Henry died. It made her feel guilty, and disloyal to Jonathan, who was a good man, and a better son never lived. She loved Jonathan dearly. It was just that their minds did not run the same way, and he tried to be too protective. She wanted to do things the way she wanted to do them, and he thought she ought to follow his pattern.

One night while Lynne and Anton were there Janie gave a family dinner party for them. It was not her idea, it was Bertha who suggested it.

"Don't you think, ma'am, we ought to have the family here one night for dinner while Miss Lynne and Mr. Anton are here?"

"Oh, Bertha! There are so many of them. How could we manage?"

"We could," Bertha said placidly. "We could get Miss Lucy Magee to help and her man to serve. And there ain't but fourteen here in town, if you stop with the grandchildren and their husbands and wives. Be sixteen if you ask Mr. David and Miss Mildred from Roanoke. It would be nice for Miss Lynne, don't you think?"

"All right," Janie said. "Get Miss Lucy Magee and let's have a dinner party."

It was nice, having them all there, dressed up and lively and apparently enjoying themselves. Janie did not pay much attention to the talk. It flowed past her but it sounded pleasant. After dinner, in the parlor, they began discussing the state of the world, and Janie listened to that. She was always interested in the state of the world. Things were pretty bad, everybody agreed, what with the Communists and taxes and the demands of labor, with juvenile delinquency and violence and immorality on the rampage, with constant talk of war and destruction. And of course the Government, even with the Republicans in power, reaching into every nook and cranny of the country.

437

Anton's was the only voice raised in hopefulness. "It is all very discouraging," he agreed, "but it depends on which side of the coin you are looking at. Turn it over and look at the other side. Think of all the progress that has been made in the last fifty years, not just physical progress—I mean, not just inventions and gadgets and machines, but progress in ideals and standards and social conscience. Think of the child labor of the last century, in England and here in this country. Think of the twelve- and fourteen-hour workday and the starvation wages of labor fifty years ago. Not even the most ultra-conservative steel magnate would advocate now the conditions existing in the early years of this century."

"Well, of course," Carey said. "We don't live in the Dark Ages, but now it has gone to the other extreme, we live under the tyranny of labor. Business can't stand it."

"Business seems to be getting on pretty well," Anton said. Then he added slowly: "Go back a little further. Think of slavery."

Janie thought, I expect we deserve that. Think of slavery. Nobody said anything, so she spoke. "Yes, nothing that we have now is as bad as slavery. And yet, Anton, for generations good people—I mean *good* people—took it for granted, accepted it as preordained by God for the sons of Ham."

"Not just the sons of Ham," he said. "Slavery has been known through all recorded history. But that is what I mean —we have changed, we have progressed. We are still a long way off, but we are nearer to the concept of brotherhood than we were fifty years ago. And that is what we have got to come to, Gram. We have just got to. We live in a different and a very dangerous world. We have got to move fast."

Anton was very earnest about this, but he was quiet. He stood leaning against the fireplace, his elbow on the mantel shelf, looking at them.

"I remember what the Bishop said about never fearing that God would allow man to destroy himself. I am sure that is true in a general sense, but it is frightening to think what we could do to ourselves now, those of us who are alive or our children as they come along. Not just physical destruction by war, but destruction of personality, of individuality, of the human self made in the image of God. We have created machines that can think, robots that can do everything but feel. Automation, Gram, can destroy all the values we live by,

438

even if war doesn't destroy us first. We know too much on one side and not enough on the other. I said that to the Bishop."

Anton always spoke of Avery as the Bishop. "I remember," she said.

"On the other hand, all this new knowledge can be used for the almost infinite enrichment of human life," Anton went on. "We have the choice. Which are we going to do and who is going to make the decision?"

"We the people," Janie said.

"Yes, we the people of the world. The choice between good and evil has been with us since Adam and Eve, individually, now we've got it on a global basis. We are all in it together. We are all brothers in danger, and we *are* our brothers' keepers, especially those who have the knowledge."

"What are you going to do about the Communists?" demanded Hugh Ames. "They don't seem to have any concept of brotherly love, and they have as much knowledge as we have."

"Perhaps that is the part we will have to leave to God," Anton said. "Of course Christianity could be the answer, if we could just learn to practice the Christianity we have been professing for two thousand years. 'By this shall ye be known as my disciples, that you show love one for another.'"

They all sat in embarrassed silence, and Janie wondered if this was an Anglo-Saxon characteristic in contrast to the other racial strains in Western civilization, this deep embarrassment at the mention of inner things, of spiritual realities. Anton was entirely without embarrassment. He stood there by the fireplace, his distinguished face and splendid dark eyes alive with earnestness, and Janie thought that he was one of the most complete people she had ever known, all in one piece, balanced; mind, heart and spirit developed. Having so little of the mind's knowledge herself it filled her with awe to realize the secrets of the universe that Anton knew. It came to her that this completeness was the purpose of life, this unity of being the thing for which each human soul was struggling. The I *am* of the Bible. The Self.

When Lynne and Anton went back to New Mexico Janie missed them very much. The house was quiet again, and empty. She missed Tom Purvis too, when he went away to learn how to be a veterinarian. Tom had accepted the money

439

with the simplicity that was a part of him, gratefully, without protestations of reluctance or pride.

"It is a secret between us, Tom," Janie had said. "Nobody is to know about it but us."

"If that's the way you want it, ma'am," Tom said, "but I would like to tell everybody what a wonderful lady you are to give it to me."

"Don't," she said. "It would not be appreciated."

Tom Purvis, the innocent, the child-man, was a misfit in the world of people, not because he lacked intelligence or courage or goodwill, but because innocence and childlike qualities could not cope with adult complexities in a world which had long since lost its innocence. And yet in her mind Avery and Anton and Tom Purvis, all so different in background, in time, in character, were yet held together by a common bond, love of God and love of man.

Janie thought about that a great deal during the months that followed. It gave her something to hold on to when she was weighed down by the irritations of the world and the infirmities of this old body which still clung to her. As a defense she adopted a motto, "and the greatest of these is love." She repeated it to herself over and over when irritation welled up in her; irritation with Bertha when she urged her to eat, with Mrs. Thompson when she was so terribly cheerful, or Jonathan when he patronized her, or Elizabeth when she talked too long on the phone; with the President or Congress or the television commentators. Bradford Long was no longer doing his commentaries on the television, she wondered what had happened to him. The twentieth century pressed in upon her more and more all the time. It would have been easy to allow herself to be irritated by its manifestations. The city had built a new airport and planes zoomed over Fairview day and night. A traffic light had been installed at the corner of Sunset Road and Fairview Avenue, where the traffic came in from Prospect Avenue. The buses and the great lumbering trucks stopped there now with a screeching of brakes; they started up again with a deep, throbbing, vibrating noise that was hard on the nerves. The papers were full of horrors. Little wars were going on in far places, men talked endlessly in the United Nations and met in conferences throughout the world. At least they talked, they were trying. The television blared at her, she usually turned it off after a few minutes. One morning nine men in Washington told the South it could no longer separate the races in public schools. When Janie first heard that decision of the United States Supreme Court bitterness spread through her. The hands of the clock had gone full circle around, she thought. The Yankees were coming again. The sound of their marching feet could be heard in the distance, the smoke of their fires stung the nostrils. She knew that she should not let herself feel that way. She would lose all that she had learned from life if she gave way to the Old Adam now, so she turned the television off, and put the decision out of her mind and thought about God and said over and over again to herself, "and the greatest of these is love." That afternoon when Jonathan stopped by to see her and paced the floor in helpless rage, speaking bitter words, she was able to sit in silence so that he thought she had gone off into her private world, and ceased his pacing and his speaking and kissed her and went away.

Janie slept fitfully now, and often her legs became numb. Bertha would have to rub them, or put a cushion under her knees when she sat in her chair. She felt dried and withered; her skin was dry, her lips were dry, sometimes her eyes stung as if they too were drying up. It was hard to smile and thank people when they told her how well she looked, but she appreciated their kindness and she tried to think of pleasant things to say to them. Gradually she found that when people let her alone she got on very well, because she was learning that by thinking about God and about the love of God and the love of man, she could push the twentieth century and her irritations and discomforts out of her consciousness, she could lose herself and become merged in God's reaction with a unity so complete that she knew only a great happiness, a wave of joy in the realization of the peace that passed understanding. It came to her that Avery had known these things all his life. He had always been able to command this happiness because he had always known how to lose himself in the currents of God's love. He had always known that only by giving up the ego, the Old Adam, could the self be realized. It had taken her ninety-nine years to learn what Avery, her son, was born knowing. Tom Purvis would say, "Why, Miss Janie? Why is that?" Janie didn't know, so she said "Why, Lord, why?"

41

As Janie's hundredth birthday approached she began to
have a feeling about it. She who had wanted to go for so long
now wanted to reach that point, a full round century. It became a symbol to her, not only of the end of a long journey
but of the completion of a long quest for the meaning of the
love of God. Leave the purposes of God to Him, you can't
understand them. You can understand His love.

Sometimes during the last months she thought she would
not make it. There was nothing wrong with her except that
the engine was wearing out. Sometimes the old heart acted
up and Bertha would have to send hurriedly for Dr. Herndon. Sometimes the old mind wandered, time merged with
time, past and present were confused. Sometimes, however,
she saw very clearly, she wished she had seen as clearly when
she was younger. There were times when she sat quietly in her
wheelchair at the front window and felt rather than saw the
life around her, the buses and trucks and cars and people on
Fairview Avenue, the families in the houses on the side
streets, all over town, all over the country, all over the world,
and a great happiness came to her, a surge of love for all
God's creation, a deep compassion for all the struggling
masses seeking and searching for the meaning of life, for self-
hood. These were the times that made her feel her own quest
was nearing completion.

So the day came, and Janie put on her gray silk dress and

Avery's moonstone brooch and sat in the parlor, feeling triumphant. The doorbell rang and the telephone rang; flowers came and telegrams. Bland Calhoun wired his congratulations from San Francisco where he now lived. Lynne had sent her a present but a telegram came also that morning, from Lynne and Anton, sending love and congratulations. They had not been able to come for her hundredth birthday because just a week before Lynne had had her fifth child, the much-wanted little girl who would be named, and called, Carolyn.

A great basket of yellow and white chrysanthemums came from Engine House No. 4. The Women's Auxiliary of St. John's Church, the Daughters of the American Revolution, the United Daughters of the Confederacy, the employees of the *Herald* and the *Evening Sun*, the bank, Mr. Harris who kept the little florist shop a block away on Fairview Avenue, old Mr. Garrett at Garrett and Wright's, all sorts of people sent her flowers. Mr. Martin, the postman, brought her a bunch of late fall asters from his yard, lovely shades of pink and lavender. Janie knew that Tom Purvis would come bringing her some small and lovely thing he had found for her in the woods. Tom was a veterinarian now, set up in a white frame house on the outskirts of town, and doing very well.

Elizabeth telephoned to say that she would be by to see her later in the day. Janie knew what an effort that would be for her. Dr. Herndon stopped in to see her.

"Just came by to say happy birthday," he said. "Good Lord, you've got a florist shop in here. An awful lot of goings-on about a mere hundred years. What will they do when you get to be a hundred and ten?"

He was not fooling her, and she knew that he knew it. His keen doctor's eyes were looking at her gravely. He felt her pulse and Janie knew very well what the pulse was saying. When he put her hand gently back into her lap they looked at each other candidly. They knew what they knew. He patted her shoulder.

"You are a remarkable woman, Miss Janie Darby. I wish there were more like you in the world, at least among my patients. But take it easy, dear lady. Don't let them push you too hard today."

Jonathan came, as Janie had known he would. She watched him park his Cadillac by the front porch and come up the steps, tall, gray-haired, well tailored, still handsome.

Jonathan always drove a Cadillac, he was always well tailored. He liked good things, well established and conservative
things. The proper expenditure of money for good living,
within the limits of his income and the bounds of good taste,
was his custom. And why not, she asked herself. Jonathan
was only seventy-two, prosperous and active. The simplicities
had not yet caught up with him. Perhaps they never would.
Perhaps simplicities were desirable only to those who had let
go, and Jonathan had not let go.

He opened the front door and came into the parlor. She
felt a wave of affection for him. Dear Jonathan, what would
she have done these last years without him. She held out her
hand, and he came across the room and took it and stood
smiling down at her.

"You're looking mighty fine today, dear," he said. "Mighty
fine. All dressed up. That is such a pretty dress."

"It has been a long time since I have worn it," Janie said.
"I felt that a hundredth birthday called for a little finery."

"It does indeed. And how does it feel to be one hundred
years old?"

"A little strange," Janie said. She began to think why, in reality, she should feel more strange today than she had yesterday. Was it only imagination or was it that she had now
reached the goal she had set for herself? She could now let
time have its way. She did not know how long she had been
thinking, but she realized suddenly that Jonathan had drawn
up a chair and was waiting patiently for her to come back to
him. He had two beribboned packages which he presented to
her. One was a bed jacket from Sara Anne. She had already
had four that day, but what more appropriate gift for a
housebound old lady? This was a lovely thing, delicate,
frothy, hand-embroidered. Sara Anne sewed beautifully. The
other was a big flat box. Jonathan unwrapped it and gave it to
her. "This is my present to you, given with much love."

Inside the box there was a tooled leather picture frame
holding a handsome group photograph. "Your great-
grandchildren," Jonathan said. "We had this taken last summer when Sally and David were here with their families. All
the children were together."

Jonathan was very proud of his fourteen grandchildren. It
was a charming photograph, grouped on the seat and arms
and the floor in front of the big Hepplewhite sofa in Jona-

than's living room. On the wall above the sofa hung a portrait of Sara Anne as she had been as a young woman. The children ranged in age from twenty-four-year-old Beverly, Carey's oldest, now married, to Sally's youngest, five-year-old Billy, whose engaging, freckle-faced homeliness stood out in the midst of what was, on the whole, a satisfactorily good-looking lot. Janie gazed at the young faces, some grave, some smiling, all looking directly and confidently at her. Here lay the future. What would they make of it, or, remembering Anton's words, what would it make of them? She had played her part in this progression; they had still to play theirs.

After Jonathan had gone Janie sat back in her chair and closed her eyes. She opened them to see Jim Thompson's taxi come up the driveway and instead of stopping at the front door go around the empty garage to the back of the house. The garage that used to be the kitchen . . . She saw Baizy standing over the old wood-burning cookstove in the brick-floored kitchen, bustling around, mixing batter, beating biscuits, scolding, teasing. Darling Baizy. She saw Mama in the storeroom, measuring out supplies for the day . . . The portrait of Mama still hung over the sofa, so pretty in her yellow dress. Janie wished there had been a portrait of herself when she was young, something to show what she had been. The only portrait of her was Jane's eightieth birthday present. Janie rolled her chair into the back parlor and sat looking up at the painting. That woman, who had seemed so old to her then, had been twenty years younger than she herself was now. She had not known much, in spite of her eighty years. Janie remembered that she had seen strength in the woman in the portrait when she first looked at her. She didn't think anyone would see strength in her as she was now, in the frail body and the wrinkled face. She knew it was there, however. Like the stream from the spring on the hillside, that Tom Purvis had told her about, it had gone underground. It had changed its nature. Then it had been strength to endure, to do, to go her own way, to hold her own opinions. Now it was strength to accept, to tolerate, to understand, to love.

Bertha came into the front parlor. "What you doing, Miss Janie?" she asked.

"Just looking around," Janie said.

Bertha rolled her back into the front parlor. "I am going to bring you some lunch now in a few minutes," she said. "And

I'm going to light this fire so's you'll be nice and warm, and here's the morning paper."

It wasn't really chilly enough for a fire, and Janie wondered why Bertha was lighting it. She wheeled her around so that she faced the fireplace with her back to the front windows and the archway into the hall. Suddenly Janie realized that this was a maneuver to keep her from seeing what was going on around her, that Jim Thompson's taxi, the comings and goings, the unexplained telephone calls, all meant that they were preparing for something. A party for her, she bet. A surprise party. Bless their hearts, but she wished they wouldn't. There would be so many people, family and neighbors and firemen and heaven knew who. So many people.

She glanced at the morning paper. She could only read the headlines now. Even with the new glasses the doctor had given her last spring she couldn't read the newspaper print. As usual, the headlines were distressing. Sixty-six persons killed as a DC-4 airliner smashed into a mountain at Laramie, Wyoming. Fighting had broken out in Morocco. There was fighting in the United Nations, France had withdrawn her delegation from the Permanent Group of the United Nations because it had decided to take up the Algerian issue. Eight men had been hurt in a shooting at a struck plant in Indiana. The Government had awarded the contract for work on the first United States space satellite. Man, so unable to control his own world, was seeking to conquer other worlds.

Bertha brought her lunch on a tray. Janie did not want it, but to please Bertha she drank a little soup and tried to eat a hot biscuit. When Bertha came to take the tray she scolded her for not eating more. "I don't know what I am going to do with you, ma'am. Don't eat enough for a bird." She patted Janie's shoulder. "Now you just sit there and take your nap. I won't let anybody disturb you."

Janie sat in the wheelchair and smiled to herself. She knew perfectly well what was going on in the dining room and pantry and kitchen. It wasn't exactly that she could hear. She didn't hear as well as she used to, but she found that as her sight and hearing failed her inner knowledge, call it intuition perhaps, increased, so now she could see the lace tablecloth and the alabaster bowls filled with flowers and the silver candelabra. She could hear the clink of glasses and silver. Cham-

446

pagne, she thought, they will probably drink my health in champagne. They are all so good to me, so kind and thoughtful. The wave of happiness that came to her so often now spread through her. She sat in the fragrance of the flowers and the warmth of the fire and the circle of God's love. "By this shall ye be known, that ye love one another." Avery, the man of God, had said that often. It was good that Anton, the man of science, said the same thing.

Presently she put her head back against the chair and closed her eyes. Her whole being was caught up in a wave of exaltation. She remembered a question Tom Purvis had asked her. "Miss Janie, ma'am," he said, "have you ever felt God?" She had not known how to answer the question then. Now she knew. Now she could have answered the question, if Tom had been there.

She thought she heard someone coming up the driveway. Perhaps it was Tom. She would go to meet him, she would like to tell him what she knew. Janie rolled her chair across the parlor and into the hall. That was as far as she got. A little later, when Bertha and Mrs. Thompson came out of the dining room to wake Miss Janie from her nap and prepare her to greet the neighbors who were gathering in the yard, they found her there. Her hands were on the wheels of the chair as she had rolled herself forward, and there was a smile on her face.

Neither woman spoke for a few moments, then Bertha said: "Call Mr. Jonathan, will you, Mrs. Thompson, please ma'am. They may be on their way here, but if they haven't left the house we should let them know."

She went onto the porch to tell the people gathered there. They stood in silence until the engine house quartet, who had come to sing "Oh, Susanna," and "After the Ball Is Over," and "The Band Played On," and such old songs that they thought Miss Janie would enjoy, sang instead "Nearer My God To Thee." They all joined in and then they went sorrowfully away, back to the engine house and the little shops and apartments.

Bertha went into the dining room to blow out the one huge pink candle that burned on top of the splendid, three-tiered birthday cake as a symbol of one century, a full one hundred years. She and Mrs. Thompson looked at each other and

447

there were tears in their eyes, not for Miss Janie exactly, because for a long time they had known that this would happen soon and you could not really mourn the going of so old a lady, but for sadness at the inexorability of time and the inevitable passing of old loved things and people and ways.